Praise for
John D. MacDonald

"MacDonald isn't simply popular; he's also good."

—ROGER EBERT

"MacDonald's books are narcotic and, once hooked, a reader can't kick the habit until the supply runs out."

—*Chicago Tribune Book World*

"John D. MacDonald remains one of my idols."

—DONALD WESTLAKE

"The Dickens of mid-century America—popular, prolific and . . . conscience-ridden about his environment . . . . A thoroughly American author."

—*The Boston Globe*

"It will be for his crisply written, smoothly plotted mysteries that MacDonald will be remembered."

—*USA Today*

"MacDonald had the marvelous ability to create attention-getting characters who doubled as social critics. In MacDonald novels, it is the rule rather than the exception to find, in the midst of violence and mayhem, a sentence, a paragraph, or several pages of rumination on love, morality, religion, architecture, politics, business, the general state of the world or of Florida."

—*Sarasota Herald-Tribune*

By John D. MacDonald

The Brass Cupcake
Murder for the Bride
Judge Me Not
Wine for the Dreamers
Ballroom of the Skies
The Damned
Dead Low Tide
The Neon Jungle
Cancel All Our Vows
All These Condemned
Area of Suspicion
Contrary Pleasure
A Bullet for Cinderella
Cry Hard, Cry Fast
You Live Once
April Evil
Border Town Girl
Murder in the Wind
Death Trap
The Price of Murder
The Empty Trap
A Man of Affairs
The Deceivers
Clemmie
Cape Fear (The Executioners)
Soft Touch
Deadly Welcome

Please Write for Details
The Crossroads
The Beach Girls
Slam the Big Door
The End of the Night
The Only Girl in the Game
Where Is Janice Gantry?
One Monday We Killed Them All
A Key to the Suite
A Flash of Green
The Girl, the Gold Watch
    & Everything
On the Run
The Drowner
The House Guest
End of the Tiger and Other Stories
The Last One Left
S*E*V*E*N
Condominium
Other Times, Other Worlds
Nothing Can Go Wrong
The Good Old Stuff
One More Sunday
More Good Old Stuff
Barrier Island
A Friendship: The Letters of Dan Rowan
    and John D. MacDonald, 1967–1974

THE TRAVIS MCGEE SERIES

The Deep Blue Good-by
Nightmare in Pink
A Purple Place for Dying
The Quick Red Fox
A Deadly Shade of Gold
Bright Orange for the Shroud
Darker Than Amber
One Fearful Yellow Eye
Pale Gray for Guilt
The Girl in the Plain
    Brown Wrapper
Dress Her in Indigo

The Long Lavender Look
A Tan and Sandy Silence
The Scarlet Ruse
The Turquoise Lament
The Dreadful Lemon Sky
The Empty Copper Sea
The Green Ripper
Free Fall in Crimson
Cinnamon Skin
The Lonely Silver Rain

The Official Travis McGee Quizbook

THE LAST
ONE LEFT

THE LAST ONE LEFT

A NOVEL

John D. MacDonald

RANDOM HOUSE TRADE PAPERBACKS

NEW YORK

2014 Random House Trade Paperback Edition

Published in the United States by Random House Trade Paperbacks, an imprint of The Random House Publishing Group, a division of Random House, LLC, a Penguin Random House Company, New York.

RANDOM HOUSE and the HOUSE colophon are registered trademarks of Random House, Inc.

Originally published in paperback in the United States by Fawcett, an imprint of The Random House Publishing Group, a division of Random House, Inc., in 1970.

ISBN 978-0-8129-8527-6
eBook ISBN 978-0-307-82708-1

Printed in the United States of America on acid-free paper

www.atrandom.com

9 8 7 6 5 4 3 2 1
Book design by Christopher Zucker

I dedicate this novel to *Travis McGee*
who lent invaluable support and encouragement.

"Extreme terror gives us back
the gestures of our childhood."
                                        —*Chazal*

The Singular
John D. MacDonald

by Dean Koontz

WHEN I WAS IN COLLEGE, I had a friend, Harry Recard, who was smart, funny, and a demon card player. Harry was a successful history major, while I passed more time playing pinochle than I spent in class. For the three and a half years that I required to graduate, I heard Harry rave about this writer named John D. MacDonald, "John D" to his most ardent readers. Of the two of us, Harry was the better card player and just generally the cooler one. Consequently, I was protective of my position, as an English major, to be the better judge of literature, don't you know. I remained reluctant to give John D a look.

Having read mostly science fiction, I found many of my professors' assigned authors markedly less exciting than Robert Heinlein and Theodore Sturgeon, but I was determined to read the right thing. For every Flannery O'Connor whose work I could race through with delight, there were three like Virginia Woolf, who made me want to throw their books off a high cliff and leap after them. Nevertheless, I continued to shun Harry's beloved John D.

Five or six years after college, I was a full-time writer with numerous credits in science fiction, struggling to move into suspense and mainstream work. I was making progress but not fast enough to suit me. By now I knew that John D was widely admired, and I finally sat down with one of his books. In the next thirty days, I read thirty-four of them. The singular voice and style of the man overwhelmed me, and the next novel I wrote was such an embarrassingly slavish imitation of a MacDonald tale that I had to throw away the manuscript.

I apologized to Harry for doubting him. He was so pleased to hear me proclaiming the joys of John D that he only said "I told you so" on, oh, twenty or thirty occasions.

Over the years, I have read every novel by John D at least three times, some of them twice that often. His ability to evoke a time and place—mostly Florida but also the industrial Midwest, Las Vegas, and elsewhere—was wonderful, and he could get inside an occupation to give you the details and the feel of it like few other writers I've ever read. His pacing was superb, the flow of his prose irresistible, and his suspense watch-spring tight.

Of all his manifest strengths as a writer, however, I am most in awe of his ability to create characters who are as real as anyone I've met in life. John D sometimes paused in the headlong rush of his story to spin out pages of background on a character. At first when this happened, I grumbled about getting on with the story. But I soon discovered that he could make the character so fascinating that when the story began to race forward again, I wanted it to slow down so I could learn more about this person who so intrigued and/or delighted me. There have been many good suspense novelists in recent decades, but in my experience, none has produced characters with as much humanity and truth as those in MacDonald's work.

Like most who have found this author, I am an admirer of his Travis McGee series, which features a first-person narrator as good as any in the history of suspense fiction and better than most. But I love the standalone novels even more. *Cry Hard, Cry Fast. Where Is Janice Gantry? The Last One Left. A Key to the Suite. The Drowner. The Damned. A Bullet for Cinderella. The Only Girl in the Game. The Crossroads. All These Condemned.* Those are not my only favorites, just a few of them, and many deal with interesting businesses and occupations. Mr. MacDonald's work gives the reader deep and abiding pleasure for many reasons, not the least of which is that it portrays the contemporary life of his day with as much grace and fidelity as any writer of the period, and thus it also provides compelling social history.

In 1985, when my publisher, Putnam, wanted to send advance proof copies of *Strangers* to Mr. MacDonald among others, I literally grew shaky at the thought of him reading it. I suggested that they shouldn't send it to him, that, as famous and prolific as he was, the proof would be an imposition on him; in truth, I feared that he would find the novel unsatisfying. Putnam sent it to him anyway, and he gave us an enthusiastic endorsement. In addition, he wrote to me separately, in an avuncular tone, kindly advising me how to avoid some of the pitfalls of the publishing business, and he wrote to my publisher asking her to please carefully consider the packaging of the book and not condemn it to the horror genre. She more or less condemned it to the genre anyway, but I took his advice to heart.

In my experience, John D. MacDonald, the man, was as kind and thoughtful as his fiction would lead you to believe that he must be. That a writer's work accurately reflects his soul is a rarer thing than you might imagine, but in his case, the reflection is clear and true. For that reason, it has been a special honor, in fact a grace, to be asked to write this introduction.

Reader, prepare to be enchanted by the books of John D. MacDonald. And Harry, I am not as much of an idiot as I was in years gone by—though I know you won't let me get away with claiming not to be to any degree an idiot anymore.

THE LAST
ONE LEFT

One

AT THE SMALL bon voyage party at the Delmar Bay Yacht Club Kip and Selma had given Howard and Junie Prowt a little brass plaque to affix to one of the bulkheads of the HoJun. It read "Oh Lord, thy sea is so vast and my boat is so small!"

Pull off the backing paper and press the gummed back of the plaque to any smooth clean surface.

Out in the middle of the Gulf Stream, at ten o'clock on the bright morning of a windy and cloudless day in May, Howard Prowt, braced on the fly bridge of his thirty-four-foot Owens cruiser, knew the precise corner of the exact drawer where he had stowed the gift, and fought the absurd compulsion to go below and find it and peel it and stick it up.

The stacks and tan cubes of Fort Lauderdale were below the horizon astern. He had plotted his course exactly as he had been taught in the Power Squadron classes, making the proper allowance for the northerly run of the Gulf Stream, and for standard deviation and compass deviation. He had computed his time of arrival at Bimini on the basis of 2300 rpm on his twin 150's. They had left Pier 66 at 8:30 and had passed the sea buoy at fourteen minutes before nine. At eleven minutes past noon the HoJun should reach the channel across the bar outside Bimini harbor.

Nobody told you how it would be. How it would feel. That was the trouble. They just said it could get a little dusty out there in the Stream. They didn't tell you about the strangeness, the alone-ness, the strange blue color and the power of it. There was an indifference about it, a lack of interest in you and your little boat. It changed the way everything looked and felt.

Howard Prowt kept trying to scan the dials, to check oil pressure, temperature, rpm's—and to check the performance of the automatic pilot against the compass, then would find himself staring, mind empty, braced for the next long lift of the hull, the teeter, the crash that would send water flashing white out to either side of the bow.

It's a good day to cross, he told himself. They build them for this.

The HoJun had felt massive, ponderous, trustworthy in all the other places he had taken her since accepting delivery last November. She had looked large tied up at their backyard dock on Heron Bayou, sizeable in the yacht club boat basin. He had learned exactly how she would respond in all conditions of wind and tide, priding himself on that gentle touch on the throttles which would ease her so close to a dock that Junie, on the bow, could step ashore with the line and put the loop over a piling. There had been several short cruises, and one long one—up to Stuart and through the lake and down the river to Fort Myers, then down the Gulf Coast to Marathon, and back home through Florida Bay and Biscayne Bay. He had taken her into some ugly chop in the Gulf, and had handled her in a tricky following sea. In his navigation he had always double-checked his course and had the pleasure of seeing the target markers, after long runs, loom out of the sea mist.

But this was not the same. It made everything else seem like pretend. This was not the same sea they had watched two years ago from the recreation deck of the little Italian cruise ship which had taken them through the Caribbean, as far down as Curaçao.

They had stood at the rail and looked *down* onto that sea. This one lifted, rose, pushed itself up into great gleaming humps higher at times than his line of vision on the flying bridge, with one in ten foaming white against the incredible laundry-blueing blue as the wind toppled the tip of it. He tensed his stomach each time the HoJun seemed to hesitate before lifting to it. Atop those long silky bulges he could see for miles, see the random pattern of the waves breaking. Then she would tilt, smash—making a jangling and thumping and clattering below, and a moment of noise, vibration and cavitation from the twin screws—then glide down the far side of the hump to that point where, as she dug her nose deep and sent water slashing back against the pilot house windshield and the fiberglass which protected the fly bridge, he could not see more than fifty feet in any direction.

He held fast against the motion, telling himself that this was not some deadly and dramatic shift in the weather pattern. It was just as the man at Pier 66 had predicted. "Wind swinging very slow, Mr. Prowt, be almost direct out of the east in an hour, and a couple points north of east by the time you're clear of the Stream. Be a pretty fair swell, nothing you can't take okay; but once it's swiveled all the way out of the north, the five-day forecast says it'll be maybe three days before I'd want to take it across. So you go now, you'll be fine. It won't have time to build the Stream up to a chop. I'd say you'll have a ten-knot breeze, freshening come evening. A pretty day to cross."

But nobody had described the absolute indifference of these swells, and the way they dwindled the HoJun to a silly little toy, and its owner to a foolish, childish fellow who had wanted to play captain.

He had listened on the 100-watt ship-to-shore, heard nothing but nasal, casual, fishing-hunting talk on one channel, Miami marine placing phone calls on another, silence on the Coast Guard Emergency channel.

One of these ponderous wallowing tumbles will tear a gas line loose and one engine will die and the spark from the other will ignite the loose gas in the bilge. Or a battery will shift and pull a cable loose and the engines will both die. Or some seam will give way in the hull, bringing in more water than the bilge pumps can handle.

Another painful abdominal cramp made him gasp and hunch himself. Great time for food poisoning. That lobster last night?

And, Oh God, here comes the biggest one yet!

She lifted up and up, toppled over the crest with an uneasy cork-screwing motion, the cavitation lasting longer, glided down the blue hill and smashed her bow deep enough to send solid water streaming back along the side decks.

Exactly what the hell am I doing out here?

"I think, honey, that next May we'll cruise the Bahamas. Get Kip and Selma to go along. Take a whole month pooting around. Maybe go over as far as Eleuthera. How about it?"

When you have enough boat to get to the Bahamas, and when you live so close, and when maybe next year they'll make you Fleet Captain of the Delmar Bay Yacht Club, then you go. Or they'll think you incompetent or timid.

So I'm timid, he thought. Outboards they bring over here. They race from Miami to Nassau when the seas are higher. Any boat has a lot of safety factor, and this one was new six months ago. But I came out past that sea buoy feeling like Horatio Hornblower, and right now I am one scared, retired wholesale grocer from Moline out in the middle of all this tumbling blue indifference that doesn't care whether I sink, blow up or make it across.

Always wanted a cruiser.

God, just get me there!

Junie, fighting for balance, clutched at his arm, startling him. She tottered away with a jolly whoop of dismay, grabbed at the pilot seat, settled into it and grinned at him. Her grin was uncharacteristically broad, her gray eyes not properly focused, her sandy-blonde hair matted damp with sea water, her color so bleached under her deep tan it gave her flesh an odd saffron tone. Above her denim halter her skin had a plucked-chicken look, so pronounced were the goose pimples.

He knew that she was both nauseated and terrified, and trying with a touching gallantry not to show either. But terror had to be stronger than the nausea, because she hated the increased swing and dip of the flying bridge, avoiding it except when it was dead calm.

Neither of us belong here, he thought. It's all some kind of pretend. She's a fifty-eight-year-old housewife and mother from Moline, and since we moved down here she's dieted and exercised and trimmed herself down, and baked herself brown, turned from gray to blonde, wears these play clothes, even talks in ways which would puzzle the placid Moline matron of two years ago. But it is all pretend for both of us—damn fools out of a yachting magazine ad, tricked finally into playing our game out here where all of a sudden it's all turned real.

"Getting rougher, darling?" she called over the sound of wind and sea and engines.

"Staying about the same. You feel better?"

"A little." The fixed smile stayed in place, even when she stared ahead.

Full fuel tanks, he thought. Full water tanks. And that damned couple of tons of provisions we carried aboard and stowed. Riding lower in the water than she ever has, and we have to get into this.

He made a businesslike routine of reading all the gauges, wearing his seamanship frown.

"Something wrong?" she called, the smile gone, her mouth pinching tight, bloodless lips sucked in, looking suddenly like an old, old woman garbed for some vulgar ingenue role.

"There's not a damn thing wrong!"

"You don't have to shout at me, Howard. I mean—I don't understand the engines and things. And it just seems to get—worse and worse."

He patted her on the shoulder. "Everything's fine. Really fine."

"Will—the whole trip be like this?"

"WE ARE CROSSING THE GULF STR—" He caught himself, changed his tone. "Honey, this is the *only* rough part."

"If you aren't nervous, why do you act so cross?"

"I am *not* nervous. I am *not* cross."

He wondered if it would be different—better—if Kip and Selma had been able to cross with them instead of flying over day after tomorrow to Bimini. Most of their gear was aboard. Kip had some kind of meeting at the last minute. Of course Kip didn't know item one about seamanship, piloting and small-boat handling. Nor did Selma. But maybe four people wouldn't get as . . .

He peered ahead from the top of a crest, saw a white object far ahead, too fleetingly to determine what it was before the glide into the trough cut off his view.

When they lifted again, he could not spot it. But the next time it was there again, and Junie said, "Isn't that a little boat?"

"I think so."

He took the binoculars out of the rack, couldn't get focused on the object on the next lift, but managed a swift glimpse on the succeeding one.

"Small open boat," he announced.

"Out in *this!*"

The spoked wheel kept turning as the automatic pilot kept searching and correcting. The distant boat would appear first a little off the port bow, then off the starboard bow, and he realized it was dead on course. He rehearsed the procedure he would follow, lock the pilot on a new course five degrees more southerly, check the time he made the change, and then when they were opposite it, return to course by giving it ten degrees more north for the same elapsed time, then put it back on his plotted compass direction. Or were you supposed to correct just five degrees and then . . .

He was reluctant to touch or change anything. He had tried some careful alterations in the rpm's to see if she would ride easier, but succeeded only in alarming himself. At slower speed she had a tendency to fall off course. Faster, she merely made a more sickening crashing sound when she came off the crest. And he could not guess how she would react to even a minor course alteration. He decided to wait and see how close they might come to the smaller boat.

Soon he could see it at every crest, an open boat, a power boat twenty feet long, or a little longer, with a sleek hull, windshield, white topsides, and a green-blue hull lighter in shade than the strange blue of the Stream. The high sun made bright gleams on the metal fittings, the controls, the chromed windshield frame. She appeared to be floating light and high, bow to the wind, moving with a carefree grace to the long steep passage of the swells.

But it was dead in the water. With the glasses he saw it was equipped with two stern-drive units, both uptilted. He could not make out the name on the transom. The boat appeared to be empty. To his immediate relief, he saw that with no course alteration, it would go by on his port at least a hundred feet away. The wind and the Stream combined to drift it northwest.

"Hadn't we ought to do something?" Junie asked.

"Do what? So it's some drunk. He rigged a sea anchor and he's sleeping it off. Or young lovers."

She reached quickly and pressed the air horn button on the control panel. That sound, so huge when he would make the turn from the yacht club basin into the channel, sounded frail out here. In intense annoyance, he slapped her hand away.

"It's a vessel in distress, isn't it?" she demanded, her face pinched into an expression of indignant anger. "Or a derelict? Aren't we supposed to do something? What if somebody is sick, like a heart attack?"

"Honey, you *started* the Power Squadron course. You didn't *finish* the Power Squadron course. I *finished* the Power Squadron course. I am in *command* of this vessel."

"Oh dear Jesus, Captain Bligh. I just mean . . ."

"I can see that she's dragging some kind of bow line. I'd say it was an anchor line that maybe frayed, maybe right down at the anchor ring so she's dragging enough so the line itself keeps her bow into the wind. So some careless damn fool loses his pretty little boat. So what if we try to come about? Ever think of that? Crossways on these swells, we'll roll everything loose, and maybe coming about we get one of the breakers just right off the corner of the stern and we broach. Then what, baby? And do you want to be the one to try to get that line with a boat hook? And what if I judge it wrong and she punches a big son of a bitch of a hole in our hull? What I'll do is report her position, and they'll send a helicopter out of Lauderdale, or a cutter or something."

"That name on it, Howard! Muñequita. Out of Brownsville, Texas?" Money-quit-ah, she pronounced it.

"What about it?"

"Howard, I swear I read something about that boat or heard something about that boat. Something in the news. Last week, maybe."

"For God's sake, June, you always want to make some kind of a big thing out of every little thing that happens."

"An empty boat out here in the middle of the ocean? That's such a little thing it's practically nothing?"

It was abeam of them and they both stared at it. She took the binoculars from the rack, braced herself with one arm hooked around the back of the pilot seat. "Gee, Howard, it's a pretty little boat, it really is. Like new."

"I'll go down and report it," he said. He went down the ladder-way carefully, anticipating the now-familiar movements of the HoJun. In the pilot house he checked the chronometer, figured the distance traveled, and, with his dividers, made an exact little prick mark on the penciled course line. He drew an X at that mark, then measured over to the chart border to get the exact position, latitude and longitude in degrees and minutes.

He rehearsed exactly how he would report it on the emergency channel. But he did not want to report it. He could guess that any skipper familiar with the Stream would have taken the boat in tow without a second thought. This was supposed to be a good day for a crossing.

"All right, Captain, why didn't you take a look and see if anybody aboard needed help? That's your obligation, you know."

"Well, I was having a little trouble myself."

"Indeed? What sort of trouble?"

"I—I was losing a little pressure on the starboard engine. Anyway, we went close enough to it to be certain there wasn't anybody aboard."

"Certain there was no one in the bunks below?"

But it probably wouldn't be like that at all. It was just a boat that had slipped its moorings somehow. And how much could they ask of you anyway?

As he turned he saw June come scrabbling dangerously down the ladderway, clutching and lurching. She had the binoculars hung around her neck. He winced as he saw them swing and whack solidly against the hand rail. He was about to tell her exactly what they had cost when he saw the frantic expression on her face.

"A hand! We've got to go back, darling! We've got to do something."

"A what? Make sense!"

"I saw it with the glasses. It came up and held onto the edge and then it let go. A little hand. A child's hand. We've got to *do* something."

Howard Prowt clambered heavily but swiftly up to the fly bridge. She was beside him when he took it out of automatic pilot. Try to get it around quickly, or ease it around? Maybe a little of both. Ease it slowly until it begins to wallow in the trough, then reverse the port engine and kick it around and gun it to get out of the way of the following wave.

Twice he brought it almost parallel with the swells, but the alarming motion caused him to head back into the wind. He resolved to do it on the third try. He got it into the trough and when she heeled over further than he would have thought possible, and when he heard a thudding and crashing below, he ran it back up into the wind again.

"At that distance, with both boats jumping all over the goddam ocean, you saw one hand?"

"I did!"

"You saw an end of a rag flap over the gunnel for a moment. Something like that."

"Can't we turn around?"

"It isn't a case of can't. Sure. But why crash a lot of gear around below because you've got that imagination of yours?"

Suddenly she turned away from him, lurched, grabbed the rail, hunched over it and was spasmed by nausea, the sea wind whipping at her damp hair. He eased the HoJun back onto course and locked it into pilot, checked his gauges. He looked at her, at the brown hide and slender legs of his life-long wife, at the regular pulsations of nausea which shook her body, and, to his mild astonishment, felt desire for her. It was an obscure and shameful pride that at a time and place so incongruous, this notion, impossible to fulfill, should come to him. Maybe it can happen from being scared, he thought, of thinking of yourself drowning and dying here in this big blue mess, and it's a way of telling yourself you're alive.

When she was through, he went below to put his call in. In the main cabin the television set had fallen out of its brackets and lay face down on the carpeting. The radio set had shifted. He turned it on. It would not light up. He could not send. Then he saw where the cable had been pulled out of the chassis.

Howard Prowt went up and told her. He looked astern, and he could not spot the drifting boat. The water was changing to a new color, to a blue that was mixed with green and gray. To the southeast he saw a southbound tanker. They were out of the Gulf Stream. The motion was easing. They were on course.

She seemed very subdued, and he glanced sidelong at her from time to time to see how angry she was. But it was a remote expression he could not read.

"Junie, honey, it's only by a freak of chance we ever came close enough to that boat to see it."

"I suppose."

"I mean, we wouldn't be *expected* to see it."

"Howard, what are you driving at?"

"Honey, on a thing like this, there can be a lot of red tape. I mean it could get us hung up in Bimini, or maybe even having to go back and fill out a lot of reports. You understand, if I was absolutely *convinced* you saw what you thought you saw, wild horses couldn't have kept me from getting to that boat."

"Yes, Howard."

"And I can't help what happened to the transmitter."

"I guess not."

"All in all, I think the wisest course is that we forget we ever saw that boat. We wouldn't want to spoil anything, you know, like for Kip and Selma."

"We wouldn't want to spoil anything," she said, and went over to begin a careful descent of the open ladderway.

"Is that okay with you?" he called.

"Is what okay?"

"To just forget it happened?"

"Sure. Sure," she said and backed out of sight. A moment later her face reappeared and she said, "I busted the binoculars."

"Accidents will happen aboard ship. Don't give it a second thought. I got the old ones aboard, those surplus ones."

Later, in calm water, he called her up to the flying bridge. When she stood beside him, he said, "Land Ho, and right on the button. Look at that range marker on shore. By God, we could damn near run that channel without taking her out of pilot."

"Very good, dear."

"Look at all the crazy colors in that water off the bar there."

"It's beautiful."

Her lean hand rested atop the instrument panel. He covered it with his and said, "That's Bimini, old lady. And bank on this—the Prowts and the Heaters are going to have one hell of a month of fun."

For a long time she did not answer. She slowly withdrew her hand. "It's going to be a ball," she said without smile or inflection. "Tell me when you want me to take a line forward." She climbed back down to the cockpit deck.

Howard Prowt cut off the pilot and took over manual control, cutting his speed another increment as he headed for the channel.

Always, coming into harbor after a good job of navigation, he had that Horatio Hornblower feeling, grizzled and sea-tough and with a look of far places.

He reached for that feeling, and for an anticipation of all the courses he would run, all the expertise he would bring back to Delmar Bay one month hence, but he could find neither.

He merely felt old. And his legs felt tired. And his gut felt uneasy. And he wished he were back sitting on the bank of Heron Bayou with a cold beer in his hand, and the HoJun tied to his own dock in that tricky way he had devised all by himself.

Damn her anyway.

Two

STANIKER, on an ever-lasting afternoon, fought off the dreams and the visions. There was some kind of a Thing, some tantalizing entity which kept launching them at him to see how he'd make out. That time in South America when they'd gone after those lunker trout in the mountain lake, those Indios had those light nets they could throw, float them out very pretty.

Dreams came like the nets, something throwing them at him, floating down to lay like cobwebs across his mind. So then each time he had to pluck off every strand. There was a way to do it. You focused on some real thing, close at hand. The sheath knife, rusting with an astonishing speed. Could you measure the days by the way the rust grew? Think of the knife and you could pluck away one strand. Look at the pile of empty shells of the sea-things you had eaten, had pried off the ragged black rocks at low tide, smashed with stones, trying to save the juice to suck before eating the creature.

Look at the crude sticks and poles some forgotten Bahamian fisherman had assembled long ago for rough shelter on this empty island, and at your own additions, poles above and a clumsy thatch for shade from each day's interminable passage of the sun. Roll over, wincing at the pain of it, and lift your head and look out across the hot white glare of the sand flats of South Joulter Cay, where you had tried to stamp the big arrow and the H E L P, because all the Nassau-Miami flights passed over here, just a little bit south, not too far south. But the white dry loose sand would not take a message, and when you put it in the packed wet sand, the tide would take it away. Look out toward the channel and remember that this was a popular place for the private boats which came flocking over from Florida in May, listed attractively in the Cruising Guide, and it was just one of those weird coincidences that not one had come by. Look over where those brackish pools are, and remember the oily and stagnant taste of the water, and wonder if the fever and the dreams came from the water or from the burns. Look at the outside of the right arm and shoulder, at the outside of the right thigh and calf where the deeply tanned skin had blistered, cracked, sloughed loose, and now suppurated and stank.

The pain of movement was a reality, as was the dull ache of the over-burdened kidneys.

These were realities, and the way he could find his way out of the bright and senseless shifting of the dreams which kept moving him to places he had been, with people who had never been there with him, people from other places who said all the ugly things from childhood. Static reality was something he could brace against, but the changing things, the birds, the airplanes, the quick lizards, he could not tell if they were part of here or part of the cobwebs.

When his teeth began to chatter, Staniker would hunch himself out into the sunlight. And then, brain a-boil, pull himself back into

the shade. Time would slip and the sun would jump three diameters
west and sometimes he would become aware of a voice and listen
and hear himself talking to Crissy, talking loudly because he was
sitting on the edge of her dock and she was swimming slow lengths
with her face closed against all listening, all explanations.

Several times there was Mary Jane's voice in that tired, whining,
scolding, hopeless sound; but of course she was three sea miles away
and a half a mile deep, her mouth at rest at last, down in the black-
green of the Tongue of the Ocean.

The dreams came oftener, and most of the time he did not mind
it, merely let them happen, and watched the colors and the changes.
But then he would fight free of the strands, and find panic again, the
awareness that everything had gone wrong, was continuing to go
wrong, could end in a death that would make all the other parts of
it meaningless.

When the sun was low, while he was in restless sleep, a Chris-
Craft out of Jacksonville came cautiously in over the harbor bar,
threading the unmarked channel, a vacationing dentist leaning over
the bow rail, reading the channel by the color of the water, using
hand signals to guide his friend, a plumbing contractor, owner of
the boat, who had the helm. It was an hour or so past low tide. The
wheels boiled up sand in the slow wake. The hull was skegged for
this kind of shallow-water exploration. In the gentle chop, at the
shallowest point, they bumped twice against the packed sand of the
bottom, then moved on into the deeper water of the natural channel
close to the key, towing the little glass dinghy astern. They came
around the point into still water. The engines droned. The chattering wives were aft, fixing the cocktail snacks. The men were studying the chart, inspecting the water, discussing where to anchor. One
of the wives turned a transistor radio to music from a Miami station.

These sounds awakened Staniker, and on hands and knees he

crawled and looked around the edge of his shelter and saw the cruiser moving past, a hundred yards away. He pulled himself up, using his right arm in spite of the pain it caused him, and cawed at them as loudly as he could. The cruiser moved on.

The shelter was at a high point, perhaps twenty feet above the water. He tottered down the narrow winding path, terribly afraid that if he should fall, he might not be able to get up. He came down to the narrow band of sandy beach which was covered at high tide, cupped his hands around his mouth and cawed again, his voice cracking to a contralto scream.

He saw them staring at him. The cruiser slowed, and the man at the helm gave it a single burst from both engines in reverse to lay it dead in the water. The dinghy came up and thumped the transom. The engines were turned off. Staniker went down onto one knee and rested his fists against the sand at the water's edge.

"What do you want?" a man called across the stillness.

"Staniker," he replied. "Off the Muñeca. Burned. Sick. Help me."

He heard their excited jabbering, and he let his head sag and closed his eyes and breathed deeply. Soon he heard the familiar snoring sound of a Sea Gull outboard, looked up and saw the dinghy coming toward him with one man aboard. The man, making clucking sounds of dismay at his condition, helped him aboard and took him out to the cruiser. In helping him aboard, they hurt him so badly he screeched and the world tilted into grayness but came slowly back. With many instructions to each other, they helped him below and got him into a bunk.

Time slipped again, and in the next instant he could feel the movement of the hull, hear the engines at cruising speed, identify the hull motion as a deep-water motion with a following sea off the port quarter. The cabin lights were on. A thin leathery man in his fifties, wearing steel-rimmed glasses, was staring appraisingly at him. Behind him, in the shadows, was a tall woman standing braced against the motion of the boat.

"Can you hear me, Captain?" the man asked.

"Yes, yes sir."

"Swallow these. For fever and pain."

The water was in a tall dark-blue plastic glass, with ice. He had never tasted anything as delicious.

The man took the empty glass and said, "I am not a medical doctor, Staniker. I'm a dentist. We have to know a certain amount of medicine. I've dressed your burns with what we could improvise. Your fever is running a hundred and three and a half. It was probably higher in the afternoon. We're making a night run to Nassau. My name is Barth, by the way. Bert Hilger, my friend who owns this boat, couldn't raise anything on the damned radio after we found you. So we're running you in where you can get hospital attention. Do you understand, Captain?"

"How—how bad off am I, Doctor?"

"How long were you alone there on South Joulter?"

"What day is it?"

"Today? Friday, the—uh—"

"Twentieth," the woman said.

"We—we blew up and burned last Friday night."

"You are a superb physical specimen, Captain. If you don't get pneumonia, I suspect you'll snap back quickly with proper care. Can you answer some questions? In case you're not conscious when we dock at Nassau."

"Yes sir."

"What happened?"

"It was—about nine o'clock. They were all below. They would have been topsides, it was such a nice night, except they were having dinner. They always ate late. Moonlight night, and we were heading for the Joulters. I was running her from the flying bridge, on pilot, and I'd turned the depth-finder on. When it began to pick up any bottom at all, I was going to cut down, take over, and find the passage I've been through before, place where there's no coral heads to bother you. On that Muñeca, you've got—you had every control duplicated up on the fly bridge. I remembered how one bank of batteries was pretty well down, and from the running time I didn't think we'd gotten the other bank charged full yet. Any boat I'm operating, I like to keep the batteries up. That would mean running the auxiliary generator after we anchored. And no reason at all why I couldn't run it while we were under way. Spoils a quiet anchorage when you have to run it at night, like of course you have to when they wanted the air conditioning on. I remember every once in a while I could just barely hear Bix—Mr. Kayd—laugh. He had a loud laugh. So I switched the auxiliary generator to the spare bank, and I pressed the button wondering if it would catch right off—it was a little cranky sometimes—and there was a big flash and a whoomp, and the next thing I know I'm in the water, choking and strangling and thrashing around, with a funny orange light on the water and the back of my neck hot. I guess I was knocked out for a little while and the water brought me out of it. When I got turned around, she was fire from bow to stern, and burning to the waterline. I was sick to my stomach from swallowing water. I saw something in the water and I managed to swim to it. It was one of those styrofoam sort of surf-board looking things with a glass place to look through. Miss Stella had brought it aboard in Key West, and she liked to use it to float around over the coral reefs, looking down at the fish. She wasn't a good swimmer on account of her leg. The board was scorched and melted along one edge, but when I pulled myself onto it, it held me all right. And about then, the Muñeca— that means doll in Spanish—went down like a rock, with a lot of hissing when the flames went underwater, and some bubbling and boiling on the surface for just a few seconds. Then it was quiet. When I could stop coughing, I started calling them. I guess I was out of my head. Maybe the only one I was calling was my wife, Mary Jane. But no answer at all."

"But wasn't the Muñeca diesel powered?" the dentist asked.

"Yes sir. But the auxiliary generator was gasoline powered, and my guess is that gas leaked into the bilge from its fuel tank or one of the tins stowed down there to fuel it with. The spark, when I tried to start it, blew the boat up, and the heat of the explosion was greater than the flash-point of the diesel fuel. Maybe I goofed. My God, sir, I'd never start gasoline marine engines without running the blowers first. But with an auxiliary, you don't think of that so easy. And maybe Bix—Mr. Kayd—goofed too, not having a sniffer installed when he had the gas auxiliary put below decks. Using a blower is something you think of when you're tied up, not running along at cruising speed."

"No other survivors, Captain."

"No sir. When I knew I was alone out there, I remembered the Muñequita. That means little doll in Spanish. It was the boat Bix picked up in Miami because the Muñeca was too big for fishing, with too much draft for some of the places they wanted to explore. She towed just fine on a long line. Snub her closer and she'd wallow and swing, but way back she rode like a church. I thought I spotted her quite a way off. I kept paddling until my arms ached, but if it was the Muñequita, she was moving as fast as I was. It's possible. With those twin out-drive Volvo units tilted up, she draws fifteen inches, and she has about an average three feet of freeboard for the wind to catch." He closed his eyes.

"Isn't this tiring him too much, Bill?" the woman asked softly.

"I'm okay," Staniker said.

"There's been a big search," Barth said. "Air and sea. I guess it started when Kayd didn't radio Nassau Marine last Saturday morning for traffic, and there were some calls in for him, and the marine operator couldn't raise him. The search has been tapering off. The focus was up around the Berry Islands."

"That was where we were headed when we left Nassau. We got into nice dolphin a few miles out. Spent a lot of time. Everybody had fun. Mrs. Kayd had been reading the Guide. She wanted to see the Joulters, and kept teasing Bix until he had me lay out a new course. He said we'd cruise from there to the Berrys Saturday afternoon."

"And on that float board you made it to South Joulter, eh?"

"I knew about where we were when—it happened. I got a rough estimate of my direction of drift from the stars, and it was too northerly and I was afraid it would make me miss the Joulters and take me on out northwest onto the Bahama Banks. I paddled due south to compensate. Paddled and rested. Maybe I passed out once or twice. At dawn I came to the bar. I let the board drift away. I walked until it got deep again, then swam ashore. Every day—I waited for somebody to come—felt worse—kept thinking about the Muñeca . . . ."

"Now there," a gentle, crooning, comforting woman-voice said. "It's all right. You'll be all right." He felt her dabbing gently at his face with some cool, scented, astringent lotion on a cloth.

He opened his eyes and saw her leaning over him in the lights of the cabin, saw it was the tall brunette, the better looking of the two, but at this closeness she was older than he had estimated.

"Do you know where you are and who I am, Captain?"

"Is it—Mrs. Barth?"

"Then you *do* know. But I'm Mrs. Hilger. A while ago you thought I was someone else. Somebody named Crissy. Or Christy. You scared me a little, you were holding my arm so tightly."

He lay very still. He breathed slowly. "What did I say?"

"I don't know, actually. You seemed to be trying to make Crissy or Christy understand something. You said something about it not being your fault. Pleading with her, or him." Her laugh was nervous. "You got quite wild this time."

"This time?"

"You just moaned and mumbled the other times. This time you rose right up and shouted. We should be tied up in another twenty minutes, Captain. Bert got through to Nassau Marine a little while ago. There'll be an ambulance waiting."

He closed his eyes. It was unfair that fever should make you talk and not know you were talking. Somebody might hear enough of the fever words to make their guesses about all of it.

You could not will yourself to be silent when the fever carried you off. But if you could make certain all they would hear would be a thickened mumbling . . .

He shoved his tongue into his right cheek, between the strong molars. He bit tentatively at first, measuring the pain. Then, body rigid, snuffling and grunting with agony and effort, he began chewing his tongue, mashing the sensitive flesh, tasting the coppery flavor of his blood.

From far away he could hear the woman shouting at him, and then she ran out and called the others. When he felt them leaning over him he pretended to be asleep. God help us, Crissy. God help us. It went wrong. I tried, but it went wrong.

Three

THE THIRTY-EIGHT HUNDRED POUNDS of the Muñequita dipped and danced on into the Atlantic dusk. Little Doll. Under considerably more power this same T-Craft hull design had won some savage ocean races. Fiberglass, teak, aluminum, stainless steel, plastic, perhaps ten thousand dollars for such a special plaything. With the twin Chrysler-Volvo inboard, outboards, 120 horsepower each, she could scat at forty-seven miles an hour, the deep Vee hull slicing through the chop, the wake flat.

With her fuel capacity increased by the two saddle tanks to over eighty gallons, at her cruising speed of thirty-two miles an hour, the engines turning at 4500 rpm, her maximum range was almost three hundred miles, without safety factor.

From the forward lift-ring a hundred feet of half-inch nylon line trailed upwind. She had been bought on whim and loaded with extras—convertible top, now folded and snapped into the boot, searchlight, rod holders, windshield wipers, bow rails, anchor chocks, electric horn, screens, a transistorized Pearce-Simpson ship-to-shore radio tucked under the Teleflex instrument panel, pedestal helmsman's seats, two bunks and a head fitted into the small area forward.

Salt had crusted on her, and had then been rinsed away when she had drifted through the rain squalls. At times when the wind and the chop were at odds and the waves broke, she would falter in a moment of awkwardness, take water, then shake herself free with almost an air of apology for such flawed grace. The automatic bilge pump had been turned on when she was rigged for towing, and when the rain and the chop brought enough water aboard, the pump would drone, working off the batteries, until the bilge was again empty.

The graceful hull was a medium Nassau blue, her topsides white with just enough trace of smoke blue to cut the sunglare.

She had lifted and dipped and danced her way with an agile grace which matched her name. Muñequita. Little Doll. The out-drive stern units were uptilted and locked in place. The long line trailing from the bow steadied her, keeping her bow facing into the wind. Yet now movement was less graceful because the northeast wind was freshening, lifting the Gulf Stream into a chop. In that balance of forces the Muñequita moved due west, stern first, into nighttime.

Even in that posture, she seemed to anticipate and avoid the uglier motions, almost as if she were aware of the look of death aboard, aware of the naked body of the girl, face down on the cockpit decking, responding, slack as a pudding, to each variation of that long and lonely dance across an empty sea.

The boat drifted into the path of a brief hard shower that moved swiftly, dimpling the swells, then spattering against the topsides and against the sunraw, blistered back of the girl. It soaked her hair and when it ran across her parted lips she made the smallest of sounds, licked with a slow tongue, moved one hand slightly.

The rain ended. The bilge pump started up, droned for two minutes and clicked off.

By midnight the boat had reached the western edge of the Stream where current and chop were diminished. The Muñequita's motion eased. She began to drift in a more southwesterly direction.

Four

ON SUNDAY MORNING, the fifteenth of May, just before noon, Sam Boylston sat in a booth by the tinted plate-glass windows of a roadside restaurant on the outskirts of Corpus Christi, looked across at the somber, pretty and intent face of Lydia Jean, his estranged wife, and knew that all the things he had said—all so carefully planned—had been the wrong things after all.

They kept their voices low. A group of idle waitresses prattled and snickered twenty feet away.

"What it all adds up to, Lyd—check me if I'm wrong—you're still in love with me in a kind of sad dramatic way . . . but we haven't got a chance in the world because I am the kind of a person I am."

She frowned. "You sum things up so they sound so neat and complete and final. But it's sort of a trick. It's argumentation, really. If you could understand what it is about you that made things wrong, and if you could—*see* yourself doing it, and if you could

understand *why* you do it then maybe you could . . . Now you have
that terribly patient and tolerant look."

"You think I need help?"

"I don't know what you need."

"I need you. I need Boy-Sam. I need the home we had five
months ago, Lyd."

She shook her head in a puzzled way. "I wish I could explain it. I
really do. You *crowd* people. You use them up, and the nearer and
dearer they are to you, the more mercilessly you spend them."

"Overbearing monster, huh?"

"You are a very civilized man, dear. You are polite. You are
considerate. You are thoughtful. But you demand of yourself an absolute clarity, total performance, complete dedication. There is
something almost inhuman about it, really. What is lacking, I think,
is the tolerance to accept—the inadequacies of others."

"Lyd, be fair. Did I ever tell you you weren't meeting some kind
of standard?"

She was silent as she refilled her empty coffee cup and warmed his
cup from the Thermos pitcher. "I've thought about it a lot. I think
it was because you were so young when your parents were killed in
that accident, and you felt responsible for Leila, and your father had
left everything in such a dreadful foolish muddle."

"Oh, come *on!*"

"No, really. Try to understand. You are only thirty years old,
Sam. What did we get married on when you got out of law school?
That old car. And barely a hundred dollars. That was only *seven years
ago!* You are worth a lot of money."

"Simple ruthless greed, darling."

"Don't make jokes, please, when I'm trying to explain something. It's because you have this terrible impatience with carelessness
and muddy thinking and laziness. You drive yourself so hard. It isn't
money hunger. You just seem to want to go around neatening up

the world. It exasperates you to see somebody operating in a sloppy way. For goodness sake, just look at Gil and that car-wash thing. He came to you as a client. Nearly bankrupt. Patent suits, wasn't it?"

"Mostly. Offered me a one-third interest if I could salvage it and get it back on its feet, help arrange refinancing."

"Now he has scores of those coin things all over the southwest, and what is your interest worth, Sam?"

"Considerable. So?"

"You neatened it up like a compulsive housekeeper. And what you demanded of me, dear, was that I be the loveliest, smartest, most charming young housewife and matron and hostess in all Texas. You were perfectly sure that because you love me, and because I had to be willing to give a hundred and ten percent to the program, I would be just that. Boy-Sam had to be the smartest, merriest, happiest, gutsiest little kid in the world, because he was yours and all he'd have to do would be live up to his potential. You demand just as much of your sister, Leila, in another way. But, right up until recently, she's had the spirit and the toughness to ignore the pressure. Boy-Sam and I, we just weren't strong enough. We had to get out."

"Pressure on the kid?"

"He adores you. He strained every nerve and muscle to please you, to do what he thought you wanted him to do. But he's just a little guy. He's only five years old. Oh, you wouldn't criticize. But when he'd fall short of what you expected of him, you'd give him a little pat and say, 'Well, kid, you gave it a try,' and walk away. He is sensitive to every nuance of your voice. You never glanced back and saw his eyes filling with tears because he felt he'd failed to measure up to the impossible standards you set him. You set impossible standards for yourself, and then you meet them, God knows how. You expect it of yourself. You take your own total performance for granted. I tell you, it discourages the hell out of us fallible types."

"You are everything I want you to be, Lyd."

"When I was little we had an old brown dog. He smiled at you. He'd get in a chair with you and when he was asleep he'd start to push. Just a little bit. He'd take up all the slack he could get. When you shoved back, he'd wake up and smile at you and go back to sleep and start pushing again. And finally it was his chair and you had no more room in it, so you moved."

"Maybe he liked closeness."

"Believe me, I could have endured. I could have kept striving to achieve perfection, kept falling short, kept seeing that puzzled yearning behind your polite smile, dear. But he's my only chick. What right have I to let him grow up with the feeling that nothing he can do is quite good enough? By eighteen he would have been a crashing neurotic, full of despair and self-hate. I hug him a lot, Sam. I give him extravagant compliments. And I don't tell him I love him *because* he can do this or do that. I tell him I love him because he is Boy-Sam."

"What's so damned unnatural about a father wanting his son to excel, Lydia Jean?"

She made a face, and a gesture of resignation and despair. "Why do I keep trying to get through to you?" She leaned forward. "Here is a perfect example of what I mean, dear. Your sister is nineteen. Leila knows her own mind. She has been going with Jonathan Dye for a long time. He is twenty-one, a fine, sensitive, dedicated boy. His teaching job in Uruguay begins in September, and I think he will be a very good teacher. They want to be married and honeymoon on the ship to Montevideo. So big brother comes onto the scene, *demanding* they prove it's the real thing by spending months apart, and you finally wore them down, dear. Congratulations! So there is Leila batting around the Bahamas on Bix Kayd's yacht, and Jonathan working as a hired hand on the ranch of some friend of

yours. To make a man of him? What are you trying to prove, pushing those kids around?"

"Easy to get sentimental about young love. I insisted for her
good, Lyd. The boy is an idealist, sort of permanently out of touch
with reality."

"With *your* version of reality."

"Give me a chance. You asked me to explain. Leila is impression-
able and imaginative. She's been absorbing the boy's do-good phi-
losophy for a long time. They were going to spend the summer in
Mexico on one of the Friends' Service Committee things, in some
village, painting huts, digging latrines, teaching English, all that
stuff. Okay, so it's a valid program. So is teaching in a backwoods
school in Uruguay. But if that kind of life is not what Leila *really*
believes in, if she only thinks she believes in it, then she could wake
up one day and find herself trapped in a kind of—sacrificial existence, a flavor of charity and penance and austerity. If she has some
time away from him, a chance to see another kind of life, maybe
she'll discover she's victimized herself with a romantic vision of a
life of good works. If it doesn't work that way, then she's probably
genuine about it. But what's the harm in making sure?"

"She's humoring you, you know. Quite a cruise for her. Bix
Kayd, and that truly poisonous second wife of his, Carolyn. And
poor ineffectual Roger Kayd. But there is a kind of sweetness about
Stella. I guess you did the Kayd family a favor, at least. Carolyn
won't lean so hard on her step-children with Leila along. So you
think the yacht clubs and marinas and the drinks around the pool are
going to make Leila skeptical of Uruguay? It's all going to make her
ache to get back to Jonathan, dear. You see, what you are doing is
not permitting them to live up to their own image of themselves.
You are asking that they live up to your image of them. And when
they marry, and they spend a year doing what Jonathan wants to do

with his life, I will bet you a dollar to a dime you'll tell them that now they've gotten the nonsense out of their systems, you have a great opportunity for them."

"Does she really know what she wants? That's the question, isn't it?"

She studied him, chin on her fist. "Sam, darling, when you suddenly look around you and see that—life itself is the basic magic, the real miracle, then we might have a chance. You are trying to impose your sense of order and fitness on the randomness of people and the illogic of fate. You want to refute the basic textures, the crazy mixture of life, and neaten it all up. Boy-Sam and I are refugees from that pattern, dear."

"I wish I could understand what you're driving at."

"So do I, dear. So do I, believe me."

She had to get back. He paid the check and they walked out to the parking lot, in the dry white heat of mid-May, walked to her red Mustang, his present to her on her twenty-seventh birthday, three weeks before she packed and left him.

When she grasped the door handle, he put his hand on the door to make her wait a moment. She turned toward him.

He said, "Remember, on that four-day honeymoon up there in the Hill Country, that day we walked up those hills beyond Ingram and you could see the Guadeloupe River?"

"Yes," she said flatly.

"I bought a forty acre piece of hillside. I had Seddon and Garvey draw me up plans for a hideaway lodge. They started construction three weeks ago. I can take some time off early in July. I'll phone you. I can pick you up at your mother's here, and we can go up there and really talk this out. I love you, Lyd. I need you. We can patch it up if we can get away together for a week, just the two of us, believe me. It will be beautiful up there then."

He put his hands on her arms just above the elbows, gave her a little shake, drew her closer. "Please, Lyd."

Her mouth softened, and her eyelids drooped with a sensual heaviness, and she took a deep slow breath. Then abruptly she pulled away, pushed her dark hair back with the back of her hand.

"No, Sam. We tried to solve too many things just that way. And I want you that way. You know that. But the other has to be talked out, and I have to know that you know what I mean. Thank God you are too honest to fake it, to pretend to understand, and throw my words back at me. Why don't you just—think about what we've said, and phone me in a month and we'll meet—in another place like this one."

He opened the car door, and she got behind the wheel and looked up at him. He said, "I'm sending you enough?"

"More than enough. You know that. It makes my pay for the part-time library job look—ludicrous. Well—do try to get *some* rest, dear. You have to understand that I *had* to do this."

"I'm taking your word for it, Lyd. You're acting like a kook. But I know you're *not* a kook. So I'm just missing the key somewhere. Take care of yourself, Lydia Jean."

"You too, dear."

"Give Boy-Sam a hug."

He watched her wait for traffic, then move into the tempo of it, heading toward the city. It seemed a saucy little car, unsuitable for someone who wasn't having much fun lately.

He walked to his car, a dusty white Pontiac sedan with the maximum power option, heavy-duty tires, springs, shocks, load levelers. He went west on Forty-Four, and by the time he turned south on Seventy-Seven, toward the valley, Harlingen, and home, he had turned the air conditioner back to low. There had been other talks during the five months. And now, as after the other times, the flavor of plausibility of the things she said faded quickly away, and it all became nonsense, a neurotic and inexplicable and corroding rejection by the woman he thought he had known so well.

Below Kingsville, recalling the many things said, he kept thinking of better responses. His attitude had been wrong. She was having some kind of girlish tizzy, and the right approach would have been to tell her that he had humored her long enough. Tell her firmly and pleasantly that fantasy time was over, there was the wife-job to do, the one she had contracted for, so let's go get the kid and the suitcases and take you home where you belong. But being with her made him feel uncertain, an unfamiliar and unpleasant state of mind, wanting to confess to crimes he could not comprehend.

He felt a tremor in the steering wheel and glanced at the speedometer and saw it resting at just under a hundred miles an hour. It irritated him to have been unaware of such high speed, and even as he accepted the need to drop down to eighty, he pushed the gas pedal to the floor, hands locked on the wheel. At a hundred and fifteen the slight tremor smoothed out. But at a hundred and twenty-five the heavy car began to feel light, buoyant, floating slightly on the irregularities in the paving, no longer under his total control. Sam Boylston felt an angry exaltation, a pleasure in an unnamed defiance. The speedometer moved upward a bit more, but so reluctantly he knew the car was at its limit. If any one of several variables went astray now, the car would stop only as smoking junk far off the right of way, and the damned woman could wonder the rest of her life how much her stupid intractability had contributed to the death of the husband.

Something attracted his eye, and when he glanced in the rear vision mirror he saw, far behind him on the long straight stretch, bleached by sunlight, the pulsing of the chase-light atop the roof of the patrol car in pursuit.

He took his foot off the gas at once. An asinine performance. Erratic and juvenile. Sober man indulging in the kind of dramatics usually reserved for the drunk or the disturbed.

But, he thought, damn Lyd anyway. I kept everything in order, kept everything moving along very nicely for three months. But for the past two the world has been going out of focus. Sudden irritability with people who haven't deserved it. Appointments forgotten. Some very sour decisions—in small matters, fortunately. A drink or two too many at the club. That curious impulse to smack Bern Wallader in the mouth last week. And, too, that sweatiness and sense of sick anticipation when I stopped at the light in Brownsville and that little chippy in her short tight skirt, rolling her hips, walked so impudently across in front of the car, glanced, half smiled and glanced again, Indio blood showing in the breadth of her face, tilt of dark eyes, stepped up on the curb, stopped there to give me the chance, turning with a certain hauteur, arching herself in display. All I had to do was reach over and swing the door open. Came damned close to it. Not over sixteen, I'd guess, more probably fifteen. Disaster in a prematurely ripe package. But the car behind me honked, the light was green, and I went on, with the palms of my hands cold and slippery on the wheel.

"What are you trying to *do* to me?" he said aloud, striking the top of the wheel with the heel of his right hand.

His speed was down to fifty. The patrol car was on his bumper and the siren gave an imperative growl. He braked and steered over onto the shoulder and stopped. The patrol car passed him and cut in and stopped directly in front of him, chase-light still revolving. The husky trooper got out quickly and as he approached, Sam was mildly surprised to see that he had the revolver ready in his hand.

Sam rolled the window down, and the man said, "Keep your hands where I can see them and get out slowly when I open—Oh! Hey, Mr. Boylston. I thought you were a flyer."

Sam looked at the weather-brown face, went back through

mental files, came up with the name. Shugg. He'd given official testimony two years ago when the son of a county judge had been killed on this same stretch of highway.

As Shugg quickly holstered the weapon, Sam looked at his sleeve markings and got out of the coolness into the highway heat and said, "How are you making it, Corporal Shugg?"

"Not too bad, I guess."

"You thought I was a what?"

"A flyer. A kid who gets hold of something with a lot of horses, the old man's, or he steals it, and looks for a long stretch where he can put it right down on the floor and keep it there. When I saw I wasn't going to gain on you worth a damn, I radioed ahead for a road block, and then I canceled when you eased off."

Sam, by an effort of will, kept his hands steady as he lit a cigarette. "Damn fool procedure, I guess. I've got a little front-end vibration at high speed, and I thought if I could pinpoint where it smooths out again, it would help them find out what it is."

Shugg looked puzzled. "I was just going to apologize for holding you up and tell you I know you got a good reason for hustling back to Harlingen, but nobody has a reason good enough for what you were doing."

"Reason?"

"You didn't hear it on the news, then?"

"Hear *what?*"

"There's a big search going on for Mr. Kayd's boat over there in the Bahamas. He didn't make a radio check yesterday morning like he did every morning, and then he didn't get to where he was supposed to be headed, and didn't make radio contact this morning either, so they started an air search and can't find a thing, not so far. Seven people aboard. The Kayd family and the hired captain and his wife and your sister Leila. I just guessed that was why you were in—a big hurry, Mr. Boylston."

. . .

He went directly to the offices of Boylston and Worth, Attorneys at Law. He hurried through the silence and emptiness of Sunday afternoon back to his large corner office, turned the Sunday setting of the thermostat down ten degrees, made certain his phone was on the night plug and alive, then looked up the number of the newspaper, asked if Tom Insley was there, got him on the line immediately.

"Tom? Sam. I heard the three o'clock news on the car radio. Have you got anything new on the situation?"

"Not a thing, Sam. Hell of a note. I know how upset you must be. But as long as I've got you on the line, do you want to make any kind of a statement?"

"No harm in that, I guess. Let's see now. Bixby Kayd's cruiser, the Muñeca, is a custom-built boat, diesel powered, very solidly constructed, with all customary safety devices and navigation aids. I understand that the weather has been clear the past two days and the seas calm. I have every confidence that Bix would employ a captain over there who knows the waters and is totally qualified. I have two guesses. One is that they had some kind of electrical failure affecting the engines and have drifted out of the area now being searched. Or, they changed their announced destination, and Bix would have so indicated when he called the Nassau Marine Operator yesterday morning, but the electrical failure kept him from so doing, and again they would be outside the search area. I have—I have every confidence they'll be spotted today, or no later than tomorrow, and we'll have an explanation of what happened. Okay?"

There was too long a delay, too much hesitation before Tom Insley answered. Sam Boylston felt a prickling sensation at the nape of his neck, that most basic and primitive warning.

"What's wrong?" he demanded.

"I guess we have a more complete report than you heard on the radio news, Sam. Bix bought another boat in Florida, a little over twenty feet, and took it in tow. It would get into places too shallow for the Muñeca. Thing is, it was equipped with a transistorized ship-to-shore. Thirty watts. And a good sea boat, fast, lots of power, the same kind of hull they use in those Miami to Nassau races. Look, I don't want to upset you any more than you are, but the Bahamas are full of pleasure boats in May. There's no news of any contact by any of them with either of Bix's boats. I can't see a simultaneous electrical failure."

"Then you better say that I am optimistic about them being found."

"Are you?"

"The reason has to be off the record, Tom."

"Too many things are, but go ahead."

"Bix Kayd never took a hundred percent pleasure trip in his life. I guess you know I did some law work for him. I resigned. We're still reasonably friendly. There were too many surprises. You can't do your best job for a client unless you know the whole picture, know everything he's fiddling around with. Bix is a promoter. He likes to stay behind the scenes. He's more secretive than he has to be because I guess he gets a boot out of it. Nobody but Bix and his personal tax accountants know the whole structure. The disappearance has the smell of one of his little games."

"How could it do him any good?"

"Think it through, Tom. Some of the things he's known to be behind could take quite a slide when the exchanges open tomorrow. Through a plausible dummy he could have set up to sell short, buy back at the bottom, and show up wearing a broad smile about Wednesday."

"Until the S.E.C. digs into it?"

"The way he moves, he doesn't leave many tracks. And there's quite a swarm of congressmen who keep coming back to his place for barbecue and bourbon."

"So you'll just wait and see?"

"A little more than that. I have some sources. I'll nose around and see if I can get some kind of a hint about what kind of business he was combining with pleasure this time."

"Will you let me know? Off the record, of course."

"That's going to depend on what it is."

After he hung up, Sam Boylston got up and walked over and stood with his hands shoved into his hip pockets, looking out the window wall, across at the empty asphalt acres of the Northway Shopping Plaza, and the new Valley Citizens Trust building beyond. He realized that he was staring at another byproduct of what Lyd called his compulsion to neaten up the world. With the increase in the size of their practice and the need for a larger staff and larger quarters, he and his partner, Taylor Worth, had started looking around.

They had found Bern Wallader sitting on this big tract, planning an eventual shopping center, fretting over traffic counts, moving all too slowly and conservatively, and planning too small. At that time Sam had just become a director of Valley Citizens and had known of the bank's need to find a new site. After a long talk with the bank president, and a confidential talk with the appropriate people in local government, and another with some people in Houston specializing in the planning and construction of suburban shopping complexes, he had boosted Bern Wallader into nervous and apprehensive action, finally getting him to move only by putting up collateral and signing notes in return for a piece of the action. Now in addition to twice the number of retail outlets Bern had thought feasible, there was the bank, the professional office building, and acres of new housing going on on the rearward land which Sam had

optioned the day he began to believe Bern Wallader could be per-
suaded to begin taking risks.

And it had started merely because they had needed more space
and hadn't been able to find anything suitable and had wondered if
anyone would build to their requirements. It was a strange knack for
commercial serendipity. Or perhaps, he thought, it was merely a
trick of objectivity. You saw what was quite logical and necessary,
and wondered why people dragged their feet, complained of digestive pains, worried about reducing their obligations before starting
something new and, when they had something feasible, had this
strange compulsion to dwarf their own concepts. With a geometri-
cally increasing increment of nearly three hundred thousand new
souls in the Republic each and every month, only the most vision-
ary projects could hope to keep pace. Most minds were dim and
dingy places, and most thinking a slow and muddied flow, full of
unidentified emotional debris, obsolete concepts, frightened rites
and superstitions.

When things did not move, you checked until you found that
point where the minimum leverage would create the maximum motion. It took time, certainly. And a cold and lasting attention to both
the details and the total objective. You had to conceal your impatience with those associates who could not keep pace, and take practical advantage of those on the other side of the table with the same
defects.

And why should Lyd disapprove of that? Wasn't it the essential
stuff of survival? Did she want softness, apathy, amiable sloth?

You had to hold on tight, or it could all go wrong. That was
something Lydia Jean didn't comprehend. He looked back across the
years to the way it had all gone bad, so quickly. He had been taking
Moon Lad, his big gray, across open country at a full run and the left
foreleg had gone deep into the unseen hole, big bones cracking like
a tree branch, and as he had rolled over and over across the turf he'd

heard the strange, breathy screaming of the big, beloved horse. It kept trying to get up and could not, but stopped the terrible noise and lay watching him as if confident he could fix any bad thing. He had taken off his T shirt and fashioned a blindfold for the horse, patting him, talking to him, because he could not use the carbine from the saddle sheath with those eyes looking at him and at the gun. He placed the slug perfectly, walking through a swimming landscape and was cried out before he got back to get the hands and the jeep with the dozer blade and the shovels and go back and bury Moon Lad before the *zopilotes* got to him.

Two weeks later, he lost the first set, but took the second and third to eliminate Rooster Hines and thus get into the finals of the tennis championship, where he would face Bill Cupp, whom he knew he could take readily. He showered and joined the group of his friends at the pool and got into a spirited game of tag. Avoiding a tag he had run and taken a flat racing dive into the pool, only to have the hefty Indrigan girl surface directly in front of him. He had put his hands palm outward, hit her massive shoulder, felt the pain like hot knives in his right wrist, and knew even as he sat on the pool apron and saw the puffing begin that Bill Cupp had the trophy by default.

And the following week the parents who would have applauded and celebrated victory were both dead.

There was a kind of infection about disasters, both large and small. They were linked somehow. Most importantly, they did not strike with total randomness. It had been careless to run Moon Lad across that kind of country. It had been foolish to play the tag game when the pool was that crowded. Ask for two, and they give you the third free.

He knew that it was not logical, and knew that superstition was a weakness. But long ago, after the world had gone wrong, he had vowed he would tighten down, that he would not let any first wedge be driven in, and if there was a small disaster not of his making, then he would be double careful to keep chance at arm's length long enough for the infection to heal itself.

But now he could sense a new darkness. Lyd's voluntary defection was a disaster which was making his days ever more bleak. The idiocy with the car was another disaster trying to happen. And it had some tenuous link with Leila, with Bix, with the Muñeca.

He hunched his shoulders slightly and turned away from the window. He was a slender man of middle height, sandy hair, gray eyes, a face just round enough to give him a deceptive boyishness. He was slight enough so that in repose, had he not had the weathered pigmentation of the range lands, the sun-squint furrows near his eyes, he might have had a somewhat frail look. But in all movement he had a wiry precision, a taut and springy economy and swiftness of those with the inherited musculature and reflexes of the athlete. This was his vanity, its outward expression the excellent fit of custom shirts, tailored business suits, and the expensive informal clothes and sports clothes.

He sat and stared at the phone and reviewed all the hints and rumors of Bix's activities he could remember hearing during the past months. He narrowed the possible sources of information down to the two most likely—old Judge Billy Alwerd down in Brownsville, and big Tom Dorra who owned all those groves and had his home place over near McAllen. He knew that they had hitchhiked in a small way on some of Kayd's previous operations, and he knew they had been seen together before the Muñeca had embarked from Brownsville for the trip up around the Gulf Coast and down around the Florida keys.

He picked up the phone before it completed the first ring. Person to person to Mr. Samuel Boylston.

"This is Jonathan, sir. Is Leila okay?"

"I probably don't know any more than you do. Just what's on the news."

"I began to worry before there was anything on the news. You see, sir, yesterday was my birthday. She was going to phone me. You know how she is. She wouldn't forget. And she'd make a real effort."

"I know."

"What are you going to do?"

"I guess the only thing we can do is wait."

"I think, sir—I'll go over there."

"What can you do that isn't being done?"

"I don't know. But neither of us liked this thing right from the start. We didn't have a good feeling about it. And—I'd just feel better if I wasn't so far away from where the trouble is. Maybe it's stupid. But we haven't done too well being sensible, it seems like."

"When did you last hear from her, Jonathan?"

"I got an airmail postcard Friday. She mailed it in Nassau. She said she was going to try to get the call through to me between seven and ten yesterday night, my time, so that's when I should stay near the phone here."

"Anything else?"

"The rest was just personal."

"I can't stop you from flying over."

"I know. I haven't made up my mind for sure, sir. I think I'll see if there's anything on the news tomorrow morning and then decide. I talked to Mr. Wing about it. He's being very nice about it. He said to tell you he hopes everything works out okay about Leila."

"Bud Wing gave me a good report on you, Jonathan."

After a silence Jonathan Dye said, "I guess the nice thing to do would be to act pleased or something. But I'm not in the mood for it. I never could get it across to you I've been doing any kind of work I could get since I was fourteen years old. I've done easier work than this, and I've done harder work than this. And nobody has ever given me any bad reports on how I do. I like Mr. Wing. But he gets an hour of work for every hour of pay. Sir, I guess we could leave it this way. If there's nothing new tomorrow morning, you'll know I'm going over there, and when I know where I'll be, I'll wire you."

"Fine. And—good luck."

After a few moments he began looking up Billy Alwerd's home phone number.

Five

CRISTEN HARKINSON CRAWLED forward in the little Dutchman, feeling the sailboat right itself as the boy, Oliver, pulled the last of the mainsail down out of the push of the wind off Biscayne Bay. He had managed it, as always, at precisely the right moment, so that the momentum carried them through the slot and into the protected private boat basin south of Crissy's house, just around the point on which the house had been built, where the basin was sheltered from winds out of any northerly quarter.

With the last of its momentum, it glided at an angle toward the dock. She stood, reached, caught the sun-warm planking, fended the boat to a stop near a mooring cleat, pulled the dock line down and made it fast to the bow ring. Oliver pulled the stern in and made it fast. He had another half hour of work, hosing her down, stowing the gear, buttoning the sailboat up, then mooring her across the angle of the dock where she would ride without rubbing.

Crissy climbed up onto the dock and turned and looked down at the nineteen-year-old boy. He had begun his work, keeping his solemn face turned away from her. With each motion he made, the big muscles bunched and slid under the hide of his broad back. The hair on his long brown legs was sunbleached to a powder white, making a strange halo against the orange light of the evening sun.

Standing there, Crissy had a sense of how they would look from the proper dramatic angle. The elegant figure of the tall woman on the dock, hair tousled, salty, bleached several shades of blonde white by all the sailing. Pale blue bikini. Black-hued wraparound sun glasses. Ratsey bag, red and white, swinging from a crooked finger. The body, youthful and taut enough for the bikini, sunned to a gold tinged now with the bronze red of the day on the water, contrasting with the leather brown of the pale-eyed, white-toothed, sailboat boy.

She stood well, remembering the lessons. Grass green, thinking the lessons would aim you right at the cover of *Harper's Bazaar,* but you ended up doing your turns and pirouettes in those schlock outfits, pirated designs, in front of the buyers who'd stroke the fabric and call you Crissy-baby, and ordered in hundred dozen lots for little chains nobody ever heard of. At a hundred yards, old buddies, the figure is still twenty years old. But put a hard-focus closeup on the face in the cruel sunlight and it will read thirty, which is just as much a triumph because that is still a half dozen and better years off the truth.

"Oliver?"

"M'am?"

He still did not look up at her standing there above him on the dock. "Now don't you go running off, hear? I owe you for the last two days, so you come to the house when you're through here."

"Yes m'am."

She went slowly and lazily up the long curve of the stone stairway—wide shallow steps hewn out of coquina rock and set into the slope of the lawn. Halfway up she made a mental wager with herself, turned her head quickly and caught him motionless, hunkered there, sail cover in hand, staring at her. He looked down quickly. Smiling to herself she climbed the last step and crossed the patio to the roofed terrace, walked to the far end of it, rolled the glass door back and went into her bedroom. It was a few minutes before six. She opened the panel in the wall of the lounge portion of the bedroom and turned the television set on. Local news at six on Saturday night.

She opened the door to the bedroom wing corridor and bawled, "Francisca! Francisca, damn it!"

In moments her little Cuban housemaid came scurrying in, eyes wide in mock alarm.

"Damn it, you *had* to see us come in!"

"I'm not watch. Honest to Jesus, Miss Creesy."

Local news had begun. "Hold it a minute," Crissy said. She moved over to the television set.

After a report of a drowning and a bloody automobile accident on the Tamiami Trail and an averted strike, he said, "As yet the large-scale air and sea search in the Bahamas for the missing yacht, the Mu—"

Crissy clicked it off and said, "Did they come and fix that damned pump?"

"Si! Yes. What was in it?" The girl frowned, wrinkling most of her delicate face. She held forefingers a few inches apart. "*Una lagartija.* Eh?"

"A what?"

"How is it a snake, but has feets?"

"A lizard. You mean a lizard got into the pump?"

Francisca's smile was full of joy. "Damn well told." She wore a bright red skirt, white blouse, gold sandals.

"Got a guest, have you?"

"Some friend only I think."

Crissy stripped off the two bikini halfs, balled them, tossed them to the girl. "Now for once in your life get your mind off your friend and see if you can do three things right. I'm only going to tell you once."

Francisca gave her deft imitation of nervous, humble fright. We're trapped in this act of ours, Crissy thought, the cruel mistress and the terrorized servant. But an act makes it easier. You know where you are.

"First, go get that green ice bucket, fill it halfway with ice and bring it here and put it on the bar over there. Next, hang around the terrace until the sailboat boy comes after his money, and then bring him here—not through the place, but by way of the terrace. Third thing, I'll be going out to eat. So go do as you please until you bring me my coffee tomorrow morning."

Her cowed repetition of the orders was marred by the little knowledgeable gleam in her chocolate eyes.

As she hurried out, Crissy stared after her, thinking: Better you don't laugh, you sexy little spook. Don't tell your friend any funnies about Mees Creesy and the sailboat *muchacho*. Don't smirk a smirk, sweetie, because everything has to add up just so, just exactly so, in a game where you don't dare take a single chance.

She went into her gold and white bath and took a very quick shower. Her body radiated the sun-heat of the sailing day, prickling to the spray of the water. She toweled her cropped hair with muscular energy, brushed it semi-dry, painted her mouth, touched her body with perfume, pulled on a Lilly Pulitzer shift, a coarse, heavy weave in a vertical pattern of wide orange and white stripes, lined with silk. It was short, almost to mid-thigh. At the shoe rack she hesitated, decided to stay barefoot.

She turned on the overhead light in her largest closet, went to the back of it, opened the hinged panel and, biting at her lower lip, dialed the combination on the barrel safe. She opened the cash box, took out two twenties for the boy for the two days of sailing lessons, then took an additional amount to replenish her household and walk-around money. The amount left was dangerously thin. She did not want to count it nor to guess how much might be there.

But it was no longer something to start up the little itchings of desperation, the feeling of bleakness and dread. Instead it gave her a feeling of excitement and tension and hope. This time it would work. It had to work. She would make it work. And it would be an end to any need to scramble, ever again.

"Bless you, Bixby," she whispered, "you big jolly Santy Claus. You ripe juicy pigeon."

She closed the safe, tweaked the dial, closed the panel and turned off the closet light as she left.

When Francisca cat-scratched at the screen panel, Crissy was carefully adding the measured ingredients for two Planters Punches in the tall glasses.

"Come right in, please, Oliver," she called, then heard the panel slide open, slide shut, heard Francisca's sandal-slap fading swiftly along the terrace stone.

Without turning from the task, she said, "Do sit down, Oliver. Anywhere, please. I want to know why I keep getting into such foul trouble when I try to come about when we're really dusting along."

"M'am, I guess it's on account of the Dutchman, it's a real tender boat, and you've got it in your head you can keep her on the plane coming about, so you try to slam her around too fast. You have to ease her, haul her pretty short when you bring her up to point, then feed it to her as fast as she'll take it and she'll get back planing. You can't yank her around. But—you're getting better at it."

She took the two tall glasses up, turned and walked toward him, saying, "Thank you, dear Oliver." The carpeting, in a pale tone of cinnamon, was laid over foam rubber sheets, and the pliancy of it under her bare feet accentuated her awareness of herself, oiled sockets of hip and knee, the shift in alternating diagonal stress lines pulling the softness of lining against the sunheated flesh, of the stronger odor of her perfume vaporized in her private warmths, of the ice-cold glasses in her hands, of the slippery lining of her underlip where her tongue-tip touched it, even of the slight heaviness and dampness of a sun-white curl bobbing against her temple in the cadence of her walk toward the boy. No western light could enter this room, but a reflected orange-golden light came in, partly from the cocoanut fronds tall enough to reach into the sunlight and turn to copper. Beyond the brown boy she could see the homing boats of Saturday, a few of them, dots on the broad bay, heading northerly to Dinner Key and to the city. In the strange, fading light she felt leonine, softly powerful.

She held a drink to him and said, "I hate these when they're made too sweet."

"Please—I got to leave, I really got to leave."

He stood awkwardly in the shorts and white T shirt, one shoulder higher than the other, eyes moving swiftly from side to side, his vision moving across her at throat level, his throat bulging in an effortful, dry swallow, his hand reaching aimlessly behind him for the catch that would free the sliding panel.

He had a bony face, and not quite enough chin. His ears stuck out, and his upper lip was lugubriously long, and even at nineteen there were the beginning signs of how the brown-dark hair would recede. Poor lamb, she thought as she put the drinks on the nearby table.

She turned toward him, with pretty sigh, query in the tilt of head, moving so that he abandoned the escape place, trying to move casually away from her, with nervous social cough. She felt sad, wise, maternal and utterly gentle. Poor ordinary chick-child, scared almost sick of all the richnesses of maturity. Poor eagle-scout child, with its mama herding it relentlessly toward the ministry. Poor trembler, facing now the fleshy actuality, quite different from all those erotic little night-thoughts it fancied so evil.

"I really got to leave," he said in the golden stillness, his voice unsteady.

"Of course, dear Oliver. I know."

Six

AT CRISSY HARKINSON'S isolated and luxurious house on lower Biscayne Bay, the servant's quarters were above the detached two-car garage and utility room. Crissy's white Mercedes convertible was in one of the stalls. The vehicle of the young sailing instructor was parked in the turnaround area, inside the open vehicle gate, near the redwood fencing, a weary and solemn car, orange rust and blue paint.

Outside stairs were affixed to the side of the carport structure, leading up to a shallow open porch which ran the length of the building. Raoul Kelly sat placidly on the railing of the porch smoking a cigar and watching the sunset, waiting for Francisca to return. From there he could see a few glints of his own car beyond the fence where he preferred to leave it, some beetle-blue gleamings between the fence boards and the broad leaves of the outside plantings.

She came swiftly from the house, grinned up at him, waved, and came hurrying up the stairs, along the porch, gave him a quick hug, a little pat, and said, "It was an excellent guess. The working classes are given a little holiday. Until breakfast. And I think noon would be a very good guess for breakfast time."

"He's a little out of his class, 'Cisca. He's overmatched."

It was their practice for him to speak English and for her to respond in her brisk Cuban Spanish. Her understanding was far better than her ability to speak English.

She leaned against a nearby porch post, hands in the pockets of her vivid red skirt. She made a face. "It is a common thing, they say, for women of her age to covet strong young men, just as fat bankers seduce school girls. I feel like an accomplice, Raoul. She had me bring the fat worm and drop it right into the web. He seemed extremely nervous. And she had set the stage very shrewdly, and dressed appropriately."

Sometimes, infrequently, he would detect in her voice some of the cadences and inflections of upper class pre-Castro Havana, the echo of yacht club, house parties, diplomatic functions.

She had been born to that world twenty-four years ago, and after the convent school and a proper marriage she would have become one of the chattering vivid young wives of Havana, all giggles and gossip and sideglance of flirtation, shopping at El Encanto and in Nassau, playing tennis and poolside bridge while the maids cared for the babies, flying to New York in the spring or the autumn with her husband. It was what the young Señorita Francisca Torcedo y Sarmantar had expected her life to be.

Had that world not changed, Raoul Kelly might even have met her there, but not as a social equal. Only child of a shop-keeper, he had been awarded a scholarship to Columbia University, had elected to enter the School of Journalism, had returned and gone to work on a Havana paper. He had heard of the Torcedo family, had not met them, knew that the wife had died as the result of a fall from a horse, knew that the father was so closely associated with Batista in certain business matters it would have been better for him to have left, as did so many others, before the bearded ones entered the city.

Later, after Raoul became a very good friend of the brother, Enrique Torcedo, during the training for the Bay of Pigs invasion, he had learned what had happened to the father. He had been too stubborn to leave. Those first days of the change of regime were days and nights of confusions, foolish acts, wildness. The papa had been clumsily and stupidly slain, not by one of the bearded veterans, but by a bewildered boy who just that day had been sworn into the militia and issued a rifle, and had thought only to threaten the man who had insulted him and the entire revolution. Francisca had disappeared at the time of the killing. Only much later it was learned what had happened to her. Crazed with grief and anger at the slaying of her father, she had run into the street with a tiny silver-plated woman's pistol and punched two bee-sting wounds into the nearest uniformed peasant flesh. They had taken her away and placed her in the stockade at a provisional military barracks outside Havana at Rancho Luna.

Raoul knew that Enrique would never be convinced that those village boys were innocent of any depravity, any bestial intent. The new day had dawned, and here was this lithe and lovely and rebellious little upper class chicken, a bonus from the benign gods of revolution. Now that all were equal, she could be given her chance to labor for the glory of the people's republic, to scrub and wash and cook and serve and carry and, inevitably perhaps, share the bunks of those young heroes of the revolution who, in turn, had the force to quell her and take her.

Once she was found, it was not difficult to arrange to have her brought out. The new Cuban Government was not eager for that kind of publicity. But there would be certain fees—and somehow they knew almost to a penny how much Enrique had managed to escape with, after everything else had been confiscated.

She was taken directly from Miami International to the hospital, dangerously thin, anemic, pregnant, alarmingly docile and submissive, and running a high fever of unknown origin. A bad reaction to the antibiotics they gave her caused her to miscarry. Old friends of the family competed for the chance to take her in and care for her. Perhaps conscience had something to do with it. During the final months of the Batista rule, they had been busily liquidating holdings and quietly and shrewdly shipping the money out of Cuba, investing it elsewhere. 'Cisca had nothing left, poor child, and she was a symbol of the brutality of the new order. And she is no trouble at all, really. Hardly says a word. The little thing just sits with her head bowed, sewing and knitting, and has that shy little smile when you speak to her.

During training Enrique had taken Raoul with him when he had made the last visit to his younger sister. He did not think she even glanced at him, or was more than remotely aware of another person present. It seemed to him then that the psychic damage had made her withdraw so far she would never return.

Apparently Enrique thought so too, because before the landing he asked Raoul to sort of watch out for 'Cisca should anything happen to him. Something happened. In the fumbled, sickening chaos of the Bay of Pigs, Raoul, diving for cover, saw Enrique run into a hammering rain that stopped him abruptly, then drove him back, emptied him, spilled him in a loose, wet, ragged ruin.

Raoul Kelly survived the invasion and survived the imprisonment on the Isle of Pines, and was exchanged for medicines, and could not find Francisca. After she had heard of Enrique's death, she had packed and gone away. They thought she was working somewhere.

He found her working as a waitress in a café in Homestead, Florida, merry and grinning and quick at her work, popular with the owners and the customers. To his surprise she remembered him at once, but she did not care to talk to him. He lost her, and then found her again, working as a live-in maid for an elderly couple in Miami Shores. She was friendlier to him than before, but not quite enough to make him feel welcome.

Six months ago he had looked her up again, and had traced her to this place. And, by now, she had been working for Crissy Harkinson for almost a year. She greeted him warmly, and he had fallen into the habit of coming to see her whenever he could.

She seemed always in good spirits, but he learned that it was forbidden to talk about anything which had happened to her before she had taken the first job. She would become very angry with him and make him leave. So he played the game on her terms. He knew the pitfalls inherent in any amateur psychiatric analysis. But it seemed to him that because she had found one identity, one existence, untenable, she had become quite another person.

Seeking clues to this new person, when he was alone in the little apartment over the garages, when the Harkinson woman had summoned her on the intercom, he would look through her belongings seeking the clues as to what she had become. Aside from her necessary identification papers and permits, the only personal things she had were some photographs of her taken with the other waitresses at the café, arms around waists, smiling in the sunshine, and the few little presents he had brought her. He was touched by the small furniture of her existence—sensible little cotton mesh briefs from Sears, simple and durable little brassieres from J. C. Penney, bright cheap skirts and blouses, supermarket cosmetics, and the blue and white maid uniforms the Harkinson woman had her buy. It gave him the saddened feeling of inventorying the possessions of the dead.

He knew her education had been good. From the things Enrique had told him, he knew she had been sensitive, imaginative and thoughtful. But this 'Cisca was a merry little thing, and her Spanish was that of the shop girls. She prattled about the plots of the television she watched, the fan magazines she read. He took her to the beaches, to outdoor movies, and to the back country to fish in the drainage canals. Being with her was undemanding fun. And it was a relief after the demands of his work. He had developed contacts which gave him reliable information about developments in Cuba and infiltration and subversion in other Latin American countries. He was doing news coverage and feature articles in this field for a Miami paper, and freelancing for Spanish language newspapers and periodicals in Florida and New York. Lately he had been doing magazine articles evaluating the total situation and attempting to anticipate trends and policies. As he attempted to be both thorough and scrupulously honest, his work had begun to attract attention on a wider scale. It was almost a blessing that his work fell into an area which was taboo insofar as 'Cisca was concerned.

When the early spring had brought the first softness in the Florida air, he had become more aware of a problem which he had been trying to ignore. On the beaches her slender thighs were golden, impossibly smooth and unflawed. There was a special and sensual intricacy of curve and pattern and texture in the way her mouth was made. The ivoried eyelid and the dense curve of black lashes slid down over the healthy gleam of eye with a meaningful perfection that seemed magical. At any casual and accidental brush of her body against his, he could feel his heart bumping against the hard wall of his chest. His jaws would ache, and he could believe the touch had left a visible weal on his flesh.

He could not sleep as well or eat with as good appetite as previously, yet he knew that any attempt to seduce her would be an unthinkable crime. Not only was he under the obligation of the request Enrique had made the night before he was killed, but he knew that only a selfish monster would, for his own need and pleasure, take the chance of smashing the adjustment she had made to the world.

Soldier rape had driven her into the shadows, and she had found a way out. But quite evidently the new personality had no memory of rape, pregnancy or miscarriage. The physical act could not help but trigger the memories and destroy the new structure of personality.

And so he endured, sometimes half sick with desire, knowing it would be far easier to stay away from her, yet feeling the need to be with her and thus punish himself for his animality.

Two months ago, in mid-March, she had solved the whole matter with a blitheness and directness that disconcerted him as much as it pleased him. He had taken her bay fishing on her afternoon off, and then they had gone to a place which would broil their catch for them and which served cold draught beer in big chilled steins. Then he had to hurry her home because she was alarmed that she might miss the beginning of what she declared was her third favorite television program.

The show did not intrigue him. He sat on the couch, dulled by the afternoon on the water, by the beer and food. He fought to stay awake. Then he was awakened by the sudden warm weight of her on his lap, her arms around his neck. The set was off, the room dark. A weak lamp in her bedroom made a path of light out through the half-open bedroom door. There was a nervous edge to her small laughter, and an anxious quaver in her voice as she said in her butchered English, "What kind of boyfriend I'm telling Rosita I'm having, eh? Sotch a trouble her boy is giving her, I tell you, every minute. I see you looking to me with the quick little eye, eh? I wait, wait, wait. Nothings, eh? I am loving you, Kelleeeee, something tough. But 'Cisca is maybe a little scare now you theenk—I'm a bad theeng."

As he held her, turned her to find her lips, telling her she was not a bad theeng, but indeed a very fine, a very splendid theeng, he realized with a shock and exultation there was nothing between the warmth of her and the clasp of his hands upon her but a wispy sheerness of short nightie.

She was shaky and nervous, and quite unschooled in her role, but eager in a rather dogged and determined way, and intensely inquisitive. They were together many times before quite suddenly, a week later, it began to be right for her; and once she knew what was sought, and could identify the earlier warnings, it became vastly right, and after many times when she indulged herself to the point of drugging herself with pure and prolonged sensation, she quite suddenly and earnestly set about learning him as completely as she had learned herself, asking intent little questions about how this was for him, and that, and how near was he now.

During this past month, the second month of their lovemaking, they had gradually established agreeable physical patterns. Yet he felt a sense of loss he could not quite identify. This supposedly ultimate intimacy was less than the intimacy he had sought. She was as merry and happy as before. At the beach he had taught her an efficient crawl. In the bays he had taught her how to manage a spinning reel and play a fish. This bed business was apparently, to her, another activity they could share. She had a casual and willing acceptance of him whenever the time and the place was suitable, and she would talk of other things at times, and then become intent when passion began to become more immediate. Pleasure made her chuckle. And she took quite an obvious satisfaction in their being able to make love quite skillfully. She would tell him, with a little shading of regret, the moment she realized she would not be able to finish, then would settle herself to making it as enjoyable for him as she could, sometimes adding mischievous innovations.

When she had been ended, she liked to be held quietly for a little while, petted and kissed, but with hardly any more emotional content than in the cuddling of a trusting puppy exhausted by play.

It was all hearty and easy and most enjoyable, but once when he was on the edge of sleep, where reality and fantasy are merged, not daring to let himself go to sleep because he knew he had to get up and leave her bed, he had the strange conviction that he had desired Francisca Torcedo y Sarmantar, but knowing the impossibility of ever possessing her, had eased the itch of wanting by taking this girl who now rested in his arms, a servant girl, one of the chunky little ones with a broad dusty pocked face, a willing laugh, a casual acceptance of him and his needs. So vivid was the fantasy that when he opened his eyes and saw the sleeping face of Francisca Torcedo y Sarmantar resting there in the crook of his arm, a face slender and delicate, marked by a thousand years of pride and breeding, he had the momentary conviction he had taken her by stealth, and should she awaken her eyes would go wide with terror and disgust, and she would sit up, arms across her delicate breasts, and scream and scream and scream . . . .

He awoke her. She smiled at him. She stretched luxuriously, held her fist in front of a yawn, craned her head and looked at the clock, then sat up quickly. "Kelleeeee, *querido!* The time!"

"I know."

And he got up sleepily and dressed, and bent over her and kissed her. She ran her fingers through his hair and patted his cheek.

"Raoul, darling, do you think you can get off early enough to come take me to the Burton movie?"

"I'll try."

"Doesn't she look to you—a little fat? Just a little?"

"Very very fat. You are much better."

"You like a woman whose ribs show? You like these poor starved little breasts, like a school girl's, *mi corazón?*"

"They, and all parts of you, are an elegance, truly."

And now, in the slanting light of sunset, on the shallow porch, he perceived that elegance of her as she leaned against the post, hands in the skirt pockets, ankles crossed. In that convent school, patronized by the daughters of the rich, they had been taught how to walk, enter a room, how to sit and rise gracefully. This training affected 'Cisca, the housemaid, only when she was in repose, he had noticed. She had somehow acquired the swift saucy walk of the shop girls, the extravagant conversational gestures of the hands, and the overly dramatic facial expressions they seemed to copy from the actresses they saw on television and in the motion pictures.

No actress, he realized, no matter how dedicated, diligent and skilled, could have immersed herself so totally in a role. One could comprehend it only by accepting the possibility that Francisca had become quite another person. It was as though the top thirty points of intelligence quotient and the top segment of emotional quotient had been lopped off. The trivia of life contented her. She had the unshakeable cheer and happy spirits it was said one could expect when a successful brain operation was undertaken to cure an anxiety neurosis which would not respond to other treatment.

Raoul Kelly tasted the bitter irony of this present relationship with her. And self-contempt. The government in Washington had wanted to set up a special study and investigation of the dynamics of the politics of poverty in Central and South America, the conditions which germinated seeds of revolt, riot and rebellion. But out of political opportunism the project had been killed in the Senate. Now a large foundation had taken over the project structure. They would base the project in California, and they had written him offering him a position of an importance which surprised him. He would be selecting, training and assigning field investigators, and directing the analysis of their reports.

He had temporized, asking for more time. A Raoul Kelly could not have dreamed of taking such a position newly wed to the daughter of Don Estebán Torcedo, and could he have done so, her value to his new career would have been inestimable. How would they accept a Raoul Kelly married to a housemaid, very lovely of course, but withal a little cheap, shrill, trivial and a bit vulgar. And with absolutely no interest in his work, nor any comprehension of it. And with a frequent turn of phrase in English which would blanch the cheeks of the foundation types and the academicians.

The question he kept asking himself was whether or not she had become less important to him now that he had possessed her. But, of course, there was the hidden side of the coin: How important and how necessary had he become to her? It was a question she evaded so completely it was as though she could not understand what was being asked.

If he could not leave her behind, yet could not take her, then this turning point in his life would have to go by default. He yearned for a position of such importance, yet was objective enough about himself to know that aside from the challenge of it, a certain matter of personal vanity was involved. He was a short, chunky man, just a few inches taller than 'Cisca. Though agile and muscular, he had to fight a tendency to put on weight. His was a most ordinary latino face, a mix of the Caribbean races—dusky, coarse-grained skin, broad nose, high hard cheekbones, dark eyes with long lashes, dark hair beginning to recede. His body was heavily pelted with dark curly hair. His shoulders were thick, and his hands had the contours of labor in spite of the softness of the journalist. The very ordinariness of his appearance was an advantage in his present work. In the cantinas of the working men he was accepted, and he was told things few others could have learned.

Yet he was aware of the almost inevitable figure of a Raoul Kelly in the future, a short soft fat bald fellow who, by that time, would have had to have achieved an important professional reputation, or would find himself among so many others who had the same look, and who sat in the small cafés in the afternoon, drinking the small cups of thick black bitter coffee, making intricate and implausible plots to restore the old order, knowing yet never admitting they were trapped in one of the little eddies created when the brute weight of history had rushed by them.

'Cisca said, "It is odd, no? Señora Harkinson seemed so eager when I was first working here to involve herself with men of wealth and importance, friends of the old politico who befriended her and built her the lovely house and died. She found no new friend of importance. She is no longer a young girl, of course. One can understand the affair with El Capitán. He is mature, powerful, handsome in a rugged manner. A convenient diversion for her, something which began before she found she could no longer afford to operate the boat the Senator gave her and then sold it. She has tamed El Capitán Staniker so he will arrive when summoned, go when she orders. In the beginning they would shout, and sometimes he would beat her. Then he became eager to please her in every way. But now why should she divert herself with this Oliver person? Her captain has been gone—it is over three weeks. She spends money on sailing lessons with the boy. I tell you, *querido*, that one does few things without purpose. And she should be busying herself to find a protector. The boat is gone, and the furs are gone, and many jewels are gone. Sometimes I have not been paid until something has been sold. Those times she was very nervous and very ugly and cruel. Now she is very nervous but very gay also. It is a difficult thing to understand."

She moved to the door of the apartment and went inside, pausing to hold the screen door open for Raoul. The architect the Senator had employed had limited luxuriousness to the main house. The little apartment over the garage was of motel derivation, formica, standard fixtures and apertures, tough fabrics, vinyl flooring. She sat in the corner of the couch and tucked her slim legs up under her, pulled her sandals off and dropped them on the floor, still frowning slightly as she tried to puzzle out Crissy Harkinson's behavior.

He went to the tiny kitchen alcove and took two cans of beer out of the midget refrigerator, pulled the tabs off, went over and handed her one, saying, "Maybe she's taking up with the kid to get her mind off worrying about Staniker."

"Eh? Oh, I do not believe that is the way it is for her, truly. From the time El Capitán departed, she became more and more agitated. She walked restlessly, appearing suddenly to tell me things to do which were not needed. If I would wake up in the middle of the night, sometimes lights would be on in the house. She smoked much. All small things irritated her. And then, last Sunday, as she was becoming truly impossible, the news came of the boat from Texas being lost somehow. She said to me she was terribly worried about Captain Staniker. But how did she act? Still nervous, but she would hum little songs while pacing, and make large smiles at me and treat me kindly. She began this matter of the sailing lessons in the rented boat. Now she is becoming just a little bit ugly again, more so each day."

He sat at the other end of the couch. "Honey, I didn't know you were all this interested in the woman."

"How not? There are just the two of us living here, no? Two women. I examine her. Perhaps it is—like the adventures in the day-time of the women of television. But they are good women in trouble. This one has the trouble of the money, and if she does not cure it, perhaps the house will go and my job will be gone. Perhaps she knows I watch her life as if it is television, but not so clear. Maybe not. She believes I am *estupida, una burra, verdad*. She asks about you. It would puzzle her, a journalist of importance visiting her maid, so I have told her you are a cook in a small Cuban restaurant. Also, I have invented others and say they visit me. It is that I do not care to have her enter my private life. It is a way—of hiding, perhaps. As, of course, she hides herself from me."

"We all do some hiding," he said as casually as he could manage.

"And what are *you* hiding, Señor?" Her look was flirtatious.

"My plans for us, chica."

"But you said if she did not need me we would go all the way to the place in Fort Lauderdale where there is the Hawaiian food! Now you do not want to?" She looked like a troubled, disappointed child.

"Not the plans for tonight. The plans to get married and go to California to that new job I've been offered."

"Oh. Do you think it would be better for me to wear high heels to that nice place, Raoul?"

He slid along the couch, put the empty beer can down, put his hands on her shoulders, held her strongly, gave her a little shake.

"Marriage, 'Cisca. Man and wife. Vows, home, kids."

"Oh, I do not care to be married."

He shook her again. "I care to marry you!"

Her face went absolutely still in a way he had not seen for many weeks. Her lips looked bloodless, and her eyes stared through him. He released her and she stood up and he expected her to say, as before, she had a headache, she did not feel well, he should leave, please.

Instead she said, "I am not one you would marry."

"Why not?"

"One does not marry this description of woman. Now perhaps you would . . ."

He got up and said quickly, taking her hands, "High heels, *almita*, might make you feel more like fiesta, ha? And you will drink one of the enormous things of rum and become very foolish. Okay?"

He watched the stillness change, quite slowly, to animation, and her eyes focused upon him, merry and mischievous. "Red shoes! Red shoes!" she cried and went scuttling off to put them on.

Later in his car on the way up to Lauderdale, she wiggled closer to him and said, "I must tell you. I make up stories about my Señora Harkinson, to make it more like the television. I do it when I am ironing, mostly. When one does not think about what the hands are doing. I have imagined it is some manner of plot, about El Capitán. It was all arranged between them the yacht would become missing, and so when it happened, then she was happy because the plan was working. And it would be money, somehow, because it is what she is so worried about. But you must help me with the story. It gets difficult."

"What do you mean?"

"In the paper on Monday there was the picture of the Señor Kayd. Oh, a very important man. I saw the picture and knew it was the one I had seen visit my Señora. He is not one easily forgotten, a giant truly, with a big shaved head and a loud laugh, a very heavy man but not fat. Perhaps fifty years old. With a white cowboy hat and boots with silver buckles and an air of importance, with a young man who brought him in a very rich car which he polished while the huge Señor was visiting my Señora. He visited for an hour, and they had drinks together and talked. His laugh rang through the house. From what I overheard, he was a friend of the Senator Fontaine and had met her when the Senator was alive and visited her here. She got out the most expensive bottles. She had me fix the small things to eat while drinking. When I took them in, they were talking quietly, and ceased when I entered. She thanked me and told me she would not need me and I could go back to my place until she called me. After the big man left she did not call me. It was the last day of March. I am sure of that."

"And what do you want from me?"

"A way to put Señor Kayd into the story, like television."

"Hmmm. Let me see now. Staniker knows the Bahamas well. He tells Crissy Harkinson he knows where there's sunken treasure, but if he goes after it he has to give a big share to the Crown. He can't finance the venture. But she has a rich Texas friend with a big boat. He flies over and talks to her. Then, three weeks ago, he arrives here with the boat and takes on Staniker as captain and they go to find the treasure. When they get the chance, they sneak off. They break contact. They hide the boat in some narrow cut and cover it with boughs. Now they are bringing up the treasure."

"And what will happen?" she asked breathlessly.

"Let me see. Oh, of course! When they have the treasure, they won't dare try to bring it out in Kayd's boat. They had a sailboat hidden too, and Mrs. Harkinson and Oliver are going to sneak over there and sail it back."

She leaned her cheek against his shoulder. "Oh, you are such a very clever man, Raoul Kelleeeee! Treasure! Mystery! Dark plots!" Then she gave that hard little bark of laughter which so often preceded her infrequent experiments with the English she had picked up at the Homestead café. "Sotch a crock of sheet!" she said merrily, and, as he winced inwardly, he wondered if she had the faintest idea what she had said.

Seven

ON THAT MONDAY MORNING after the news of the missing cruiser had been announced, two men sat waiting in a second floor office in Brownsville, in a mottled old stucco building two blocks from the old bridge across the Rio Bravo to Matamorros. The windows faced a narrow street where the mid-morning heat was increasing. The windows were closed. The noisy compressor on the old window unit set up a sympathetic resonance in the metal cover of the air conditioner and in the glass of the window, a resonance that built and faded like engines out of sync.

The wooden furniture was heavy, scarred, marked with the burns where cigarettes and cigars had been forgotten. The grass rug was scuffed thin, broken in places. Only the file cabinets looked new, three of them aligned against one wall, thick, gray, fire-resistant, with combination locks. Below the office was a small grocery store and bar, specializing in Mexican food, Mexican beer. The juke music was always turned high, but over the sound of the air conditioner only the repetitive thud of the bass could be heard.

The girl rapped at the door and came in from the outer office without waiting for a reply. She brought letters in and silently placed them in front of the older man who sat behind the desk. He read each one slowly and carefully, lips moving, before signing it. A straw ranch hat was pushed back from a scramble of untidy white hair. His moustache, thick and unkempt, shaded from white at the hairy nostrils down to a stain of yellow at the lips. He wore khakis, the shirt sweated through so many times the pale streaks of salt formed overlapping patterns at the armpits. In the frigid air of the office the sharp stale smell of him was still detectable.

He signed the last letter and the tall, frail girl picked them up from in front of him as he leaned back.

"Francie," the old man said, "you go on over to the courthouse and get them two notorial certificates the fella over in Tulsa wants."

"I could take the deeds along, Judge, and mail them from there."

"You do that, Francie. And leave that door there open so as we'll know it when Sam Boylston gets here."

She nodded, and as she turned and walked out, she gave big Tom Dorra a sidelong, speculative glance. Tom Dorra stared at her hips and legs as she walked out. He dwarfed the oak armchair he was slouched into, a man big enough to be stared at in the street, five inches over six feet, broad as a man and a half. He added almost another foot with the heels of his western boots, and with the very high crown on the custom Stetson. He was half Judge Billy Alwerd's age. Their skin was almost the same shade of brown, but whereas the Judge's looked desert dry, Tom Dorra's hide looked oiled. His tailored khakis were pressed and fresh. His belt buckle was a half pound of ornate Mexican silver.

After the outer door closed behind Francie, Tom Dorra said

lazily, "Your Francie, she give me the look about one more time, Billy, even though she got no more ass on her than Fred Astaire, I'm going to purely run her over to the Orange Tree Motel and give her my message."

The Judge yawned. "Don't you mess with her, Tom D. I need for her to keep her mind on her work, not wobbling around all sprung and breathing hard. After Milly died, I run through four of them before I found Francie. She's no Milly, God knows, but she keeps track. Get back to what you were starting to say when she came in."

"Oh. Here's the way I see it, why Boylston wants to see us both together. It figures that Bix Kayd cut him into it too, didn't tell us he was in, but told Boylston we were. So what's happened has got him a little jumpy too, and he wants to know what we plan on doing."

Judge Billy shook his head slowly, contemptuously. "That kind of thinking is the best reason in the wide world you better keep checking everything out with me, Tom. First off, young Sam hasn't got the yen for anything too tricky, and that's why he give up doing any law chores for Bix, knowing that if he didn't know the whole story and anything went a little sour, he could spend a lot of time in tax court, explaining. Second, that means that Bix wouldn't be about to beg Boylston to come in on anything, because the way Bix likes it is having folks lined up and itching to let him he'p them get rich. Third off, that young Boylston is handling himself smart enough he doesn't rightly *need* to come in on a little piece of a big one when he can do just as good taking a big piece of a little one and running the show himself."

"But you said he said on the phone it was about Bix."

"So he smelled something out, figured you and me had something riding this time, and wants to know what the hell goes on because his little sister is on that cruise, boy, or maybe you forgot."

"Do you think we ought to tell him anything?"

The Judge chewed at the corner of his moustache. "I think I'm going to wait and see just how he comes at us, and then I'm going to make up our minds for us, Tom D. One thing to bear in mind is that young Sam don't have a lot of real weight yet, but come a few years from now the way he's going, you and me could find ourselves needing a favor."

Tom Dorra looked bleak. "I sure God hope old Bix didn't get careless about anything. It would give me a case of the shorts for some spell. And you tell me, Billy, just why in the world old Bix had to turn it into some kind of damn game, making it look like a big old family cruise, when by God, he could have fly over and got it all settled in three, four, five days at the most."

The Judge took a half-eaten cigar from the top drawer of his desk, bit an inch off it, put it back, chewed slowly. "Now you know how Bixby Kayd is. He doesn't like for anything to look like what it is. He wants the whole world wondering and guessing what's up his sleeve. Besides, taking his own boat makes the transportation problem easier in one sense. Then, too, the delay would like to make that pack of limeys a little edgier and readier to deal. And being there like that would give him a chance to do some thinking on just how the whole thing should be operated once he's got hold of it. Bix likes to put on a show, but dog knows he's no fool."

He stared at Tom. "Am I keeping you awake?"

"Huh? Oh, I heard what you were saying. I was just thinking back on the onliest time I ever did see that little sister, that Leila Boylston. About four years back, which would make her about fifteen then. Wally and me had flew up to Ritchie's spread to look over some blooded stock, and that Leila was up there visiting the youngest Ritchie girl. The little Leila, she came riding along with us when we went looking for that stock. She set that roan real nice and pretty, and goddam, Judge, she was dressed like for a street parade in white britches so tight she could have set on a dime and told which president it was. Now a gallop was right interesting, and a canter was something to see, but when that roan moved at a slow walk, that little round can on her, it tippy-tilted back and forth so sweet and fine. I could have fell off my horse like the sun stroke and lay there howling and a-tearing up the sod. That roan liked to stay out in front, and I tell you that Leila was prime. There don't one like that come along every year. I swear, we stayed there one more day, I'd have slung her under my arm and took off up into Ritchie's high timber and never been seen since."

Judge Alwerd sighed, spat into his tin waste basket. "One day, big Tom, you'll find out how it quietens and eases a man to get past all that stud time of life."

"Sounds a little too quiet to me," said Dorra.

Judge Billy shook his head. "A fifteen-year-old girl child you saw that one time four years back. Agitates you to this day. And going on about my Miss Francie. You with seven kids. Makes me wonder if you got enough attention left over for business."

"Now, Billy, you know I . . ."

"All I know is we'd better be talking about money around here." He began to say more, but stopped as Francie touched the buzzer to signal the Judge that Sam Boylston was on his way in.

As the door opened, Billy Alwerd said, "Come on in, Sam. Come in and set. You know Tom D. Pull the door shut, you don't mind."

Sam shook hands with them and took an oak armchair about the same distance from the scarred desk as Tom's was. He wiped his forehead on a handkerchief and said, "Summer seems to be starting up earlier ever' year. Tom D., you gained some weight?"

"Not one bit. Just seems like I must always look bigger than folks remember. I stay just under two ninety like always, Sam."

There was a silence as they waited for Boylston to decide how he wanted to bring it up. Sam clicked his lighter shut, huffed smoke and said, "One of the things I learned when I did a little work for Bix, he hates having his name in the paper. I remember when there was a little trouble, he was paying a man to keep it out. Now he's in the news, and he's on the front page. The papers keep calling that cruiser a yacht. Bix would be stomping and cursing, wondering how many IRS boys might be wondering if he was being audited close enough. But then again, I was wondering if something might come along that looked good enough so that he wouldn't mind being in the papers, if it was necessary."

"Have to be real, real good," Judge Billy said softly.

"Good enough, I guess, so that you and Tom D. would be glad to have a piece of it?"

"If it was something like that," said the Judge.

Sam looked over at Tom Dorra. "It would ease my mind if I knew all this publicity was something Bix decided he'd just have to put up with. On account of Leila being along, if he'd wanted to be considerate, he could have let me have a little hint. But it isn't too late for a little consideration. It's something a man could give without having to say anything else about anything, wouldn't you say?"

"Billy is doing the saying," Tom said.

The Judge swiveled his chair and sat staring out the window. He turned back slowly. "I guess I tell you that we're edgy about it too, you'd have to know more."

"I guess I would."

"What you do is keep it in mind that Tom D. and I are coming right out with it, without being cute, just because your little sister being a guest on that boat kind of takes it out of the business picture and makes it friendship."

"I won't forget it."

"The way it started, you know Bix has been getting into resort operations outside the country. Sunshine Management, Incorporated. It's a nice tax picture. He had an eye on the Bahamas. He found an outfit based there that was in trouble. Ventures, Limited, set up as a Bahamian corporation. They'd moved too fast, picked up

too much land in too many places, but a lot of it right choice. Some
kind of legal tangle was keeping them from selling off some of the
beach land and islands to get even. It was all pledged against the full
amount of the loans they'd gotten, I guess, and they'd borrowed to
the hilt and no way to issue more paper to get development money.
The only way out was to sell all the holdings at once, in one package, pay off the debt, and have something left to distribute to the
shareholders. Eleven million five was the asking price. Bix muscled
them down to ten three, but it was still too much he figured. He had
it figured that about nine flat would be about right, but that was getting near the danger point because at that price maybe a lot of other
promoters would have started to get interested. So he started snuffling around. He got a man who could deliver the whole board, a
majority of the board, if he could have some leverage to work with.
The leverage they worked out was eight hundred thousand cash,
under the table. For that piece of money, Bix's pigeon could get an
affirmative vote through the board to take Bix's cash offer of eight
million seven. That makes the total nine five. He's been working on
it a year and a half. All he could scrape up for the under-the-table
money was four hundred, in a real quiet way without attracting any
attention. So Tom D. here and me, we came in for two hundred
each. Bix's program was to keep them sweating and see if he could
get them to go along for less than the eight hundred, and if it was
less, we'd all cut our ante the same percent. Sam, there's no need to
go into how we stand to make out. We worked it out with Bix, and
let's say it's enough to make a man smile some. When there's risks
something could go wrong, and when you come up with the kind
of money you keep in fruit jars, you want it should fatten up pretty
good. So, considering, when the news came through, Tom and me
started feeling some edgy. There isn't a scrap of paper we've got to
show, not even any way to write it off. It isn't like Bix to get careless
with any kind of money."

"So the Muñeca left here with eight hundred thousand dollars in cash aboard her!"

"More than half of it hundreds, all the rest in fifties," Tom Dorra said. "All banded and marked and packed neat in a suitcase, not a big suitcase, little bigger than one of those dispatch cases. Those boys on the board who were going along with it, it was going to make them well, but the others were going to get burnt and figure everybody got burnt."

"Who was his contact?"

The Judge said, "A Canadian name of Angus Squires, has a place in Freeport and some kind of a hideaway fishing lodge on something called Musket Cay in the Berry Islands. The way it works, Bix had moved the eight million seven into a Nassau bank and had some lawyer in Nassau with a limited power of attorney who'd make the offer and when it was voted in, pay by bank check and take over the deeds to the holdings in the name of Sunshine Management, Incorporated. Squires would call an emergency meeting of the board in Nassau. On his way from Freeport to Nassau he'd meet Bix at Musket Cay. Bix would give him some of the cash money and show him the rest. When the deal went through, Squires would stop at the same place on the way back to Freeport and pick up the rest of it, the eight hundred, or whatever Bix was able to work him down to. Bix said he wasn't going to hustle the deal through. He said he'd cruise around the islands some. He said the longer he dragged his feet, the more Squires and his crowd would be hurting. Last I heard from him, Sam, he give me a call from Miami when he got there, just about almost a month ago."

"Who is that Staniker and his wife?"

"Now that would be the fella he took on in Miami. He said he'd want to get somebody who knows the waters. Bix and his boy, Roger, took it around the Gulf to Miami from here. He said he'd want to get a cook aboard too once they took off from the states.

Reckon he found a couple that suited. Bix would check them out pretty good, that's for certain. The thing is, Sam, there is no reason on God's earth Bix would want to turn up missing this way. It's a good safe boat, and he'd have a good safe place aboard for the money, but eight hundred thousand and no sign of the boat at all, it starts a man thinking, and it keeps your food from settling real good."

"Who is the lawyer in Nassau?"

"Near as I remember, he didn't mention a name."

"What have you been planning to do, Judge?" Sam asked.

Tom Dorra said, "Earlier I was saying to Judge Billy we don't hear anything in another couple days, I just might go on over and get that Squires off in private and dance him up and down some to see what might come loose and fall off him. But Bix didn't talk like he was dealing with any hard case. What are you going to do?"

"Clean up a few things and see if I can get out of here by tomorrow night and get on over there and see if there's anything they could be doing they're not doing. I can take a look at Squires and let you know."

"We would be most humbly grateful, Sam'l," said the Judge.

"I'm grateful you told me what's going on."

"Just saved you a lot of digging is all, I expect. I sure hope that—everything is all right aboard that boat. You boys want to walk an old man down the street and let him stand you a touch of the nerve tonic?"

"Thanks, but I'd best be getting back up the line."

"Nerve tonic is what I need most," Tom said, rising to his full height, straightening his pale hat. "By the way, Sam, I was talking to old Goober the other night and he said he seen Lydia Jean a week back still up there in Corpus. Her old lady must be having some long spell of the sickness, I guess."

"Can't be helped," Sam said.

"Can get tiresome, tending the sick. I got to go up to the regional meeting of the growers next week, and if I get a chance, I could give her a ring and cheer her up some."

"You do that," Sam said evenly. He said goodby to them and walked out. Tom D. started to follow along, but the Judge called him back in and closed the office door.

"Now what the *hell* were you trying to do, bringing that up about Lydia Jean?" Billy asked angrily.

Tom D. sprawled his bulk and weight back into an oak chair and said, smiling, "Now Billy, half the Valley knows Lydia Jean run out on him and he can't seem to sweet talk her into coming home where she belongs. Thought I'd give him a little something to think on."

"A little game, eh? Like learning to jump out of airplanes without a chute, or picking up rattlesnakes by the back of the neck with your teeth. What makes you so damn dumb anyways?"

Tom Dorra looked angry and upset. "You've got no call to talk to me like that. Sam Boylston's just another one of those nice clean little lawyer fellas."

Judge Billy tilted his swivel chair back and looked at a far high corner of the room. "Been around a long, long time. Seen a lot of them come along. Don't you get twitchy thinking on that free drink I offered. You set and listen. Might help you some day. Got any idea why Lydia Jean run for cover? Tell you what I think, big Tom. She's trying to see if she can slow him down some, make him look around and see folks instead of things, and like the fella says, get him to learn to stop and smell the flowers."

"Do you honest to God know what you're talking about, Judge?"

"Won't work, of course. Not with Sam Boylston. He's in a dead run. Can't stop. Won't stop. Scared to stop. That's the way the big ones are. He ain't real big yet. But he's moving as fast as you'll ever see. Twenty years when he's Bix's age about, line 'em up side by side, Bix Kayd is dime-store goods, a clown-man. You can feel the power in Sam'l. He's got the stillness, hearing all, seeing all, tucking it away. When you ragged him some about Lydia Jean, I seen something look out of his eyes at you, something I wouldn't fool with."

"You're scaring me to death, Judge."

"Me, I won't last long enough to see him as big as he's going to get. But he's a-going to own this whole Valley, as just a first step. Oh, not by title and deed, but there won't be anybody with land worth in six figures on up stupid enough to cross him. What he wants done gets done. And tucked back in his brain is the memory of how you did him today. He won't come after you just to pleasure himself. He can't waste his time on earth like that. But one day there'll be money he can see on the far side of you, and he won't go around you. He'll go right over the top of you, stompin' as he goes, and you won't be a person to him because nobody is real to him but Sam Boylston. If I was you, I'd start thinking on cashing ever'thing in and moving far enough away so he won't likely come across you."

"Billy, what's wrong with you? The land my great grand-daddy settled is smack in the middle of my holdings. I got friends close and true in six counties. Nothing Boylston can ever do to me, a little lawyer-man like that!"

"Lydia Jean may slow him a little bit for a little time, but then he'll come on faster than ever. He thinks he's like everybody else. It's just he don't have any softness slowing him down. God knows I ain't got much, but what I got makes me smaller than I could have been. You got more than me by far. But if Sam Boylston had a thing to gain by rendering you down into cooking oil, he'd stoke the fire, boil you good, skim the fat into a bucket and tote it off. It saddens me thinking you're the last Dorra going to own land in this county, and I might live long enough to get brought down with you if I'm standing too close, so we've come to an end of drinking together, and now it's time we start winding up all the things we're into together, so let's start dickering on who buys who out of what and for how much."

"You got to be kidding, Billy! Your old brain is cloudy. I got a bad case of the shorts. Do that, and you'll be running me out of some prime stuff, and you damn well know it. We been friends a long time."

Judge Billy Alwerd blinked and smiled like a lizard on a rock. "All of a sudden being friends with you is too dangerous, Tom D. Anything you want to take over, I'll take back mortgages, but I'll discount 'em right off. We're going to be arms length all the way."

Tom stood up and leaned over the desk and said, "Do me this way, and I'll crack your spine, old man!"

"I will. And you won't." He chuckled. "In a manner of speaking, boy, what's happening to you right now is Sam Boylston's doing. You tweaked him about his woman, and you come down with a hard case of finance-yool leprosy. Don't mess with Francie on the way out, you hear?"

When Sam got back to his office there was a note that his wife had called him. He called her back, knowing the call would be about Leila, and that she had heard. He told her that he didn't know anything new, and that he was going over to the Bahamas the evening of the next day. When she asked about Jonathan, Sam said that Jonathan might be in Nassau already, but he certainly would be there by the time Sam arrived.

When she was silent for a few moments, Sam said, "Aren't you going to say it?"

"Say what, dear?"

"If it wasn't for me, she wouldn't have been on the cruise."

"There's no point in you blaming yourself, Sam. You had no way of knowing anything would happen. And why do you think I'd say anything like that to you at a time like this? Do you think I go around looking for chances to be nasty?"

"I don't know what to think about you, Lyd. I don't know how much resentment there is. There has to be some, wouldn't you say? Or you'd be home where you belong."

"That isn't the kind of attitude that's going to make me hurry back."

"I should get used to your new rule, I guess. No matter what I say, it's going to be wrong."

Her long sigh was audible over the line. "Darling, let's start this conversation over. We both love Leila. We're both very worried about her. I would appreciate it if you would let me know what you find out. And I hope everything turns out for the best, and that she's safe. And—please don't take any chances over there, like flying around in some little airplane in bad weather looking for her."

"I want to make certain they're doing everything."

"Please be nice to Jonathan."

"For God's sake, Lydia Jean!"

"Don't try to shut him out. He's as concerned as you are."

"I'm not the one who goes around shutting people out."

"We have such happy talks, don't we, Sam?"

"So let's try a new area. An old friend of yours will be looking you up next week."

"Really? Who?"

"He had the needle out. And he was enjoying it. Maybe you can tell him your troubles."

"Who are you talking about?"

"Big Tom Dorra."

"Damn you, Sam! Damn you!"

"Did I say something wrong?"

"He is not an old friend and you know it. Do you really think I'd talk to *him* about *us?* He is physically repulsive to me. He looks— buttered. And he is absolutely convinced he's God's gift to woman-hood."

"You're a legitimate target, Lyd. You turned yourself into a target by leaving me. So you've got to expect Tom Dorras to come around. And there isn't a damn thing I can do about it."

"Do you think I'm incapable of handling the situation?"

"Does it make any real difference? Tom D. will have a little smirk and a little wink for anybody who asks him if he saw you when he was up in Corpus."

"So what fools believe is more important to you than what you know is true?"

"A lot of things I thought were true haven't turned out so good."

"So I'm supposed to come home just to keep you from feeling inadequate?"

"Honey, I'm adequate. Some day Tom Dorra will sign a testimonial to that effect if anybody asks him to. What's the matter now?"

"I'm crying. Do I have your permission?"

"For the love of . . ."

"I don't want to spoil the Sam Boylston image. Oh God, I thought we were getting somewhere the last time we talked."

"The day you tell me exactly where we are supposed to be getting to, then we can start getting there. Try writing it down. It might help."

"Good luck about Leila."

"Thanks for calling."

"Don't mention it," she said and hung up.

After thirty thoughtful seconds, he picked up the hand microphone, pressed the dictate button, and began to work his way through the stack of correspondence on his desk. After one false start, he pushed Lydia Jean and Leila back into storage cupboards in the back of his mind and closed those doors which would isolate them completely until he would be free to once again give them his attentions.

Eight

CRISSY HARKINSON AROSE a little before noon on the day after first taking the boy, Oliver Akard, into her bed. The double thicknesses of draperies kept the room in semi-darkness, the switch on the bedside phone had been turned off, and the little Cuban maid had long since been taught to work in silence until the coffee summons from the bedroom of the mistress released her from such constraint.

She remembered that her last glance at the luminous dial of the radio clock, just after the boy had slipped out onto the dark terrace and closed the sliding door, had shown that it was just four in the morning.

She trudged slowly, solidly, heavily, through the dressing room alcove and into her bath, touched the silent switch and, when the cruel lights flickered and went on, she stared mockingly and mercilessly at herself in the mirror, at the tangle of her hair, deep smudges of fatigue under her eyes, face slack under the tan, mouth pale and swollen—pulpy looking. Her body felt stretched and wearied and lamed. At thirty-six, my lady, she told herself, such a romping takes one hell of a toll, and he lives up to Kinsey's report on that age group, and you have got your work cut out for you to hew your way quickly back down to that twenty-eight you damned well have to make him believe.

She started with an amphetamine, and then a long hot sudsy languid shower, turning to a very brisk cold shower. Then harshly astringent lotions, a soothing gentleness of cream, subtle care with the eye makeup, including the drops of magic which made them shine with the imitation of youth. The amphetamine had begun to hit, lifting her spirits, taking away the weariness which had seemed bone-deep, and after she had brushed and poked her almost-dry hair into the casual and youthful style which seemed to do the most for her this year, she selected and put on a pale, fitted, silver-blue housecoat with a fussy girlish frothiness of lace at the throat. She turned this way and that, smoothing the fabric down over her hips with the backs of her hands, moved a little closer to the mirror and gave herself what she called her Doris Day smile.

"You might just make it, kid," she whispered.

She went to the bedroom intercom, pressed the lever and said, "Francisca?"

She heard the quick light sound of the girl's approaching footsteps and then the merry voice of first greeting.

"I think maybe you could squeeze about three or four of those big oranges. Enough for a tall glass. And a pot of coffee."

She went over and pulled on the drapery cords, hand over hand, opening the whole side of the bedroom to the bright day. She bent over the low broad bed and balled up the tangle of pale yellow sheets, carried them in and stuffed them into the hamper. From the linen closet she selected pale green sheets and pillow cases and tossed them onto the bed for Francisca to make it up. From the rug beside the bed she picked up the orange and white striped shift, shook it out, reflected with bitter humor she hadn't gotten much use out of it this time, took it in and hung it up carefully.

When Francisca knocked and brought the tray in, Crissy Harkinson went to her chaise and sat and swung her legs up, and gave the maid a mechanical smile as she reached and took the tray with its short legs and set it across her thighs.

"Was come for a school theeng," Francisca said. "Small girls on bicycle. Teekits to send off the music somewheres. One dollar from the bockus I give. Hokay?"

After a pause for comprehension, Crissy said, "That was fine, dear. Would you do the bed now, please?"

She unfolded the morning paper. Friday. The twentieth day of May. Her heart tilted for a moment, and she felt sick. It was beginning to be too long. Garry had guessed it might be two days, certainly not more than four. God, if it had gone wrong somehow, then the big chance was gone, and it was the only one you'd ever get, girl. The years are running the wrong way for you. If Garry messed it up, then you're back to sweating out the other choices, all of them bad. There's only one big thing left to go, and that's this house, and when you sell it, you have three choices. Live the way you like to live on the money you get, and it will last maybe four years and then you are forty and you can decide whether it will be the sleeping pills or a cruddy little job, a cruddy little room, sore feet from standing all day behind a cruddy counter. Or invest the money and get some funny little income for life, and go see if any of the old contacts were still in the business and, out of pity or sentimentality, wanted to make room in the circuit for a one-time upper-level hooker who'd retired too many years ago, at the personal request of State Senator Ferris Fontaine. Or take the house money and make the gamble of building a front with it, maybe the tragic, youngish widow, obviously well provided for, demure as hell, visiting Hawaii or Acapulco or some damn place to try to take her mind off her grief, and then sort out the possibles and take dead aim at some old goof with a fat portfolio and stampede him into marriage, hoping his heart isn't too damned sound. But what if the pigeon turned out to be canny enough to get her checked out first? Or what if he happened to be putting on a front with money as small as hers? Or what if he kept living another twenty-five years, so that when she finally got it— the total freedom and total security she'd wanted all her life—she'd be over sixty years old?

No. Garry Staniker had worked it. It was the only way things would come out fair. The Senator had not really meant to cheat her. She knew she was probably the only toy the old boy had ever bought himself in his whole chinchy, skinflint life, the only time he had ever spent real money with any kind of pleasure at all. Over seven years of a good honest return on the investment too. You spend money on what's important, and she remembered how strange it had seemed to her, when they had met, that an old guy with so much power and influence in the state would be so uneasy and ashamed and apologetic.

It had been one of those long weekend arrangements, six of the kids supplied on request and flown down to Key West where some kind of contractor had a big house with a wall around it and was putting on a special house party with the idea of softening up some politicians who were in a position to do him some good. It came to three hundred each after the usual cut was taken off the top, and that was better than good during the slow season, and there was some iced champagne on the company plane that ferried them down, so all the kids were in a mood to have fun.

When they were sorted out, she turned out to be Fontaine's, and she remembered how, to the twenty-seven year old woman she was then, he seemed older than God, though later she found out he was sixty-one then. But as she got to know him, he seemed funny and sweet and nice. He was very courtly and old-timey. When they were alone was when he got all shy and strange and funny. She finally understood from what he was saying that it would not make any difference in the money arrangements, and he would just as soon have his friends believe that she was earning the money as expected, but it just wasn't possible, and that was that, and he did not care to talk about it any further.

There was just the one double bed in the room they'd been given, a bed with a huge carved Spanish headboard. After the light was out she got him talking again and got him around to talking about the problem, which he seemed to find easier to do in the dark. He said, no, he hadn't been sick. He had just gradually become—incapable a couple of years ago, and he did not care to go through the dreary experience of proving it again. He told her about his life. He had married young. There hadn't been the time or the money for play. He said there had been some episodes, as he called them, during his middle years when he had become successful as a rancher. His home base he said was at one of his ranches, a long way east of Arcadia. Twenty-six thousand acres. Brahma and Black Angus.

She made her cautious beginning by explaining to him that she could get to sleep much easier if she was close to someone, and after certain reluctance he held her with his arm around her, and her head on his shoulder. She kept thinking of twenty-six thousand acres, and imitated deep sleep, a purring snore, but a restless sleep in which she shifted, burrowed against him, put her round arm carelessly across him, a great fan of her soft hair—much longer then—across his throat. She wondered at the increased knocking of his heart, but was not sure there could be any ultimate victory until, at last, she felt him with infinite stealth move his hand, bit by bit, until he could touch the strong round breast of the girl he thought asleep.

Ten days later at his telephoned request, she took a commercial flight to Miami where he had registered them both on the same floor of one of the big beach hotels. She sidestepped his attempts to talk of future arrangements until she had managed to prove to his satisfaction and hers that what had been thought impossible was becoming easier at each opportunity. The next day he sent her, alone, to look at the apartment he could arrange if it suited her.

Over dinner in his one-bedroom suite that evening they struck their bargains. She could count upon his visiting her for a couple of days on the average of once each month. It might be oftener at times or less frequent, but it would probably average out that way. He wanted total discretion on her part. He said he felt he did not have the right to demand physical faithfulness of her. He would leave that up to her, stipulating only that she was not to have anyone visit her at the apartment, nor was she in any direct or indirect way to sell herself. The apartment lease and the utilities would be taken care of. He would give her money to open a checking account, and she would give him the name of the bank and the account number, and a deposit would be made, untraceable, to her account each month. What did she think it should be?

"Fifteen hundred dollars a month," she said.

"You trying to gouge me, girl?" he asked, scowling.

"Senator, I don't think it's nice to argue about money. I told you what I need. I don't *have* to argue about money. I can remember from high school, from economics class, a monopoly can set its own rates because there's noplace else to buy what it's selling. I'm going to gouge you pretty good, but I'm going to give you fair value. If you don't want it that way, let's call the whole thing off right now."

He stared at her, and he chuckled for a long time, shook his head, chuckled some more, and from then on did not deny her what she asked. By the time she picked out the land and the house was completed, he had regained a virility which, he claimed, seemed like unto what he could dimly remember of himself as a bridegroom. With the house went a stolid square humorless but efficient Swedish woman. Ferris Fontaine had hired her, and when Crissy made mild objection to her, she gathered that Fontaine had once done her delinquent son a favor of such magnitude the woman's personal loyalty to the Senator was beyond measure. Crissy gradually became aware that Fontaine had been testing her discretion and her judgment in small ways for some time. When he had satisfied himself about her, the Biscayne Bay house, because it had been located and designed for total privacy, became a place where he held secret meetings of men with whom he was involved in various intricate business affairs. Crissy acted as hostess, knowing when to absent herself to let them talk, learning from the Senator which drinks she should make a little heavier than usual. Though the relationship between Fontaine and Crissy could not help but be obvious to all who were invited there, the Senator never permitted other girls in the house.

Three years ago, perhaps as a reward for how well she had handled things when he used the house for meetings, and perhaps out of the money which had been the result of such meetings, he had bought her the pleasure cruiser, the handsome Odalisque, and had hired Garry Staniker to captain it and maintain it.

"Use it all you want and any way you want, honey. It's registered to you, but I'll be using it now and then. Some of the cagiest ones will loosen up a little when you get 'em off on the water."

By then the Senator was sixty-seven. Though he seemed far more vigorous and vital than when she had first met him, she knew it was time to take the final step, and one evening when they were there alone, she brought it up with more of an air of casual confidence than she felt.

"It's been six years, darling," she said.

He sipped his ale, belched comfortably and said, "Six very wonderful years, little girl."

"Thirty-three makes a pretty old little girl, Fer."

"By God, you sure don't show it a bit."

"Thanks heaps, but the fact remains. Also the fact remains that I think about it. And I think about you being sixty-seven."

"Mmmm. Let's say I show it, but I don't feel it."

She went to him, sat crosslegged on the floor close to his chair, took his hand in both of hers and looked earnestly up at him. "Fer, I'm not going to bring out any violins and give you any crap about the best years of my life."

"But?"

"I think the word is settlement. Some kind of a settlement. You are a tough old monkey and I think you are going to live forever, but I think you would feel better if you knew that if something did happen, you wouldn't leave me behind cussing you up down and sideways for not setting up some kind of an arrangement to keep your little girl off the streets when the money runs out. Fair is fair."

She waited in the silence while he thought it through. "Fair is fair, sure enough. It isn't the easiest thing in the world to set up, Crissy. By God it isn't. I can't just go sticking you in my will. The wife and the kids and all the grand kids would rise right up and bust hell out of any codicil like that, especially if it was as big as what you'd need."

"What do I need, Fer?"

"Pretty good piece." He went inside to her desk and worked it out on scratch paper. He called her and she went and stood beside him, her hand resting on his shoulder. "Little girl, if you was to live exactly as good as now, with the upkeep to pay on everything and what you have to spend, and if it was set up so you'd live off investment income, it would take four hundred and fifty thousand dollars put away into a good balanced program."

"Good Christ!"

"But that would mean you'd eventual leave behind a pretty fair estate, going to somebody I don't owe spit. So it's got to be worked out on a lifetime basis, so you live fat and die broke. Okay?"

"Sure, Fer."

"Lump sum life annuity, I guess. And some way to transfer this house out of your name but giving you the right to live here as long as you live. That would pay some of the bite on the annuity. The thing to do is get ol' Walker Waggoner scratching around seeing what he can come up with. Then the smart thing would be to get you started on it and me pay the gift tax or whatever, then there'd be no fuss from anybody after I'm gone. When I know what it will come to, then I can figure out the best way to scramble it together. Fair is fair, little girl. You said it true."

Some months later she had to take a complete physical and sign insurance application papers. More months passed and when nothing happened she queried Ferris Fontaine.

It had irritated him. "Little girl, I am doing the damned well best I can, and it is going to get done when a lot of things that affect it one way and another get sorted out."

Fifteen months ago he had come to stay with her on the middle days of a windy week in January. He complained of indigestion. She heard him get up in the middle of the night, and she could not tell how much later it was when she woke again, reached and found him still gone, and no body heat remaining in his side of the bed. She found the bathroom lights shining down upon him on the floor near the toilet, in the pale blue pyjamas she had once bought him. He had reached up and had unrolled an entire role of flowered toilet tissue, pulling it down upon him so that she had to brush it to the side to see his face and know that it was a dead face. He had told her once what she would have to do if he ever should become very sick at that house, or die. She did not think she could manage it. Then she remembered the loyalty of Bertha, the Swede. Bertha understood at once. The two women dressed the body, Bertha with silent tears running down her square pale face. Crissy packed his suitcase. They put the body in the front seat of the navy blue Continental, and the suitcase in the trunk.

Bertha got behind the wheel and Crissy followed at a cautious distance in her white sports car. They left the Lincoln on a dark street in downtown Miami. When no cars were coming, they tugged the body over behind the wheel. The motor was running, the windows down, the headlights on. Bertha tipped the Senator forward and as the horn began to blow, she trotted heavily to the sports car and climbed hastily in beside Crissy.

They did not speak all the way back. When they got out of the car Crissy said, "Thank you—for helping."

Bertha said, "I'm giving you my notice now, M'am. I'll stay thirty days if you haven't found anybody by then, but then I'll have to leave."

"Suit yourself."

"I came with him because he asked me to, only."

"Don't bother to explain."

"But I am a decent woman."

"Congratulations," Crissy said and went into her house. She stripped the bed, remade it fresh, showered, made a stiff drink and went to bed and waited for tears. There weren't any. She had liked him well enough. He had paid well for what he wanted from her. But the old floof had let her down where it counted most, maybe.

After the Senator had been buried by his family, with suitable fanfare and an attendance so large that it was rumored that half of them came not to mourn but to assure themselves he was dead, Crissy drove all over the state seeing in privacy those men who had been members of the inner clique, trying to use the leverage of her special knowledge to pry loose some promise of support.

But they seemed more amused than distressed, and she gave up quickly after one of them, eyes gentle as flint, alternately squeezing and stroking her shoulder, said that they sure didn't want to upset anyone Fer had been fond of, but they'd have to rig up something to give her a nice long stay up to Chattahoochee to ponder it all out some. You had it right nice for a nice long time, considering . . .

So she had hurried back to the house, aware of having been a fool, of having attempted a dangerous game. She had to learn wariness all over again, after these past lush years. She knew it wouldn't be difficult. The practice had started early, maybe way, way back when they took you from the grammaw-house to the Home, and you knew it was a terrible mistake and you were too little to explain it to them, but you knew somebody would remember you and fix the mistake. Then you gradually realized it wasn't a mistake, and it wouldn't be fixed.

You learned wariness when you were a child bride and the New Orleans cop bounced a slug off the pavement into the back of Johnny Harkinson's curly head as he was racing off with a snatched purse. Wariness during the thousand nights Phil Kerna owned you, and you were his luck, sitting back out of the cone of light, watching the poker sessions. Owned you and then loaned you, when the markers came due. Wariness in New York, sharing the apartment with Midgie and Spook, the three of you modeling Frankal's cheap wholesale imitations of high-fashion items, and hustling the buyers but giving them a fair and full return because Frankal didn't want any repeat business ruined. New lessons in wariness when you pulled stakes and went down to Savannah with Midgie and used her contacts to get lined up with that Friendship Club, a telephone operation, hundred-a-week dues. Once they couldn't come up with it and spent ninety days working in the prison laundry, ruining their hands and teaming up to fight off the old bull dykes. From then on you make certain you always have your dues.

Drifted to Atlanta, where it was closer control, a straight percentage action. Wariness in the slow realization that it had stopped being something you were doing for just a little while for kicks. You were a seasoned hooker, and you'd turned twenty-seven, and because your score on repeats was falling off because of competition from the kid stuff just breaking in, you had no more choice left on who, and damn little choice left on what. So, in your wariness, you knew that a really big score was the only way out. So when you got picked for the Key West duty, one of the six packages picked up by the company airplane, one of the steadier types, and the chance with the Senator opened up, you begged and bargained your way loose, using tears and money saved up.

But in the end it was only a partial score, girl, because you turned soft and sweet and trusting. And that was the final lesson. The long years shot and no time to work on any score that would take more years. No time for mercy, girl, and who showed you any? The thing about this score, it had developed out of the Senator thing. You could say it was even a part of it—a chance to more than make up for not having really put the pressure on that old goat sooner and harder. Should have put security on a pay-as-you-go basis right from scratch, when finding out I could turn him back into a man was such a miracle to him, I could have made him crawl on broken glass all the way from his twenty-six thousand acres to where he had me stashed. Every year, old man, you lay fifty thousand on good, fat, blue chips in little girl's name, or the fun stops.

Spilled milk. Oh God, Garry, if you messed up my second chance at the jackpot . . .

She heard the latch of the sliding glass door and turned her head and saw the boy, Oliver, peering in at her and sliding the door open as she had told him to do.

As he came in, closed the door, turned to her, she held both her hands out, her smile brilliant, and whispered, "Darling, darling, darling. Come here, dear. Sit right here where I can look at you."

The shyness of translating last night's intimacy to broad daylight made him approach her with a most curious gait, partially a humble shamble, partially a self-conscious strut.

She took his hands, turned her face upwards, eyes half closed, soft mouth demanding the kiss. He bent hastily and clumsily, got his nose in the way, managed to kiss the corner of her mouth and, in sitting back on the chaise lost his balance, squashed his weight down onto her knees, shifted off them, apologized hoarsely, sat there blushing sweatily and intensely. She noted the way he was dressed, and guessed it had been the result of anguished decisions. He wore sand-colored skinny stretch jeans, and a dark blue sports shirt with the sharp creases of brand-newness still in it, buttoned down the front with small brass buttons. He seemed able to look everywhere except at her.

"Olly, my darling, I have been sitting here waiting for you and trying to believe that what happened really happened. It all seems so fantastic and incredible. It was so—completely unplanned. When you woke up did it seem as unreal to you?"

"Yes. I guess it seemed that way to me too."

"What is happening to us?"

"It—sort of just happened."

She gave a sharp tug at his hands. "What's the matter? Can't you look at me? Can't you say my name? Can't you tell me how you feel?"

She saw him force himself to look into her eyes. His deep tan was suffused with the pink tinge of his blush. With his somewhat indistinct chin, and with those eyes set a little too closely, he looked at her fixedly with an expression of such wondrously enthralled goofiness, she came dangerously close to laughter. His adam's apple slid up and down his throat as he swallowed. In a huskied and very uncertain voice he said, "I—love you, Crissy. I love you."

It was what she wanted to hear him say, and it had come sooner than she had expected.

She leaned, lifted his right hand to her lips, kissed the heavy knuckles one by one, feeling him tremble. "I don't know whether I love you, Olly. Love is a very precious thing. It is a lot more rare than people think. But when you find it, and it's for real, it is worth the most terrible sacrifices. I don't know if—if we're strong enough."

"Strong enough?" he asked, puzzled.

"If you think I'm going to keep us some kind of a state secret, dear, if I decide I do truly love you, then you are making a mistake about me. I am going to be proud of us. People are going to know about us. And they are going to say very cruel things. Are you strong enough for that? And for the pressure your family will put on you? We have to be so terribly sure, Oliver. After all, I'm twenty-eight years old, and I've been married. And widowed."

"I'll be twenty in July."

"The world will say wicked things about us. And a lot of people will even laugh at us. That's why we have to be so sure."

She could sense that it alarmed him. Poor bunny. So many things to alarm him and fascinate him all of a sudden. In empathy her memory went all the way back to Phil Kerna, and the strangely dazed, swooning, hypnotic feeling she'd had after that first time with him, when after that night and day and following night in the Reno motel he had left her there alone and gone back to the poker table. Having been married to Johnny for a year had left her as innocent as a child in comparison with what Phil had been able to make her experience. Now it would be just the same with Olly Akard, who had come to her with only the experience of a couple of years of furtive intimacy with his little steady girl, Betty, had come to her with that curious conviction of the male of limited experience that his role was that of sole aggressor, full of determined anxiety to perform properly just as it was written in the books, and with the pitiful belief that the one small pleasure he had always achieved was all his body was capable of.

She knew how deeply he had been confused and frightened, first by her, and finally by the unexpected and wild and savage intensity of his own guided response. Curious guilts and shynesses made him feel very awkward to be with her in daylight, knowing she too remembered all the tumbled deliriums and grotesqueries of the unending night.

Though she knew she had brought him far enough for there to be little danger of his being frightened away now, she laughed softly and fondly, hitched herself closer to him, put one hand on his powerful shoulder, laid her right hand against his cheek and with her thumb stroked the furry sheen of his eyebrow.

"But no need to look so scared already, dear little bunny rabbit boy," she said. "I won't want to parade you on display until I am absolutely certain. And meanwhile we will be dreadful sneaky sneaks. Like the page sneaking into the quarters of the sexy old queen. My little maid is discreet. And this home of mine was designed to frustrate nosey people."

He said with overly casual and clumsy curiosity, "I—I suppose that's the way the Senator wanted it."

She looked at him in blank astonishment. "I beg your pardon?"

"I mean—well, I guess he wouldn't want people to know he was . . ."

She narrowed her eyes and firmed her lips. Then she got up quickly and strode away, whirled and pointed a finger at him. "See? See what they do? So *that's* what they made of it, eh? My God! Really! And you had to find out if those dirty little fibs were true, didn't you?" She moved closer. "I built this house to suit *me!* I built it with money from my husband's estate. Ferris Fontaine was an old and dear friend. When he asked if he could use my home for little political meetings now and then, I was *glad* to say yes. I was *honored!* That's the reward for friendship. My God, it's really pathetic! What foul little minds people must have to really believe I was dear Fer's mistress. A man so *old!* How *could* you believe it, Olly?"

"I didn't," he said earnestly. "Not really. Before I ever even met you, I didn't believe it."

She sat by him, smiled, patted his knee. "Thank you, dear. Let's change the subject. It makes me angry. Are your people curious about why you got home so terribly late?"

"I coasted the last half block and into the driveway with the lights and motor off."

"That was very clever, dear."

"Nobody said anything about it today."

After a silence she leaned her forehead against his shoulder and said in a small voice, "Do you know what you do when something keeps on seeming so unreal? You find out just as soon as you can if it was really real."

She walked her fingers up his broad hard chest and, starting at the throat, undid the first three brass buttons.

"Right n-now?" he asked hoarsely.

She straightened and looked at him. He had gone pale enough to make his tan look odd. He wiped his mouth on the back of his hand.

"My darling, we'll try to get along without any rules at all, but there should be one rule. Whenever we want each other as desperately as we do right now, we'll never let anything stand in the way. Be a dear and go pull those draperies. The cords are over at the right."

She turned her head and looked at the clock radio near the bed and saw that it was three thirty in the afternoon. She rolled her head back on the pillow and saw that the boy would soon be fast asleep.

She bit her lip and debated changing the schedule she had planned for him. He was adapting more swiftly than she had estimated.

Funny, she thought, how often Phil Kerna kept coming back into her mind. All tenderness and cajolerie and sweet words until he had slipped the collar around your neck so deftly you hardly noticed it. Then he could risk the flat hateful stare, give the harsh commands, knowing a humble obedience was your only choice.

"Oliver!"

"Uh?" he said, and opened his eyes, focused on the face so close to his.

She hitched herself up, resting her weight on her elbows so she could look down into his eyes in the half light of the draperied bedroom. She studied him with a flat, bright, questing stare, unsmiling, until he asked her if something was wrong.

"I was wondering about something, Oliver."

"Wondering what?"

"Perhaps I was wondering if you think this is some sort of a game. A little diversion."

His eyes widened. "Honest, Crissy, I . . ."

"You must understand that I am a very intense person, darling. As soon as I'm certain that you mean as much to me as—I think you mean right now, there aren't going to be any half measures for me. For me it is going to be a hundred and ten percent. Or nothing at all."

"But . . ."

"Let me tell you the whole thing, dear. I told you we would be dreadful sneaks until I *am* sure. And that gives you an opportunity to have your cake and eat it too, you know. I was wondering if that is the kind of man you are."

"I don't know what you mean."

"Have you forgotten the long talk we had in the middle of the night? I guess you could call it the confession hour. As I understand it, if you weren't lying, I'm the second woman in your life, and Betty was the first. Did I say 'was'? Excuse me. We're keeping us a secret from the world, for a little while. And from Betty. That gives you quite an interesting life, doesn't it? Two women saying yes to you. Does it give you a sense of power, Oliver?"

"Crissy, believe me, that wasn't anything like . . ."

"Correct me if I read you wrong, dear. You said that you and your dear little Betty have been going steady for three years, and two years ago you—ah—slipped. Wasn't that the word you used? And you vowed, both of you, it would never happen again, but it did. And you finally, after you'd slipped enough times, decided that as you were to be married eventually anyway, you might as well enjoy each other."

"But it isn't . . ."

"Perhaps I'm jealous, darling. Do you mind terribly? When you aren't here with me, there's absolutely no reason why you can't be lifting her little skirts. She's probably very attractive. And quite a lot younger than I am."

"It was just kid stuff. I know that now, Crissy. It didn't mean anything."

"And you'll never touch her again?"

"Never. Honest. I swear I won't."

"Thank you, dear. But I do think you should put temptation out of your path."

"What do you mean?"

"Break it up, dear. End it. I don't care how you manage it, but I think it should be all over within—three days. If you are going to get a hundred and ten percent of me, I demand a hundred and ten percent of you. I don't share, dear. I don't believe in sharing. You might be tempted to—find out if she is just the way you remember."

"That's—awful fast. What will I say to her?"

"My God, haven't you two ever quarreled at all? Don't you know by now what she gets mad at? Get into a brawl with her and walk out. Or just tell her very coldly you've out-grown her. There must be dozens of ways."

"It's going to hit her pretty hard."

She thought, picked her words carefully. "I love your gentleness, and your kindness. But I want my man to be strong. If I can't ask you to do such a small thing as that, how do you think it makes me feel? Secure? Loved? Perhaps—you're not really *ready* for the big leagues, dear, where the grown-ups are. Maybe you'd be better off with your little Betty person after all."

"No! Listen. I'll *do* it. I just said it's going to be hard on her. She thinks we're—you know. All set. There—there isn't *anything* I wouldn't do for you."

She lowered herself, dug her face into his throat, sighed comfortably and said, "We have to be strong, dear. Both of us. Strong and selfish. We have to remember that there isn't anybody or anything else in the world that means a damn, not really. We're all that counts. You and I. Oliver and Cristen. Hold me, darling."

Soon, in an automatic and almost absent-minded way she began the little trickeries of arousing him, thinking as she did so that he would get rid of Betty just as he had promised. It was the first small test of how strong his infatuation was becoming. It was astonishing how compulsive the flesh could become when it was their first affair with a mature woman, rich, ripe and skilled, and so startlingly without shame or reserve, so unexpectedly frank in the giving and taking of pleasure, so impatient when her cues were misunderstood or overlooked. Then, as their clumsiness and timidity diminished, they were made ever more blind by sensation until, finally, it was such a necessary thing for them to keep experiencing, they would sacrifice everything else in the world to sustain it, and, finally, would reach that stage wherein all of life outside the bedroom walls was a vagueness, a dream-walking hallucination, a place of those shifting shadows which had once been real people, real objects, real goals and ambitions.

The practices demanded only a portion of her attention, and her thoughts ranged far as she pleasured the boy. There was one daydream that was becoming more real to her each time she experienced it. It happened a long time from now. It happened after everything had gone just as she had planned it, and after she was safe, and far away. There would be the years of heats and wanting, and at long last that too would be all burned away, and peace would come to her.

It will be a faraway place, she thought, a house above a lagoon, and I shall be old. I shall be wise. I will have young servants, brown and beautiful and smiling people who love me. There will be legends about me, none of them true. When the fires are burned out, then what is left will be goodness and kindness, and I will be able to forgive them all . . . .

The boy slid into the heaviness of spent sleep, and she got up and freshened herself, went back and set her alarm for six thirty and was soon napping comfortably beside him.

Nine

BY NOON OF THAT SAME FRIDAY, Samuel Boylston had been in Nassau forty-eight hours. He had not been able to get away as quickly as planned, hoping each hour would bring word of the fate of the Muñeca, and had arrived Wednesday noon by Pan Am from Miami.

Before he left he had received a wire from Jonathan Dye saying that he was staying at something called the Harbour Central House on Victoria Avenue. Sam had arranged to have a rental car reserved for him and waiting at the airport. It was a small Triumph sedan, weakly air conditioned. The rental clerk gave him a Nassau map and he studied it for a little while before driving off. He had been in Nassau at other times for both business and pleasure, and it did not take long for him to refresh his memory of the layout of streets, and it took no longer than the trip from Windsor Field to the city for him to adjust his alarm system to driving on the wrong side of the street.

He found the Harbour Central House two blocks up the hill

above Bay Street and parked in front just as Jonathan came with long loose lanky strides up from Bay Street. He was a big knuckly young man with coarse black hair and that variety of tough, under-privileged-looking skin which remains pale despite all exposure. He had a calm dignity which Sam interpreted as an infuriating kind of self-approval.

Sam got out for the awkward measure of the handshake and said, "Any word yet?"

"No sir. It's sort of—slacking off."

"How?"

"There's only about so much area to cover. I can show you on the chart I've got, sir. It's not they're not anxious to do everything. There's the Aircraft Crash and Rescue people, a lot of them volun-teers. And the commercial aircraft people. And the Marine Operator telling all the pleasure boats to be on the lookout. The people at the Ministry of Maritime Affairs have been wonderful. But the weather has been perfect, and they know exactly when the Muñeca left Nas-sau last Friday morning, just 5 days ago today, heading for Little Harbour in the Berry Islands. They didn't take off until maybe ten thirty in the morning, and Mr. Kayd didn't call in at nine on Satur-day morning. They cruised at sixteen miles an hour and usually got where they were going before dark. So the search area wouldn't be more than a hundred and twenty or thirty miles across. But they've covered three times that much area, sir. The wind has been out of the east and the northeast just about every day, and they've allowed for drift. They haven't said it to me, and they won't say it to you, but you get the feeling—they think that somehow it sunk in deep water. They're going through some motions still, but . . ."

Sam saw the pure misery in the boy's eyes as he turned away and stared down the slope of the street toward the harbor.

"What kind of a place is this where you're staying?"

"Simple. Clean enough. Sixteen shillings."

"You could get your gear and come along with me as my guest. I've got a reservation at the Nassau Harbour Club."

"I guess I'd just as soon stay right here, sir."

"Then get that chart of yours and ride on out with me while I register. We'll talk some more and I'll bring you back."

The room they gave him was on the second floor with a small balcony overlooking that part of the harbor. Sailboats with blue sails were racing around a marked course in a windy chop.

From the side windows there was a view of the free-form swimming pool below, of tidy tanned girls swimming, of waiters bringing drinks to round metal tables. At the long docks with their finger piers were the pleasure boats, clean and colorful, bright work winking in sunlight, moving and lifting against the mooring lines to the push of wind, tide and chop.

Jonathan spread the chart out on one of the twin beds. There were patterns marked on it in different colors of crayon.

Jonathan said, "One of the Aircraft Crash and Rescue people marked it up to explain how a search pattern works. This is a square pattern here. It's a spiral with square corners. They know how far they can see from the altitude they fly at, and on each leg they overlap about a third of the area they could see the last time past. When they go down to check something, they use loran to get back to the point where they broke off from the pattern. Anything they see floating, they check it to make sure it isn't debris from the Muñeca."

"How would they explain two seaworthy boats disappearing with no trace at all?"

"Well—fire and explosion is one way. The Muñeca was diesel powered, but the smaller boat Mr. Kayd bought in Florida was gasoline. If it was tied alongside the big boat something like that could have happened. Then there are coral heads. The navigation charts of the Bahamas aren't real accurate. A coral head can build up from the bottom maybe fifty feet down, and the top of it might be only a foot across and two feet under water, but they're hard as granite. At cruising speed one could open up the bottom of a cruiser so that it would go down in seconds practically. If they went plowing into a whole area of coral heads, maybe it would open up both hulls."

"So that would bring it down to the question of just how competent that Captain Staniker might be, and how well he knows the waters and the special problems of the area."

"From what I've found out I guess he knew what he was doing, sir."

"I'm her brother, Jonathan. Would it be at all possible for you to call me Sam?"

"I guess so. I guess I could—Sam."

"She wouldn't have been over here if I hadn't leaned on you two. I suppose you keep thinking about that."

The boy sat on the bed, looked down, frowning. "I guess you do too, sir. Sam. But what's the good of saying if this and if that? There's that saying, if your aunt had wheels she'd have been a tea cart. Leila and I, we talked about it a long time before we agreed to play it your way. She was a lot more indignant about it than I was. I made her see it from your point of view. You were motivated by love for her. When the motivation is okay, you can overlook lousy performance."

"Lousy performance?"

Jonathan looked up at him, slightly surprised. "You want to deny people the privilege of making their own mistakes. It's like you don't want to give yourself or anybody else any leeway. Leila said you were pushing us around just for the sake of pushing us around. It could look that way, you know. I said you were concerned about her having a good and happy life. She put her finger right on the flaw in that one. She said there must be a thousand definitions of what constitutes a good and happy life, and so it was a thousand to one that what you wanted for her would relate to what she wants for herself. Certainly it was a lousy performance, because there was no need for us to prove anything to each other, and certainly not to you. You see, Sam, if Leila and I had any doubts or reservations, we'd have taken a leave of absence from each other to check it out. At nineteen and twenty-one we're both a little tougher and more mature than the average. What we want to do with our lives is not sacrificial. For us it's self-seeking, because that's where the satisfaction is. And what could make our lives full might sound like nonsense to you." He paused. "Just as your life sounds like nonsense to us, Sam. You do what you do very successfully. But there are people who are the best in the world at juggling flaming torches, or dancing on ice skates, or collecting old Roman coins. It doesn't mean everybody should get the same charge out of it."

"So you went along with it because my motives were pure."

"Because if we didn't, it would have been years before you and Leila would have re-established a good relationship. She said it didn't matter. I said you are the only blood kin she had and it does matter."

"At this point it is an academic discussion, Jonathan."

"If—it's as bad as it could be, I am going to try not to let myself hate you, Sam. Because what was true is still true, no matter what happened."

"Why didn't the three of us have this kind of a talk seven weeks ago?"

"We tried to. You weren't listening."

Sam stared out at the boats, finally turned and said, "That is perfectly accurate. I wasn't listening. And I might learn to regret that most of all. Now then. What did you find out that makes you think Staniker qualified?"

"He came here with his wife ten years ago with enough money saved up to make a down payment on a big ketch that had been built here in the islands. He and his wife did a lot of the work themselves, fixing it up for charter. He got all the necessary papers and permissions. He was based at Yacht Haven, just down the road from here. They lived aboard. He operated it on charter for five years. They made a living, but they didn't make much more than that, I guess. Five years ago they were out on charter and heading for Eleuthera and a waterspout took the sticks out of her and opened the seams and smashed the dinghy. The water that came in drowned the auxiliary so he couldn't transmit. She drifted down to Cat Island and broke up on a reef there. He got everybody ashore, and he was cleared of any blame when they had the investigation. The ketch was a total loss and there wasn't enough insurance money to start up again. He went back to Florida and got a job as a hired captain. I guess that when Mr. Kayd was looking for somebody to run the Muñeca over here and cruise the Bahamas, he'd be a pretty good choice."

"If he was such a good choice, why would he be available? Why wasn't he already employed?"

"I wouldn't know. I guess it would be easy enough to find out in Miami."

"Why didn't he make a better success of the charter business right here?"

"The people I talked to at Yacht Haven, the ones who were there when Captain Staniker was, they gave me the idea he was a good sailor but not a very good businessman. I got the impression that it was his wife, Mary Jane, who sort of held the whole thing together."

Sam and Jonathan went down and had lunch in the coffee shop. After lunch Sam drove into town, dropping Jonathan off on the way. He had dealt on a prior visit with a Mr. Lowry Malcolm with the law firm of Callender and Higgs on Bay Street. He took a chance on catching Malcolm in, and after a ten minute wait was taken back to Malcolm's small office. Lowry Malcolm had gotten out the file on the previous business matter.

"This is something else entirely," Sam said. "I'd like your help in

tracking down some information. One of the law firms here repre-
sents Mr. Bixby Kayd either under his own name or the name of
Sunshine Management, Incorporated, a United States corporation."

Lowry Malcolm was a languid, remote-acting man, thin, pale
and balding. He raised his eyebrows. "Ah, the poor chap who's been
lost at sea?"

"My nineteen-year-old sister, Leila, was aboard."

"Oh, I say! That *is* hard lines. Terribly sorry to hear it. Saw the
names in the paper, of course, but didn't make the connection. I do
hope the vessel will turn up safe and sound."

"Thanks. Will it be a lot of trouble to find out exactly who would
be representing Mr. Kayd?"

"Shouldn't be. Shall we give it a try?"

On the fourth call he found that the firm was Kelly and Dawson,
only a block away. Before calling there, Malcolm said, "When I get
the chap on the wire, what should I say?"

"Tell him that I want to speak to him on a matter of great urgency, as soon as possible. Tell him I am an attorney from Texas and
you have had dealings with me and can vouch for my reputation and
integrity—and you will appreciate all the cooperation he can give
me."

After he had made the call, Malcolm said, "That firm is the Bahamian headquarters for Sunshine Management. Thought I'd seen that
bloody name on a plaque on someone's building. The chap you
want is Kemp Rodgers. Know him well. All my life, actually."

"Would you call him an honest man?"

Malcolm's jaw sagged. "What an odd thing to say!"

"Sorry I haven't got time to work up to it gradually, but it is important that I know."

"Kemp is a dear fellow. He is absolutely straight. Never fear. Actually he might have done far better at the law had he not considered
it—a necessary nuisance to provide him funds for unspeakably sav-

age little motor cars. He lives for Race Week when he can risk his neck in all that snarling, sliding nonsense. But I must say, if one can endure the racing part of it, it does provide one a rather remarkable choice of lively ladies. He will see you as soon as you can get over there, Boylston. He's shifting his appointments to make space. If you need more help . . ."

"I'll be back. And thanks."

Kemp Rodgers was a trim man with a large, guardsman moustache, bright blue eyes, oversized hands, and two shelves of race trophies.

His first impression was that Sam Boylston was connected in some way with Sunshine Management. When he learned there was no connection, he was reluctant to give out any information.

Sam Boylston called upon that special and directed force he used rarely, in fact could not use except when a great deal was at stake. He could not fake it. He would feel a curious stillness within himself, and he would have a sense of something coiling and gathering. His voice always became softer, with the feeling that he heard it from a distance, and observed the scene from a distance. It was a force he seemed to be able to aim with his eyes, and he had watched varied and strange effects it had upon people.

Usually they seemed startled, and then alarmed. As if some familiar and unremarkable object, such as a paperweight, had suddenly grown a viper's head, impressive fangs, and had begun waddling across the desktop toward them with every evidence of malignant determination.

Out of the stillness he said in a careful voice, "I do not need to be reminded of the ethics of my profession, Rodgers. I know what privileged information is. My sister was aboard that cruiser. I am not going to beg, and I am not going to be very patient. Have you seen Bixby Kayd recently? Did he have anything to say about buying the

land holdings of Ventures, Limited? Was a large sum recently trans-
ferred to the local bank account of Sunshine Management?"

The blue eyes tried to look fierce. They became vague. The
moustache twitched. The large hands began washing each other.
"Really, I couldn't—ah—it was thirty-one hundred thousand odd
pounds. Told Kayd there was no reason to think Venture would
settle for that little. He roared with laughter, gave me a great bloody
bash on the shoulder and talked about positive thinking. We fixed
up a limited power of attorney."

"For what purpose?"

"His offer was, in your money, eight million seven. He said Sir
Willis Willard—he's the Chairman of the Board of Ventures—
would be calling a special meeting to consider the offer. I would be
advised to attend and make the offer official, and hand over the
cheque if they approved. Not bloody likely, I told him."

"I'd like to talk to Sir Willis."

"He's a very busy chap and . . ."

"I'm sure you can arrange it."

"But I don't see what the connection could be between . . ."

"If you don't mind. It can be at his convenience."

With visible reluctance, Rodgers reached for his desk phone. He
arranged an appointment for Sam Boylston with Sir Willis Willard
for the following morning, Thursday morning, at ten o'clock in Sir
Willis's offices in the Imperial Bank of Commerce on Parliament
Street.

Rodgers said, "Sir Willis is a lovely old boy. He's done so very
well with almost everything he's touched, this Ventures mess is a
thorn in his side. I gather he's trying to liquidate it in such a way
none of his associates in it will get too badly hurt."

"As far as you know, no special meeting was called."

"I expect if it were to be called to vote on the Sunshine Management offer, I'd have been notified."

• • •

Sir Willis's offices were spacious, paneled in pale wood, decorated with cheerful accents of primary colors. The girl ushered Sam in and pulled the door shut as she left. Sir Willis was a wispy man, white hair, pink skin, bright blue eyes. He seemed no larger than a child behind the absolutely empty expanse of pale desk. And he looked like a child who had been mercilessly scrubbed, carefully dressed, and sent off to a party with many warnings about how to behave.

"Whichever chair might suit you, Mr. Boylston. The straight one or the soft one. You heard Rodgers's half of our conversation, I believe. This is all something to do with Kayd, poor chap, and Sunshine Management, but you are not associated with either."

Taking the straight chair, Sam had his first chance to look directly at those old blue eyes. There was nothing childish about them. They had seen a great deal, understood most of what they saw, and had stored away only what seemed of any possible future use.

"I may startle you with what I have to say, Sir Willis."

"I vaguely recall hearing something which startled me in nineteen fifty-eight, or possibly fifty-nine. As I recall, I rather enjoyed the experience."

"I have no proof. So I am not making—accusations. I'm going to ask for your advice."

"I'm most generous with it, Boylston. Generous to a fault. But, of course, the supply is unlimited. Old men have vast stores of it."

"Did Angus Squires request a special meeting of the Board of Ventures, Limited, to consider another cash offer from Sunshine Management?"

Without hesitation, Sir Willis said, "He did indeed. Last Wednesday. One week ago yesterday. And suggested tomorrow. Friday seems to be the traditional day for Board meetings for some reason which defies logical analysis."

"There will be such a meeting, sir?"

"My young ladies out there are indignant. They properly notified the other nine members of the Board. Then Squires phoned
again on Tuesday, day before yesterday, shortly before noon, and
withdrew his request. You understand that any Board member can
ask for a special meeting. And so my young ladies had to telephone
the other nine chaps and cancel. At least they did not have to inform
young Rodgers. They had not gotten around to notifying him."

"Do you know what Sunshine Management was offering?"

"I believe Squires's expression was 'interesting enough to merit
consideration.'"

"Eight million seven hundred thousand."

"My word! That *would* have been a waste of time. I see no reason
why we should go lower than ten million five. Kayd knows that was
our firm figure."

"He was confident your Board would accept it."

"Rather a fool then, what?"

"I don't think anyone could safely call Bixby Kayd a fool. I did
some legal work for him a few years ago. When I finished it up, I
refused to do any more work for him. He was a little too tricky for
my taste. He believed your Board would accept the offer."

"But what could give him *that* impression?"

"I believe, sir, he had a certain amount of faith in the eight hundred thousand dollars he was carrying in cash aboard the Muñeca. It
was to be a little private gift, as I understand it, for Mr. Squires and
some of the others on your Board."

Sir Willis Willard placed his little hands palm down against the
top of his desk. He stared at the far wall of the room, high above
Sam's head.

"I congratulate you, Boylston. You have indeed startled me. Very
cunning indeed. And quite merciless, of course. Aside from myself,
three other men are quite well situated, and they are willing—as I

would be under other circumstances—to take their losses, recoup a sizeable portion of their investment and put it to work elsewhere. I have voted against them because the other seven, including Squires, are not in a position to absorb such a percentage loss of investment capital. And so, to swing it, Squires would need only to corrupt two other men. It would give him six votes in favor. And it would mean a very serious loss to the other four men I have been trying to protect. Excuse me a moment, please."

He opened a drawer in his desk, took out a folder, pencil, scratch pad. He turned to a tabulation in the folder, then did some rapid computation. "Certainly!" he said. "Assuming Angus Squires would take four hundred thousand for himself, and give two hundred thousand each to—the two I suspect would be most susceptible, accepting an offer of eight million seven would give Squires nearly a quarter of million of your dollars in profit, and give his friends fifty thousand net profit each. And by getting it all for a total of nine million five, your Mr. Kayd would be undercutting our rock bottom offer by a million dollars."

"My informants told me Kayd had evidently been dealing quietly with Angus Squires for some time," Sam said. "On the same day the cruiser was reported missing, Kayd was going to rendezvous with Squires at a fishing lodge Squires owns on Musket Cay in the Berry Islands. I'd guess Squires would want to make certain Kayd had the money, and perhaps take some of it along to bring here to Nassau to turn over to the men who'd agreed to sell their vote. I suppose that after the deal went through here, Squires would get the rest. He'd want some sort of safeguard. Dealing with Kayd can make anybody uneasy. My sister was a guest aboard that boat, Sir Willis. And there was over three quarters of a million dollars aboard. Four women and three men and money for a bribe. Bribe money has no past. It doesn't appear on the records. And if nobody is left to report it missing . . ."

"But evidently someone *is*."

"I got my information from two men who—go into things like this with cash the revenue people overlook. There were—certain reasons why they were willing to talk to me. But they won't want to raise a fuss if it's gone forever. They took a chance. The return was going to be high. They'll moan a little, lick their wounds and keep their mouths shut. If somebody did go after the money, I can't believe the information came from them, or from Kayd. I am curious about Squires. If he might be in so much financial trouble he would take—a bigger risk."

"Who knows about all this, Boylston?"

"You and I, sir. Squires. The two men I questioned. And perhaps the two men on your Board who were going to go along with it."

"And Rodgers?"

"I didn't talk about it to him. My guess would be no. Kayd wouldn't tell him anything he didn't have to know."

"If Kayd had mentioned it, I am quite confident Rodgers would have terminated representation and come immediately to me."

"Sir Willis, do you think Angus Squires could have . . ."

"Done them all in? Highly unlikely, I would say. If he needed money badly, he would have gotten more out of the whole thing by going ahead as planned. And, as you know, we have no tax upon income here. I was a bit dubious of his coming in with us on this Ventures thing. Heard some rumors, you know. But no proof, of course. He's one of the Canadian chaps who got in on that Freeport arrangement in the beginning. And, if you meant could he have mentioned it to anyone capable of violent acts, you must remember that Squires would not talk freely about anything so certain to damage him should it come out. As it has, of course."

"How much could it damage him?"

"Badly. Both him and the others involved. You Americans have taken quite a fancy to the phrase 'power structure.' Ours here is small, but very strong. One generally knows who might be doing what, and how well they are managing it. I shall merely trap the likely ones into revealing Squires's plan and activities. It shouldn't be at all difficult." He smiled, made a small chopping gesture with a small hand and said, "Then we shall make quite certain everything they touch from now on shall turn out very badly indeed. Squires and friends accepted that risk. And lost. I am grateful to you for a most interesting talk."

"Could I ask a favor, Sir Willis?"

"Of course!"

"If it wouldn't be too much trouble, I would like to know Squires's movements last Friday, Saturday and Sunday—where he went and who might have been with him."

"No trouble at all, my dear fellow. And I should like to know as well. Ring me here at—this same hour tomorrow and I shall have it for you. I have been wondering, and perhaps it is none of my affair, if the authorities might conduct a—a more productive investigation were they to be told of the money carried aboard?"

"If it's possible, Sir Willis, I'd like that kept quiet. If—it was taken, and there was a lot of publicity about it, it might drop out of sight for a long time. And it seems to me it is getting a lot of publicity right now. I had a television team with a movie camera and lights trap me just outside the Harbour Club this morning. From a Miami station. They wanted a statement. It would seem to me that—a public mention of the money would compound the confusion. And anybody with any useful information might get lost in the crowd of crazies who would come forward. I'd like to go at this quietly. If, in the future, I think a lot of new attention would help, then I can bring it up. Sometimes—special information can be a good lever."

"And if whatever happened had nothing to do with the money?"

"I have to keep remembering it might have been that way. It's hard to think clearly when—you're emotionally involved."

Sir Willis appeared to look more attentively at Sam Boylston.

"Forgive me, Boylston, but I've rarely been exposed to Americans who make that distinction. Makes doing business with them a bit of a bother at times. Judgments based on emotions are quite valid, of course, if one happens to know what he is doing and why." There was, Sam felt, a considerable power in this pink and white doll-man, a knowledge of the flaws in others and himself, a readiness to take any kind of advantage so long as it did not offend his own image of himself as an ethical man.

This immaculate little old man was going to quietly dismantle all the works and dreams of Squires and friends, burn the rubble and sow their lands with salt. And some phases of this program would enrich Sir Willis in one way or another. In a sudden, expanded comprehension of self, Sam Boylston realized he had made exactly this same decision himself, had made it about big Tom Dorra and old Judge Billy Alwerd. Though their role had been peripheral, their actions had been illegal enough to give Sam his rationalization. There had been an icy little focus of satisfaction and anticipation in the back of his mind whenever he had thought of them since finding out about the money loaned to Bix Kayd. When he had time to devote to them, he would find out their every area of income and investment, and see to it that small things began to go wrong. A man in a boat who has to devote all his time to caulking the seams, bailing, working the pump, has no time for careful navigation, no time to look for the reefs. If Dorra and Alwerd were to respond with total speed and energy and calm intelligence to every challenge, he could do them no real harm. But those two were hunch players, drifting at half efficiency through a haze of myth, superstition and self-approval. Shrewder than most, perhaps, but capable of fatal mistakes in judgment if too many things started to go wrong at the same time. And, when they began foundering, he could reach into the chaos and pluck out a few useful things at sacrifice prices.

As his intent became more apparent to himself, Sam saw the similarity between himself and this scrubbed old man with the eyes as cold as Burmese sapphire. And he felt a curious contempt for Sir Willis and for himself.

As Sam left, amid the expressions of mutual gratitude, Sir Willis said, "Perhaps one day we might talk about the special advantages of setting up business interests here in the Bahamas. I suspect, dear boy, we might find some unexpected mutual benefits—of the sort you chaps from your province of Texas seem able to appreciate."

"I'll look forward to it," Sam said, but knew from a flicker in cool blue depths he had not quite carried it off. The original feeling of affinity had faded away.

He telephoned Sir Willis at the bank on Friday morning at ten. Sir Willis said, "Bear with me, Boylston, if I seem a bit—indirect. Our friend was expecting a radio message from your fellow countryman Saturday morning. It did not come. Saturday afternoon he went to his vacation spot from his home base by float plane, and was left off there, along with a young chap who is in the way of being a personal aide and secret'ry. On Sunday evening our friend used his marine radio there at his place to ask the float plane to come by Monday morning and take him off. He went back to his home base, leaving the secret'ry chap alone there, should anyone come visiting, I expect. By now he has returned also, but I do not know precisely when. As to the friends of our friend, I had a chat with the one I thought most likely last evening. It became rather an ugly conversation, but it was all confirmed. There were two of them, as I suspected, beside our friend. I can guarantee silence on the part of the one I talked with. Much better if our friend has no inkling that I know of the nasty bit of work he hoped to arrange. Is all this sufficient for you?"

"I'm grateful to you, Sir Willis."

"May I offer my hope that things will turn out far better than—

you have reason to expect at the moment. Do let me know if I can be of any help. Matters which you might find difficult I could probably arrange quite easily. We are quite a small community, actually. And it would have been a great pity had anyone of your countryman's special—talents acquired such substantial land interests here, particularly in such a manner. It would have been troublesome to oust him, as we most certainly would have, sooner or later."

Sam Boylston's room phone rang at ten o'clock Friday evening as he was pacing restlessly, uncertain as to what he should do next.

If it had been—as he was quite certain Sir Willis would term it—foul play, it had to depend on word of the money leaking out. The leak could have come from careless talk in Texas, in Nassau, in Freeport, possibly even in Miami. With a promise of a share of that much money, some very savage talent could be recruited along the lower coast of Florida. Small cruisers came over at will, and several men masquerading as sports fishermen could monitor the calls from the Muñeca and trace her and intercept her at the proper time and place.

But the timing of it seemed almost too close. The Muñeca had left Nassau Friday morning. Kayd had planned to meet Squires on Saturday. But he had not made his routine radio contact on Saturday morning.

Kayd's shrewdness had to be taken into account. He would make certain that information about the fortune aboard didn't leak out. He would certainly keep it from his family. And he would not take aboard any hired captain who had not been checked out very carefully.

What if the Muñeca had arrived at Musket Cay earlier, say by Friday evening? They were headed that way. The cruiser could make it comfortably. Just because Squires had arrived Saturday afternoon, it did not mean he had not arranged for a little reception party to arrive there, possibly by private boat, a day or more earlier. Or perhaps somebody in Squires's confidence had arranged it without Squires's knowledge. It seemed to fit the timing. Perhaps the logical course was to go to Freeport first, then back to Musket Cay.

His mind would travel in logical patterns and rhythms, but at intervals he could not anticipate, he would suddenly realize that every conjecture was based on the assumption all aboard had been slain and the bodies stowed aboard to sink with the boats into the great black depths of the Tongue of the Ocean. Logically it was an acceptable assumption. Emotionally he could not believe such a thing could have happened to Leila. She was too vibrant, too spirited, too totally alive to be wasted so mercilessly, so prematurely. In those moments remorse and grief and rage combined into an emotion as strong as a physical illness, darkening his vision, clogging his throat, giving him ripples of nausea which made cold sweat on his body and made his legs feel too weak to support him.

He was recovering from one of those moments when the phone rang and he heard Jonathan's excited and unsteady voice say, "Sam? Are you there, Sam? They're bringing Staniker in."

"In where? Who is?"

"Some people on a boat. They found him somewhere, on some island, and they've asked for an ambulance to meet them."

He reached the Prince George Wharf area in time. He found Jonathan in the crowd. A cruiser was angling in, spotlight trained on the dock area. A man was trotting, waving them along to a place inside the main wharves where the dock levels were suitable for small boats. The big cruise ships with their festival lights dwarfed the Chris-Craft. The ambulance was waiting. The cruiser edged in. Lines were heaved to the men on the dock. As the cruiser was moored, there was a silent lightning of flash bulbs and strobe lights, and the doctor and the ambulance attendants stepped aboard, carrying the stretcher.

Ten

BY FIRST LIGHT on Sunday, in the sea mist, on the incoming tide, Corpo was wading the flats east of his island, hunting scallops, humming tunelessly, speaking greetings to each one as he shoved it into the gunnysack fastened to his belt. He had guessed it would be time for them to be in, and knew he had to get out there before the tide deepened it too much.

And it pleased him to have the silence and privacy of the mist and the dead calm. They couldn't see him from the mainland shore, from all their candy-colored houses. No doll-wives shading their empty little eyes to stare out at old Corpo as if he was a bug who'd moved too close.

"Not a damned house back then," he said, as if speaking to someone a dozen feet away. "Who was here first? I ask you that, man to man. Who was here first? Sergeant Corpo, that's who."

Sooner or later they'd work themselves up and get up some kind of damned petition. Like before. Potentially dangerous. Squatting on public lands. Health hazard. Known to be violent. Get one of their bloody writs, send the sheriff boat around, make a lot of trouble for nothing. Hell, the nearest part of the island to the mainland shore was a good half mile, and with a private channel five feet deep between the island and the shore anyhow.

Would mean losing the beard again, and all the itching when it was growing back in. Sit there in court in a white shirt with all the candy people staring at him, wishing they could snap their fingers and he'd disappear. The Lieutenant would have to handle it again, like the other times. It was hard to follow what he said, and some of it didn't seem the way Corpo remembered it, but it was good to listen to.

"If it please the court, I would like permission to reconstruct the circumstances which brought Sergeant Walter Corpo to this area. He was a platoon leader in my company in 1944, an infantry combat veteran by then, a young man who had enlisted in December of 1941 after one year and a few months of college. I led a patrol of fifteen men into the small village of Selestat near the Rhine. We were ambushed. Sergeant Corpo took cover by a fountain in the square and gave us covering fire to enable us to withdraw, with little hope of being able to retreat in turn. He was not ordered to cover the retreat. It was his instinctive reaction. We got out with but three casualties and came back with the entire company. Sergeant Corpo was believed dead. It was obvious he had kept firing after being hit several times, gravely.

"A shard of metal, possibly a mortar fragment, had penetrated his skull. A corpsman detected a pulse and had him removed to an aid station, though believing he would soon die. From there he was taken back to a station hospital and then to a general hospital, both installations thinking his chance of survival remote. I believed he had died. I put him in for a posthumous decoration, and he was awarded the Silver Star. The war ended. I returned to law school. After graduation I entered the practice of law here in the city of Broward Beach. In 1948 the Veterans' Administration got in touch with me and asked me if I would go over to Bay Pines Veterans Hospital near St. Petersburg on a matter regarding Sergeant Walter Corpo. He had asked for me.

"I discussed the case with his doctors. He was in excellent physical health. The brain injury, however, had left him with certain disabilities. Complicated instruction confused him. His attention span was short. He would say exactly what he meant in every circumstance, a trait our culture does not find palatable. They did not consider him dangerous. But they had noticed an increasing unrest in him, an increasing irritability at being forced to live in such close quarters with so many other men. They doubted he could earn a living. But he was eligible to receive a total disability pension. He had no relatives close enough to take any interest in him. Could I be of any help?

"He knew me. He was glad to see me. He was absolutely certain I could get him out of that place. He had saved my life twice. I brought him back here with me. He lived in my home. I had an outboard boat and motor. He had a taste for being alone. He began to spend longer and longer periods on the water. After he was gone for three days I demanded an explanation. He took me to that small mangrove island in the bay, approximately ten acres in area, nameless at that time and now known as Sergeant's Island. He had, with what must have been incredible effort, hewed a curving channel back through the mangrove to a small hammock of palmetto and cabbage palm, and he had used the outboard motor to wash the channel deep enough to use. He had constructed a crude shelter out of driftwood, tarpaper, tin cans hammered flat, and some battered windows scavenged from the city dump. He said it was what he liked and what he wanted, and he wouldn't be in anyone's way.

"I will now present for the consideration of the court, two documents. The first is from the Trustees of the Internal Improvement Fund giving Sergeant Corpo permission to reside upon that state-owned land until such time as title passes into other hands. The second is also dated in November of 1949 and is signed by the Chairman of the County Commission, and grants Sergeant Corpo all the necessary zoning exceptions applicable.

"Once a month Sergeant Corpo comes to the mainland, picks up his disability check at my home, cashes it at my bank, buys provisions and returns to Sergeant's Island. Over the years he has considerably improved his cottage. Should he not appear for his check, I would go there at once to see what happened to him. He is in splendid physical condition. He wants merely to be left alone.

"There has been talk of violence. There was one such incident. Seven years ago a pack of teen-age boys came to the erroneous conclusion that Sergeant Corpo was a drunk, and that the cottage might well contain a large supply of whisky. There were five of them. They decided to raid the island. They thought Sergeant Corpo some sort of harmless nut. I could have told them that Sergeant Corpo grew up in the swamplands of Georgia, that when he was twelve and thirteen he would go into those swamps hunting and be gone a week without anyone worrying about his safety. I could have told them how silent and deadly the Sergeant was on night patrol duty.

"They raided him on a Saturday night. He heard them coming. He turned his lanterns out. He went outside, circled them, found their boat and cast it adrift. Then, in the night, he took them one at a time, lashed them to the mangroves with pieces of rope, spacing them far enough apart so they could communicate only by shouting to each other. Then he went back to his cottage and cleaned up all the mess and litter and breakage they had caused. He did a good job. Then he came over here to the city and asked the authorities to come pick up the boys. It was dawn when they gathered them up, cowed and terrified, their faces grotesquely puffed by insect bites, eyes swollen shut. They were of good family, had been in trouble prior to the raid, but to the best of my knowledge, have stayed out of trouble ever since.

"I submit that these petitioners who are making a new attempt to dislodge Sergeant Corpo are expressing not any feeling that he is a public nuisance, but rather a social judgment, and wish to penalize anyone who is unwilling or unable to conform to their particular standards of housing, habit, dress and deportment.

"Your honor, I am reminded of the prim lady who lodged a complaint against the owners of property adjacent to hers on the grounds that it was being put to immoral use as a nudist colony. The officers who investigated were confused by her statement of carryings-on right out in plain sight, having noticed the high wall, the large size of the adjoining grounds, and the remote location of the nudist establishment. When asked what she meant by plain sight, she said, 'Right from my roof with my husband's binoculars, you can't hardly miss it.'

"When the only room left in our society for men such as Sergeant Corpo is inside an institution, it will be time for us to re-examine our goals—and our humanity."

"Hoooheee, how the Lieutenant does go on," Corpo said. "And how you this fine morning, Mr. Scallop? Excuse me. Pop you into the sack with all your folks. Get your tribe thinned out some before the mist burns off, and the Sunday damn fools come roaring around here in circles, pulling other damn fools on skis, scaring the fish and stirring up the mud."

He turned and looked back at his island, a vague darkness in the mist, and turned back to his chore, only to find himself staring at a blue hull inches in front of his eyes. It had appeared so suddenly, with so little warning, his first impression was that he was being run down, and gave a hoarse yell and sloshed backward in the thigh-deep water, stumbling, catching his balance.

"Dumb fool!" he shouted. Then he saw how it was moving, almost stern first, slightly crabwise, a line trailing from the bow. With no wind, and with the tide moving as it was, it had to have come in through the inlet to be moving across this flat. It had drifted right across the waterway and into his bay. Fine boat. New looking. Florida number on the bow.

Corpo reached and caught the bow line and started gathering the loose end in, coiling it as he did so. There was enough weed entangled in the line to convince him the boat had been adrift a long time. He put the coiled line up on the bow. He sloshed around the boat. He could not see into it, it had so much freeboard, but he reached high, slung his sack of scallops over the gunnel, lowered it and let it drop the final few inches.

At the transom he spoke the name and port aloud. "Muñequita. Brownsville, Texas. And that's for sure one hell of a drift. No, you got a Florida number. And that's weed from the ocean out there. Got your little propellers tilted up clear of the water. End of all that bow line too unraveled to tell much how it parted. Say you must have been riding an anchor, swinging too much maybe. Get a tide change and slack and you put a loop over a fluke, then when it comes tight again, it could fray. You're pretty new, aren't you now? Not a mark on those propellers. Walk you home and tuck you under my front stoop and find out how bad some poor fool wants you back."

Suddenly Corpo noticed a little folding bronze step plate at the transom corner, just above the waterline. He folded it down on its hinge, got a foot on it, reached up and caught the grab handle and pulled himself erect on the step and stared into the teak cockpit.

"Motheragod!" he said, launched himself backwards, landed, stumbled and fell, came gasping to his feet in water deeper than he had expected. Wind riffled the water and the boat moved on. He hesitated a moment and then floundered after it, jumped and got the grab handle, knee on the folding step, worked his way up, sat on the broad transom, swung his legs into the boat.

As he took two strides toward her, he wiped his hand on his sodden pants, bent over and laid two fingers on the side of her throat just under the angle of the jaw. There was something there. A faint thing. A flutter. Not the bump-bump-bump you always felt when they weren't hit bad.

He looked with consternation at the brightness, knowing the mist was burning off. Looking straight up he could see the first blue glaze through mist.

He went around her to the controls, pulled the nylon cover off, wiped his hands on his thighs as he studied them. Both keys in place, brass-bright. Quarter turn right for on. These little toggles should drop the props into the water. Hiss and chunk. Okay so far. Throttles in neutral? Starter buttons. Try it, Corpo.

One caught very quickly. The other ground for several long seconds and caught. He revved them with several quick hard bursts on each one, then at slow speed slipped them into gear. The boat moved. Exhaust bubbled astern. Water whispered along the bow. He turned the boat, tried more throttle, startled himself with the way it jumped. He pulled it back down. Just as he eased it slowly into his channel he looked west and saw the candy houses beginning to show through the mist, looked east and saw a motor sailer moving south down the Waterway toward Fort Lauderdale.

He had trouble in his narrow channel. At the turns the stern would swing too far, brush the roots. The channel widened at the cabin, where for so long he had used the very lowest tides at the time to chop out the dead roots, grub out the muck, sand and dead shell and use it to build up the land around the cabin. With engines off, he glided slowly under the platform porch, nudging his skiff rudely aside as he scrambled forward, fended the boat off the house pilings, then made it fast at bow and stern.

He picked up the damp sack of scallops and went up the stairs, pushed the trapdoor open from below, climbed into his living quarters. He dumped the scallops into a shallow washtub, went out onto his front porch, dropped a bucket on a line, pulled up enough water to cover them. They began to move around in the washtub.

"Taste the best that time I fried you with the butter and onions, didn't you now?"

He wondered when would be the best time to eat them. They'd keep fine. Maybe late in the day.

"Got me a good mess of you scallop folks that time I found that girl in that boat, too."

Now when was that? Last year, or yesterday, or was it something going to happen, or by God, was it now!

He went to his think place, put his hands around the poles he had cut for supports, rested his forehead against the wall timber. He closed his hands as hard as he could, hard enough to make his shoulder muscles creak and pop. The poles were shiny where he had grabbed them a thousand times, the timber stained where he had rocked his head back and forth on it.

Everything would open up for you and turn loose, so you didn't know where you were. You had to pull it back and lace it down. You had to shut your eyes and think of a row of poles closing you in like a fence on each side of you, so that tomorrow was ahead, and yesterday was right behind you, and last month and last year were way back. Then you could get the shape of yesterday and the day before, and from that you could make it into now.

Yes, she was down there right now.

Clucking with exasperation at himself, he stripped his bed, flipped the mattress over, got the other sheets out of the box and made it up fresh.

He took a clean cotton blanket down to the boat, spread it on the deck beside the girl, and gently rolled her over onto it, trying not to look directly at her. He wrapped it around her, slid his hands under the blanket and stood up with her, astonished at how light she was. It was easier to carry her out and around and up the front way. He put her on the narrow bed and went back and closed his screened door, noticing the last of the mist was burned away.

He opened the petcock and ran some rainwater from his roof cistern into a basin, washed his hands with the sliver of yellow soap, dried them on sacking. He ran rainwater into the pot, pumped the little gasoline stove, lit the burner, put the pot on. Then he went over and sat on his heels and looked at her. Pretty enough little face, but the bones behind it looked sharp enough to come right through the skin. Skin worn off her cheek, mound of her forehead, edge of her jaw. He puzzled it out and decided it could have been rubbed against the teak deck just that way if the boat moved around much. Scrawny little arm about as big around as a turkey leg. He felt her forehead and clucked again, and said, "Just like a fire inside there, missy. You've got a fire that's burning the meat right off your little bones."

When he turned her head gently, he found the worst place. Where the fair hair was matted and tangled dark, above her ear. He fingered the hair pad away, separating it, and found the wound, perhaps two inches long, gaping almost an inch wide in the middle. It had been rain-washed, and had a skin of healing over it, but the lips of the wound were swollen and granular. He sucked his mouth in and held his breath and prodded at it with a gentle finger, but he could feel no give or shift of the bone under the wound, no fatal sponginess.

"Missy, you got a good hard little skull, or somebody didn't get a good solid swing at you with that rifle butt. What that needs is some sewing, and maybe I can and maybe I can't. All depends."

When the pot of water began to sing, he dropped the handful of tea leaves in it and took it off the fire and swirled it. He filled a tin cup, tasted it, blew on it to cool it, put two spoons of sugar in it, stirred and tasted it again, and took it over to her. He supported her with one arm behind her, thumb and finger at the nape of her neck. He poured hot tea into her slack mouth and it ran out and down her chin and onto his blanket. He tried twice more with the same result.

He shook her, and yelled, "Swaller it, God damn ya! Stop messing up the bed!"

When he tried again, her throat worked and it went down. A sip at a time, he got it all down her and lowered her gently and said, "Missy, when I yell you got to understand it comes out before I think a thing about it. Now I got to see how that back looks. Kindly excuse me."

He shifted her over onto her face and peeled the blanket away, tugging carefully where it had adhered to the drying fluids that leaked from the burned flesh. He swallowed hard at the faint sick-sweet smell of infection, and said, "Now you lie still there. It's not so bad at all, missy. There was a boy in my outfit, when we got pulled back there in North Africa to get some rest, can't recall his name, blond boy, he got dog drunk, passed out on the beach, didn't wake up 'til afternoon, and he looked worsen you."

He examined her carefully. It was easy to see what had happened. She'd had a pretty good tan, but not across the buttocks where skimpy pants had covered her, and not across the band across her skinny back. There the burn had bitten deep, had blistered, cracked, suppurated, and was now a strange dark rough red, marked with random areas of yellow and yellow-green.

He pondered the problem. He went and got the little jar of the sulfa ointment he used when he got an infection from a barnacle scratch, or a catfish spine, or a bug bite. Damn little of it. Piece it out some. So he opened one of the small tins of butter, put about two parts of butter to one part of the salve in a bowl and mixed it thoroughly. Next he got his half bottle of snakebite whisky from under the bed, took a sheet of paper from his scratch pad and crumpled it, rolled it between his palms. He sat on the edge of the bed, soaked the paper ball with whisky and, after hesitant moments, began to scrub the bad-looking areas, breaking the crusts, rubbing down to a healthier rawness.

He thought she made some small sound, but could not be certain. "Got a poor sad little can on you, missy, all crumpled in and the bones showing, and these here little knobs down your back, like in that labor camp we took over that time. And your belly is puffed the way it is on the starving folks. Now that's the worst of it for a little time, and I can butter you down now."

He smeared her back glistening with the mixture he had concocted and then began rubbing it in. He hummed to her and he closed his eyes and he began to rock slowly back and forth, thinking that even starved down, hurt and burned, she was a soft, sweet and tender little thing. Suddenly he realized he had begun to breathe quick and high and shallow, and he jumped up and covered her over and paced back and forth, cursing the evil for wanting to come out at such a time. He wiped his hands on the toweling, settled himself down, and tried to think of some kind of covering for the burns.

Remembering he had some fine netting somewhere, he looked until he found it, cut squares of suitable size, boiled them, wrung them out, and pressed them onto the contours of the burned areas, turned her very gently onto her back and covered her over with the edge of the blanket.

The head wound took more time and trouble. He had to light the bright gasoline lantern and bring it close. He had to soak the matted hair, lather it, shave it with great care. He put a needle and some braided nylon line in the saucepan to boil clean. But what to put on the wound. Not a thing left.

Suddenly he jumped up, swatted himself in the forehead and said, "There's a damn fool in this world every place you look, missy." He hurried down and got aboard the fine boat and located the first-aid kit in one of the stowage areas in less than a minute. It was a good one, a big new one, the seal unbroken.

He put a strong antiseptic on the head wound. He sewed it neatly and solidly, pulling the edges together where they belonged. He put a gauze bandage on it and taped it in place. He had a wealth of medicines and instructions. The instructions were hard. He could get them into his mind, but then if he read further, the first part would slide right out of his mind. He found another burn remedy, and plenty of gauze and tape for her back. And some pills for fever, for infection, for a lot of other things which sounded as if she might have them. He settled for four different kinds, and decided two of each would be about right. Getting them into her was another problem. He found he could put her flat on her back, pull her jaw open, holding her tongue down with his thumb. Then put a couple of pills as far back as he could get them at the base of her tongue, poking them back in place with a finger. Then if he closed her jaws and poured tea into the corner of her mouth, making a little pocket for it, she would swallow.

He looked out and was astonished at how much of the day was gone. He read about exposure and sunstroke and dehydration and head wounds and shock, and the treatment for some of the things

seemed to be just opposite to the treatment for others. He read the
words aloud, puzzling over them. There was one certain thing.
Nourishment and plenty of fluid.

He boiled the scallops, mashed them to paste, made a thick gruel
out of them, gradually got all of it down her. And more tea. And
boiled rainwater. And brandy he found on her boat. When there was
a sharp ammoniac odor and a spreading stain on the blanket he had
a feeling of pleasure. Get her full up enough so it starts running out
the other end, you're making some progress.

When night came he fixed the screens and made himself his first
meal of the day. He lighted his other lantern. In the kerosene flicker
she looked pretty, the way he had brushed her hair back and over to
hide the shaved place. Her lips weren't as swollen and cracked.

Heartily he said, "Got to make sure, little missy, there isn't some
hurt place I overlooked. You understand that, don't you?"

He took the blanket off her and looked at her in the lamplight.
Pretty little breasts, hardly bigger than teacups. Not as big, even.
Little orangey buds on them. Poor little belly still swole. All resting
sweet now on the clean bedding. Hands half curled into fists. Tufty
little tan-color bush of hair down there, childish sweet and trusting.
Safe as can be with old Corpo.

And he saw his big hand move slowly out to finger the little
breast. He had nothing to do with it. It just moved by itself. He gave
a huge coughing groan and jumped up, covered her, went over to his
think place, grasped the supports, chunked his head solidly, three
times, against the timber, grunting at each impact.

"What you trying to do?" he asked. "Who you think you are?"

He opened his eyes and turned and looked across at her, and at
that instant the strangeness happened to him again. It happened
sometimes when he was upset. It was like taking a half step backward into some bright busy area and looking from there into his life,
seeing it as a dim and funny old movie. At such times he looked with

disbelief at the boxes where he kept things, the dingy empty clothes hanging from nails, the straw chair he'd found afloat after the storm, the structural braces he had meant to fix in some better way. And the strew of pans and cans, floats and nets, and the things he found on the beaches after storms—a hatch cover, most of an awning, a white plastic dog, an empty keg, the row of colored glass bottles on the board over the wooden sink he had built—bottles frosted by the slow abrasion of the surf.

In this strangeness he always wanted to ask: What are they making me do? Why are they making me be like this? In the bright busy area things moved too swiftly for him to see them, but there were faces and places, books and buildings, words spoken too quickly to be understood. As always before it faded away, leaving him back in his own place, the memory of how it felt fading as quickly as the sensation, but knowing he would recognize it at once when it happened again, the way you recognize a dream you've had before.

He went over to the wall where he put the girls. Each month after he cashed his check, he would buy that magazine. And when it was a girl he thought would be nice to be with, a lively girl with a lot of fun in her, then he would cut out the folded page, print her name in the corner so he would not forget it, tack her onto the wall and introduce her to the others. Doreen, Ceil, Jackie, Puss, Bernadette, Connie, Judy Jean, Charleen. And they all smiled right at him, every one. The earlier ones were mottled by the dampness, the colors bleaching out of them.

Slowly and methodically he tore them free, making a neat packet, leaving a few corners tacked to the plywood. He held the stack in position to rip it in two, but could not because it suddenly seemed like tearing through all the tenderness of flesh. He folded the pictures, pondered in what box they might belong, put them in the box with his go-to-the-bank clothes.

Squatting there, he looked at the girl and said, "Too much light on your face, missy. Must have wore you out with all the aid station work. What the corpsmen used to say, don't go moving them around too much. Do what you got to do right where they fall. You'll know soon if they can stand moving, or'll turn dead."

He moved the lantern away from her, and in doing so momentarily put more light on her face, and was made uneasy by the immobility of it, a look of the skull. He set the lantern down, put his fingertips under the shelf of the jaw, felt nothing.

"So you *died* on me!" he yelled. "All I done for you! Hard as I worked, you damn little bitch! Just what the hell is the Lieutenant going to say? Missy, why'd you do such a fool thing?"

Her mouth seemed to move. He stopped, bent, peered, laid his two long fingers against her throat again.

"Now why should Corpo be cussing you out? There's that little heart going along nice. Tump, tump, tump. Just put his fool fingers wrong and missed it, because it isn't real hard and strong, but anyway it don't have that bird-wing feeling any more, that fluttery stuff. Missy, you sleep deep and sweet, and Corpo's going to be close by."

He blew out the lanterns, waited for his night vision, then went out, crossed the little clearing, climbed the ladder to the driftwood platform he had built in the highest branches of the only live oak on the island, a water oak impervious to the salt water into which it thrust its roots.

Corpo sat crosslegged, looking out over the interwoven crown of the dense mangroves. From there, off to his right, he could see the blinkings of the range lights along the Waterway, see the light on the sea buoy out there beyond the Inlet channel, see the clutter of neon of the resort lights over on the beach side. To his left were the lights of the houses that ringed the bay, and back over his left shoulder were the city lights of Broward Beach. The night breeze was freshening out of the northeast. One of the nocturnal waterbirds flapped across the island, and made a sound like hoarse drunken laughter. He heard a rat-rustle in the cabbage palms, then a great surge and slap of a large fish just outside his channel, and the rushing sound of the smaller fish it had startled into flight. When the breeze would die, the marsh mosquitoes would cloud whining around him. He opened the wooden box he had nailed to the platform, took out the small bottle of oily repellent, greased his arms, neck and ears, annoyed at the odor of it which masked the night smells. Shortly after moving to the island he had stopped smoking, and the smells had come back until they were as strong as when he was a kid, able to find where the swamp cats slept, where owls had fed, where the swamp rattlers were nesting. This wind was a good one for the night smells. From other directions too often it had the smell of the meat they burned behind their candy houses, or the swollen stink of the city buses, or a smell from the dump fires beyond the city, a smell that to him seemed to have a color—a thin sulfurous green-yellow. Burned meat smelled purple. Bus stink was red-brown.

When he went down the ladder, yawningly ready for bed, as he crossed the clearing, he was startled to see the big pale shape of a strange boat under the porch platform, and after a puzzled moment, it all came tumbling back into his head. He hurried up the steps and into the cabin, knelt on the floor beside the bed in darkness, leaned his ear near her lips, felt and heard the weak but steady exhalations. Her breath was sour, and, through the sharper odors of the medication, he could scent the smell of sickness, a smell like fresh bread. He put the backs of his fingers against her forehead. The heat still came from it, and maybe it was a little less, but he could not be certain.

Suddenly he realized he could sleep on missy's boat, in one of the two forward bunks. All day, and he hadn't given that boat a real good look. It could have some good things on it, in a lot better shape than if it had gone down and they'd come washing onto the beach.

Once he was aboard he remembered seeing the flashlight in the same stowage locker where he had found the first-aid kit. He found it by touch, a good chunky one with a big lens, a red flasher, and one of those square six-volt batteries.

He found a lot of good things. Masks, fins, snorkels, spear guns, spinning rods, tackle box, nylon dock lines, fenders, charts, boat hook, bedding, several bottles of liquor, towels, bathing suits, hats, boat shoes, fire extinguisher, cans of engine oil. And, carefully wrapped against dampness, two guns. A twenty-two caliber target pistol and, broken down, a four ten gauge, single-barrel, automatic shotgun. Fool guns, he thought. Play toys. No punch at all to knock them down if they're coming on you fast. He admired how neatly everything was stowed, and how the stowage compartments were fitted in.

Come daylight, he would figure out the electrical system and how much fuel she had, and how the little toilet worked. He opened the foredeck hatch for ventilation and figured out how the screens worked. He decided he would not use the bedding, just sleep on top of the plastic bunk cover. Crouched double under the low overhead, he stripped down to his ragged underwear shorts, turned the flashlight off and stretched out.

Immediately he began worrying about her. He went up and looked at her, came down and went back up again. Finally he tied a piece of cord around her ankle, ran it over to the trap door, let it hang through, and to the dangling end tied two empty tin cans, then dropped some small sinkers into them. When he tweaked the cord they made a splendid clatter. If she worsened, she might thrash around some, and if she woke up, it would give him warning so he could get to her before she got too scared waking up in a strange place.

The Lieutenant would be proud to know how well his sergeant was handling things. Saving everybody trouble. Why, if he ran that sick little girl over to town, they'd start yelling at him and get him all mixed up. And then all the candy fools in their candy houses would be signing up papers again, making trouble for the Lieutenant. And the Lieutenant had said not to get mixed up in anything at all, because give them half a reason they'd move him off the island for good. The Lieutenant would understand he couldn't have just looked into that fine boat and seen her and then shoved the boat away to float on off into the mist. It was a poor damned excuse for a soldier didn't look out for the wounded.

But, he thought, it might be the best thing of all to keep the Lieutenant out of it until it was all over, one way or another. If the little thing died, in spite of all the nursing care, he'd make up a nice box and bury her nice and say the words, and keep some fresh flowers over her for a time.

If she come out of it, she would be poorly for a time until the strength came back to where she could go driving off in that boat, smiling, waving back, calling out Thank you, Sergeant, Goodby, Sergeant, Thanks for everything, until her girl-voice faded into the distance.

Clothes! Now either way there'd have to be clothes. Not a thing on this boat except the naked little swim clothes. She'd have to have something to wear as she was getting well. And she'd want the other girl things too, comb and lipstick and such, and a purse to carry them in.

Until he could get it worked out, maybe one of his two good white shirts would come long enough on her so it could be sewed into something to cover her decent. Some pretty white nylon line off this boat for a belt. For a little bit of pretty, she could have that pin he'd found on the beach, with the red stone.

Later he could work out some way to get her the necessaries. Get some woman to buy things he could bring back. One of the girls in the bank where he cashed the government check every month? No, she might tell the Lieutenant. Then one of the women that hung around Shanigan's Waterfront? Every once in a while, maybe not as often as every two months, those women would start coming into his mind no matter how hard he tried to keep them out, and then one night he would open the box and take out a twenty and a five and go over in the skiff and tie up at Shanigan's and sit at the bar, and by the time the five was mostly drunk up, there'd be one of them handy to take him on back past the lady's and men's, into the store-room, onto that busted old couch jammed up into the corner, making sure she had the twenty before she'd take off her skirt and pants, all beefy white meat there in the same light that always came in the little high dusty window, blinking red and white, red and white, over and over, fast as a heart beat, from Shanigan's sign that hung over the docks. The light always the same, and the itchy need for it always the same, and no matter how different they looked out by the bar, in the little room it was always like exactly the same one, thick white belly and thighs, the dark smudge, big handfuls of the softness, and no poor damned way in the world to slow it or stop it or change it until too sudden it was over.

No, not one of them night women. Not one of them who took the money and made fun. Dumb Corpo. Herman the Hermit. Where's your medals, Sarg? Going back in the skiff he'd have to fight to stay awake, and the whisky would have turned sour on his stomach, and all the next day he'd tell himself he'd never go back there, not ever again, no sir. There wasn't a one of them fit to pick out clothes for the Missy, even touch them.

Just at the edge of sleep he was brought back by a frightful and familiar sound, and he knew one of the big owls had drifted silently into his clearing, carrying in its talons one of the small white terns from the sand spit at the inlet. The victim shrieked and squalled its panic, seeming to beg for mercy, and audible under the terror cries were the owl sounds, a deep hoo-ha-hoo-ho-ha, a rich continuing throaty chuckle of satisfaction. The tern sounds weakened to a whimper, ended with a final whistly squeal. In the silence the owl chortled a time longer before settling to the feast.

Better explain to Missy about that before it happens some night when she's on the mend.

Eleven

THE WIRE-SERVICE stringers in Nassau, as a result of interviewing the Barths and the Hilgers, the two couples aboard that Jacksonville Chris-Craft which had taken Captain Garry Staniker off South Joulter Cay and rushed him to Nassau, were able to phone in reasonably complete accounts of the disaster in time to hit the Saturday morning newspapers.

CAPTAIN SOLE SURVIVOR IN YACHT EXPLOSION was the page-one head on the Miami *Record*. Raoul Kelly, eating a late lunch-counter breakfast noted that the paper had rerun a photograph an alert reporter had unearthed earlier in the week, taken at a Miami marina by a boat buff who had been far more interested in the lines of the custom cruiser than in the people aboard. It had been taken moments after the lines had been taken aboard. Staniker, at the wheel on the flying bridge, was half turned, backing the Muñeca out of the slip. Mr. Bixby Kayd, looking enormous in swim trunks and a terry beach coat, and wearing big dark glasses and a baseball

cap, stood on the cockpit deck, leaning over the rail, fending off a
piling with a big hand. Roger stood near the bow rail, making up a
line. Carolyn Kayd—and few news reports failed to mention she
had been first runner-up in the Miss Texas contest four years ago—
lay supine on a beach towel spread on the trunk cabin roof, one knee
hiked up, the briefness of her bikini and the camera angle giving
more than ample reason for the approval registered by the contest
judges. The little dark daughter, Stella, was up on the flying bridge
standing by Staniker, looking back as he was. Just visible toward the
stern, beyond Stella's father, was the boat guest, Leila Boylston, a
very trim and pretty young lady, making up one of the stern lines.
Only Mary Jane Staniker was missing, and could be presumed to be
below engaged in housekeeping duties. On an inside page Raoul
found a simplified map of the central portion of the Bahamas, showing New Providence, the Berry Islands, and the Joulter Cays at the
north end of Andros. The artist had marked a spot to the right of
the Joulter Cays with a tiny symbol of a boat with little streaks
erupting from it to indicate explosion.

Raoul read the whole account carefully, ordered more coffee and
read it through again. Staniker's condition was fair. He had some bad
burns. He was in Princess Margaret Hospital, and had been unable as
yet to confirm what he had told the Jacksonville couples after being
rescued.

One small detail bothered him. It said that prior to their being
employed a month ago by Bixby Kayd, Staniker and his wife had
operated Parker's Marina south of Tahiti Beach on Biscayne Bay. He
had learned from Francisca that Captain Staniker, Crissy Harkinson's frequent visitor, had been working somewhere not too far
from Crissy's home, but he had not known what it was. He had
passed Parker's Marina enough times to remember it as a dreary little
beer-bait-boats place.

With the newspaperman's instinct for just how much coincidence was acceptable, he felt something a little curious about the interrelationships involved. Ferris Fontaine, Crissy Harkinson, Kayd, Staniker. Staniker had been sneaking away from the drab little marina to continue his red-hot affair with the lady who had sold the Odalisque out from under him. Kayd visits Crissy in March. Why would Kayd hire somebody who apparently couldn't locate another job as hired captain? Why couldn't Staniker find another job? The cruiser the Senator gave Crissy had been sold in early January.

He shrugged and pushed it out of his mind. Obviously, if there was something fishy about the whole thing, any attempt to unravel it would involve 'Cisca because she was the only one who could swear to Kayd's visit to the Harkinson woman. And what would that kind of fuss do to 'Cisca's precarious adjustment? What would it do to her to be taken to a place full of men in uniform and asked questions?

It is, after all, gringo trouble, and none of our business, he thought. The attitude filled him with a mocking amusement. The refugee attitude. Or, more accurately, the peon syndrome. Let the rich slay each other at will. Each one is one less.

When the phone call came, a little after noon that Saturday, Crissy was on her back on a sun pad beside the sailboat tethered in the boat basin below her house. She had folded and tucked her bikini to the smallest possible dimensions, and she held her face upturned, the sun glowing oven-red through her eyelids, her face and body oiled, trickles of sweat diluting the oil. Francisca came pattering down the stone steps to say a newspaper was on the telephone.

It was a call she had expected, and to give herself time to go over probable questions and answers, she told Francisca to tell the man to phone back in twenty minutes. When he called again she had showered and just gotten into a robe. She took it on the bedroom extension, stretching diagonally across the large low bed, prone, propped on her elbows.

"Weldon, on the *Record*, Miz Harkinson. This Captain Garry Staniker, have I got it right that he worked for you?"

"Yes, that's right, Mr. Weldon."

"And the name of your boat was the Odalisque. Right? What was the size of it?"

"Not very large. It was a thirty-four foot Hatteras. Why are you asking me this, please?"

"Well, I guess you know he's been found and . . ."

"Yes. It must have been a terrible thing."

"The reason for the questions, there's going to be some kind of investigation, find out if it was his fault. What we're doing is trying to get the jump on it, trace him back a ways, see if people he worked for thought he was a good captain. How long did he work for you?"

"I guess you could say two and a half years, approximately. Nearer three. A little less than a year ago I put the boat on the market. I wasn't using it very much, and the expense of the insurance and maintenance and dockage and fuel and the captain's salary was just too much. When I put it on the market last April I paid him through May. I gave him excellent recommendations, but I guess jobs like that aren't easy to find. Anyway, I kept reducing my asking price until the boat was sold last January. I got about half what I expected."

"How did you happen to hire Staniker?"

"Actually a friend found him for me. The Captain had been operating a boat for a company my friend had an interest in, and they had decided to sell the boat."

"Do you mind telling me who this friend was?"

"If I don't tell you, I suppose you could find out easily enough. It was State Senator Ferris Fontaine. I'm afraid if you print this people might misinterpret it. I had an arrangement with the Senator whereby he had the use of the Odalisque and her captain whenever he wanted, letting me know in advance, of course. And he contributed to the upkeep. That's why, a few months after the Senator passed away, I decided the Odalisque was costing too much for the number of times I was using it."

"Were you satisfied with the job Staniker did?"

"Oh yes. He kept her in very good condition, ready to go on a moment's notice."

"Did he ever get into trouble with the boat?"

"What do you mean?"

"Well, damage it in any way while running it."

"There was just one little insurance claim. He went aground with the Senator and a party aboard up near Stuart, coming out of the St. Lucie Canal and heading out through the pass into the Atlantic. But I understand that is very tricky water up there, and the sand bars keep shifting. He ran aground at slow speed right in the Channel and bent a shaft and a wheel."

"Did he drink while running your boat?"

"Sometimes when we went deep sea fishing and it was very hot, he'd drink some cans of cold beer. Nothing more than that as far as I know."

"How about safety precautions?"

"The Odalisque was powered by gasoline engines, and he was always very careful about gassing up, always opening the hatches and turning on the blowers and being very firm with anybody who forgot and took out a cigarette. And he had a bilge sniffer installed when I first got the boat, with a warning buzzer. We passed the Coast Guard inspections without any trouble."

"Then you were perfectly willing to give him a good recommendation when he was looking for another position?"

"Yes indeed. I gave him a letter, to whom it may concern, when he went on half pay, saying he had worked for me for such and such a period of time, and I was selling my boat, and I would be happy to answer any questions any prospective employer cared to ask about him."

"Did many ask?"

"I think there were six or seven. I praised Captain Staniker to the skies, but I guess the jobs just never materialized. When I had to put him on half pay, Mrs. Staniker found a job at a little marina to make ends meet."

"Did you keep track of how he was making out after your cruiser was sold, Mrs. Harkinson?"

After a careful moment of hesitation, she said, "I would say that I was kept better informed than I cared to be, Mr. Weldon. When he couldn't find anything and began to lose his confidence, he seemed to begin to feel that I had some sort of responsibility to find him something better than working in that little boat-rental place. So he would stop by and tell me his problems. I felt too sorry for him to tell him to stop bothering me."

"Did Mr. Kayd check with you before hiring him?"

"No, he didn't. But I believe that Mr. Kayd was a friend of the Senator, and I think they had some mutual business interests. I didn't know Mr. Kayd personally, but there is certainly a good chance he could have gone cruising on the Odalisque with one of the groups Senator Fontaine would take out, and he certainly could have talked to Garry Staniker and liked him, and found out that Garry ran a charter ketch all over the Bahamas for five years. And he would realize that Senator Fontaine would not—well, I guess you know the facts of political life, Mr. Weldon."

"I see what you mean, sure. A boat is a good place to have a quiet little conference. Fontaine would have known Staniker was loyal and discreet when he recommended you take him on, and known he was competent. That should have been good enough for Kayd. Did Staniker tell you he'd landed a job?"

"He called up to tell me. He was very pleased and excited. He said it was a marvelous cruiser and fine people. But in the next breath he was complaining about it being a temporary job, perhaps six weeks, a little more or a little less. He said his wife was worried about giving up their job of operating the marina to take a temporary job, and he said that even though it was very good pay, maybe she was right. I told him that he should do the most marvelous job he could, and there was the chance Mr. Kayd might keep them on permanently, and without any children to tie them down, there was no reason they couldn't take the Muñeca back to Texas. And even if Mr. Kayd didn't want a permanent couple aboard, certainly he might recommend them to some of his Texas friends with yachts. It seemed to cheer him up. Frankly, it was a relief to me to know he'd found something, and he wouldn't be heckling me for a while."

"You read the story of what Staniker told those people, about the way it happened. You seem to know boats pretty well."

"Not really. I only had that one cruiser, and I don't think I'd want another one. They're too much expense and responsibility. I've been learning to sail lately, and loving it."

"When you read that account, Mrs. Harkinson, did you feel Staniker had maybe pulled a bad goof?"

"Not at all. It's sort of natural to turn things on when you're running. Blowers and bilge pumps and so on. And with that boat being diesel powered, and with a switch up on the fly bridge to turn on the generator and bring the other bank of batteries up, I'd think it would be a normal thing for anyone to just switch the generator on. A good captain tries to make everything as comfortable as he can for the owner and the passengers, so he would be thinking of the noise the generator would make if he had to run it at an anchorage after he'd set the hooks. Cruisers are very complex things, and there's an old saying that no single thing ever goes wrong. It's always three things going wrong at the same time. Things go wrong that you can't anticipate. Like when the Sea Room blew up last year."

"Something about bottled propane?"

"They finally figured out what had happened. That woman had found a piece of brain coral on the beach, worn almost round, and she put it in a saucer on top of a cupboard in the galley. When they came in through the pass the boat rolled and the hunk of coral fell and hit the copper tubing to the galley stove just right, and the gas leaked out and being heavier than air, filtered right down into the bilge, and when there was enough of it to ignite, that poor woman happened to be sitting on the cockpit hatch cover, and it broke her back and threw her into the sea."

"I gather you think they'll clear Staniker."

"I think any other action would be terribly unfair."

"There's one thing for sure. Nobody is going to get a look at what's left of the Muñeca. She's a couple of thousand feet down. I'm grateful to you for giving me so much of your time, and being so frank and helpful, Mrs. Harkinson. It'll give us a good chance to do a report in depth when we cover the investigation, and I'll make sure there isn't any wording in it that might embarrass you in any way."

"I'll be very grateful, Mr. Weldon. It certainly is getting an awful lot of publicity, isn't it?"

"These things depend on the ingredients. Texas millionaire, young beauty-contest wife, crippled daughter, pretty young guest, luxurious cruise in the tropic isles, and pow! And the captain is the only one left. How long the media keeps leaning on it will depend on how soon something else comes along with juicy ingredients. Thanks again, and if I come up with a question I forgot to ask, can I get back to you?"

"Of course. It's been nice talking to you."

She reached and replaced the pink Princess phone on the cradle in the recess built into the headboard. It had gone well. And now if Garry was only playing his role just as it had been planned.

She remembered drilling one thing into him. "You are going to be stunned, sweetheart. Shocked and stunned. You'll have lost a boatload of people, including your own dear Mary Jane. So slow yourself down. You won't be tracking well. You won't seem to hear some of the questions. Give yourself lots of time to answer. If you let anybody trick you, it could be my neck too."

"You're so right, baby."

"And when the time and place is right, do it, and don't let yourself stop or think until that part of it is all over, and then for what happens next, *keep thinking every minute!*"

"Stop worrying!"

"Go over it for me now, every little thing."

"Again? For God's sake, Crissy!"

"Again, yes. And again and again and again. Lover, this means clover forever. This is big casino. Every chance you've had, somebody or something has messed you up. A man like you! Who should have had the whole ball of wax. You're *due*, Garry!"

It was strange how gradually it had dawned upon her that Staniker could be turned into a weapon, and used. When Fer had told her he had hired a captain to go with the gift cruiser, and they had gone to give her her first look at it and take the first short shakedown cruise, she had been startled and slightly amused at the Senator's selection of a captain. Garry Staniker was a familiar type, one of those big, easy-moving, outdoor studs, in fact almost a caricature of the breed. Big brown craggy face, an acre of shoulders, bulging wads and pads of muscle, boyish lock of brown hair to fall across the seamed forehead, dimming tattoos on the powerful arms, a slim waist and even his work clothing tailored to display the power of his build. The crinkles around blue eyes had been shaped by weather and amusement. He had that lazy, half-mocking assurance of the man whose animal magnetism has given him his choice of women wherever he had roamed. And he looked at her with interest and approval, which did not displease her. It did not seem plausible that he could be so theatrically decorative and still be able to run the boat. He looked as if Central Casting had dug him up to play a bit part, a smuggler in the China Sea, a gun runner in the Indian Ocean.

But he could take the Odalisque in and out of tricky dock spaces in wind and tide with the casual competence of a taxi driver stealing a parking place. He maintained the cruiser beautifully, doing all chores not only with a tidy efficiency, but with a manner which seemed to say that he was indeed from Central Casting, but had learned the procedures aboard his own series of luxury vessels.

Ferris Fontaine obviously liked him and trusted his ability and judgment and discretion. On longer cruises Mary Jane would come along to take care of cooking, buying provisions, bunk-making, laundry. She was a plump, subdued, busy and docile little woman of about forty. Her only flaw as an employee was a somewhat uncomfortable anxiety to please. She obviously adored Staniker. He had an amiable manner toward her most of the time, the gentle, condescending attitude one might have toward a house dog one is used to and fond of. When displeased with her, he would put an edge in his voice which would make her jump as if stung by a lash. Crissy, by getting Mary Jane to talk a few times, learned that when they were married Garry had just gotten out of the Navy, and she was working as a waitress in San Diego. It had been mostly her savings they had used for the payment on the Bahamian ketch. After two stillborn babies and a series of miscarriages, her tubes had been tied for reasons of health. She said she often felt homesick for the Bahamas. It had been hard work. But so lovely. From little nuances when Crissy was able to get her to talk about her husband, she could guess at the emotional adjustment Mary Jane had achieved. Her rationalization was that women threw themselves at her husband, and men were often weak and did not have very good sense about women.

On cruises, sunning herself, Crissy often felt Staniker's eyes upon her. She wondered what sort of approach he would make. She intended to fend it off with vivid directness. Finally she tested him by having him take her, alone, down the Waterway, inside the Florida Keys and anchor overnight in the seclusion of protected Tarpon Bay. Not only did he make no move, but the situation seemed to unnerve him. She made him join her for a nightcap out on the stern deck while the Odalisque swung at anchor in the moonlight, and got him talking enough to confirm her growing suspicion that he was not going to take any chance which might lose him the job. It paid five hundred a month. His small triumphs seemed to be all in the past. He had some vague conviction things would get better, but he was frightened by any idea they might get worse. Studying him the next day she saw more clearly how his forty plus years were eroding his image of himself. Pucker of flesh under the chin. Slight discoloration of the whites of the eyes, a little softness bulging over the tight-drawn belt. When she was alone on the boat she poked around in the crew quarters forward and found his little bottle of hair dye, and the gummy little applicator brush. The evidences were plaintive. As with athletes and beach boys and beefcake movie stars, the years were nibbling away the morale by corrupting the image, and he had to convince himself that nothing had really changed, that nothing really would, ever.

After Fer's sudden and badly timed death, and after she had failed in her clumsy effort at blackmailing Fer's cronies, she knew she ought to sell the Odalisque as quickly as possible. The money had stopped. She had a few thousand in a checking account, and half that much in her safe in the back of the closet wall. But the money had stopped.

Yet when Staniker, obviously troubled about his own future,

sought her out and said that he guessed she would be getting rid of the cruiser, she found herself staring at him in an imitation of astonishment, and heard herself saying, "Why should I sell my lovely boat, Captain?"

It gave her a sour amusement to let him believe Fer had left her enough money to live in the same style as when he was alive. She had him take her cruising alone, knowing she was wasting money because of this foolish game of impressing her own hired captain, yet reluctant to end it. For a time she sought to solve the problem by making the job so unpleasant for him he would quit. She gave him the most menial chores and complained constantly about everything he did. But he refused to let it upset him and did all she asked with that amiable tolerance of someone humoring a child or a sick person. She learned, by talking to other boat people, why Staniker endured the abuse. He had captained the Odalisque for two years and more. And it was on his record that he had lost his own vessel in the Bahamas. Without a solid and impressive reference from the owner of the Odalisque he could not hope to find another position as good.

She stopped persecuting him. Weeks passed and she felt caught in a strange lethargy. She would not look directly at her future, at the step she would eventually have to take. While she still had the money to finance the venture, she would have to go hunting, posing perhaps as the stunned and tragic widow, going alone to some likely resort area where she could find a man of years and means and loneliness, a man who would believe every detail of the history she would invent, and who would marry her.

At her age she knew marriage was far safer than any other arrangement. She had no doubt of her ability to find such a man and, having found him, capture him completely regardless of all protestations by relatives and advisors. But she would be trapped then, for good. The contract would have to be honored, because her past could not stand the close scrutiny it would receive if any divorce action was brought. And the old man, she suspected, would live forever. She had not felt trapped in her arrangement with Fer. But he had not been with her day and night. She knew she needed the sense of freedom, whether she used it or not. Her mirror told her that she was attractive, vital and exciting. Yet she knew in her heart that when her looks began to go, they would go very quickly no matter how desperate her efforts to save them. She could not settle for less than marriage, and, in marriage, for less than what Fer had planned to give her.

In her mood of listlessness, in April, three months after Fer had died, she had Staniker take the Odalisque on down to the keys. In a bemused, half-hearted way she seduced Staniker, overcoming a suspicious reluctance on his part that it might be a trap, an excuse for firing him. She had not been with a man for months, nor with a man like Staniker for years. Yet he was just as she had expected him to be, a powerful, sensuous and domineering animal, very knowing and skillful, lasting, heavily built, quickly resurgent. She matched his pace and needs, and they remained at anchor in the secluded bay for a week, using each other up, dwindling at last into that softened drowsy lethargy of the slack and emptied faces, the smudged eyes, the little sorenesses and stiffnesses of the flesh.

For a time she amused herself by seeing if she could turn his simple carnality into self-destructive infatuation. But he was an old dog who had trotted down a thousand alleys, and had learned that some of it was good and some of it was better. She knew that in their topside roles of owner and captain he was totally aware of her as Crissy Harkinson. But down in all the tumble of the broad bunk in the master stateroom, he was aware only of Female, of her as an anonymous volunteer in an ancient army, a familiar ritual of arms, heat, gasping, holding and bursting, varying from all the others in such minor detail of skill, endurance, demands and size he was not aware of any difference at all, and aware only of himself after all.

The episode made it seem pointless to continue any pretense with Garry Staniker. On the way back up Biscayne Bay she told him she had to get rid of the Odalisque, that she couldn't afford it, or him, and she was going to take her personal belongings off it and turn it over to a broker. She said she would pay him through the month of May. The abruptness of it soured him, but she saw him work to bring his temper under control and guessed he had remembered the recommendation he would need from her.

Three days later he stopped at her house to pick up the promised letter. She was irritated at the broker's pessimism. He had said, "It's a good make and a good year. It's in good shape. Two months ago, if you'd brought it in then, I could have moved it in maybe a week. But now—I don't know. Things might not perk up until the season starts again. It's hard to say. And you're asking top dollar on it, you know."

"I checked around. I looked at what they're asking for boats like mine."

He had shrugged. "Sure. They're asking that. And the boats are right there waiting for a customer, right? I'll do the best I can."

She was further displeased to learn she would have to pay a monthly fee covering dockage, insurance and maintenance. It was considerably less than her costs had been, but she had not realized there would be any expense at all.

Her mood was not improved when Francisca woke her from a nap to tell her Staniker was in the living room. She had forgotten to write the promised letter. She went out and said, "Come back to-morrow, will you?"

"But I need it now, Crissy. Please. I can wait. You take your time. I'll wait right here. Okay?"

She went back to her bedroom desk and started to write the To
Whom it May Concern letter. After writing a paragraph she stopped,
tore it up and took a fresh sheet of her note paper.

"Should anyone wish to know the reason why Captain Garry
Staniker is no longer employed by me, I shall be happy to explain it
over the telephone." She wrote her phone number and signed her
name. She took it to him and, smiling, handed it to him. He started
to thank her, then stopped in the middle of a word.

"What kind of a letter is this?"

"You can read, Captain. It's the very best kind."

"But the way it sounds . . ."

"But it's so *much* more personal than a letter, Garry. *Really!* I'm
not good at letters. But when someone phones me about you, I can
give you all kinds of marvelous recommendations."

He was dubious and suspicious, but he had no choice but to accept her way of doing it. An elderly man phoned her at noon the
next day and put his wife on an extension so they could both talk to
her. They started off quite enthusiastic about Garry Staniker. But at
the end the life had gone from their voices, and she knew they
would not hire him. Yet she could have repeated every word she had
said and Staniker would have approved. What he could not know
was the timing and the intonation.

"Did you ever have any problem about drinking on the job, Mrs.
Harkinson?"

" . . . No?" The long pause then a thoughtful No with a slight
question. "No. None at all. I would say . . . no problem at all." Very
emphatic, yet with another curious pause.

The game amused her. After she hung up she had a fleeting sense
of mild guilt, but she shrugged it off. Let Garry sweat it out too.
This was the year for it. The Senator was gone, and the party was
over. Why should anybody land on their feet? Mary Jane Staniker

had found a job at Parker's Marina. It wasn't as though Garry would
have to stop eating.

When she came back from a shopping trip in the late afternoon
he was waiting for her, pacing up and down the terrace.

"What did you tell the McMurdies?"

"Don't yell at me, Garry. It annoys me."

"It *annoys* you!" She carried her packages into the bedroom, and
he followed her in, talking all the way. She dropped the packages
onto the chaise and turned to him and said, "Did I ask you to come
in here, Captain?"

"Crissy. Please! They were okay, and then they phoned you, and
then they said they'd let me know. But I could tell it was off. Damn
it, that was a *good* job. If you put the knife in me, I've got to know
why. And I've got to know what I have to do so you won't do it the
next time."

"What's the matter with you? Every single word I said about you
was a top recommendation. Why should I do anything else?"

He sat on the straight chair by her desk and shook his head dole-
fully. "I don't get it. I don't know what turned them off then. What
you have to understand, it's a time thing. There are more guys with
the papers than there are owners who want a hired crew. You come
off one job, that's when you have to move into the next one. You try
to line something up, and the owner finds out you've been on the
beach two or three months, he thinks you're a clown. I thought—
you were sore at me for something I'd done or didn't do. Look,
could you give me a regular letter? Please?"

"Okay," she said. "Sure, Garry." She went slowly toward him,
feeling a quickening of herself which grew more immediate with
each step. She knew it was not a specific desire for a specific indi-
vidual named Garry Staniker. It was a way to turn off all thought.
He was a hiding place. He had the weight and skill and enough

special knowledge of her ways and wants to turn the world off, and out of his anxiety would come a doggy earnestness to please. Then sleep would be deep. She had not been sleeping well.

When the next prospective employer phoned her she was prepared to recommend Staniker highly, but the man who phoned was the personnel manager of an electronics firm which owned a corporation boat, and in a most contentious and irritating way he cross-examined her over each answer she gave. "How do *you* know that?" "What makes *you* think he's competent in *that* area?"

She said, "Little man, you seem confused. I'm not applying for a job."

"It's my job to double check these things, Mrs. Harkinson. Please don't tell me how to do my job. When the safety of the executives of this corporation is involved . . ."

His voice faded as she reached and dropped the phone back onto the cradle.

Through the hot months she lazed and drifted in a self-indulgent stupor, baking herself in the sun, getting fuzzy on the midday drinks, taking long naps in the cool darkened bedroom, watching much television in the evenings. She told herself that she could not really make any plans until the cruiser was sold. The money was going. She knew she ought to get rid of Francisca, perhaps try to rent the house, make an effort to get a good price for the jewelry she had left. But she would push those thoughts aside, stretch and yawn and shout for Francisca to bring her a drink.

Several times through the hot months and into the coolness of the beginning of a new season, she became aware of the dangerous softness and heaviness of her body. Then she would spend days in the disciplines of exercise, diet, abstinence. She would try on everything she owned and leave the bedroom and dressing room heaped with clothing for Francisca to put away.

Staniker had gone to work at the marina where his Mary Jane worked. The man who had been working there had been caught pocketing some of the boat-rental money. The marina was not far away. There were no set hours when he had to be there. He and Mary Jane lived in a cottage on the marina property. Staniker stopped by to see Crissy quite often, arriving in his old car or in one of the rental outboards. He complained constantly. He said he was looking for better work all the time. Yet when she asked specific questions, he became vague and evasive.

They would drink together. Sometimes they would go to bed. They quarreled often. She had lost a measure of control over him when he realized she was no longer capable of helping him find a job. Sometimes he became ugly when he drank too much, and a few times he struck her and hurt her. At those times he told her she was his bad luck. She had spoiled everything for him forever. For a time she could not understand why, after she would become so angry with him she would tell him never to come back, he would make such humble and earnest efforts to regain her favor.

She realized one day that she was a necessary part of his status, of the fiction he made of himself. As long as he could come without invitation to this beautiful and isolated house where lived the attractive blonde ex-mistress of an influential man, and drink her liquor, be brought food by her maid, swim in her pool, pull her into bed, then he was maintaining one final contact with the golden world of yachts and ports and parties, and the inner image of the bronzed captain on the fly bridge, nodding down with amiable and knowing grin at the banquet of girls spread sun-struck on the foredeck.

So long as this relationship could be maintained, he could pretend that the dreary little beer, bait, outboard rental marina was but

a temporary setback in the shining career of youthful Garry Staniker. And she could guess that, for the sake of his self-esteem, he
would by nod, wink, nudge, veiled phrase, let the people know that
Staniker had a good thing going.

In January the Odalisque was sold. She had cut the asking price
several times. The offer she accepted was still lower. The expenses of
sale were heavy. And there were bills to pay out of the cash she
received, including back pay for Francisca. The amount she had left
was frighteningly small.

Still she could not seem to stir herself to change anything. There
was still the house itself. Prime waterfront. It would sell for a good
amount of cash. She did not try to find out how much. She did not
want to think in exact terms, because if she knew how much, then
she would begin to work out how long it would last her.

In sleep she began to dream quite often of old times, before she
had met Fer Fontaine. It was a life where you were told what you
would do and where you would be. Punishment was brutal and immediate. She would awaken from such dreams with a curious sense
of regret and nostalgia. It had not been a mode of life she had sought,
or even realized what currents of chance had drifted her into it. She
had told herself it was something she was doing for a little while.
But the little while had been years.

And then, as if awakening from another kind of sleep, she came
out of the long lethargy of waiting on that last day of March when
Bixby Kayd came to see her. He had been at the house several times
when Fer was alive, when a small group of men were quietly buying
up raw land, marl deposits, gravel pits and central mix plants along
the route for a big new highway later to be announced officially by
the State Road Board. As a familiar index of the man's importance,
Crissy knew he had also gone on some of the Senator's little cruises
aboard the Odalisque, those cruises which would include the more
special members of the larger group, the ones capable of making

those special arrangements which would make their share a little richer than the shares the smaller fry would get.

Bix had phoned her and arrived a half hour later in a rental limousine. He sat in an armchair, facing her, in the living room beside her slate fireplace—a big, brown, beaming man with a loud jocular voice, custom-tailored suit in western style in sand-colored twill, elaborate stitching of boots, pale stetson on the floor beside his chair, the bourbon on ice she had fixed him looking dwarfed by the size of his hand. His hair, with the light behind him, was a sandy stubble a quarter inch long covering those places on his big skull which had not gone bald.

Francisca, as she had requested, brought in the tray of small crackers, the spiced cheese melted and hot atop them, slightly brown by the broiler flame, passed them, put the tray down within Mr. Kayd's reach.

It was a time of mutual appraisal, as Kayd offered belated sympathies about the Senator, said how pleased he was to find her still living here, had phoned on the off chance, killing time between the flight from the Bahamas which had brought him into Miami International and his jet flight to Houston, where his own plane and pilot would meet him to take him back home to the Valley.

She was alert to all familiar nuances in the male attitude. He had that automatic courtliness, that appreciative manner of the self-confident man who finds himself alone with an attractive woman. She considered, and dismissed, the possibility he had come to check the possibility of sampling wares he had found interesting back when Ferris Fontaine's presence made all curiosity academic. It was not that sort of visit, nor was it a social call.

Finally he gobbled a cracker, wiped his fingers on a paper napkin, took a large swallow of his drink and, hunching forward, lowered his voice to what, for most people, would have been the normal conversational level.

"Fer Fontaine was a damn careful man, Crissy. That's why it was a pleasure doing business with him. That and having his handshake worth anybody else's notarized signature. That's how I know if you were the kind that runs off at the mouth, he wouldn't have kept you around a week, much less all the time he did keep you. And he wouldn't have left you fixed up pretty good like this, with the house and all. So I can ask your help in a little private problem I've got."

"I'll help any way I can, Bix."

"Fer wouldn't have had anybody around who wasn't solid. So the times we did business aboard that boat of his, that fella I chatted with, that captain that ran it, with the chunky little wife who could cook up a storm, they had to be just as reliable as you. For the life of me, I can't remember his name."

"Staniker."

Kayd snapped his fingers. "Right! Larry? No. Garry. And is her name Jane?"

"Mary Jane."

"I remember him telling me about knowing every foot of water in the Bahamas. Do you know if he's still in this area? Do you think you could locate him?"

"I don't think it would be difficult."

He lowered his voice a little more. "When you find him, you tell him Bix Kayd wants to hire him and his wife for six weeks, maybe a little longer, starting sometime after the middle of April, to work aboard my boat for a long cruise in the Bahamas. Tell him it's a fine boat, fifty-three foot, custom built in North Carolina, twin diesels, every extra and navigation aid you can dream up, comfortable crew quarters. Name of it is the Muñeca. Soon as I get back, we're going to get her ready to go and take off. She's in Brownsville, Texas, right now, and me and my boy Roger will bring her around the Gulf, and my wife and daughter will be aboard, maybe a friend of Stel's too. Stella is my daughter. Once we get here, we'll buy some kind of runabout and take her in tow, so we can get to places too shallow for the big boat, and so the kids will have something to horse around with, skin diving and water skiing and so on.

"Now I know that a man as good as Staniker around boats must be working for somebody, and to get loose, he'd have to locate somebody reliable to take his job while he's with me. So when you talk to him, you tell him I'll pay him three thousand for the six weeks, him and his wife, and if it runs longer, I'll pay him at the same rate. You line it up for me, and I'll phone you from New Orleans or Biloxi on the way around the Gulf, and I'll give you a little present for your trouble, Miss Crissy."

"You don't have to do that! I'm glad to do it, for old time's sake, really. But . . ."

"What's bothering you?"

"You know what he's going to say. He's going to want to know why you're willing to pay so much."

She got up and took his empty glass and her own over to the drink cupboard. He remained silent and thoughtful. When she handed him his new drink he said, "My pretty little wife is itching and aching to see the Bahamas. I've been too busy for a vacation. Stel and Roger are my kids by my first wife. I've got an interest in some resort land over there. Trying to do business with some people who aren't what you'd call eager to take the bait. You tell Staniker I might have to meet some of those people on the sly, maybe on one of the Out Islands, and offer a little sweetening their partners might not get to know about. So I'd be paying extra for I'd guess the same thing Fer wanted, a real bad memory about where we went and when we went and who might have come aboard. I remember him being bright enough to buy that."

"I'm sure he is."

Kayd looked troubled. "There's one thing he doesn't have to know. But it's the reason I want a man Fer was willing to trust. It isn't likely Staniker would ever have to know, but there's always the off chance him or his Mary Jane might find out somehow that I've got all that sweetening aboard, a stack of it I sure wouldn't want to risk having a pick-up captain or ship's cook knowing about."

"And there's no point in letting even Staniker know about it if you can avoid it."

He looked at her warmly and appreciatively. "Fer sure found himself a smart gal. Don't ever tell anybody one word more than they need to know. Decided to tell you because what I want you to do, if there isn't enough, I authorize you to boost it on up to where he'll say yes. But not over five. I pay for what I need, but I don't want somebody trying to guess what the traffic will bear. If you know all my reasons, you can do a better job on Staniker. Maybe, later on, if things work out right, and you've got the time, you could go over there to Nassau on a little vacation once in a while and do me a little favor now and then. You'd get some little presents. Enough so as to know you weren't wasting your time."

"Little favors?"

"A man on my payroll with some cute ideas about what he can get away with, seeing as how I'm so far away, might want to put on the brag to some pretty tourist gal who never heard of Bix Kayd. Or some old boy who didn't land a contract to barge building materials to one of the islands I hope to buy, might tell the big-eyed tourist gal how the boy who did get the contract is making kick-backs to the builder. When I get to wondering about something I get to fretting about it. A smart, pretty woman is the best pair of ears a man can buy. I'm into a lot of things, scattered here and there. I get the big sell from these investigation firms. They want me to put in what they call a security system. Screening, lie detectors, concealed microphones, psychological tests, plant some investigators on the pay rolls. Know what they never understand? Why should I pay some outfit forty or fifty thousand a year to find out everything about what I'm doing? Who do they sell *that* information to? I have a few smart gals here and there. They do little favors. I make a little present. They like it, the smart ones. It's kind of a game. And nobody knows they've got any connection at all with Bix Kayd. It's a little excitement. Something different."

He looked at his watch, gulped the remainder of his drink, put the glass down and stood up. "Don't want to miss that flight." He took an alligator billfold out of his inside jacket pocket, fingered ten hundreds out of what he was carrying, said, "Here. Give it to Staniker so he'll know we've got a deal."

"I hope he isn't off somewhere on a cruise, Bix."

"Do your best, Miss Crissy."

She thought about it all night long. Staniker did not come by. She paced and thought and drank and nibbled at the knuckle of her thumb. She would stop and study herself in her mirrors. The excitement kept starting in the pit of her belly, coiling up through her to burst like bright rockets in her skull, dazing her. In the bright dawn she closed the draperies and went to bed to sleep heavily for several hours.

She awakened not knowing for a little time where she was. Then it came tumbling back into her head. She got up and went to the money Bix had given her. The money made it real. The money made all the rest of the money possible.

She willed Staniker to come to her. He came strolling in at four thirty in the afternoon, smelling of beer, complaining about the condition the rental skiffs had been in when they were returned. The terrace was in shade at that time of day. They sat at a table, and she fixed drinks and brought them out. She had told Francisca she would not need her. At last Staniker noticed how unresponsive she was. "Is anything wrong?" he asked. "You sore about something, Cris?"

"How's the job hunting?"

"Something will turn up."

"Oh, certainly. Because you make such a marvelous impression these days, Captain. Let me list your charms. You're getting a beer belly. You missed a couple of places on your jaw when you shaved. You smell sweaty. Look at your fingernails. It's been a year, Captain, a whole year since you ran a good boat for good pay. And downhill all the way. Haven't you noticed?"

"What the *hell*, Cris!"

She leaned toward him and said with a slow and deadly emphasis. "Do you know what's going to turn up for you? More of the same, Captain. More of just what you've got. Nothing. Ten years from now your Mary Jane will be working as hard as she is right now. And by then you won't even pretend to work. You'll hang around the marinas with the other old nothings. You'll tell lies about the navy and about the Bahamas and about me. I'll be somebody you used to know, Garry. Just lies, my friend. Beer and dirt and no money and fancy lies that not even the other old bums are going to believe. Starting today I think I'm going to become somebody you used to know. You never had it. I guess that's the secret. You always looked as though you had it. You acted as though you had it. But on the inside, Garry, nothing. Nothing *I* need. Nothing *I* can use."

"What are you trying to *do* to me?" he whispered.

"Me. You're doing it to yourself. You just haven't noticed. You're a slob. Everything you've touched has turned to nothing. It's your great talent, wouldn't you say?"

"I had some bad luck, but . . ."

"Your luck is going to change? Why? Because you're so young and competent and charming? Staniker, you are a silly, stupid, middle-aged man who puts dark goop on his gray hair and keeps forgetting to hold his belly in when he stands up."

"Do you know what you are!"

"Go ahead. Say it. It will help me decide."

He hesitated too long. "Decide what?"

She laughed. "It's all pretty funny, you know. We've run the string out, you and me. We're both on the long downhill ride. The big chance came along, and it's too late for us to try to grab it. Maybe back when you had some guts left and some pride. When you still *wanted* things badly enough to go after them."

"How do you know how bad I want things? What do you mean, big chance? What are you talking about?"

"You're not hard enough, Garry. Believe me, you couldn't carry it off. I couldn't take the chance. Not with you. You'd mess it up somehow. And the sad part of it is that I haven't got time to find the right man for it. A hard man. One I could trust. So instead of a big, beautiful cake, all you get is a couple of crumbs. You might as well have the crumbs. He *did* ask for you."

She reached into the pocket of her slacks and took out the little packet of bills Kayd had given her. They were folded once. She flipped them onto the table. "Go ahead. Pick them up, Captain. You've got a job. That's an advance on your salary."

His big hands shook as he counted it. "A job?"

She forced a yawn. "Running a boat. What else? You aren't able to do anything else, are you? Six weeks, or so, beginning about the middle of this month. Oh, and he wants your wife aboard too, to cook. He wants to cruise the Bahamas. He said it's a fifty-three foot cruiser, custom built, twin diesels. He's bringing it around the Gulf from Texas and when he gets in touch with me I'll tell him how to get in touch with you. He'll pay three thousand total. That's five hundred a week for the pair of you."

"Why does he want to pay that much?"

"He knows you. His name is Kayd. Bixby Kayd."

Staniker looked puzzled. "I know that name—Oh, great big fella? Big voice?"

"Himself. One of Fer's pack of old buddies. He guessed that if you didn't know how to keep your mouth shut, Fer wouldn't have kept you on. So the big fee includes keeping your mouth shut. That means it's some kind of a business trip."

"A thousand dollars!" he said in a reverent tone.

She stood up, fists in the pockets of her slacks. "So run along, Garry. Let's pretend it's been nice. Anything you might think I owed you, this pays it off. Right? Just stay away from me. Don't come around any more. It would just remind me of how close I came to the jackpot."

As she had hoped, he pleaded with her to tell him what she was talking about. She refused, chopping at his pride as savagely as she dared, sometimes making his face turn sallow under his lifelong tan. She let him follow her into her bedroom.

Finally, in a blazing imitation of anger, she said, "All right! All right! I'll tell you, not that it is going to mean a damned thing because you're not man enough to even recognize a chance like this. And you wouldn't have the guts to grab it if you did. It's too rough for you. It would take more than you've got. More than you've ever had. You see, Captain, you'll have four and maybe five people aboard. Kayd and his second wife. His two children from his first marriage. Maybe a friend of his daughter's. And because he was idiot enough to trust me, I guess because Fer trusted me, he told me something you're not supposed to know. He's going to bribe somebody in a big land deal. With cash money. And he'll have that aboard."

"How much?"

She had given careful thought to what figure she would tell Staniker. She knew it had to be a very substantial figure to make Kayd edgy about carrying it or having the hired captain know about it.

"Four hundred and fifty thousand dollars," she said mildly. "Cash money. Bribe money. The kind nobody knows about and it can't be traced. Forget it. You'll never even get a look at it."

"That much cash?" he said incredulously.

"There was twice that in this house once," she said. "One of Fer's deals. You know how it works with men like that. They have tax angles to think about. Anyway—you can see why there's no point in talking to you about it."

"It's a lot of money, Crissy."

"And only one way to take it. You'd have to fake a disaster, Captain. An explosion or something. They'd have to go down with the boat, every one of them, dead because you'd have to kill them. And you'd have to hide the money somewhere in the islands, in a place so safe we could leave it there for months and months. You'd be the sole survivor. You'd have to have a good story and stick to it no matter how hard they tried to trick you. And when it all quieted down, you'd have to find a way to slip over there and pick up the money and bring it back. We'd split it down the middle, my friend. If you were gutsy enough to give it a try. And then we wouldn't go hand in hand into the sunset, Captain. We'd head in different directions. I know what kind of a life I'd buy with it." She tilted her head. "You'd probably go somewhere where you could buy a big old crock of a seagoing motor sailer and stock it with a couple of adventurous little floozies and go to the far islands of the Pacific. You could be their big daddy, their seafaring hero type."

She threw her head back and gave a loud jeering laugh. "You! Good God! Can you imagine a meat head like you bringing off anything like that? You're too small time, Captain. You'd wet your pants even thinking about it. I can tell from the look on your face that the idea of killing six people is making your tummy-wummy turn over and over. Do you know the difference between you and a *man*? A *man* would remember that a lot of things can happen to people. Hell, their airplane might crash on the way back to Texas when the cruise is over. Mary Jane might slip on that dock some dark night and crack her skull on a rental boat. A *man* sees a chance and takes it. You know, Garry, your trouble is that you'd *rather* live small."

He reached her in three strides, clopped the side of her head with a big open palm and knocked her to her hands and knees, her ear ringing. "Get off my back!" he yelled.

She looked up at him. "Get out of here. You bore me. You want to talk about it. That's all. Just talk about it and scare yourself like a little kid at the horror movie. Go away, Chicken Staniker. Get out of here."

At midnight she lay in darkness on her bed, aware of the invisible bulk of him beside her. He sighed and said, "It's the only chance I'll ever get."

"Talk talk talk. But you won't do it."

"How many times do I have to tell you I . . ."

"Maybe you could. If you really want to. But I don't think you want to."

He put his arms around her and pulled her close. "If you'd stop riding me and start helping me, honey. Maybe I can't do it. Maybe I can. If we get it all planned out, maybe I can. I—I think of that much money and I feel sweaty. You know? Things have never gone right. It wasn't my fault things didn't work out so good. Luck evens out, maybe. A big one, to wash out all the little ones. But—what you should be doing is building me up, not tearing me down. Come on. Let's talk more about it. Don't fall asleep."

Her heart bumped with an almost painful excitement as she put her arms around him and smiled into the darkness. "I don't want to play kid games, Staniker. Not with so much at stake. Not with two hundred and twenty-five thousand apiece on one big roll of the dice. Six people. Can you do arithmetic in your head? How much apiece, baby?"

After a few moments he whispered, "Thirty-seven thousand five hundred."

"Suppose you could go to a place and walk in and they'd hand you thirty-seven thousand five hundred, no questions asked. All you'd have to do would be take them Mary Jane's head in a brown paper bag."

She felt him shudder.

She lunged over and turned the lights on. She bent over him and shook him. "I have to *know!* If you could fix it so she wouldn't feel a thing, could you do that? For the money I gave you today, thirty-seven times over. Could you?"

He squinted in the light. His face was sweaty. He wiped his mouth on the back of his hand, looked at her and looked away.

"Yes," he said in a husky voice. "If she—wasn't in any pain. And I wouldn't get caught for doing it. Yes."

She dug her nails into the slabs of muscle on his shoulders. She stared into his eyes. Barely moving her lips she said, "You know, we might be home free. We just might."

"You—you've got to help out."

"Garry, you'll know every move. Believe me. You are going to go through it so many times that when it really happens, you won't even have to think about it. It will be as if you were watching something happen. Trust me."

She watched his eyes. Long long ago Phil Kerna had taught her to watch for the special signs when a player decided to back his hand to the limit. Phil could tell when they had filled on the draw. When he believed that he had the better hand, and when the player was on his left, Phil would dawdle over his bet, keep scowling eyes on his cards, clatter his chips. That was his signal to her to study the player on his left. There was a point when the decision was made, to go all the way with the hand. The jaw would firm up, throat bulge with the dry swallow, chest lift in a long, deep breath, lids droop slightly to hide the eyes. Then, out of the cone of light over the table, too far away to see any cards of course, she would uncross and recross her legs, a motion Phil could see out of the tail of his eye. And with that signal he would bet into the do-or-die type.

"Like a kid jumping off the barn, baby," Phil would say. "Once they decide to go, they go no matter what. They don't stop and think again when I bet into them. They just boost their bet that much."

When she read the expression wrong, he would thrash her after the session was over. She saw it now on Staniker's face. She saw the instant when, in his mind, it changed from speculation to resolve.

"I—I got to do it," he said, and his heavy face looked slightly astonished at the realization there was no longer any other choice.

She got up then and went into her dressing room, so filled with a strange hard exultant glee she did not dare remain close to him for fear it would erupt into a wild laughter that would upset and confuse him. She turned on a single light on the dressing table, and paced swiftly and silently back and forth, in and out of the area of light, across the soft, resilient carpeting. She saw distorted shadows of her naked body against the pale doors of closets and wardrobes, and caught glimpses of herself in the triple mirrors, lithe and swift, stalking and turning. Her legs felt springy and tireless and sweet. She set her teeth into her thumb knuckle, made a tiny snickering sound, whirled and sat on the dressing-table bench and smiled at the three images of herself, accepting their smiles in return. She arched her back and lifted her arms, pulling the solid breasts high. And then she identified what it was she felt. It was the sense of being young. All the time since Fer had been old, old, older. It was very, very good to be young again.

· · ·

Now, remembering, and sitting at the dressing table and putting on the last careful touches of makeup to create the desired impression on Oliver Akard, she gave herself a bright little nod. It disconcerted her to do such a thing without thought of plan. Lately there had been too many of these puppety little actions, too many grotesque images flickering through her mind. Time to take a tight hold, girl. A lot has been done and there is a lot to do, and when it is all over you can act as batty as you please. This was going to need all her attention. It was the first time she had seen Olly since the news of Staniker's rescue.

"Crissy?" Oliver called softly from the bedroom. "Crissy?" She had not heard him slide the glass door open or shut it again.

"In here, darling. In the dressing room. Come here, darling." She made her voice drag, made it sound dispirited enough to match the eyes she had so expertly smudged.

Forty minutes later the scene was developing as she had planned it. He had kept asking what was wrong, and she kept denying there was anything wrong, and finally, as he began tremblingly to couple with her, she gave a cry of despair, wrenched herself away, went in a stumbling tearful run to her bathroom and locked herself in.

When at last she came out she put on a dark robe and sat on the chaise and made him sit on the foot of the bed, ten feet away.

"I had no right to fall in love with you, Oliver. Please go now, while I've got the strength to send you away. Forget it happened. I don't want to hurt you. I have to get out of your life."

After he pleaded and demanded for a long time she said, "All right. Maybe it's a kind of punishment. You won't want to touch me ever again after I tell you. It will make it easier for you to go. You see, I was playing a game of pretend. I made myself believe he was never, never coming back, and so that gave me the right to something—decent."

"He? Who?"

"Staniker, of course. Garry Staniker, that brutal bastard who somehow got to own me, Oliver. I kidded myself. I thought I could lift my head and begin to live again. I cheated myself and I cheated you. I'm so—so terribly ashamed."

Then she told him the story of a silly woman, of a short cruise on the Odalisque, a faked breakdown, a lonely anchorage, too much to drink, of fighting him off until it seemed easier to let him have his way. The boy looked stunned and sickened. She sighed, "After that, I guess I stopped caring for a while. I'm a mature woman. I had a married life for a time. He's a very clever sensuous brute, you know. It was purely physical, dear, not like what you and I have. But I can't lie to you about it. I got pleasure from it. He saw to that. Finally I realized I had to get out of the trap. I tried. God knows I tried. I thought that by selling the boat I'd be rid of him. So he started coming here. I fought it. Believe me, I fought it. But he is a strange man. I think there's something sick and wrong and dangerous about him. He'd laugh at me when I begged him to let me alone. When I irritated him too much, he'd beat me. He's told me that no woman he's ever had has walked out on him, and no one ever will, and that until he gets tired of me, I have no choice at all. When he comes back, Oliver, it will all be the same as it was before. There's nothing either of us can do about it. I even tried to kill myself once, but I didn't have the courage."

The words bowed his strong, young shoulders, made his face pale and sweaty, gave him a nauseated look.

"You've been a miracle I didn't deserve, Oliver. I should have known it couldn't be really true, to have you make me feel so proud, and so cherished. Please leave, dear. Right now. I'll never forget you."

"I *can't* leave you!"

"Now is the time to leave me. He's hurt, and it will be weeks, maybe, before he comes back. His wife is gone now. I think what he'll do is move in here with me, and there's no way in the world I can stop him. I'm a coward, dear. He's trained me, with those beatings. He knows all the ways to hurt."

He came lurching to her, bungling and clumsy, to hold her and make his groaning sobs and protests, his young heart in a terrible agony and, she knew, under the agony was the sly desire to keep on having her as long as he could.

With great reluctance she at last accepted the compromise she had sought. "All right then. We'll be selfish, Oliver. We'll crowd our whole lifetime into whatever time there is left before he comes back. From now on we'll pretend there isn't any ending to us."

He began to make brave sounds about how he would drive Staniker away from her and keep him away. "Shush, darling. Let's not spoil the time left by talking ugliness and silliness and things that won't happen. Just—love me. Make me forget everything but you."

Afterward, she studied his face in his heavy sleep, in the indirect glow of the bedside light. He looked haggard, yet very young, like a child after too much carnival, tickets for every ride, the belly queasy under the weight of candied apples.

As she got up and closed the interconnecting doors so she could take her shower without awakening him, she remembered how Spook used to talk about them. Spook had acting talent and a sense of mischief and a contempt for the men she could hook. "Look, kid, what have they got? They've got the drearies, these sad dull little jobs and houses and wives and irritating kids. The movies and the TV people have these huge, glamorous problems, and the marks feel left out. So along with the trick I give them a little theater, like maybe my old man is a U.S. Senator and he's spent thousands trying to find me, or I have a rare and unusual kind of blood disease I caught in Arabia. I like to cry a little. Where else are these drearies going to buy genuine romantic stuff? Put them through the wringer, kid,

174 JOHN D. MACDONALD

and you establish a nice repeat business and a little bonus on the sly to help you out with your problems."

As she was lazily drying herself after her shower she found herself reaching further back into memory, back to one of the games of her childhood. It had been years since she had thought of it, and she did not know what had brought it to the surface just now.

Each Sunday at the Home, when they filed out of the hall after supper, there would always be a bowl of those round hard candies on the table by the door, and old Satchel-ass would be sitting behind the table watching it like an eagle. If you had a dining-hall demerit that week, you got waved on by. If not you could take one, picking it up between thumb and first finger with the other fingers curled out of the way so you could have no chance to get more than one. They were each wrapped in a twist of white waxy paper, so that the color showed through, but if you hesitated to look for a color you wanted, she'd wave you by and your chance was gone.

Some of the kids chomped theirs up as they walked out of the building, and others rolled it on their tongue to make it last a long time, and if you stuck it back in the pocket of your cheek behind your teeth, it would last practically forever. But she had always saved hers for the games of Last One Left.

About nine or ten girls was the best number, each putting in one candy, and you had to look inside the paper to be sure nobody had wrapped up one already sucked a little. You drew the hopscotch squares on the cement playground with the edge of a piece of shale, with one candy in a corner of each square, making the jumps hard enough so that on the very first time some would jump onto a line, or lose their balance when they picked up one of the pieces, and it would be weeded down until only the winner was left, and the nine or ten pieces belonged to her.

Crissy won more consistently than anyone except a tall spry skinny colored girl named Shacks. When Shacks won she would stand and whinny with crazy laughter, and go whinnying off with the candy, until finally she got on everyone's nerves so badly Crissy and three others had cornered her in the john after lights out. It had taken a long time and a lot of effort to make her start crying, and it wasn't until then they found out she was so damned dumb she'd thought it was Laughs One Left, and the whinnying was because she thought it was the name of the game.

Crissy remembered the pleasure of being the Last One Left, and often, after winning she would save the treasure until lights out, and then unwrap as many as six in a row, putting each one in her mouth and trying to identify the flavor, then roll them around with her tongue until all flavors blended, and finally chomp them all into sweet splinters and powder and juice, knowing that in all the nearby beds the ones still awake could hear the night feast and know what it was.

Twelve

ON SATURDAY AFTERNOON, the day after Staniker was brought back to Nassau, when Sam Boylston returned to his room at the Nassau Harbour Club, Jonathan Dye seemed unchanged in any way. He was still sitting in the straight chair by the desk, hunched and miserable, arms resting on his knees, knuckly hands dangling.

His color was poor, eyes puffy, his beard a dark shadow on the angular jaw and long throat.

He looked up and nodded absently at Sam, then directed his stare back toward the nubby texture of the gray rug.

Sam put a package on the bed and said, "I've got permission to talk to the Barths and the Hilgers. Sir Willis fixed it up." The boy did not answer. Sam said, "You can see their point. The reporters got their story from those people before the police could stop them. It was second hand. Nobody can be certain it's what Staniker actually told them. They could get some details wrong. So it's better to wait for the results of the interrogation of Staniker and keep reporters away from those people. People usually have a tendency to dress a story up when they're the center of attention. It makes them more important. They've been questioned by the authorities now. But the results of that won't be released to the press. Their boat is tied up at Yacht Haven. Want to go down there with me in a few minutes? Jonathan!"

"Sir?"

"Do you want to come along with me and talk to those people who brought Staniker in?"

"I don't know. I guess so."

Sam unwrapped his package. It was a small, expensive tape recorder, an import from Japan, transistorized, built to operate on nine-volt batteries at a recording and playback speed of one and seven-eighths inches per second. The monitor speaker could be detached to reduce bulk even further. The shop had shown him how to use it. A switch could put it on continuous record, or, in the other position, set it so that it was voice-activated with a dial to adjust the sensitivity. He had purchased extra reels and extra batteries.

He set it up and turned it on. He counted to ten, moved six feet back and counted to ten again, and went over to the door and counted to ten, a third time. He rewound the tape and played it back. Within the cycles-per-second range of the human voice, it had good fidelity, better than it had sounded in the shop.

He saw he had aroused Jonathan's interest. "What's that for?"

"I used to do some trial work. They kept telling me I did it just fine. But I couldn't get to like it. I learned one thing. You think you are listening to everything, but you always miss a little. You catch it when you play it back. Sometimes it's important."

"What good is it going to do?"

"It's a pretty good little machine."

"I mean what's the point in talking to those people?"

"They saw Staniker in bad shape. Conscious and in bad shape."

"So?"

"So maybe they heard something he won't talk about when he gets his health back."

"You're playing games, Sam."

"How's that?"

"Maybe to keep busy, go through some motions. What difference does it make how it happened? Maybe Staniker screwed up the details. The only thing that matters is that he thinks he's the only one who escaped. I guess maybe you think so too. So you want to go thrashing around to find out how it happened. Why? Who cares about *how*? There's just one thing I care about. She's alive! No matter what Staniker might think, Leila is alive!"

"Easy, boy."

"God *damn* it, don't give me that look of pity! I haven't flipped. And I am not that kind of sentimental jackass who thinks the virtuous survive and the evil ones die." He stood up slowly. "And I think—I really think I'm strong enough to endure losing her. It would rack me up for a long time, Sam. But eventually I'd work my way out of it. Listen carefully. I sat in that chair for most of the night. And a lot of today. And I've said to myself that she is dead. Leila is dead. There isn't anything anybody can do about it. Dead and gone and you'll never see her again. And only a damned fool would think anybody below decks could survive explosion and fire. But something keeps me from really believing it. Almost as if she were standing over there in the corner behind me and shaking her head sadly and wondering how I could be so stupid. You know how she was in the water. Dazed and burned and half-conscious, she'd keep afloat by instinct. Somehow she was thrown clear, I swear it. We were close, Sam. As close as people ever get. It wasn't kid stuff. We were lovers. For over a year now. And that was good, but it wasn't the basic part of us. It was just a way to—say something to each other about what we were to each other. If she's left this world, my heart would be a stone. But it isn't. But if I don't find her soon enough, one day, all of a sudden, I'll know she's gone." He sat again, face in his hands, made a single dry sound, a cough like a sob.

Sam Boylston poured a half tumbler of Canadian whisky from the bottle he'd bought in the package store in the lobby. He dropped in two cubes, swirled it, took it over and fitted it into Jonathan's big hand. "Knock it down," he ordered.

Jonathan drank half, coughed, finished it, gagged and shuddered and handed the glass back. Sam once again debated telling the boy about the money. It would justify Sam's interest in finding out just what had happened. Yet it might be the final proof that Leila had died. If somebody had gone after the money, there would be no survivors. If the money was the target, then Staniker was in on it. And Sam knew that one of the rarest traits in the world is the ability to tell a complex lie time after time without slipping somehow.

The boy did not realize that his conviction she was alive was merely a device to protect himself from a blow he was not yet ready to endure. Sam realized it would be quite easy to explain it to the boy and tell him about the money. Irrational reactions had always made him impatient.

"I sound like a nut," Jonathan said. "I can't help what I believe."

"What are you going to do about it?"

Jonathan looked mildly surprised. "Go look for her. Now I know where to look." He got the chart and opened it up on the bed. "Here is where it happened. Here is where they found Staniker. So Leila had to get carried onto the Bahama Banks to the north of the Joulters. It's all shallows. There's supposed to be at least two thousand little hummocks of sand and rock, some with vegetation, that are still out of the water at high tide. I'm going to go to Andros, get some kind of a little boat and—go find her. She wouldn't panic, you know. She'll manage to stay alive long enough. Long enough for me to find her. And she looks fragile, but she's tough. She could endure a lot."

It was his obvious duty to point out to the boy that such a search was pure fantasy. He had no useful experience with boats and the sea, and no first-hand knowledge of that area. It was pure damned foolishness. And what good was this sort of idiotic hope if in the end it would finally collapse.

As he began to choose his words, he saw himself in the mirrored door of the bath. And he could remember other times, other mirrors, when he began to choose those words which would open the paths of logic for Leila, or for Lydia Jean, or for Boy-Sam. Why in God's name were the emptiest dreams the very ones they thought most important? They wrote their stupid little melodramas and then were so terribly terribly hurt when you didn't come on stage and say the lines they'd written for you. Did they want humoring? Did they want accomplices in utter sappiness to make themselves more secure in delusion?

So this time, he thought, instead of turning off the stage lights and dropping the curtain, I'll play it their way. He turned toward Jonathan and said, "If you say that's where she is, then that's where she is. And the more help I give you, the sooner you'll find her."

"I—I guess that's right, sir."

"I'll pay the shot on leasing a decent boat with a crew who know those waters. If the boat doesn't draw much over three feet, she can thread around through the channels. And you can use a dinghy with a kicker for shallower work. Can you handle it, or will it take both of us?"

"I can handle it. Is it okay if I see what I can do right now about lining up a boat?"

"Sooner the better."

The moment the boy left, Sam Boylston felt irritated at himself.

Humoring them involved a curious kind of weakness, and created an uncomfortable obligation. Once you started the game, you had to keep on playing it. And it was a game which could bring you nothing.

Now, with his visit to the Barths and the Hilgers aboard the Docksie III, he was beginning a game more to his liking. It would have an ending, and in the ending there would be a hard and merciless satisfaction. After that would come time to mourn the sister lost. But was not his game as pointless as Jonathan's, actually? That fragment of insight jarred him, and he thrust it aside. Delicate little philosophical comparisons were good parlor games for people like—Lyd, Leila and Jonathan. Any man who went around inventing doubts and reservations was emasculating himself. Neither compulsion, his or Jonathan's, would bring Leila back. But his might well keep someone from profiting through the loss of her. When a man released his clasp They snatched everything from him forever.

At quarter to seven on Monday morning, Sam Boylston tapped at the door of Apartment 6, Harbour Heights Apartments. In a few moments the door opened as far as the safety chain would permit, and the girl in white looked at him through the gap.

"Sam Boylston," he said. "I know I'm a little early. If it's inconvenient I can come back . . ."

She closed the door, released the chain and let him into the small, bright, tidy living room. "Yes, you are early, Mr. Boylston, but perhaps it is better. I might not do this thing you want. Would you have some coffee with me?"

In her speech she had the Bahamian trait of emphasizing the unexpected word. Her face was too narrow for beauty, black bright eyes set too closely, her skin dusky sallow in the way of the mixed blood of the Islands. But she had freshness and style. Special Nurse

Theyma Chappie was assigned to the daytime trick, eight in the morning to four in the afternoon, caring for Captain Garry Staniker in his private room at the Princess Margaret Hospital.

She brought his coffee to the table by the windows where she had been eating her breakfast, and they sat facing each other.

"I understand, Nurse. There's no way I can force you."

"It is what I said to my brother. Sir Willis has been very good to him, very helpful. If he had not been, perhaps I could not have had my training. But I am a professional person. There is an obligation to the patient. Also to the hospital. And there could be trouble with the officials too. To take a risk, I told my brother, I would have to believe it is a good thing to do, perhaps a necessary thing. We have been ordered to say nothing to reporters. Perhaps this is lies. A trick."

He took out his wallet, unsnapped the packet of identifications and handed it to her. "I am exactly what I say I am, Nurse, a lawyer from Harlingen, Texas." After she had looked at the identifications, as she handed them back, he handed her the color snapshot of Leila he took from another compartment of the wallet. "This is my kid sister. She was a guest aboard the Muñeca."

"So pretty!" she said, and in a little while handed it back to him. "But they will question this captain carefully, no? What is the need of what you wish me to do?"

"There is one reason I cannot explain either to you or to the authorities, a reason to believe that Staniker may have—with or without help—killed those six people aboard and sunk the cruiser."

She looked shocked. "But he does not seem such a person!"

"I want to know how he responds to questioning. I will be looking for things they will not be looking for. I think they are worried about carelessness. I am worried about guilt."

"Then why not tell them your reasons, Mr. Boylston?"

"Because then, from their questions, he will know they know

that reason. And he will be much more careful in his answers. It is a standard interrogation procedure, Nurse. If you pick up a murderer and charge him with a small robbery that happened on the same night, you will learn more than if you charge him with murder."

"If I help you will it become—evidence in a court so it will come out how I helped you?"

"No. Maybe it was an accident. Maybe the boat blew up. If I learn anything that makes it seem otherwise, I'll have to get him in some other way."

She studied him. "He is like a thing to you. Something to hunt."

"Do you think people should get away with mass murder?"

"Of course not. But if you want—too badly to believe he is guilty of something, maybe you will believe what you want to believe."

"I'm not like that."

She tilted her head. " . . . No. Perhaps not." She took a quick look at the gold watch pinned to the bodice of her uniform. "I guess you must show me now how the machine works."

"You'll do it then."

"But if it is found, I will have no idea how it came to be there."

She marveled at how small the recorder was. She caught on very quickly as he explained the operation. She said that there was a deep shelf in the bedside stand, and she could place it on the back of that shelf behind a stack of fresh face towels, a place where she could easily turn it on or off.

When he asked her opinion of Staniker's condition, she said, "He is a very strong one. He went a long time without help. For many persons, it might have been too long. There could be bad luck, perhaps more kidney damage than Dr. McGregory thinks. Or a pneumonia which will not respond to antibiotics, or a pulmonary edema we cannot control. He seemed dazed. And the tongue is very bruised and lacerated from the convulsions. He speaks with difficulty.

Maybe the Doctor will permit an interrogation today. I would guess tomorrow. It will depend on his condition, of course."

She fitted the recorder into her white shoulder bag, patted it. "I am glad it is such a small thing. And works so silently." She looked amused and said, "Perhaps I can borrow it one day and find out if Helena entertains someone I know here when I am on a night shift and she is working days." She flushed and said, "We share this place. There were three, but that is too many. The other went to an out island clinic. Now we must go, or I shall be late."

Down on the street level, he watched her trundle her pale blue motor scooter out to the curb, kick down upon the starter lever and move away into morning traffic, her slender back very straight.

He had a professional uneasiness about the little electronic ear she carried with her. It was an eavesdropper with total recall. The slow considerations of the law have not kept pace with the technology, and so the explosive expansion of listening devices and techniques exists in a gray area. Inevitably, when the law lags too far behind the realities, an eventual permissiveness is achieved through the mere weight of investment, employment and universal use. The average citizen, when he thought of it at all, saw nothing wrong in the good guys bugging the homes and offices and phones of the bad guys. But history had the queasy trick of constantly reversing the roles. Had the redcoats been able to bug G. Washington's winter encampment, he could have been fatally surprised on the shores of the Delaware.

The clever and compact little microphones and transmitters could spy on all sounds. The polygraph could, in a sense, spy upon the mind itself. And there was a dreadful inevitability about that day in the future when the state of the art obsoleted the business of affixing the sensors to the subject, the day when polygraphs could be taken without the knowledge of the subject. This would be the final and deadly invasion of all privacy.

He could recall the precise incidents which had led to his feeling of uneasiness. He had consented to handle a divorce action for an old friend. It was an area of the law he found distasteful. The old friend showed up with the specialist he had employed. The specialist had traced the wife to the particular motel where she would go with her lover. He had then installed equipment in a particular room and arranged that the couple be given that room. With obvious professional satisfaction, the specialist, in Sam Boylston's darkened office, had projected his infra-red 8-mm movie film, taken by a camera mounted inside a ventilator grill, and had concurrently played a tape captured by a mike and transmitter affixed to the underside of the motel bed. He heard the voice of the woman whose parties he and Lyd had attended, saying in a moaning and gritty voice, "Now! Now! O God! O beautiful! O beautiful!"

When the film ended, the expert had turned off the tape and opened the blinds. As he rewound tape and film onto the reels, the only sound in the office had been the muffled hacking sobs of his friend sitting there with his face in his hands. Sam had told him to find another attorney, one who would be willing to use this inadmissible evidence as a club to beat down any demand the wife might make for support. The expert was not angry or upset. Merely very very puzzled. Without such brutal and clinical proof, the marriage might have been mended. But once exposed to the fleshy explicits, the husband could not endure the thought of any reconciliation.

The second incident occurred when a small corporation in San Antonio, engaged in a proxy battle, had engaged him to find out how all their strategies became known before they could put them into effect, and what charges they might bring against the raider.

By employing another firm of investigators, a branch office of a national organization which made much of the number of ex-FBI agents they employed, he learned that the internal security had been penetrated in an unusual manner. An expert had imbedded a sensitive and shock-resistant induction mike and transmitter into a ball of sticky putty-colored material the size of an English walnut, and from outside the security fence, at night, had used a sling shot to paste it against an upper panel of one of the third floor windows of the conference room where, every morning, the executive committee of the Board of Directors met. The transmitter had a thirty-six hour life, and the substance in which it was imbedded took about the same amount of time to dry out and fall from the pane. The tape recorder, voice activated so that no attendant was necessary, had been placed along with the receiver in the store room of a diner well within the five-hundred-yard range of transmittal. Realizing the difficulties of taking legal action, Sam had recommended that the executive committee meetings be continued in such a way as to provide information that would seem valid but would mislead the opposition, and that the actual battle plans be arranged in secret meetings off the plant premises.

To protect himself professionally against this ever more sophisticated electronic invasion, Sam had employed the agency to give him a thorough grounding in the advanced techniques, and had also contracted to have his offices "swept" from time to time at random intervals to determine if any devices had been planted therein.

The third incident was far more subjective. It happened after Lydia Jean had been gone from home for two months, living with their boy in Corpus. And one night as he was going to bed, he had the sudden thought of how easy it would be to employ an agency to install phone taps and keep track of her movements and make regular reports. He knew that the thought was not as sudden as it seemed. It had that special flavor of thoughts which lie on the floor of the mind for a long time before emerging into the conscious mind.

It was a wretched idea. If she could not be trusted, there could be little point in yearning for her to come home. If she learned he could do that to her, his chances of ever getting her back were that much less. As he discarded the idea, he realized that ever since he had learned of the new marvels in electronic espionage, he had been gradually accustoming himself to speak less openly to everyone in his own offices and in those he visited. He had thought of it as merely a sensible precaution. If one assumed everything was overheard and recorded, one could cease worrying about what might be safe to say. It made a life more drab, more guarded, more ceremonious. All men of any degree of responsibility had begun to speak for the record, for the unseen audience, and old intimacies had withered because closeness must depend upon the exchange of the innermost thoughts. Orwell, in *1984*, had not considered the consequences of such a diffusion. An ever-watchful Big Brother could be outwitted, but a gnat-throng of little brothers could only be endured. Miniaturization of electronic circuitry was effecting that great change in human relationships which, in other cultures, had been created only by using secret arrest, imprisonment and torture to turn brother against brother.

He got behind the wheel of his rental car, but before he could start the engine, another of those strange spasms of grief and loss squeezed and twisted his brain and his heart. Chin on chest, eyes tightly shut, he grasped the steering wheel with such strength it numbed his hands and started a tremor in his arms and shoulders. It was more like a combination of terror and anger than like a sense of loss. During those few moments when it was most intense, the three women of his life merged into a single entity, something which was sister-dead, wife-lost, mother-dead, fading swiftly, leaving him to stand chilled and alone, like a small figure in a barren landscape in an old book.

He came out of it and, as before, found that the spasm had dulled

and slowed his mind. Daylight had a cinematic unreality, and he had
to reconstruct the schedule he had set himself, putting each errand
into its proper place, like stacking tumbled blocks of great weight.

When Sam Boylston returned to the Nassau Harbour Club there
was a message for him to call a Mr. Cooper at a number in Austin.
Yandell Binns Cooper, known throughout the southwest as Stuff
Cooper, father of Carolyn, Bix Kayd's second wife. Sam returned
the call and braced himself for the force and weight of Stuff's imperative personality.

But after the secretaries had put him through, Cooper sounded
vague and mild. And old. "Sam? Sam, boy, I tracked you down
through your office. Is it like all the papers and television got it?"

"I'm afraid it is, Mr. Cooper."

"Damn all! Ever' one of 'em, eh? All the time I was thinking it
was some kind of thing ol' Bix was pulling. Everybody knowed he
was upsot having to let go too much of that Bee-Kay stock a couple
years back. What I figured it for, he wanted to turn up missing so as
some of his people could buy it in cheap. Thursday it had fell off to
eleven something and I picked up some on a hunch. When he calls
me back I know what my broker man is going to tell me, he can't
find any takers noplace. Damn over-the-counter stuff. Sam?"

"I'm here, Mr. Cooper."

"Sam, I can't believe it. I keep on seeing her. She had that special
smile for her daddy. I keep on seeing Carrie the way she was when
they made her queen for that bowl game, way up on the float, all
them flowers, ruffly dress, holding that *booq*uet, a-wavin' and smi-
lin'. It ain't right, boy. You *know* that."

"I know it."

"And that pretty little sister of yours, and those kids of Bix's from
before. I didn't want her to marry Bix. Hell, he's only five years

younger'n her daddy. You know what I wanted, boy. I made it clear enough. When you and Carrie were going together."

"I know. It just didn't work out, Mr. Cooper."

"I keep thinking she'd be alive if they had. You can't blame me for that now. Lydia Jean is as sweet as they come for sure. Maybe a better wife than Carrie would have made you. What she wanted most, I guess, was being the wife of a big man, so she could go in any store and they'd all jump and come running up, rubbing their hands and smiling. I told her one time that was just what she'd get with you. It would mean waiting a little spell, that's all. You've been proving me right, boy. I'm glad for you, but it don't help much right now. You about to head on back?"

"Pretty soon I guess."

"You being a lawyer I guess you can imagine what kind of a mess it's going to be for a long long time. It wasn't just Bix not letting his right hand know what his left hand was doing. He was more like that Hindu gal they got statues of, three or four arms growing out of each shoulder, and not one of them hands knowing what any other of the hands was up to. Everybody connected with him in any business way is plain scrambling right now, like trying to run acrost the front of a landslide. He'd set up his private affairs pretty complicated too, from a couple things Carrie told me. All kind of insurance trusts and residuary trusts and holding corporations and foundations and so on. I bet he covered every possible contingency except a common disaster where him and Carrie and Stella and Roger all passed on at one and the same time. I bet you the state boys and the feds and the lawyers don't get it all unwound for twenty years and more. Sam?"

"Yes sir."

"Nothing I'm doing is going to make much point to me for a time. What do you say, you come on back and we'll set it up to go down there to Yucatan and get those same guides and horses I told you about and see if we can get us a jaguar. Might be Ollie Sloan could be talked into coming along. He's been in sorry shape since his wife died, and you know him pretty good, don't you?"

"Well enough, Mr. Cooper. I'll let you know."

"You do that. And if there's any red tape over there about that accident, anything I can help with, you call me, hear?"

As he hung up he felt sorry for old Stuff Cooper, and he also felt exasperation and an old guilt about Carolyn Cooper. It was one of Stuff's myths that Carolyn and Sam had "gone around together" at the University. Sam had been in his first year of law school and Carolyn had been four years younger, a sophomore. At that time Sam had not met Lydia Jean. Carolyn, her daddy's darling, was vivid, outgoing, arrogant and beautiful, and came complete with white Cadillac convertible, hefty allowance, and an impressive capacity for vodka gibsons. There had been a weekend party at a ranch. At the last moment his date caught a virus and couldn't make it. He went alone. And the party turned into one of those gaudy brawls which provide several years' worth of gossip. After Carolyn's date passed out, she became blankly, blindly, helplessly drunk. Sam was on his way to his car when he came upon two boys hustling the stumbling girl toward the outbuildings. They objected to having their plans changed. It took him four or five minutes to encourage them to see it his way. By then Carolyn was sitting in the grass, hiccuping.

He picked her up and took her to her white convertible, stepping over one of her escorts as he did so. She toppled over and began to snore. He went into the big ranch house and found her purse and the suitcase she'd brought but hadn't unpacked.

He drove her car over two hundred and fifty miles to the Cooper ranch, arriving at first light, stopping inside the gate, a good mile from the ranch house. When she woke up, she looked wanly at him, then scrabbled her way out of the car throwing up down the front of her dress as she did so, then falling to her hands and knees.

At her suggestion he opened a cattle gate and they drove across pasture land to a water hole bordered by a stand of live oaks. He put her suitcase on the hood of the car. He turned his back as she stripped and walked barefoot across the hoof-marked mud and immersed herself in the clear water, holding her dark hair up out of the way as she dunked, scrubbing her face with her free hand, rinsing her mouth. After she came out, he stood with his back toward her still, and told her what had happened and what he had done.

When she told him he could turn around, he found her standing beside the hood of the car and the open suitcase six feet from him. She had made up her face. She was brushing her dark hair, and looking at him in challenge and expectation. She had posed herself in the first red-gold rays of sunrise, standing hip-shot, half turned to the sun so that it glowed against naked thigh and flank and across the faint round of belly, and against the side of one breast, leaving the other in the half shadow of the gray light of morning, nipples rigid with the sensuous stimulus of displaying herself to him.

"Thought you were too meechy-mild to come on man-size, honey," she said, taking slow strokes with the brush. He could hear the crackle of static electricity in her black hair in the windless morning.

"So what are you proving, Carrie?"

"It's what you're up to proving, isn't it? Ol' Stuff keeps saying I should find me a man to steady me down before I get messed up for sure. From what you said, I came too scary close. I've been telling him I want me an older man, somebody making out good, not some boy."

"What makes you think I'm making out so good?"

"Oh, Sam, you haven't got a pee pot, I know, and you're not as far older as what I had in mind, but you'll have the law degree soon, and Stuff can put tons of business your way, and I notice people do what you tell them to do mostly. Maybe you could tell me too and

I'd listen. It's what I need, I know. Not some boy with the only thing on his mind getting it day and night. Maybe it's my time right now, and you came along just right—for the both of us."

Leaning against the car boot, looking at her, he had thought of how it would be to marry Yandell Binns Cooper's darlin' girl. He would get the law work from Cooper and his whole crowd eventually. Title work and land grants and water rights. Ranch tax work, and mineral rights, and options on sections, and grazing rights. It would lock him into a secondary power structure, and he might work up to a hundred thousand a year gross, but he would be one of Stuff Cooper's hired hands, and Stuff's sons would get the land, because that was the feudal way of doing it.

She turned toward him with a half smile, and tossed the brush into the suitcase and said, "The only way I can make out is after being looked at. So it's like two birds with one stone, Sammy. You get to know if the deal is worth it, the looking and the rest too, and you must have seen that old pink puff quilt in the trunk when you taken my suitcase out, then we'll get Concita to fix us up a breakfast like you never saw before, and tell Daddy-Stuff when he comes downstairs his worries are done."

"Better put your clothes on, honey."

"Nobody'll come by here."

"Get dressed, Carrie."

"Me being sick like that put you off? I feel real good now, Sammy. Think of it like it's a reward for you saving me like you did and getting a good thump under the eye for your troubles. It isn't black yet but it's going to be." She approached and put her hands on his shoulders and tilted her head.

He did not move or touch her. "Get dressed!"

When she swung he leaned back just in time, but a fingertip hit the tip of his nose, stinging it, making his eyes water. She dressed, used a stick to poke her soiled dress into a patch of brush, slammed her suitcase shut and threw it onto the back seat.

At the ranch house Stuff Cooper was already up. His approval of Sam Boylston was immediate and obvious, and Carolyn, to make Sam uncomfortable, hinted to Stuff they had been seeing a lot of each other. When Carolyn went up to bed, Stuff warmed up the Cub and flew Sam back to the house-party and landed on the ranch strip there. It was too early for anyone to be stirring.

As Sam Boylston drove his old car back toward the university, he kept thinking of how she had looked in the first sunlight of the morning, and he thought of that off and on for quite a long time, then had met Lydia Jean and hadn't remembered it again until the invitation to the wedding of Carolyn Cooper and Bixby Kayd had arrived.

There had been a few times when he had wondered if maybe it wouldn't have been better to have grabbed that chance. But after he knew he was doing better than he could have done by marrying Carolyn, he found he felt grateful to her in a strange way. When you make a choice you have to do your damnedest to make certain you did the right thing. You have to make your choice come true. And later he had appreciated how shrewdly the nineteen-year-old girl had gone about it, how sound her instinct had been in judging a man she did not know at all well. She had pretended to be the wanton, and had made him desire her so badly it had bloated his throat, knotted his belly and made his knees feel watery-weak. He had come within a half heartbeat of taking her, and she had so clearly stated the bargain beforehand, he would have honored it had he done so, because he could not permit himself to live with that obvious a flaw in his self-image. The girl had known that about him, had guessed at the severities of his self-disciplines.

He shrugged off the memories of Carolyn, unboxed the duplicate tape recorder he had bought before returning to the Harbour Club, and began listening once more to the tape of the Hilgers and the Barths answering his questions aboard the Docksie III. He found it uncommonly difficult to keep his attention in close and careful focus. It irritated and puzzled him. One of the abilities he had found most useful was the knack of shutting out everything except the task at hand, and never permitting any random thought or distraction to intrude.

And this kind of listening was part of his profession—to listen to the words people said and weigh the nuances, guess at the deletions, evaluate the inconsistencies. Verbal communication was astoundingly inexact. People seldom listen to one another. But the truth was always there in some form, sometimes only a shape seen through layers of mist.

He began tape and stopwatch again, brought himself into a total focus, and began to jot down a log of the portions needing a more careful evaluation. The segments to study were when Dr. Barth, the wiry sunbrowned dentist with the steel-rimmed glasses was answering questions, and where Lulu Hilger, the tall brunette wife of the owner of the cruiser, was speaking. They had been the only ones in the cabin when Staniker had explained what had happened.

When Jonathan Dye knocked at the door, Sam emerged from his work, was instantly aware of hunger and was surprised to see that it was two o'clock in the afternoon.

Jonathan strode about the room full of restless energy and explained that he could make a deal with what seemed to be the right boat and man, if Sam approved.

"His name is Moree. Stanley Moree and he's from Nicholl's Town at the north end of Andros, Sam. He knows the Great Bahama Bank like the back of his hand. He built a boat he could use on the Bank.

It's a sailing catamaran and he can set the rudders up so it draws less than a foot of water. He's got a way to fix a little five-horse Seagull motor on it, and he built in a fresh-water tank too. He's even got a little one-lung gas generator he can start up that'll run a little marine radio. When we find her we might have to get help in a hurry. He says that if I buy the provisions, he'll charge me four pounds a day. Or twenty pounds a week. That's only fifty-six dollars. It's seaworthy. He's brought it over here and taken it back a dozen times. It's here now. And he can leave any time. It's only twenty miles, a little more, from the tip of New Providence to Nicholl's Town and from there we're only twelve or fourteen miles from the Joulter Cays. Some friends I've made here say he's a good man. Is it okay with you, Sam?"

"It's fine with me. I brought some cash along out of the office safe." He went to the closet and took his billfold out of the inside pocket of his jacket, and with his back to the room took four hundred dollars from the amount in the back compartment, hesitated, added another two hundred. He handed the money to Jonathan saying, "I didn't know what I might need it for. Renting a plane or a boat. Something like that."

Jonathan counted it. "This is—quite a lot. Thanks, Sam. I can get some other things I was thinking about. Some more first-aid stuff. And a good pair of binoculars. Some flares. And I want to see if I can find one of those bull-horn things that run off six-volt batteries."

"Take some salt tablets for yourself. And sun lotion. Get a good sleeping bag."

"Stanley Moree is going to phone me here in a few minutes. To find out if it's okay. Then I'm to meet him at the boat in an hour."

"There's some interesting things on this tape. Want to hear them?"

"If you don't mind—I mean, I can't get very interested in what Staniker said or didn't say. It's sort of—after the fact. Sam, could you tell him I'll meet him down at the boat, and everything is all set?"

After Jonathan was gone, Sam Boylston went out onto the small balcony into the sun heat from the air conditioning. He leaned his palms on the cement of the balcony wall. The great clowns, he thought, were great because they could give you a pungent taste of that curious emotion, that fringe emotion where tragedy and comedy overlapped, could make your eyes sting while you guffawed. Jonathan, in his tall bony, sallowed, half-clumsy toughness, in all his earnestness and his self-delusion, would glide through the crystalline Kodachrome shallows in the homemade catamaran, lift the bull horn to sun-cracked lips and send that forlorn electronic bray across the nubbins of sand and rock and weed, startling the crabs and the sea birds. LEILA LEILA LEILA.

He looked over at a group of young people at tables on the far apron of the pool. They were locals, children of people with memberships. These were sailboat people, race-week people, sports-car people, raised in the big and gracious old homes which faced the sea. Colonial British, raised among such a flood tide of tourism they accepted it as that sort of inconvenience one puts up with without rancor or particular attention—as Arab children accept the flies in the marketplace. He heard a girl laugh, and her voice had the extraordinary clarity and timbre peculiar to the English woman, and he singled her out as she walked toward the pool, a limber young thing, red-gold tan, sunbaked hair, brief dusty-pink swim suit, looking back to laugh again at her group. A boy got up to follow her and swim with her, a young man muscled and poised, totally assured of himself and of his place within his world. He was older than the others, the same age as Jonathan perhaps. Sam realized that in some past existence he had wanted, for Leila, some Texan counterpart of such a young man. Now, with a sudden feeling of revulsion, he saw how such a one would take the news of the sinking of the Muñeca.

Pain and grief, of course. But a manly acceptance, tinged with a certain subconscious unadmitted pleasure in the martyr role, the public image to sustain of having loved and lost. "Damned shame, sir. Bad show."

Far better the grotesquerie of disbelief, the absurd search, Don Quixote with bull horn and Japanese binoculars, peering and braying across the ten-thousand-year silence of the shallow Bank, giving not a damn for image, for impression, for status of any kind.

And I care too much, he thought. So much that I blush for a kind of madness I should cherish. So much I have pressured them all—Leila, Lydia Jean, Boy-Sam—trying to turn them into Carolyn Coopers and fellows full of sleek and watchful assurance . . . .

The room phone rang and he went in, closing the glass door, to tell Stanley Moree he had a firm contract and Jonathan would join him at the boat. He then ordered food to be brought up to the room. After he had eaten, he listened again to Lulu Hilger's voice in a sequence which interested him.

"I was watching over him. Bill and Bert were topside. Francie had been with me, but it made her too nervous watching him. And there was an unpleasant smell where the burns on his arm were infected, even after Bill Barth had dressed them, and Francie is always just a little queasy when she stays below in any kind of a sea. It never bothers me.

"He was sleeping, but he would thrash around sometimes and groan and mumble. Bill took his temperature before, and it was over a hundred and two. And his pulse was very fast. I wondered if he was getting more fever. I was sitting on the foot of the bunk. I leaned way over and hitched closer and put the back of my hand against his forehead. He gave kind of a convulsive jump and grabbed my arm just above the elbow. He sat right up, staring at me and breathing hard. I can't remember exactly what he said. He had terrible strength in his hand. I think I almost fainted from the pain.

See? I'll have these bruises for weeks. He called me Christy. He seemed to be pleading with me to understand something. And like he was almost in tears about it. He was saying something like, 'It wasn't that way! You've got to understand that, Christy. You've got to help me. You've got to.' He seemed terribly agitated. Then he slumped back suddenly, letting go of me. He was breathing very deeply and very fast. His eyes were closed. His face was covered with beads of sweat.

"I had some lavender-flavored rubbing alcohol, and I sopped a little hand towel with it and swabbed his face off, keeping it away from his eyes. His breathing slowed down. Then he opened his eyes and he was himself and he knew who I was. I asked him who I was. I said he'd called me Christy."

"What was his reaction to that, Mrs. Hilger?"

"I guess it scared him to know he'd been out of his head. It would scare anybod—"

"No. I mean exactly what did he do and say?"

"At first he didn't say anything. He closed his eyes. He pushed my hand away from his face. Not roughly. Just slowly and gently. Then he asked what he'd said. I said he was trying to make Christy understand something and he was asking her for help. I said that people in delirium don't make sense. I said he was just a little wilder this time."

"And there was a special reaction then?"

"I don't know what you mean by special, Mr. Boylston. He seemed surprised. 'This time?' is what he said, lifting his head off the pillow. I told him that the other times he was just moaning and thrashing and mumbling."

"How soon after that did he go into convulsions?"

"It wasn't long after that. Four minutes. Five. It scared me half to death. I thought he was dying. I know what I should have done, but I didn't know it then. You're supposed to wedge something across their teeth, as far back as you can get it, so they won't chew their tongue to ribbons. I ran and yelled to Bill and he came hurrying down. By then Captain Staniker was quiet again. Asleep or unconscious. He was like that without any change when they took him off and put him in the ambulance."

He put the tape on fast wind, all the voices sounding like a nest of agitated mice, and, with a couple of pushes on the rewind button, located the resonant and antagonistic baritone of Bert Hilger, plumbing contractor and owner of the Chris-Craft named Docksie. He numbered himself among the boat-people. Sam Boylston was an outsider. A batch of boat-people had been lost at sea, and he resented technical questions from someone who did not know the bilge from the binnacle, yet was compelled to answer because of the familiar gratification of imparting expertise.

"Check and check and check again," he said. "You stay healthy if you don't depend on the gadgets, Boylston. You mistrust them every minute. Duplicate everything and check the gadgets against each other. I run on gas, so I got two sniffers in the bilge, independent of each other. But before I make a run I still crawl down there and hold a cup with a few drops of gas in it next to the probes to make sure the buzzers and blinkers work on both of them. I'm wired for separate electric on both engines, independent fuel supply, and I watch fuel consumption, battery levels, rate of charge like an eagle. I check the compasses against each other and against the charts. I got two big hooks rigged so I can drop them fast if I get into trouble. I listen to every piece of weather I can find on the dial. I carry spare wheels and a wheel puller. Hell, things have gone wrong. Things always go wrong. But if you don't trust anything, you don't get into bad trouble. When the sea is building, you'll find the Docksie in a protected anchorage with all the water and supplies we need to wait it out."

"Then you think the Muñeca *should* have had a detection device for gas fumes."

"The question doesn't mean anything. She was diesel. If I was diesel and had a gasoline generator and gas cans of fuel for it below decks, I would have had a sniffer. Some perfectly sound boat owners I know wouldn't have. Most of them, maybe. It's how careful you want to be."

"Suppose Staniker was at anchor and wanted to turn on the generator."

"Then without even thinking about it he would have opened some hatches and run the blower first. He wasn't some Kansas clown on his first cruise, you know. He was running, and when you're running you don't think of any accumulation of fumes in the bilge, not with a diesel, because you've got air movement through the bilge. You pick it up with a bow ventilator arrangement and it runs through and comes out somewhere near your transom. But the way I see it, he ran into a freak situation. He had a following wind and sea at about the same knots he was making. So he was running with dead air below. It wasn't moving."

"And the explosion that blew him into the water could have ignited his diesel fuel?"

"I wouldn't know about that. As I understand it, compression creates heat, and I've seen some of those custom jobs they make for heavy duty work up there in North Carolina. They're solid. Any fuel has a flash point. Put enough heat on it all of a sudden, and it will go. And if it did, the only place anybody would have a chance would be if they were on the fly bridge. And even then you'd get seared pretty good, the way he did."

"Does it seem odd to you that no other boat saw the fire?"

"Why should it? Let me show you on the chart here. He was north of Andros according to the approximate position he gave me, up beyond North Goulding Cays far enough so no one would see him from Morgan's Bluff, Nicholl's Town or Mastic Point. He was moving in toward coral head areas, and it was night, and nobody who didn't know how to sneak through there, as he did, would be well clear of it, way out in this area, far enough away so they'd see a glow, but if they did, the normal guess would be some kind of fire on shore."

"Mr. Hilger, could you show me a few other places on this chart where it would be the same sort of situation, I mean where a fire at sea would attract so little attention?"

"Well—let me see now. Mmmm. No. I guess you could say that was another part of the way his luck was running. When your luck goes bad on the water it seems to go bad in every possible way."

"And it would be deep water there they tell me."

"It's the Tongue of the Ocean, Boylston, and it comes in pretty close to the eastern shore of Andros. It's a steep one. Within a hundred yards, say you're heading east, you can go from forty feet of water to six thousand. That's why they've got that experimental base at Fresh Creek on anti-submarine warfare. That's down the coast of Andros, about forty miles south-southeast of the Joulters."

"Thank you ver—"

He thumbed the button that took it off playback, then pressed the rewind button. He put the reel back into the original box and put it into the drawer in the bedside stand. He loaded a new reel on the recorder, and put the little machine into the side pocket of his jacket as he left.

It was almost five thirty when Theyma Chappie admitted Sam to the tidy little apartment in the Harbour Heights development. She had been home from the hospital long enough to shower and change. Her dark hair was undone, ribbon-tied, spilling down her slender back. The ends of it were damp, and she smelled of flower perfume and soap. She wore a sleeveless rose-pink knit shift in a coarse soft weave, gathered at the waist with a narrow belt of the same material, flat white sandals with gold thongs. Her mouth was made up a little more abundantly than in the morning. She had a warmer, livelier look.

He accepted her offer of a drink and said he would take whatever she was having. It was gin and fresh fruit juices in large weighty old-fashioned glasses with a sprig of fresh mint. He sat on a severe couch upholstered in pale gray fabric. Under the glass top of the coffee table in front of him was a display of exotic seashells. She sat on a low footstool on the other side of the table, arms wrapped around her knees, and in reply to his question, she gestured with a tilt of her head toward the recorder, the one she had taken to the hospital and brought back. "Oh, it was a most easy thing. But I was frightened all the time it was there. You can see. Most of the tape is used up. He was much better today. Except for the speaking. His tongue is swollen and bruised. It is painful for him to talk or eat. He must speak carefully. But they did question him today. Dr. McGregory permitted it. The fever is gone. Sub-normal, actually. Pulse slow and strong. No rales in the chest. But these things can turn bad quickly."

"How much questioning?"

"I would say forty minutes this morning. And almost an hour later in the day."

"Officials?"

"Yes. I could not say who. The head nurse brought them and asked me to leave."

"Did any newspaper people interview him?"

"Oh no! And they are eager ones, I tell you. All manner of sly tricks. Oh, I say I could have made very much money today, to help some of them sneak into the room. Or to ask the Captain some question and then tell someone what he answered. One of them offered me five pounds to take a little camera in and take a picture of him. Stay five feet from him, the man said. Look through here. Push this little button. Bring the camera back to me. The flash bulb is all

ready." She frowned. "When I said I could not do such things, all
the time I knew what I had hidden near the bed behind the towels."

"It isn't the same, Nurse."

"Best you keep telling me that, Mr. Boylston."

"If there was any trouble about it, I guess Sir Willis could inter-
cede for you."

She made a face, took deep swallows of her drink. "My brother
asked this. I think we may leave Sir Willis out of it. The great man
would not bother his head. You know? It would offend him, I think,
to be asked to help such an unimportant little female person. He
would say, Oh my God, what will they ask of me next? And he
would worry about what all his important friends might think if
he came to the rescue of . . ." She stopped quite suddenly and gave
him a look of challenge he could not interpret. "It does not matter.
One learns to look after oneself, yes?"

"What's the matter?"

"Is something the matter?"

"All of a sudden you ducked behind a wall."

She pondered that, then smiled. "I rather like that. Yes. I went
behind my wall. Perhaps I forgot my place for just one little moment. Sir Willis is Bay Street. And so are you. A Bay Street in Texas.
You have the look." She pressed her fingertips to her cheek. "I heard
what it is called there, I think. A touch of the tar brush? Perhaps it is
uglier there than here. But ugly here, too. At least here we are not
something one lays with to change one's luck."

"I reckon we've got our share of people who like to suffer on account of the color God happened to be handing out at the time."

"Ah. Cowboy talk! It is beautiful! I have made you angry. Why
should you be angry? I am doing you a favor. I am giving you a very
nice drink. Who are you to get angry if I say the world happens to
be round?"

"What gives you the right to classify me?"

"Ho! So back there in your Bay Street of Texas, you are some bold crusader, yes? And so you go rushing out from your big office to defend some poor nigger girl because she has this so touching confidence in you, yes? Ah, you are a very valuable fellow!"

He stood up quickly with his drink and went and stood at the windows, staring out, eyes unfocused, at the distant vista of Nassau harbor. She came and deftly took his empty glass from his hand. She rattled ice in the small kitchen, brought him a new drink.

"Is the world round, Mr. Boylston?"

"Sam. It is very damned round."

"I am Theyma, Sam. And it is too bad it is so damned round I think."

"My wife left me over five months ago, Theyma. Not for another man, or because I was mixed up with another woman. Nothing like that. I seem to be a little less than her ideal. One of the things she threw at me surprised me. About a year ago the brother of a woman who worked for us got into a cutting scrape down in Brownsville. The woman's name is Rosalie. Short, dark, plump, cheerful, not too much English. She's Mexican-American. She asked me to defend her brother. I did the sensible thing. A lawyer in Brownsville owed me a favor. He does a lot of that kind of work. I asked him to take the case. The brother got off with ninety days, which was pretty good, considering. Rosalie acted huffy about it. When my wife left me she said that was one of the times I let her down, when I let Rosalie down. I said I wasn't that kind of a lawyer. She said there were apparently only two kinds of lawyers. I thought it was a lot of romantic idiocy. Until you shook me up, Miss Theyma."

"Have you lost her for good?"

"I don't know. I hope not. I miss her, and I miss the kid. He's five now. I can't let myself think she's gone for good. This is a stronger drink."

"It seemed like a good time for the drinks to be stronger."

"I was wrong about Rosalie's brother?"

"If she trusted you, yes. It is a matter of honor, of her being part of your family. If you appeared in court and he went away for a year, she could still be proud."

He turned toward her, smiling, and said, "Miss Theyma, why does so much of the round, round world make so damned little sense?"

And as he tried to keep the tone light, to his dismay he felt his eyes filling with tears. He tried to hide it by finishing his drink. But when he lowered the glass, she took it from him and set it aside and took his hands in hers and stood, head tilted, looking at him in a troubled way.

"I did not mean to hurt you, Sam."

"I don't know what the hell is wrong with me!"

"Sam, I was being naughty. That is all. To give you—what is it?—needles. I did not mean to hurt. To hell with the roundness of the world, Texas Sam."

"Okay."

She studied him. "You know what I think about you? You are a very severe man. Very strong, very rigid, very honest in your own fashion. Too much is happening for you now. The loneliness of no wife and boy. The pain of the sister. Hatred for that Captain. Be careful, Mister Sam. A man can break, and he can do mad things and spoil everything forever."

The directness of her sympathy made his eyes begin to smart again, and in a clumsy and unexpected way of hiding his face from her, he took her into his arms. She stood rigidly, but without protest, and he had the feeling she had stopped breathing. Then her arms slipped around him. She inhaled tremulously, pressed the warm wiry slender strength of her body against his, her fingers prodding into the muscles of his back, rolling and twisting her hips against him, nipples suddenly hard as little pebbles against his chest, through fabric. As he felt the planes of her slender back, the small ripeness of her hips, he inhaled in her crisp hair and soft throat an incongruous scent from childhood, suddenly recognizing it as the smell of vanilla Necco wafers. As he searched for her mouth, she suddenly gasped, thrust at him, wrenched herself away, ran to the couch and sat on the very edge of it, head bowed, back deeply curved, fists on her tawny knees, breathing audibly.

He went to her, touched her shoulder. She reached up and put her hand over his. "Sorry," she breathed. "Sorry."

"My fault."

She stood up, gave him a wan smile and went off to her bathroom. It was a full five minutes before she came back, in full possession of herself.

"Sam, there are too many ways a thing can go wrong, I think."

"How do you mean?"

"You must know how naughty I really was. You were very attractive to me. The look of you and how you move, and the color of your eyes. I thought it would be a very pleasant matter, you know? This pretty shift, and nice drinks, and then I would challenge you in some small ways so you would notice me as I am, and then we would take the challenges to bed and turn them into good sport. See? I have no shame. To arrange a thing so coldly, I can do it only if the attraction is strong and if—it can be—unimportant. So we spoiled it."

"Did we?"

"Of course! I have concern for you, Sam. Too, too quickly we have some meaning for each other. The chance to be casual is gone. I cannot risk anything that would be more than that. Or would you." She grinned. "In your marvelous language, who needs it? Now please put a new tape in your little machine and go away, my dear Sam, before we become damn fools and forget how round the world is."

Thirteen

ON TUESDAY AFTERNOON Staniker was awakened from his nap by the muted clacking of the slats of the blinds as his day nurse opened them. Just outside the window was a vivid bough of bougainvillaea, the sun lighting the petals from behind, turning them to hot flame.

He lay with lids half closed, idly watching her do other small housekeeping chores around the room. With a remoteness and objectivity alien to him he noted that she moved well, with a high-tailed, saucy, frisky, promising look. It was a flavor he had always appreciated in a young woman, and over the years he had come to learn that more often than not, it indicated a considerable amount of sexual energy.

Nurse Chappie stopped and made a frowning inventory of the room, to see, apparently, if anything had been overlooked, and as she did so, she fingered her slender, tea-tan throat . . . .

Throat! He closed his eyes. He had a new image of what the

inside of his head was like. It was a smaller place than ever before. It had dwindled because he had been forced to erect a square framework inside it from which he suspended a heavy fabric hanging from ceiling to floor on all four sides. He had dragged all harmless things into the lighted area, that cube wherein he sat. But things stirred in the darkness beyond the fabric. They could be summoned by a certain kind of thought, and then the shape of them would begin to bulge inward against the fabric, and you knew that if it kept up, they would come crawling under the fabric from out of the unspeakable blackness. So you gave your thoughts a quick twist and aimed them in a safe direction, and the things would quiet down and the fabric would once again hang quite motionless. When danger was over you could take deep breaths, unclench your belly muscles, and let your eyes open.

He had escaped them this time by aiming his thoughts at the motor sailer he was going to buy. It would be like the one he had seen last year in Miami, up for sale because the owner was ill. Teak and mahogany hull built in Hong Kong, and then glassed and finished and rigged in Sweden. The diesels and electronics and navigation aids had been mounted aboard in Germany. A blue water sailer, with power winches, enormous fuel and water tanks, big generators, freezers, air conditioning.

He walked her decks and, young again, he stood at the wheel balanced against the easy movement of her, outward bound from Wellington to the Loyalty Islands, and sprawled atop the trunk cabin, bikinied and sun-drowsy, but smiling at him with a happy and grateful warmth, was one of those superb and vital New Zealand girls, a truly great one, greater than the very best of all the ones he could remember. A great vessel and a great grinding girl, and all the money packed into the barrel safe so carefully hidden down below it was no worry at all to him.

When Mary Jane got a look at that money, she'd . . .

It took a violent twist to turn swiftly enough into a new direction because that had made a great stir behind the fabric.

"You slept well, Captain?" the nurse said, not knowing how helpful it was to have her speak at that moment.

"All I seem to do is sleep," he said.

"Ah, you speak much better now," she said, leaning to slip the thermometer under his swollen tongue. She laid the pads of her fingers against his big wrist, and, frowning, watched the sweep second hand of the gold watch pinned to her white nylon bodice as she counted.

After she had put the thermometer back in alcohol and was marking his chart he said, "I'm expected to live?"

Her smile was quick and bright. "You are not actually in a dying condition, mon. Now you must have water again."

"How many gallons will that make?"

"Dr. McGregory says we can stop keeping track of the fluid balance now. He's satisfied there's no kidney damage. Here. Drink this now, and then you may go on a journey. With some help. All the way to the water closet."

When he was seated on the edge of the bed, in the short gown, she worked his left arm into the sleeve of the robe, then hung it lightly over the shoulder on the burned side. She helped him up with a considerable wiry strength, and, from his left side, her right arm around his waist, his left arm heavy across her narrow shoulders, she walked him in small steps to the private bathroom about eight feet from the bed. She left the door ajar, saying, "If there is any faintness or dizziness, Captain, call out. And do not forget the specimen. The bottle is there on the shelf over the lavatory."

He was again astonished at how weak and how frail he felt. Better than yesterday, at least. So better than this tomorrow. When he came out, she helped him to the armchair and, after she had finished making his bed up, helped him into bed and took away his robe and hung it in the shallow closet. She went off with the sample to deliver it to the lab, and when she returned, young Dr. Angus McGregory was with her. He was sunburned and portly, with a ginger-gold moustache of RAF impressiveness.

He nodded at Staniker, studied the chart, jotted some new instructions on it. "Confirms what Nurse Chappie here tells me. Grotesquely healthy, Captain. An affront to my profession. So let's have a look at the arm first. Nurse?"

They had him straighten his right arm. She held it in one hand by the unburned fingers and helped McGregory unwind the overlapping gauze. Staniker looked at the outside of his right arm as it was exposed and felt his stomach dip. The whole arm had a strange blue-gray sheen. It looked dead. He expected a grunt of alarm from the doctor.

Instead McGregory said, "Marvelously ugly, what? New spray technique. Porous enough to let air in, but it won't let fluid out. Sulfa derivative in it. Otherwise inert. And one can see through the bloody thing to see how you're mending. It'll dissolve as new skin forms, hopefully at about the same rate. Leaves less of the typical burn scar, that shiny puckery look."

He leaned closer to study it inch by inch. "Very, very good! Oh, you'll have scar enough, dear fellow. We had to snip away quite a bit of bad meat, but very little muscle tissue. No functional impairment. What you must do, Captain, is keep working and flexing the arm. Not vigorously. Same with the leg. It will slow the healing at the joints somewhat, and hurt a bit, but you'll maintain a better muscle tone and the skin won't draw tight on you at the joints. Now let's have a look at that right thigh and calf, Nurse."

After they were through, McGregory said, "Those types tire you this morning?"

"Not too bad."

"They should be the last of the official lot. The insurance wallahs wanted a go at you this afternoon, but I said absolutely no. Tomorrow morning should be better. Then by Thursday it will be up to you who you care to see, if there's no hitch in the way you're coming along, Staniker. Press people. Magazine people. And a very odd little telly batch from Miami with monstrous lights and cables and such. But I could give you a word of advice on all that."

"I would appreciate it, Doctor."

McGregory gave the nurse a meaningful glance. She nodded and left the room. McGregory lighted a cigar little larger than a cigarette and sat in the armchair. "None of my affair, I suppose. But were I you, I would give a bit of thought to number one, eh? Work in your line might be hard to come by for a time. Reason I know of the situation, a chum of mine got innocently involved in the Profumo mess. Buggered his income for a time. But he had the wits to sell his exclusive story. Chain of newspapers. They put a writer fellow on him to shine it up. Made a handsome package out of it. Eight hundred pounds if I remember. Actually, poor Harold didn't have much to tell. Been pronging one of those wenches and had the bad luck to get bashed about by her dark-hued chum. But the bits he did know, he kept to himself so as to have something to peddle to the papers. Painful to you, perhaps, but all the little clerks and shop girls would want to read the Captain's personal story of the last cruise of the Muñeca. And you are, you know, under no obligation to give your story away to those clots who are so anxious to get in here to see you. Oh, they'll tell you one must speak to the press. That one has to. Lot of bloody nonsense. More you tell them, the less you can sell the rest for. So among the rabble are a few chaps with contracts in their pockets. Were I you, Captain, I'd make every one of those people send up a note about what they want of you. I'd weed out the ones with an idea of paying for an exclusive story, and see them one at a time, get their names and addresses, sign nothing, and when you get back to Florida find some nimble chap to represent you. There is no hurry. My word! Texas millionaire, beauty queen, yacht, tropical islands, castaway—the story should intrigue the masses for years and years. And I fancy your picture would not hurt the female readership level one bit. As I said, none of my business. To give you an idea. One bloody fool offered *me* fifty pounds to give an exclusive story about *you*. And Nurse Chappie has been under pressure also. But she is a sound one. Very sound indeed."

"I'm grateful to you, Doctor. I really am."

"We can protect you long as you're here. But of course the moment you're released, they'll swarm upon you like May flies."

"When do you plan to release me?"

"To decide, I must know if there is someone to look after you for a bit. Your wife is gone, I know. Would there be a relative, a close friend, someone to take you back to Florida?"

"I'm sorry."

"I won't be held to it, understand. But if you have to do for yourself, I should guess I might let you go a week today. A good thing your Mr. Kayd carried such splendid insurance. I see no reason also why we cannot keep your day nurse on until we let you go. She'll keep the pests away from you. I've canceled the midnight to eight one, and after today I see no need for the four to midnight lassie."

"I haven't even got clothes I can wear out of here."

"The marine insurance fellow could give you a bit for that I should think. And Nurse Chappie could do a spot of shopping. If they are paying for your flight back, they can't expect you to board a BOAC affiliate naked as an egg, now can they?"

"You're very helpful, Doctor."

"Nervous twitch. Typical of the trade, I expect. Probably why we get into it in the first place. I might get carried away if you can't work something out with the assurance company, and advance you a few pounds myself. You could send it back when they've arranged for the pay you have coming."

"There's money in a savings account in Miami but it's in my wife's name. And there's a small policy on her life. So if I have to ask you, I can send it back as soon as I—arrange everything."

McGregory stood up, rubbed his cigar out on the sole of his shoe and dropped it into the white wastebasket. "You're a hardy one, Staniker. Good thing. Few men could have survived the effects of that week on the island, much less come out of it with no complications. I'll stop by and have another look in the morning."

After he had been gone ten minutes, the slender nurse came back in and told him the choices for the evening meal and helped him decide. She was past her usual time of leaving. She said the other special nurse was in the hospital and would be along shortly. She rolled the night stand around and tidied it, adding to the stack of face towels. With her purse clamped under her arm she stood by him, ran the backs of her fingers along the line of his jaw.

"Tomorrow, Captain, you will have to shave yourself. A blessing, I suppose. I am not very good at it."

"Nobody is very good with a dull razor, Nurse."

"I shall even buy a blade for it."

She was standing at the left side of his bed. He reached and put his left hand on her waist, thumb and first finger clasping the narrowest part of it, hip socket fitting the palm of his hand, the other three fingers splayed against the swell of roundness of her hip.

For an instant she stood absolutely motionless. He felt a faint tremor and then she jumped back far too violently, something oddly like terror on her face.

"Come on, now," he said. "It isn't that serious, is it?"

"It—startled me. That is all." She moistened her lips. Her smile was quick and unconvincing. "It proves you are recovering, Captain."

• • •

In the evening, after he had eaten, he thought again of how she had reacted. As if brought suddenly face to face with a monster. But it could not mean anything. She was of a certain type. That's all it meant. They look knowing. They have saucy little hips, sharp little breasts. Their eyes are incurably flirtatious. But the slightest touch panics them. Her reaction was far less distressing to him than his own. He had touched her deliberately, coldly, experimentally, hoping that the girl-feel of her, the flesh-warmth under nylon, the rounded meaning of the young waist and hip would awaken him. In all his life, ever since puberty, except during those brief times when he had achieved total sexual exhaustion, he had not been able to look upon a woman who had even the slightest trace of physical desirability without being aware, in an absent-minded way, of his own physiological changes, a sense of heaviness, a slight swelling of the neck and hardening of the shoulder muscles, an impulse to yawn, the very slight beginnings of tumidity. Yet even when she had walked him, her arm around his waist, his arm across her shoulders, in spite of her warmth, scents, desirability, there was no reaction at all to her. He could have been made of cold bread dough. He had hoped the deliberate caress would restir the familiar heats. But he could have as well been resting his hand against a palm bole or a traffic sign.

It's something about the burns, perhaps the medication. Or having so much fever. It had been the same as always during those long days aboard the Muñeca, and at the anchorages. Nothing wrong then. Carolyn Kayd had known just what she could do to him, passing him in the narrow areas of the boat, swaying that muscular butt just enough to give him a solid thud with her hip when they were opposite each other, then excusing herself with such a laughing innocence.

. . . but then slack and loose as a bag of butter, moving with the roll of the dead boat as he looped the length of quarter inch nylon

line around her and threaded it through the lift ring of the hatch
cover, snugged her down there so tight, made her so fast that the line
dug into the softness of her waist and . . .

"Nurse!"

"Captain, what is wrong? What is wrong?"

"Could—I have a drink of water, please?"

"Of course, sir."

And he realized that he had just gone through the worst of it. It
could not happen again, not that dangerously. The dark movements
beyond the four walls of fabric had been unbearable because of the
weakness. He felt thankful. It reminded him of a time when, in Key
West, with a hurricane coming, a drunken hand off a shrimper
which had put in for shelter backed him slowly into a corner of a
bar, holding the knife blade low, with that slight professional upward tilt which seeks the belly. All sound in the bar had stopped,
and then he had seen in the man's eyes an inability to use a knife on
living flesh. It was the same kind of relief and gratitude, awareness
of the narrowness of the escape. He had sidestepped, chopped down
at the wrist as he hammered at the face. He had kicked the knife into
a corner, snapped the wrist bone, and had been with the shrimper's
woman through the twenty-hour scream of the wind of the hurricane which had missed the town by a narrow margin, the eye passing twenty miles south, heading for Texas.

Now, in the center of his mind, he was able to bestir himself,
stand up and stretch, walk about, anticipate the task of taking down
the frame and the fabric. He knew the names of the black things out
there, and he could let them in, one at a time, and tame them. They
were called Throat, and Fan Motor, and Head Nodding. Once
tamed they would begin to blur, and some day they would be difficult to recall.

He closed his eyes and once again he examined one of the objects
he had dragged into the safe area. Suitcase of medium size, aluminum

in a dull finish, ribbed for greater strength. Trade name—Haliburton. Good gear for the heat and damp of tropic cruising. The catches were designed to exert enough leverage on the double rubber seal inside the lip to make the suitcase airtight. The fourth key he had tried had fit the stowage locker. The second little brass key fit the suitcase. It all rested in there in such orderliness, such dignity. Official paper belts around the middle of each packet. There were two rows of stacks of the packets, six in each row, arranged vertically, across the long dimension of the case. To fill the additional width there were three stacks of packets placed end to end. Fifteen stacks of banded money, to a depth that filled the case to about two thirds of its depth.

The amount in each packet was imprinted on some of the bands, rubber-stamped upon others. The top layer of packets was made up of packets of fifties and packets of hundreds only. On the hundreds the band said $10,000. The other bands were marked $5,000.

In the dim yellow-orange of the stateroom light, it had a look of remoteness, impartiality, indifferent dignity. It was like cathedrals, like long gleaming conference tables, like the crackling, hissing recordings of the voices of famous men long dead. Until he had opened the lid, he was not entirely convinced she had been right about it. The top layer was level, indicating the same number of packets in each stack. He pulled a stack free. Seven packets. He pressed it back into place, closed the case, fastened the pressure latches, carried it topside, lurching, banging it against the bulkhead as the dead vessel rocked in the trough.

In memory he jumped ahead to that moment when, in the shadows of rusty iron, he had finished burying it deep in the dryness of the drifted sand, and with great care had smoothed and swept and patted the surface until he could see no trace of his efforts.

Only much later, two days or three, he had fought the pain of the burns and the illusions of the fever by trying to estimate if there was

as much there as she had said there would be. The fact of two de-
nominations made it difficult to figure it out. Finally, scratching on
the dirt with a twig, he figured out what would be in the case if
every wrapped bundle contained only fifties. No matter how carefully he worked the arithmetic out, it came to $525,000.00. But at
least half the top layer had been bundles of hundreds.

Finally his fever-dazed brain found a possible answer. On the
bottoms of the other stacks there would be bundles of twenties and
tens. And it had been merely accident that the stack he had examined had been made up of all fifties and hundreds. He decided the
sensible thing to do was go up, dig it up, count it all—when the sun
was lower, and when the pain wasn't so bad.

The nurse told him it was time to go to sleep. She tried to help
him to the bathroom. He said he could manage. She hovered close to
him. When he came out she had cranked the bed down, plumped
the pillow, tidied the bedding and turned it back into that cool and
exact triangle shape of hospital welcome. She reminded him that
after midnight, until eight when Nurse Chappie would be back on
duty, he would have no special nurse. She pinned the call button to
the sheet near the pillow. She took pulse and temperature, gave him
the mild nightly barbiturate. She said goodby to him, saying that she
had been taken off the case beginning tomorrow. He thanked her.
When she settled herself into the armchair, the only light in the
room was the cone of her reading lamp shining down on her knitting. The wool was pale gray. The needles ticked as steadily as a
clock, and he heard from afar the long hollow mournful whonk of
a large vessel signaling as it left Nassau harbor.

Fourteen

CORPO HAD PROPPED her up on the narrow bed, almost to a sitting position. He had put his best white shirt on her, folded a blue bandanna diagonally, knotted it around her small waist as a belt, folded the cuffs of the shirt back until they were at her wrists. He had combed her hair in a way that looked quite good to him, gently fashioning it over the shaved and bandaged place.

He had cleaned up several areas of the littered room, stacking the things in boxes he had saved. On an upended crate beside the bed were some of the brilliant red blossoms of flowering air plants in a small glass jar.

He could not tire of looking at her. Her eyes were sea green, with little flecks of amber near the pupils, her skin flawless where it was neither burned nor bruised nor abraded. He liked to lean close and look at those eyes, and the way the little dark lashes curled, and the way the pale hair of the eyebrows was laid so neatly and cleverly, the blonde head hair springing so vitally from the white scalp where the curve of the gentle forehead ended. She had small even teeth, a narrow upper lip and a full protruding lower lip, and a small cleft in her chin. All the neatness of the way she was made reminded him of birds he had picked up, freshly killed, the feather patterns and the down of the soft underside.

He sat on the broken chair near the foot of the bed and admired her. She went on and on and on, in a light sweet breathless voice, her expressions changing often. She was by far the prettiest thing he had ever seen.

"And you sure are a talker, Missy. You sure do go on and on."

He could not understand much of it. Sometimes the words didn't fit together in any way that would make sense. It didn't seem to matter whether he was there or not if she felt talky. She talked to a lot of different people. Sometimes she'd seem to be talking right to him, but when he moved off to the side she'd keep talking to the place where he'd been. She'd doze off. Sometimes it would be a good heavy sleep. Other times she'd toss and twitch and whine. She'd get all sweaty, and he'd wipe her face off.

He liked it when she'd laugh. It would make him smile and sometimes laugh with her. She had a lot of different kinds of laughing. Sometimes like a tea party, and sometimes teasing, and sometimes a real belly-buster, deep and hearty for such a little mite of a thing.

It began to seem to him as if he was getting to know the folks she was talking to. She'd wait and listen to them answer, and she'd nod, and he'd find himself straining to hear what they were saying to Missy. There was Stel and Roger and Mister Bix and Carrie. Then there was Captain Stan and Captain Staniker which could be the same one. There was a Mary Jane, and Jonathan and Sam, and other people she didn't say often enough for him to remember.

Sometimes when she was talking real clear and straight, he would put his hands on her shoulders and give her a little shake and say, "What's *your* name, Missy. What do these folks call *you?*"

But she would keep carrying on as if she hadn't understood a word. She talked about fish and reefs, and whether she ought to go back to the Island Shop and buy that blue sweater. A couple of times she just sat there and cried, not making much noise about it, but he just couldn't stand it and he had to get out of there because it like to broke his heart hearing it. He went down to clean some fish and in a little bit he heard her tea party laugh a couple of times. He shook his head in wonder, and decided he'd boil her up a nice thick fish chowder for her supper.

Once he got angry enough to try to join in. Missy was talking in a whispery little voice to the one called Stel, trying to get Stel to stop crying. He figured it out from what she said that Stel had a game leg, and the one named Carrie was being mean to her. Missy didn't seem to care much for Carrie either. So he said it was a pretty sorry person that'd pick on a little gimpy gal, but Missy went right on without hearing a word, and it all turned into nonsense words and she fell asleep all at once, leaving him with the idea that it was a good thing Captain Stan was being especially nice to that Stel, because she sounded like somebody who could use friends.

It tired his head trying to sort out all those people. And he was beginning to feel impatient with her for not getting better faster. Those heavy sweats and the moaning in the sleep made him nervous.

He had the uneasy idea he ought to go right on over to town and get the Lieutenant. But then they'd put her into the hospital. But hospitals had that funny thing about what to do when your head was hurt. They might never let Missy go. There was another thing too. The Lieutenant might get upset about the girl being there on the island with him all this time. And the people in those candy houses over there would get real puckered about it, and get dirty ideas. No use trying to explain to them there'd been just that one little slip, and he was sorry it happened, his hand just reaching out that way for a little feel of that pretty, dainty, little titty. If that hand got away from him again, he was going to go down and lay it on the fish cleaning block and whack a couple fingers off it with the axe.

They wouldn't even try to understand he was busier right now than he'd been when he was building the place all by himself. It was so hard to keep track of all the things he had to do, he kept falling behind on one thing or another and racing around trying to catch up.

What with washing out the bedding, scrubbing the place, burning the trash that piled up on him, patching up the place where the night bugs could get in to pester her, he still had to keep track of the nurse chores.

He'd boiled the boat sponge clean, and when she made a mess, after he'd put the bedding to soak, before he'd slip her into the fresh sheets, he had to swab her off clean and nice again, using the sponge and soap and warm water, keeping his head turned and going by touch so as not to look at her, then drying her nice with the soft toweling. Good thing the brief rains had been heavy or he'd be short on water.

Food was a real problem too, getting something down her that would give her some strength back. A can of chili looked just too dark and heavy for a sick missy, so you thin it down with powdered milk. Put the spoon to her little mouth and she'd open up like a baby bird, and that was the way to get the pills into her too, stuff them into those first few spoonfuls. When she got all she could handle, you couldn't get the spoon past her teeth and she'd make a tired whiney sound and roll her head back and forth to get away from the spoon.

Had to watch her back to see how it was coming, and the last time he greased her it looked fine, except for two little bad spots left on that sunk-in little white butt, to be pinched open and scrubbed clean and covered with the medicine.

Then he had a name for her. She was talking to that Jonathan and said, "Leila Dye. Leila Dye. That will be funny after all the years of being Leila Boylston, huh?" Celebrate, he thought, with a good chowder for her so thick you could stand a spoon in it, plenty of chili powder and that spic sauce to give it some life. Stir a whole damn tin of that Aussy butter into it to start her fattening up. Count every little rib she had. Fever melts it right off them every time. Never thought she'd be as much as nineteen. Boylston girl, with a teacher fellow to get married to. Teacher, don't you sweat too much. Ol' Corpo's fixing her up fine, and she'll live right here with him until she's dancing and laughing and singing the whole day through, and then she'll let you know how it's time to come get her, and you can let on to that brother Sam she's in good hands.

While fishing he was taken far off, and came slowly back into himself to find that he was drifting through the Inlet, out toward the breakers, holding a rod with an empty hook. He started the motor on the skiff and came home, and coming around the last turn, saw the strange boat under his place, couldn't fit his mind around what he was supposed to know, because it had been there before and he couldn't remember why. Then he remembered the girl all of a sudden, and why he'd gone out. He yanked open the bait well lid and saw four good fish, enough, thank God, and couldn't remember catching them. He squeezed in beside her fancy boat, moored the skiff, ran up to take a look at her. She was out of the bed and on her side on the floor sound asleep, her head in a corner. He clucked and went over and felt of her, and was pleased to find out she felt almost cool to the touch for the first time. He lifted her easily, put her back on top of the rumpled bed, tugged the tails of the shirt down to cover her decently. He went down with the cook pot, cleaned the fish and cut them into chunks and dropped them into the pot. When he carried it up, she was sitting on the edge of the bed, and he said, "You feeling a lot better, Missy?"

"But you can't expect me to be absolutely *useless*, darling! It doesn't make any *sense*. I've done some of Sam's work at home for ages, and I'm a whiz typist, and pretty dang good at speedwriting too, and certainly *somebody* in Montevideo needs typing in English. So all I'm asking, darling, is for you not to get all proud and stuffy, and write to them and just *ask* them to fix up the permissions and things I'll need to earn any money down there . . . What difference does that make? When we have babies I'll stay home. Darling, it's a *tiny, tiny* apartment, and you'll have long hours and I'll go slowly mad. Do you want me wandering the streets or something? . . . Certainly I like to be alone with you, Jonathan, but I also like to be with people too."

"Sorry I asked," Corpo mumbled, and spiced the fish generously, added water and powdered milk and set it to boil. When he looked over at her, she was on her feet, tottering feebly across the rough flooring, her hands held out for balance. He dropped the spoon and hastened toward her.

"Did anyone see Jonathan?" she asked in a higher voice than usual, thin, plaintive—a little-girl voice. "Did anyone see Jonathan? I have to talk to Jonathan. It's about Mrs. Staniker. It's about Mrs. Mary Jane Staniker. She scared me awful. Her hair is wound up in the fan. Her face is like plums and her tongue is sticking way out and her eyes are bugging way out and her lips are like sausages. I got to find Jonathan. I thought it was firecrackers. For a joke. Jonathan!"

He caught her by the wrist as she started to run. She wheeled toward him, and he knew that she saw him. She looked at him, and her eyes were different. They saw him. They went wide. She stared down at herself, looked wildly around the room, and then began screaming and screaming and trying to yank free of his grasp. She was much stronger and wirier than he could have guessed. He tried to keep her from hurting herself. In her struggles she fell, and kept trying to crawl away from him, her screams dwindling to tiny rasping squeaks. Suddenly she seemed to faint. He put her back in the bed. She lay on her back, snoring softly, her mouth sagging open. She felt hot again.

After he had stared at her for a little while, he looked until he found his mirror and propped it in its place on the two nails over the sink. He studied himself for a long time, slowly combing the beard with his fingers. He looked around the room.

"Damn, damn, damn," he said softly, and went to the box where he thought there was a good chance he would find the razor and the soap stick and the little scissors he'd need to chop it short enough to shave and to chop his hair close enough to grease it and comb it.

That Wednesday night, down on the port bunk aboard the Muñequita, Corpo felt mildly disconsolate. Nice how much of that chowder he'd gotten down her, and she'd cooled off some. But she'd been talking to a mess of people he'd never even heard of before, waving her hands some, giggling and smiling and bobbing her head. And he'd wanted her to look right at him once more and see there was nothing to be so scared of. Think he was a wild man or something. A good beard keeps the bugs off. Man had a right to shave or not shave. But she hadn't been able to see him. She was looking past him mostly, making him feel as if there was a room full of people behind him. "My name is Leila Jane Boylston and I am eleven years old, and I like tennis and swimming best," she had said in her little-girl voice.

He heard the rain coming, moving across the mangroves, hissing more loudly as it approached. It was a good rain for ten minutes, leaving the air washed clean when it ended.

He told himself that it was no good. She had gotten a little better and now she was worse. It went that way a lot of times. They'd get hit bad, so bad it wouldn't look as if there was any point in trying to get them back to the field hospital. The corpsman would plug up the holes as best he could, put on plenty of sulfa powder, squeeze those ampules into the casualty's arm. Before the morphine took hold, they'd sometimes brighten right up, ask for a butt maybe, look around, and then all of a sudden they'd go. Just like that. Life filled a man up, and when it went out, he sagged like a kid's balloon losing a part of its air. But slower. The dead would just dwindle and flatten, and their uniforms would look too big; and if the outfit had been saddled up without a break for a few days, the whiskers would look artificial, little wires poked neat and careful through the silent skin. Every dead knew it couldn't happen to him. Even if the whole platoon was wiped out, he'd be the one left. It's what they had to think or they wouldn't be there at all, and if they were, you couldn't get them to keep moving. If any one of them ever knew his odds were no better and no worse than anybody else, then how in hell could you get him to take the point? How could you get anybody to work their way along a hedgerow close enough to lob grenades into a machine-gun position with a good field of fire? After a while you got to understand that it was exactly the same with the krauts, and they could do the things they did, the damned fine soldiering, because theirs was just the same dream, each one of them accepting the idea of a wound, maybe a bad one, and pain that could be bad, but not accepting that final listening-look some of them got and the shrinking down into a still thing smaller than the clothes it had worn. If you kept them on the move too long, then the ones who had all their springs and strings pulled a little tighter than the others; they would start to figure it all out, start to know that what kind of luck was coming up for them, good or bad, had not a damn thing to do with who they were, or what they thought, or how they felt. Then they had to make do with the idea of being nothing. Just something moving and breathing in a bad place. That's when they'd flatten out and try to work their way down into the safe, black, warm ground and never stand up again. They gave it a word. Combat fatigue. What it really was was the knowing of it, finding out you were some kind of a bug, killing other bugs, and if God paid any attention at all, it was more like he'd look down and shake his big sad head and say, "What the *hell* are they up to now?"

Right there toward the end, he thought, before they busted my head, I had me some workers. Ever' one had been through the mill, got over believing he could depend on some kind of magic, knew that the onliest way to have any personal luck was to give it a chance to work by being as quick, smart and sly as a weasel. Slide like a snake through every little fold in the ground. Bust every place that even smelled like a sniper would like it. Ears to hear the incoming mail before it made any sound at all, like a dog whistle. But I was losing them too. One at a time. Something always happens you can't count on. And then I lost myself. Knew I was getting hit. Glad it didn't hurt. Felt like somebody hitting you with a stocking full of sand. Sort of a jar, and then a warm running feeling where the hole was. And then it just winked out. Like back in the rest area when the movie film would break. All of a sudden nothing except a white light on a white screen.

And that boy upstairs there, that fresh meat from the repple depple, he never had time to get smart . . . .

Corpo knuckled his eyes and shook his head in a familiar disgust with himself. Sergeant, if you're getting so you can't tell a pretty little girl from a dumb recruit, them candy people are sure to God going to haul you off in the funny wagon.

He crawled out of the cramped forward section of the Muñequita and straighted up on deck, snuffing the clean night. Wrap her up and tote her down here and use this fine boat and run her down to the city pier. Or wait a bit, do all you can, then make her up a nice box out of the good boards you've been saving, pretty her up, say the words, and bury her deep and neat and quiet. And take this fine boat out on the first misty night and let it loose with the tide moving out.

It could have happened by now, he thought. He went up and moved close to the bed, sat tirelessly a-squat on his heels, reached and laid the back of his forefinger against her forehead. It felt so unexpectedly cool he was certain it had happened, then the breath caught in her throat in a half-snore. She coughed, sighed, turned onto her side, her back toward him.

"Cain't quite make up your mind to live or die, huh?" he whispered. "If you're making a choice, Missy, living is better, hear?"

He thought of going back to the bunk aboard the white boat, but he had the feeling that if he left her, something that was hovering over her might pounce. He stretched out on the floor beside the bed, and awoke in first light, feeling a little bit stiff and sore. She was still cool to the touch, and he leaned over her face and snuffed at her, nostrils wide. That sick-smell was almost gone, that soury new-bread smell. He went fishing and came back and she was still asleep. He fixed breakfast and then ate it all himself when he could not wake her up enough to eat it. This was her heaviest sleep of all, and when it lasted through midday it began to worry him.

He had his back to her, and he was patching a hole in a window screen when she started yelling so loudly he nearly went through the window. He spun and saw her sitting straight up and trying to squirm back away from something. "No!" she yelled. "Oh God, no! Please! Please! Get away from me! No!"

He trotted to her, wiping his hands on khakied thighs, and grasped her shoulders and tried to ease her back down onto the pillow, saying, "Now there, Missy. Nothing after you. Everything is fine, Miss Leila. Just having a bad dream there, Missy."

And all of a sudden he realized that those wide green eyes were staring directly at him, wide scared, wondering eyes, and her lips were sucked white. He released her and stepped back.

• • •

She knew it was another part of a dream, exceptionally vivid, trapped in some kind of a terrible shacky place in some kind of a jungle, with some huge weird type staring at her, scary pale eyes, and that dent in his forehead so deep it made her stomach turn over. She willed herself to wake up, willed the man and the shack to fade away.

"Are you awake now for sure, Missy?" he asked.

She closed her eyes and opened them to an undeniable reality which, if it were a dream, was more carefully detailed than any she had ever had. Yet, she thought, if I am ill, maybe a dream could be like this.

"Missy?"

"Awake? I don't know. I can hear my own voice. I'm awake I guess. But nothing makes any sense."

"You had the fevers, Miss Leila."

"I feel kind of vague and floaty," she said. She pushed a sleeve up to scratch her arm, sensed a strangeness about it, looked at her arm, and felt a sudden wild alarm. "What's *happened* to me! I'm like a skeleton! What's *happening?*"

"Now don't you be scared. Please don't you be scared. You're doing real fine, Miss Leila. You're a-looking real good today."

"Who are you?"

"Why, I'm Sergeant Corpo, Missy."

She looked slowly around the room. "Why am I here? What *is* this crazy place? Where is it?"

"Well, this is my place. I built this place. This is my island. Everybody calls it Sergeant's Island. I've been here a *long* time. The Lieutenant fixed it so I can stay on here for good."

"What are we close to, Sergeant? Are we near Nassau?"

"Nassau? That's a good piece from here. The closest place, where I buy supplies, that would be Broward Beach, twenty minute run to the south in my skiff."

"Florida!"

"It surely is."

She lay back abruptly, thin forearm across her eyes. He thought she was going to sleep. She said, "Sergeant?"

"Yes, Missy."

"You've got to help me. I don't know what questions to ask. You've got to just tell me why I'm here, and what this is all about. Please."

He came closer and sat on his heels by the bed. "Missy, it was Sunday morning, early, real misty morning, and I was wading the flats to the north of my island, and you like to scared me half to death, come floating right up to me in a big pretty boat, line dragging from the bow, weed tangled in it. There you were laying on the deck when I took a look, jaybird naked, excuse me, and sunburned terrible bad, and that big open place on your head I had such a time sewing up nice."

She took her arm away, stared at him, then lifted her hand and reached unerringly to the healing wound and touched it tenderly with her fingertips. It felt alien to her, a great thickened clumsy welt, with a dull inner pain when she touched it. How in the wide world, she thought, would I happen to be drifting around naked in a boat in Florida? It has to be some kind of a complicated joke. Or a plot.

"What kind of a boat?"

"New and nice, Miss Leila. Blue and white color. Kind of a greeny-blue hull, white topsides, twin stern-drive engines, name Muñequita registered out of Brownsville, Texas, but it's got a Florida number and a seal on the bow."

He seemed so very anxious to please and reassure, but there was an oddness about his eyes that made her wary. "When did this happen, Sergeant? When did you find me?"

She saw him press both fists against his forehead, then rise and wander aimlessly, go over and start looking through bits of paper fastened to a post which supported a crude beam. He turned toward her and with a shy smile and hopeless gesture said, "Near as I can make it out, it had to be last Sunday. That means this is Thursday. And that would make it the twenty-sixth of May."

She felt her mouth go dry, and she went back into the confusing corridors of memory, searching for a date. She found a Friday she knew. The sixth day of May. Twenty days gone without a trace! She could remember the day clearly. They were at anchor at Southwest Allen's Cay in the Exumas. The island was a long oval barrier of sand and rock enclosing a broad anchorage with but two good entrances for a boat of the draft of the Muñeca, one to the east and one to the west, almost opposite each other. A long still day, dazzlingly bright. But not one of the good days, because Carolyn had been whining at Mister Bix again. She had wanted to go further down the Exumas, and Captain Garry had figured out how far they could go and still get back to Nassau again on the tenth for some kind of business meeting Mister Bix had. But then she had changed her mind and decided she wanted to get back to Nassau sooner. She had apparently agreed to staying at the anchorage another day and a half or two days and arrive back at Nassau on Sunday, and then she had begun complaining about the heat, a rash on her throat, running out of the good sun lotion, a stone bruise on her foot.

By then the pattern had become familiar. Carrie's pattern. It set up the usual side effects. Carolyn would be poisonously and damagingly sweet to Stella, ignore her husband completely, and flirt quite openly with Captain Staniker. Bix, suffering rejection, would take every chance to stomp on his son Roger's pride, pointing out everything Roger seemed incompetent to do, from catching a fish to making a drink. Roger would go about with the stiff-mouthed look of someone fighting tears of helplessness. Mary Jane Staniker would keep her head down and go about her chores with a scuttling look. Staniker, by making an extra effort to be protective and gentle with Stella, would inadvertently add to Carolyn's sour mood. And Leila would make an extra effort to stay out of everybody's way. She was in awe of Carolyn's special talent to make six other adults as miserable as herself.

In the morning Carrie had Staniker launch and rig the little sailing dinghy, and she went off alone, up and down the protected waters in the light air, managing to look rigidly discontented as far as the eye could see. Mister Bix and Captain Staniker went off in the Muñequita to troll on the Atlantic side, Bix making it clear that Roger would be an unwelcome nuisance to take along. Leila had put her writing materials in a plastic bag and swum ashore. She went to a pebbly beach at the south end of the island where the slope of rock and scrub growth behind her concealed the anchorage where the Muñeca lay. As she sat with her bare back against a smooth and comfortable slant of stone, she could see Stel on her plastic float-board paddling slowly back and forth over a coral reef, looking down through the little glass porthole. She finished another two pages of a letter to Jonathan, thinking she would probably add more before mailing it from Nassau.

The heat of the sun finally made her uncomfortable enough to think of getting back into the water. Stella came paddling to the beach and came walking ashore, carrying the light foam board under her arm.

Stella limped badly. She had been Leila's friend for years. Leila had realized in the very beginning with this strange, shy girl that any kind of special consideration made her become remote. So she had treated her as if there was no handicap. And, indeed, there was far less of one than Stella believed. Leila knew the history of it. It had been a difficult delivery. The nerves of the left leg had been damaged. By the time the specialists had achieved a sufficient regeneration to give her the use of it, the leg was smaller around and shorter than the other leg, and it would never be very strong. Both legs were pretty, slender, shapely. They did not match. That was all. Her figure was very good. She had a delicate and sensitive face, lovely eyes which seldom looked directly at anyone. She had a dark, brooding look, and only the very few who knew her as well as Leila knew the quickness of the hidden humor, the taste for the absurd.

Only once on the cruise had Leila made an effort to comfort Stel. Carolyn, one night at dinner, had been exceptionally, cleverly vicious. She talked about bringing "poor Stel" out of herself. She seemed incapable of saying her name without adding the "poor," and she would jump to Stel's assistance when she least needed it. Leila awoke in the night in the cabin she shared with Stel to hear the smothered sound of weeping. So she had stepped over to the adjoining bunk and slid in with her and held her. Stel had been rigid at first, and then had softened and clung and wept herself out. It had made Stel strange toward her for the next few days, but then they had found their way back to the casual warmth they knew best.

Stel dropped the board and sat on it and said, "Madame the Queen is really winging it today."

"Whatever it is, if somebody could bottle it, you could use it to destroy empires. Your father ought to give her a good thumping."

She made a face. "He'd rather thump on Roger. My dear daddy made his own bed like they say. I guess the daughter-daddy bit clouds my vision, but he acts so damned—goaty about her. She keeps him on the hook. She makes his hands shake. Years married and still it goes on. He's scared to thump her, Leila. She wouldn't let him near her for a year. Anyway, thank God Garry's got the sense to steer clear of her."

"It's Garry now? Gracious me!"

"Oh, come *on!* He's a nice guy, Leila. A really truly nice guy. And
this cruise is rough on him and his wife. I'm glad they're getting paid
well at least. A happy ship. Ho, ho, ho and a bottle of arsenic. Honest, I'm sorry I dragged you along, but I think if you hadn't been
along, I'd have jumped overboard a long time ago."

"Oh sure. You know, for a guy who's supposed to have been cap-
taining for years, Staniker seems sort of keyed up and twitchy to
me."

"Darling, the Kayd family does that to everyone. It's our proud-
est boast." She paused. "I guess what really gets me is what Carrie
does to daddy. He is so strong in every other way. And she keeps
him groveling around whenever she feels like it. She keeps putting
the knife in me to see if she can get a rise out of him. When he
doesn't do a thing to get her off my back, then I resent him. And
when he crushes poor Rog, I resent him more. I know what she's
doing. She's cutting us loose from him. Uncontested possession.
Anyway, I'll tell you one thing. This is the last cruise of the Kayd
family. As a happy united little group at least. Rog can keep taking
it if he wants to. Leila, maybe we ought to jump ship in Nassau and
fly back home."

"Mean it?"

"Mmmm. I don't know. It's nice to think about."

Leila sighed. "There's not enough cruise left to make it worth-
while to stir up the fuss. Let's stiff it out, kid. Let's show 'em we're
tough. Honey, I have to get into that water before I begin to smoke."

In the late afternoon of that day at Allen's Cay, with Bix and Staniker still not back, Carolyn napping, Stella reading in the shade of a
tarp Roger had rigged over a part of the cockpit deck, Leila swam
ashore again and wandered, looking for shells. She came upon Roger

standing in the shallows and casting out over the reef where Stel had paddled before lunch, using light spinning gear. When she asked him if he was having any luck, he lifted a stringer of gaudy fish out of the shallows and said, "Mary Jane'll know which of these can go in the pot."

Fifty feet further along the shore she came upon big and curious animal tracks and called to Rog in an excited voice. He came hurrying and looked and said, "Hey now! Garry said there might be some on this cay. Iguana. This groove is where his tail drags. Let's see where he went."

"But those feet look pretty big. Don't they bite?"

"Garry said they're timid unless you corner them and try to grab them. He said there used to be thousands and thousands up and down the Exumas. But they're delicious. Like chicken."

"Lizard steaks? Gaaah!"

"Come on."

They followed the track for several hundred yards, losing them in the rocks then picking them up again in a sandy patch further along. At last they lost them for good. He had driven a driftwood sliver into the arch of his foot, in the middle of the sole. He sat on a flat stone, and she knelt and picked carefully at it with thumbnail and fingernail until at last she got a firm grip on it and pulled it free. She held it up in triumph and said, "You will walk again!"

He laughed. His teeth looked very white in the saddle brown of his lean face. Of all aboard he was the only one to take a tan as deep as Staniker's. He had dark hair, like Stella's, and the same mobile sensitivity of feature, the same hint of vulnerability. Yet he was unflawed in any physical way, slender, muscular, moving with sureness and precision and grace, except when he had to perform any task when his father was watching him. He wore pale blue briefs, a ragged hat from the Nassau straw market.

They were in a cleft in the rocks, with a sand floor, with walls rising eight sheer feet behind him. It was like a small room which had been cut in half diagonally, looking south across the blue of the depths, turquoise of shallows.

"Thank you, Doctor," he said, and his smile faded away. He looked at her in a way which made her aware of the skimpiness of her one-piece suit, cut to a deep oval in back almost to the base of her spine.

She rose with a bright smile and said, "Ol' Iguana is probably back there chomping up your fish, Rog." As she turned away he caught her, hands on her waist, pulling her back, burying his face in her hair.

"Knock it off, Roger. Please."

"Leila, Leila, Leila."

"I *mean* it! Stop it right now."

He turned her swiftly and tried to put his mouth on hers. She wiggled and twisted and pushed at him. It was all so stupid and unexpected and ridiculous. When struggling seemed to only excite him more, she decided to go dead. She took a deep breath and let it out. She let her arms hang. Except for keeping her lips tightly compressed, she went limp. He would give up in a moment. Her eyes were closed. His hand clasped the back of her neck, his arm against her back holding her tightly against him. He slid his other hand down inside the low back of her suit and, fingers splayed wide, hand cupping her bottom, pulled her against the hardness of himself. The sun came red through her eyelids. He smelled of sun-flesh, wind, salt and maleness. She felt a dreaminess, an inner turning, a loosening of her mouth, a yearning for Jonathan's body so wretchingly vivid she felt as if her heart had been torn loose. As she put her hands lightly on his shoulders, pressing herself into him, with coughing catch of breath, suddenly all the textures were wrong, and in shame and fright she plunged free of him, stumbling in the sand, to come to her feet and find herself trapped in the corner of the V.

He prowled toward her, hands low, his face as blind as the stones around them.

She felt a stone move as her foot brushed it, and she snatched it up, held it to strike, and yelled, "Roger! Roger!" He was in some far place where he might hear her.

He halted, still in a half crouch, then slowly straightened and wiped his mouth with the back of his hand. He looked at her and turned away and went to the flat stone where he had sat before. He rested his arms on his knees, lowered his head to his arms. She saw him in profile, chest and belly expanding and contracting with his fast, deep breathing.

She dropped the stone and walked out to where she could not be trapped again. She saw a movement of his hunched shoulders and thought for one incredulous moment he was laughing at her.

"I don't—know why," he said. "I'm sorry. I'm—so sorry."

She sighed and went closer to him. She felt very tired. "Just don't cry. It doesn't matter that much."

He looked up, frowning, eyes wet. "I had the feeling—it would be—some kind of an answer to something."

She understood. She moved closer. "It could be, maybe. Not with me, though. It's what he's doing to you, Rog. He won't let you have any pride. He won't let you have—manhood. Or maleness, maybe is a better word. He's getting you to the point where you don't know *what* you are. So this was—trying to find out, maybe. I don't know anything about these things, Roger. Maybe he is trying to—emasculate you because she's emasculating him. Could that make any sense?"

"I don't know. I hate him. I keep getting the feeling I'm going to do some terrible thing. I guess—I almost did." He tried to smile.

"You were very scary, you know. I don't know if I could have hit you with that stone or not. I didn't even know you. If I couldn't—stop you, you were going to rape me."

"Maybe. I don't know."

"If you could hate him, Roger, it would be better for you."

"I despise him!"

"Sure. That's why you keep straining all day to do something that will please him. Something to make him proud. And the harder you try, the worse things get. Roger, listen to me. Please. You've got to get out from under. Because, if you could—try what you tried, you haven't got things under control. You *could* do some terrible thing. You're a man. You shouldn't let him make you doubt it."

"I feel so ashamed, Leila."

"It's over. Okay? Don't keep on making some kind of a thing out of it. People can start enjoying remorse. Come on, Rog. Get up. Nothing happened. Nothing will. Nothing has changed. I've forgotten it already."

She could remember going back to the rocky beach with him, remember making him laugh, finally. But she could not unearth any other parts of what was left of that day. It seemed to fade out somewhere between the beach and the cruiser.

Now in this narrow bed in the clutter of the shack, with the Sergeant watching her, she wondered if it had been a very bad decision to do nothing about Roger's attack. Perhaps, when he had the next chance, when they were in the Muñequita together, he had come at her again and she had not been able to stop him. She had read that a severe blow on the head resulting in concussion could temporarily or even permanently wipe out all memory of the incidents leading up to the moment when the injury occurred. The Sergeant said she had been naked when he found her in the drifting boat. The boat had a good range. She remembered Captain Staniker saying it would go two hundred and something miles on full tanks. That could account for her being in Florida. When it was done, and the madness dwindled, Roger would have tried to wake her up. If he couldn't, he would panic. He would head for the states, abandon the boat, and try to run away and hide. But they'd find him. Maybe they already had. She wondered how large the gap in her memory might be, how much time had passed between that day when things faded out to the time she had been injured and abandoned.

"I guess they've been trying to find me, Sergeant Corpo. I guess there'd be a big fuss about it in the papers and on the air."

"Now I wouldn't rightly know about that, because there'd be nobody coming by here to tell me. Don't have a radio or get a paper. Lot of noise, foolishness, gets people all stirred up."

She tried to smile. "You're kidding me!"

He sat on a rickety wooden chair and tilted back dangerously. "One time some kids came and messed this place up for me. But they won't be back. And the Lieutenant stops by to see how the place looks, maybe once a year. But I go on in every month to town to cash my army check and stock up on what's needed. Have to go back sometimes when I forget something. Damn—excuse me, Missy—nuisance."

"Then you're a hermit!"

The chair legs came down with a thump. He looked aggrieved. "Hermit? Some nutty old man in a cave? Miss Leila, what I am is a veteran on a pension. Having people around gets my head to hurting. Maybe on account of getting wounded in the head. I couldn't say. When I was a little kid I liked to go off by myself. Go into the big swamp and stay in there for days."

She sat up straight and swung her legs out of the bed. The look of them shocked her. They were like old pictures of people in concentration camps. The backs of her legs were pink and tender where the deep burn had shredded away the tanned skin of cruising.

She looked at the improvised garment, the rolled and knotted blue bandanna which served as a belt. She saw the brilliant red flowers in the glass jar on the crate beside the bed. She saw the piece of cheap costume jewelry pinned to the front of the white shirt. Red glass mounted in a brass brooch. It was like someone dressing a doll, a tender game which made her feel shy.

"You—you've been taking care of me since Sunday morning? Alone? You've been doing everything that had to be done?"

He got up restlessly. "Missy, I had a long time in them hospitals, believe you me. What has to be done has to be done. You were burning up and clean out of your head."

She tried to stand up but the room swam and darkened and she fell back as he hurried to her. "Now don't try a fool thing like that!"

She sat in a huddle of misery and said, "I—I have to go to the bathroom."

He covered his eyes with his left hand and began snapping the fingers of his big right hand, making a very loud cracking sound. "Now just a minute. Now you wait. I had something worked out. Oh!"

He spun and hurried out. A spring slapped the screen door shut. She heard him clumping down outside stairs. Soon he was back looking pleased, carrying an old-fashioned chamber pot. Water sloshed in it as he set it down close beside the bed. The lid was from a small green garbage container. He said, "You get well enough to walk, I've got a privvy about a hundred feet from the cabin. I recalled finding this pot a long time ago, and I kept looking till I found it. Brush grown up around it and a mess of other stuff. I sand-scrubbed it clean as a dollar." He moved the chair over next to the pot. "You just kind of ease yourself over, and take it slow and easy so you don't get faint, Missy. You need me, you just yank on that cord there and it'll jangle some cans I've got hung below. When you get settled back into bed you jangle them anyhow. I've got to cook you up a good dinner. You slept on through breakfast today, and you should be next door to starved."

After she had crawled back into the bed and covered her legs with the sheet, she lay quietly, her eyes stinging, fingertips resting on the absurd piece of jewelry. It sounded too dramatic to tell herself she had fallen into the hands of a madman.

What had happened to everyone? Where were they?

Suddenly ravenous, she reached and grasped the cord and jangled the cans vigorously.

She heard his distant voice. "Coming, Missy. Be right there."

Fifteen

THAT FRIDAY, the twenty-seventh day of May, was a very hot still day. A mist hung over the land, a broad area of silvery glare showing where the sun was. The mist caught and held the aroma of the fires of the drying, dying Everglades, a faint stink—like a memory of disaster. The mist held the sharp pungencies of a hundred thousand tail pipes. Days such as this in Dade County, infrequent, corroded the broad leaves of tropical plantings, stung the eyes, smudged white roofs, and lay an almost invisible scum on the motionless water of ten thousand swimming pools. Off-season tourists, lard white from the long midwestern winter, would be deceived by the overcast look, spend hours on the beaches, and a certain predictable number would die days later of the merciless ultraviolet burns.

Raoul Kelly had worked all morning in his rented room in the heart of the Cuban colony along Southwest Eighth Street in West Miami. His second-floor room in the peeling stucco building had four windows across the front overlooking Eighth Street. They were double-hung windows, all with the bottom sash opened as far as they would go. He had taken the screens out and stacked them against the wall as invitation to any elusive breeze. Eighth Street was also Route 41, the Tamiami Trail, and the big diesel tractor-trailer trucks halted by the traffic signal a half block away, made a blue stench and resonant fartings as they worked their way back up through the gears, overwhelming the piercing nasal agonies of the gypsy singer on the big stereo juke in the cantina underneath his room.

His desk was a four-by-eight sheet of marine plywood laid across three two-drawer filing cabinets. On one wall he had scotch-taped detailed maps of Cuba, the Dominican Republic, Haiti, the Caribbean, Mexico, Central America, South America, Venezuela. He had made marks on all the maps, a private alphabetical and numerical code cross-referenced to file cards which were in a personal shorthand meaningless to anyone but himself. He had improvised an open bookcase of boards and cinderblock, and it was stacked with reference works, the overflow piled on a table beside the shelves. On another wall he had hung a big cork board to which he thumbtacked working outlines, notes to himself, reminders of appointments.

He had a sagging bed, a chest of drawers, a noisy floor fan, two straight chairs, a fraying grass rug, a shallow closet, a key to the bathroom at the back of the second-floor hallway, and an old rebuilt Underwood standard. He was a very fast four-finger typist, using unlined sheets of yellow legal-size paper. He turned such sheets in at the editorial desk at the paper. For the magazine work, he would take his final draft down the street to the bakery where Señora de Onís, wife of the owner, would type them properly and carefully onto white bond with two good carbon copies for twenty cents a page. In Havana she had been a private secretary in a large insurance agency.

Raoul Kelly had worked all morning in his underwear shorts, the floor fan hurling the stifling air at his naked back. Sweat found its tickling way down through the thick mat of black hair on his chest and belly. The sheets of copy paper stuck to the undersides of his forearms when he rested them on the desk, and had to be peeled away. Just within reach was a little radio with a cracked gold and white plastic case. He kept it at a station which announced each news break with a grandiose blast of trumpets, kept it at a volume where he could hear the trumpets and nothing else, and would hear them and reach out without conscious thought to turn the volume up.

He was doing an article in *depth*—a phrase which never failed to irritate him—about the background, present, and guessable future of subversion in Venezuela. From time to time he would refresh his memory by finding the right portion of the three hours of tape he had recorded during an interview with one of El Caballo's underground agents who had defected after two years in Caracas, had slipped into the states illegally, and had been fingered for Kelly by the sister of the man who was hiding him.

Though he knew it would annoy his newspaper, he had decided to place the article in, he hoped, *The Atlantic*, and let the wire services pick up the news breaks from the text when it was published.

It was going reasonably well, but his concentration was shaky because of the letter in the shallow straw bowl he used as an in-basket. If he could decide how to answer it, then he could forget it.

It was on the creamy bond of the Waterman Foundation:

> *My dear Raoul Kelly,*
>
> *I am afraid I must be more explicit about the special problems of organization we are facing here in setting up Project Round-Table. Not least among the many reasons we asked you to join with us would be to have you, as an Area Coordinator, help select, recruit and train those field investigators who would work under your direction.*
>
> *There is an increasing pressure upon us from the Director and*

*the Board of Trustees to establish an operational structure. By
dint of special pleading, motivated by my respect for your work
and knowledge of your background, and also by the enlightening
two days I spent in your company, I have induced my colleagues
to grant one small additional grace period, but I fear that if we
cannot have your affirmative answer by that date, we shall have
to extend our invitation to the alternative choice, the man I told
you about.*

*You must make a decision on or before the fifteenth day of
next month, and the sooner you can decide, the more helpful it
will be to me. We need you.*

> *Cordially and hopefully,*
> *G. Emmett Addyson, Deputy Director*

I can make out, he thought. I can keep on doing what I am doing,
which is, in effect, a one-man version of their Project Round-Table.
In a world where the semantics of politics is like smoke in the wind,
nothing is gained by ringing words, exhortation, cries of alarum.
Facts move the world.

He turned back several pages and looked at one of the facts in the
article he had just finished:

> Just after dusk on November eighth last year an esti-
> mated seven tons of weapons and explosives was ferried
> ashore from the Polish freighter *Trogir* and offloaded on
> the beach five miles east of Rio Caribe on the Peninsula
> de Paris in the province of Sucre, where approximately
> twenty men with pack animals, under the direction of
> one Ramon Profeta, a Cuban national, accepted delivery
> and transported the material to a secret arsenal near Cu-
> manacoa. Among the supplies were five 60-mm mortars

of Chinese manufacture and four hundred rounds of
ammunition, including one hundred white phosphorus
mortar shells.

Orderly, triple-checked, plausible and ultimately provable, as
was the shameful illiteracy rate in the Republic of Panama, the record infant-mortality rate, and the recorded voice of the President
of the Republic saying, "The question is not *whether* we will have a
Castro-type revolution, but *when* we will have it."

But he yearned for access to the great flow of economic and so-
ciological and political information the huge grant by the Waterman
Foundation could create. Facts could then be interrelated, time-
tables predicted, causes isolated, countermeasures recommended.
Facts in abundance, fed into the twin computers of the human mind
and the transistor could illuminate all the misty patterns of conflict
and change. Otherwise it was all blindfold chess where the oppo-
nent's moves were neither announced nor recorded.

Yet he had promised, on his honor, to look after Francisca.

Just as he finished his penciled corrections, he heard the trumpet
call of news once more and turned the volume up.

Furious debate in the Senate on the proposal to recruit mercenary
combat battalions in Japan and the Philippines, uniform them in a
distinct fashion to sustain nationalistic pride, staff the battalions
with American officers, and use these people to fight the brushfire
wars which were promising to last a hundred years, giving each man
after twenty years of service the option to return to his home place,
or accept United States citizenship. Mercenary was as dirty a word
as empire.

And then the announcer said, "The official investigation and
hearings on the Muñeca tragedy in the Bahamas which resulted in
the death of Texas millionaire Bixby Kayd, his beautiful young second wife, his grown children, Stella and Roger, and his daughter's

guest, Miss Leila Boylston of Harlingen, Texas, have now ended. Captain Garry Staniker has been cleared of any suspicion of negligence. His wife, Mary Jane Staniker, also perished in the explosion and fire which sank the yacht a few miles north of Andros Island on the night of the thirteenth, just two weeks ago today. Staniker, who was marooned for a week with serious injuries before being rescued by a pleasure boat out of Jacksonville, was earlier listed as being in critical condition, but improved rapidly enough to be interrogated earlier this week, and it is expected he will be released from the Princess Margaret Hospital at Nassau sometime next week. In a prepared statement released an hour ago, Captain Staniker said he was pleased at the decision of the Board of Inquiry and felt it was just and fair. He refused to answer any questions about the tragedy or about his future plans."

Raoul Kelly tilted his chair back and slowly scratched at the sweat-damp bristle on his chin. Damn the pack-rat mind of the newspaperman, he thought. Grab everything that has a curious shine to it and stuff it into the back of the nest. And then, in odd moments, keep trying to fit the little pieces into a pattern.

After the weather news—thunderstorms during the night, clear and cooler tomorrow with a northeast wind—he turned the volume down. He had not gone hunting for background on the Staniker story, but he had read everything he had come across, from the two columns about Mister Bix in *Time* to Dud Weldon's carefully researched history of Staniker's maritime career in the *Record*.

He recalled the way, in Weldon's feature story, Cristen Harkinson had given Staniker a clean bill, and that Weldon had not exercised his considerable talent for innuendo in trying to make something of the fact she had been Senator Fontaine's special friend, and Kayd was known to have been associated in some vague business way with men Fontaine knew well. So it meant Weldon had put his own stamp of approval on the Harkinson woman.

There was a long scream of rubber, a janglingly expensive crunch. He leaned out of a window and saw two cars partway up the block, their front corners merged and locked in a tangle of torn metal, two men getting out of the two cars, starting to wave their fists at each other. Tempers ran short in this weather.

He turned his chair to sit facing his fan. He could not dismiss his uncomfortable awareness of certain facts which, had Dud Weldon known them, would have given him leverage for a far fatter feature.

Kayd had visited the Harkinson woman on the last day of March, over two weeks before he had returned aboard the Muñeca and hired Staniker. And Staniker and the Harkinson woman had been having a lengthy affair.

The Crissy-Staniker setup was not likely to be known. Even without the planned isolation of the house Fontaine had given her, an intimate arrangement between a woman and her hired captain was not anything which would be likely to attract any interest in the steamy social climate of the Miami area, even if the affair continued long after the lady had given up boating. It would be of moment only to those it happened to affect in some way—Crissy Harkinson, Garry Staniker, Francisca, Mary Jane Staniker and one sweaty Cuban newspaperman.

"And so what?" he said aloud. What has it got to do with anything? He's been cleared.

And, of course, one could not take any chances with 'Cisca's hard-won adjustment. The only *possible* reason for opening up the can of worms would be to find out if some sort of curious conspiracy had resulted in the sinking of the Muñeca. And, if so, the whole story would suddenly become twice as big as it had ever been. 'Cisca would have to testify as to Kayd's visiting the house, as well as to the relationship between Crissy and the Captain. All news media would zero in on one emotionally disturbed girl, and they would unearth every portion of her personal history. It was obvious she could not endure that sort of exposure, that intensity of focus of public interest.

He leaned and picked up Addyson's letter, scanned it again, flipped it back into the basket. Dilemma-time, he thought. Problems with no solutions.

Just as he was trying to stop thinking about the whole thing, an inadvertent process of logic took it one step further. If there was indeed some kind of dangerous and deadly motive underlying the loss of the Muñeca, it would surely occur to Staniker and the Harkinson woman that Francisca had seen Kayd in Crissy's house, and that she could verify the Staniker-Harkinson relationship.

Assume a maximum shrewdness and deadliness, and you had to suppose that they would further guarantee their own safety by effectively silencing the little Cuban maid, no matter how stupid Crissy assumed her to be. In fact they might think stupidity more dangerous to them than guile. It would be natural to tidy up now the most immediate danger was over.

So get her out of there, Kelly, just in case. And before el Capitán returns to his pussycat.

He showered, shaved, put on a fresh sports shirt and slacks, left the manuscript at the bakery, and drove down to the Ingraham Highway, heading for the Harkinson place.

In the development house of his parents, a cement block house with a red tile roof on a small lot beside a weedy canal, Oliver Akard lay upon his bed in his underwear shorts, the last of the daylight coming through the window beside the bed making oily highlights on the gleam of perspiration on his long muscular legs. His hands were laced behind his head. When there were two hesitant knocks at the closed bedroom door he did not answer. The door opened slowly and his mother peered in, then came into the room, closing the door behind her.

"Sonny? Did I wake you up? I'm sorry."

"It's okay, Mom."

She came and sat on the foot of his bed, facing him. He moved his legs to make room for her. He felt a remote fondness for her, tinged with nostalgia, as if he were looking at a picture of her long after she had died. But he also felt a restless irritation at what he knew was coming. She verified it with a long long sigh.

"What's happening to you, dear? What's made you change so?"

"Why should something be happening?"

"We're so worried, Sonny. Your father is terribly upset. You've always been such a good boy. We've always been so proud of you, dear."

"Oh, for God's sake!"

"There's no need to take the name of the Lord in vain, son."

"If he'd get off my back he wouldn't have any reason to get upset, right? He kept riding me, didn't he? I've got cuts coming, and if I want to use them, that's my business."

"Betty told me you haven't been to classes all this week."

"So I haven't been to classes. So?"

"What makes you so cruel and hard? What makes you be so ugly to your own parents, Oliver? It just isn't *like* you."

"Betty had to come running to you, didn't she?"

"Sonny, she's worried about you, the same as we are. You hurt her dreadfully. I guess you know that. She's a fine girl."

"The very best. Yes indeed."

"We've always been able to talk things out. And I think I know just a little bit more about the world than you give me credit for knowing."

"What's that supposed to mean?"

"You're an attractive young man, Oliver. And you've always been easily led. The world is full of idle, vicious women who take their pleasure in corrupting young men like you."

"What in the world are you talking about?"

"Maybe you'd like to tell me what I'm talking about. I think you know what I'm talking about."

"I haven't got the faintest idea."

"You don't seem to be keeping your sailboat at Dinner Key these days, Sonny. It hasn't been there for weeks. And your sailboat friends haven't seen you for weeks either."

"Betty isn't all nose! She's half mouth!"

"If you're not doing something you're ashamed of, why are you upset?"

"What I do with my time is my business. I earned the money for my car, and I earned the money for the Dutchman. It's none of Betty's damn business what I do."

"Or my damn business either?"

"You said it. I didn't."

"Where *is* your boat, Oliver?"

"It's moored at a friend's place."

"A new friend?"

"Okay, okay, okay! What else did she have to tell you?"

"The last time any of your old friends saw you out on the Bay was some time ago, apparently. Betty didn't find out until she started asking. You had a blonde-headed woman in your boat. A girl from school named Cricket saw you. Cricket told Betty the woman was nearly naked, a very cheap-looking type, and as old as I am."

"She happens to be twenty-eight."

"I can imagine. I can just imagine."

"What's that supposed to mean? Sarcasm or something?"

"Oh, Sonny, it's so *easy* for a clever woman like that to amuse herself with a boy like you."

"You don't even know her, so you don't know what you're talking about. How could you know what she's like?"

"I know this. To change you as much as you've changed in these past weeks, she has to be an evil creature. A slut!"

He sat up. "You watch it!"

She reached and turned on the lamp on his homework desk. "Don't yell at your mother," she said calmly.

"Don't call her names and I won't!"

She stared at him until he averted his gaze and lay back once more. "You've gotten seriously involved with her, haven't you?"

"Well—she's a pretty tremendous person."

"Is she married?"

"Her husband died. They didn't have any kids. He died a long time ago."

"Sonny, look at me. I am going to ask you something. If the answer is yes, I promise I won't tell your father. It will be between you and me. Have you had—sex with this woman?"

"We're in love."

"I knew what the answer had to be. What else could a person like that possibly want of you? Oh, Sonny, she's got you twisted around her little finger. You don't know up from down, right from wrong. Behind your back she snickers at you, believe me. She's callous and vicious. She's just *using* you. You just happened to be handy. How many other strong young boys have there been?"

"You're out of your mind. You don't know how it is. You don't know what you're talking about."

"You were going to dedicate your life to the service of God."

"Let's say it isn't going to work out that way. Okay?"

"You've got hate in you now. I can feel it. You never had it before. Sonny, will you get down on your knees with me right now and pray to God for the strength to break the hold of the flesh that she has over you?"

"Knock it off, will you?"

"This is a good Christian home."

"That could be the trouble with it."

"What is that supposed to mean, Oliver?"

"I'm grown up. To you I'm still twelve years old or something. You and Betty. My God! Thanks but no thanks. I don't even belong here any more. So don't count on me staying here. And the more you keep twisting things and bugging me, the sooner I go. Okay?"

"Why warn me, son? What didn't you just leave without a word? That would be more like the new Oliver Akard, wouldn't it? You're cruel and cold and—h-hateful."

"I knew that was coming next. The weeps. Oh how could you! Oh dear. Oh what am I going to do."

She tilted her head and stared at him, her cheeks wet with tears. "Where have you *gone!*" she asked wonderingly. "What has happened to my son?"

He felt a sudden fullness of his throat, a smarting of his eyes, and he had the impulse to reach to her and be taken into her arms. But he made himself laugh to hide any look of potential tears. "Where'd he go? Your little boy grew up, lady. Too bad. But they all do. So get used to it. Take up something else, huh? Bridge lessons maybe?"

In a sad and wondering way, as she stood up slowly, she said, "I don't *know* you. I don't even *know* you." She moved slowly toward the closed door. She stopped a few feet from it, head lowered. She turned quickly, startling him. Standing slightly crouched, her face contorted, her fists clenched, she said, "You got into that chunk chocolate that time! Two whole pounds of it! Aaah, you gobbled it, you did. You crammed it down. Chocolate smeared all over your face and your clothes. Aaah, how sick you were! Vomiting, vomiting. I held you while you were emptying yourself. Do you know something? You disgusted me. I worried about it. I wondered if maybe I didn't have enough mother love. You DIS GUS TED MEEEE!"

She ran out and banged the door shut.

"Mom?" he said, but too quietly to be heard. He was propped up on his elbow. He lowered himself back to the pillow. She had slammed the door so hard it had jingled the row of little trophy cups on the high shelf over the doorway.

It was night. The light on the desk reached far enough to show indistinctly a slow movement of the three scale-model aircraft suspended from nylon filaments, hanging from the ceiling over his tall chest of drawers. Spitfire. Hurricane. B-29. Atop the chest of drawers in a narrow chromed frame was the picture of Betty. He could not see it, but he knew exactly how it looked. *I looked right into the lens, darling, and pretended I was looking right at you. Happy birthday, darling. Happy, happy birthday.*

This was his room, he thought. He won those trophies. He made those models. He slept in this bed. That was his girl. It was a strange kind of sadness.

There was no way they could understand. Not any of them. How could they be made to see how special and how terrible it was, last night when Crissy had clung to him, weeping hopelessly, like a little kid afraid of the dark. She did not have anyone else. Their time was growing short. She kept saying there was nothing they could do. Nothing. But the idea of Staniker having her again was unendurable. She had made those funny little hints. And she had said, "Don't you see? This was all we were meant to have. But it's so much more than most people in their whole lives, my dearest. There's one clean way to finish it. If we have the strength."

And then later, all too casual, turning away when he tried to look into her eyes, she had said, "There's some horrid, big, brown rats living in the tops of my palm trees, dear. They're getting terribly bold. Do you have a gun you could bring over? You could shoot them for me, maybe?"

It wasn't much of a gun. He had checked to make sure it was still in the back of his closet. His father had given it to him one Christmas, when he was fifteen. It was a single-shot 22 rifle chambered for longs. Montgomery Ward. It threw high to the right. The half box of shells was in the back of the bottom bureau drawer.

The best way, he thought, would be to take the bolt out and wear those khakis which were roomier in the leg, and put it down his pant leg, muzzle down. In a little while. It was their bowling night. If they went, he could carry it out to the car without any pantleg nonsense. They might not go. Just to show him how upset they were. See what you've done to us? You're spoiling everything for us, Sonny. After we've devoted our lives to you, boy.

He yawned and stretched. When he was away from her it was like being half alive. Everything was in monotone, like an old movie. Thoughts moved slowly, and his bones felt old.

Once again he let himself float back into sensual reverie, the images of the flesh, halted when his mother had knocked at his door. He knew that he could never have guessed how difficult it could be. Sometimes he would feel powerful as a giant, and, gathered into his great hands and sinewed arms, she would feel so sweet and little and whimperingly fragile, he would take her with a measured care, such a cautious awe and tenderness it seemed to make his heart melt and flow. And other times, in the tumbly striving gloom, she would seem to grow to an overwhelming weight, a huge warm bulging of thighs big as trees, belly like a meadow, furnace-door mouth, breasts like dunes, and the strong pulling of her arms would dwindle him to a little stick-figure of a man, drowned in the softness, held in purring, chuckling hunger, ticked close, and at last made to go into the scary puppety leapings that was not like pleasure but like all the world pulled down to a whine of bright lights, a shrillness of a single vivid and indescribable color, a grating and drawing and diminishing that was like the sense of falling which comes at the end of dreams.

When Sam Boylston walked into Staniker's hospital room on Sunday afternoon at one thirty, the Captain was sitting in the arm chair in a cotton robe. Theyma Chappie was fixing a bowl of tropical blooms on the deep windowsill, pinching off the dead blossoms and dry leaves. She gave Sam a swift sidelong glance.

"I shall be down at the floor-nurse station, Captain," she said. "Ring if you need me, please."

As she was leaving, Sam went to Staniker, started to put his right hand out, changed to his left hand. As Staniker took it, Sam said, "I appreciate your giving me some time, Captain."

"Sit down, Mr. Boylston. Sit down. I know how you must feel. Miss Leila was a fine little lady. It was a terrible thing to happen. You just never know. One minute everything is fine and the next minute—You just never know."

Sam sat on the straight chair by the bed, readjusting his mental image of Staniker to fit the reality. The man was both bigger and better looking than he had expected. And there was a certain flavor of earnestness about him, of staunchness, one might easily find attractive. Yet there was something about him which reminded Sam of someone he did not like. It took him but a few seconds to pin it down. Big Tom Dorra, who along with old Judge Billy Alwerd had invested half the cash in Bix's venture. Staniker did not have the hugeness of Big Tom, but the impact seemed strangely the same. There was the same flavor of a lazy gentleness which underscored rather than diluted an almost tangible maleness. The Captain and Tom Dorra both projected effortlessly that same promise of brute masculinity which had given some extraordinarily wooden actors long long careers in motion pictures. And just like Big Tom, in spite of the weather wrinkles and the smile wrinkles, the eyes themselves, pale, with coarse lashes, had the empty, bored distant malevolence of the bull elephant, the ruthless look and pattern of the stud.

He noticed an odd thing about the hair at Staniker's temples. It was gray at the roots, gray for the first half inch, the dividing line between new color and old almost mathematically precise.

"Was my sister having a good time on the cruise, Captain?"

"That was a fine comfortable vessel, Mr. Boylston, and Mr. and Mrs. Kayd had me take them to interesting places. It would be a nice experience for anyone who didn't know the Islands."

"Did she seem to be having a good time?"

Staniker scowled in heavy thought. "I guess you'd want to know just how it was. She'd get moony about her boyfriend back in Texas. But that wasn't all the time. There's another thing, and I've run pleasure boats enough years to see it happen over and over. You put people on a boat and what it does, Mr. Boylston, it makes any little differences a lot bigger, especially if it's family. Stella was a meek little thing, and that Mrs. Kayd, her step-mother, seemed bound on making that cruise pure hell for that little girl. Nasty nice. You know?"

"I know."

"And Mr. Kayd kept criticizing his own boy every chance he got. Not a bad kid, that Roger, but his old man didn't give him much of a chance. I guess Mister Bix kept getting the uglies on account of his wife was forever whining and complaining at him. When things got rough, Miss Leila would sidestep pretty good. She and my wife and me, we had to stay out of the line of fire. They'd keep trying to get outsiders to take sides in family trouble. I don't mind telling you, Mr. Boylston, off the record, that Carolyn Kayd was real trouble. I think she liked things all messed up. Hell of a good-looking piece of woman, and she started giving me the eye after we'd been cruising a week or so. Just to needle Mister Bix. Even if my Mary Jane hadn't been along, I've been around too long to walk into any kind of a setup like that. Maybe I'm making it sound worse than it was. Your sister had some good times. She hung one bull dolphin that like to give her fits. He spent more time in the air than he did in the water, but she got him up to the gaff, and when I yanked him aboard and he started going through all those colors as he died, she said she was sorry she hadn't lost him. Nice little girl. A nice happy little girl. The Lord giveth and the Lord taketh away, as the good book says, but it doesn't seem to be worked out too fair sometimes."

"I guess my friend Bix Kayd conducted business as usual."

"That man was on the horn ever' single morning. I bet he put enough on that credit card in phone calls to damn near buy another boat the same size."

"And conferences too, I imagine. Meeting people here and there."

Staniker stared down at his big left fist and then looked at Sam with a troubled earnestness. "He met with some men, sure. And only he and me knew about it. That was most of the reason why he bought that Formula 233 boat in Miami. He told me what kind of performance he wanted in a small boat we could take in tow, and I picked it out for him. What he'd do, we'd leave the big boat in a good anchorage and the two of us would take off in that Muñequita, with billfish gear, and meet up with people like he'd arranged it. But I wouldn't feel right about talking about that, Mr. Boylston. The way Mister Bix set it up in the beginning, he was paying me a big wage partly for keeping my mouth shut. He had reason to know I could. Now God knows it doesn't matter to him any more what I say to anybody one way or the other. But perhaps it could matter to some of the men he had dealings with. I've signed a contract to tell the whole exclusive story to a man who's going to write it up, but I'm going to leave out all of the business stuff, because I expect to stay in the business of hiring out as captain, and if you get a reputation for too much mouth, jobs get scarce."

"I appreciate your point, Captain. You know, it's a funny thing. If my sister hadn't been aboard, I'd be upset about something that doesn't seem important at all to me now."

"What's that, sir?"

Watching Staniker closely, Sam shrugged, smiled wryly, and said, "I had a deal going with Bix. A couple of hundred thousand dollars of mine went down with that boat."

Staniker stared, eyes wide. "Cash money?" he said in a hushed tone.

"Cash money. And a lot more that Bix put in the kitty."

Staniker shook his head. "Now why would a sane man take a chance and tote that much money all over the Bahamas on a fifty-three foot boat?"

"Sometimes, when something is for sale, cash is the only way you can buy it. Cash doesn't leave tracks, Staniker."

"I never had any *idea!*" Staniker said.

"I wouldn't have mentioned it. But when you told me you felt—a moral responsibility not to discuss his business dealings, I knew there wouldn't be any harm in it."

"I'd never mention it to a soul, Mr. Boylston, I swear."

Sam sighed. "Funny thing. I had a hunch about that cruise. I should have followed it. I felt a little edgy about having my kid sister go along. Careful as Bix was about everything, there was a chance somebody might figure out he had it aboard. Nobody knew except me and Bix. If somebody went after that money, I thought, it would be a damned poor place for Leila to be. Oh. Correction. Two other men knew it would be aboard, even though Leila and nobody else in Bix's family knew. The other two are business associates. Known them for years. They stood to make too much out of the deal to try anything tricky anyway."

Staniker poked very gently at his burned thigh, biting his lip. "Mr. Boylston?"

"What?"

"I was wondering. Is it going to come out there was all that money aboard? I mean through the estate or insurance or anything?"

"For personal reasons, Staniker, I hope not. But there's always that chance, isn't there? One of our associates might try to set it up as a casualty loss. But I don't understand, Captain. Why should any publicity about it be upsetting to you?"

Staniker stared blankly at him. "Upsetting? Oh, no. Listen, maybe you don't like it, me making a few bucks by signing that contract. Maybe you think it isn't right to make money out of a terrible accident like that. But it's going to be hard for me to get work. I got to worry about how I'm going to keep eating. My contract has book royalties in it and movie rights. Now I swear to you I won't tell a soul about that money. You can trust me all the way in a thing like that. But what I was thinking, the reason I asked, if it *did* happen to come out, it might mean a lot more money for me out of that contract. You can hate me if you want to, but nobody is going to look after me except me."

"I understand." Sam stood up. "Thanks for giving me the time. You coming along all right?"

"Better than they thought I would, I guess. They're letting me leave Wednesday. That's what? June first? Yes. I got a little advance on an insurance settlement. I might maybe try a hotel a couple days to get used to getting around, then fly on back to Miami. But I guess it will be a long time before I really get over this thing, or maybe never. It's a nightmare for sure, Mr. Boylston."

On his way to the stairway he saw Theyma Chappie coming along the corridor toward him. He beckoned her into a small alcove.

"Do you now see what I was trying to tell you?" she asked in a low tone.

"Yes. I see it."

"Some terrible thing hides behind his eyes. When he put his hand on me, after I jumped away, I felt so cold for a long, long time. That was when I knew he could do what you say he did. Then I was sure."

"He's good, Theyma. Believe me, he's damned good. It's a great front, all that bumbling slowness and sincerity and troubled manner. There aren't many ways. Trick him, or trap him, or break him. I don't know how it can be done. But I have to do it."

"What will doing it do to you, Sam?"

"Balance the ledger."

"God's business, no?"

"With man's help sometimes. Your place? Five thirty?"

"Good."

"Just get the recorder out of the room, and that's the last of it. I'm grateful to you for taking the chance."

"Perhaps it would have been better not to. I think. For you. I am not sure. But—it is done. And you go tomorrow. Sam, go all the way home. Go all the way to your Texas and your Lydia Jean."

"This evening I'll play you something I put together out of all those tapes."

"Perhaps I do not wish to hear it, eh?"

"I want you to."

She made a face. "Why should such things you want matter to me in any way? You bully me, Mr. Boylston. It is a disgrace. Excuse me. I must go tuck your monster into bed for a nap." She pulled her shoulders high, canted her head, gave him an odd look. "I watch him asleep. When his lids quiver and his hands twitch and his mouth changes shapes I know he dreams. And I wonder."

Sunday afternoon after Leila awakened from another of her long naps, she fought back the insidious lethargy and drowsiness and told the Sergeant, sweetly and politely, that she felt she would be more comfortable aboard the Muñequita. Had he not said it was moored under the house? Then it would not get too hot. There were screens which could be zipped in place, a bow hatch propped open for ventilation, a marine head, bedding in a locker under the port bunk. She said he would then have his own bed back. She would be able to do more for herself. The suggestion seemed to displease him, and he went out without a word. She felt herself sliding back into sleep, fought it for a little while and then let go. Never had she slept so heavily and continuously. She wondered if the blow on the head had anything to do with it.

She had seen herself in the mirror he brought her when she asked for it. It had frightened her. Her cheekbones looked sharp enough to poke through her sallow-tan skin. Her eyes were sunk back into her head. Her matted hair was clumsily brushed over the shaved area of the wound. Her lips were swollen, pulpy, pale, cracked and split.

She knew everybody would be looking for her. She could not sustain a sense of urgency longer than a few minutes before sinking back into that lethargy that was so like having had too many drinks. He brought her bowls of spiced, rich, heavy food, big mugs of hot tea. She would feed herself until her arm tired, and then he would take the spoon and feed her, coaxing her to take more, making little clicking sounds with his mouth, the way some people speak to horses.

Once she had awakened—yesterday? the day before?—to find she had been turned face down, the improvised night-gown pulled high, while hands that were at once strong and gentle rubbed a pungent ointment into her back, working from high on her shoulders all the way to the backs of her calves and back again. In that disjointed world of half-sleep, Daddy was once again putting on that stuff that stopped the terrible itching-burning of the poison oak. Sam didn't get it as bad as I did, she thought.

Then she heard the stranger-voice, crooning to itself, " . . . enough skin come off to build a whole new gal, I do swear . . . no bad places left . . . coming pink and new like a baby . . . pore little burned ass ain't board-flat no more, plumping up again . . . ."

Just as her body began to tighten in alarm, he had given her a little pat on the shoulder, grunted to his feet, spread the clean white shirt down over her, pulled the sheet back in place. Her thought of protest faded into the velvet dark of sleep.

Remembering, as she wondered why the Sergeant had left without a word, she reached a hand under the back of the shirt and felt of herself, felt on her back and buttocks, under a slight oiliness of medication, an ugly random pattern of welts and lumps and ridges instead of the familiar smoothness. There was no pain, yet here and there a special tenderness.

After a long time she heard him clumping up the outside steps. It took a moment to remember the name of the song he was singing without words. Lili Marlene. "Dum dum dah *dum* dah—dum ti dum ti *dah*."

He told her the boat was ready. He wrapped her in a blanket and picked her up. From the top of the stairs she had expected to be able to see water beyond the shoreline of the island, but the trees were too high. The light hurt her eyes. The world seemed far too huge and bright. The steps looked unsafe. She clung to him. She saw the small boat basin, like a pond in a swamp, the water black and still, and saw the channel where it entered the thick mangrove growth and curved out of sight.

Over his few dum-dah-dum bars of the song, repeated over and over, she heard the tiny song of mosquitoes around her ears, face and throat. In the shadows of the mooring place under the house he stepped lightly aboard the Muñequita from his sheltered dock. The overhead was far too low for him to carry her into the forward cabin space. He set her down and steadied her as she backed down the step and clambered weakly into the bunk he had made up. He came in, closing the screening behind him, sat on his heels and sprayed the

mosquitoes which had come in with them. The hatch was propped
open overhead, the screening in place.

He flicked on a weak bulb over her bunk, turned it off again.
"The batteries are charged up pretty good, Missy, so if you're wan-
tin to use the light it shouldn't take it down much, and the gas is full
near to the top so as I can run the engines in neutral and recharge,
comes to that. And you can run this little fan too I'd say, when the
air gets too still."

He pressed a switch. The little rubber-bladed fan began to whir.
She felt the wind against her face, glanced up at it, and a picture
formed quickly in her mind and disappeared, leaving an aftertaste of
fear and despair she could not identify. She had too brief a glimpse
of the dark, bloated, horrid face of the woman to identify her. Eyes
bulged from the sockets. Thickened tongue protruded from the
mouth. And a long strand of her hair had been caught in a small fan,
wound around shaft and blade. The fan did not move. It hummed
and stank.

"You all right, Miss Leila?"

" . . . Yes. Yes, I'm all right."

After he left her alone she made herself get out of the bunk and
look for the things she had hoped to use. The search did not take
long. The little pistol and the shotgun were gone. The spear guns
were gone. Both bronze keys were gone from the ignition switches
and from the compartment under the instrument panel where the
little Japanese transistorized ship-to-shore radio was locked away.
She stretched out on the bunk and wept for a little while. Then she
collected from the compartment under the other bunk a few things
she could use. Towels, insect repellent, a terry beach coat which belonged to Roger, one of Stel's swim suits, the yellow one with white
trim.

There's one way, she thought, when I'm strong enough. Put this
suit on and slip over the side and swim out his crazy channel to the

open water. Even if it's five miles to shore, I can make it. So I better work it into the conversation sometime that I can't swim.

But there was another thing to try first. And planning it, she fell asleep.

On Monday, far stronger than she had hoped to be, she was able to walk halfway up the steps, clinging to the Sergeant before she tired and had to be carried the rest of the way. With his primitive sewing kit, she had fashioned herself underwear pants from a piece of sheeting, a short skirt from a beach towel, a bandeau top from a smaller towel. After she had rested and eaten well, she said, in polite accusation, "You should have taken me to a doctor right away, you know."

"Missy, you don't know about head wounds. You don't know a thing." He touched the sickening dent in his forehead. "After I was sound as a dollar, they kept me in that place *three whole years!*"

"But this isn't the *same!*"

"Well—there's another thing I expect you better know about. If it wasn't for the Lieutenant, all them pretty little people in those little houses over there on the mainland shore, they would have got me stuck back into that place long ago. I get mixed up a little sometimes. One of them fat little sons of bitches—excuse me—he stood right up in court and he asked the judge that time how they had any garntee I wasn't going to sneak over there some dark night and kill them all in their beds, like I was some kind of maniac. I don't bother them. Why'd they want to bother me like they do? Missy—from the minute I found you, I had that on my mind. You understand? What if I took you to a doctor and you were dead when we got there? What if you died and never come to? All those people over there would jump right onto a thing like that and say Sergeant Corpo, he hurt that pore girl and he should ought to be locked up. Missy, the onliest thing I could do was nurse you good as I could and hope."

"But what if I *had* died?"

"I had a spot picked out, and I got lumber to make a good box, and a Bible to say words over you. I would have took that good boat out on a dark night on an outgoing tide and let it go on out the pass into the ocean. It would have been the best I could do, Missy." He gave a single loud clap of his hands. "But what good is this kind of talk? Here you are setting up, smart as paint, and everything is fine as can be."

She smiled at him. "I'm very very grateful to you, Sergeant. It's nice things worked out this way. Now I'd like you to take me to Broward Beach in the boat so I can get in touch with my people."

He leaned forward and stared at her. "What's the matter with you, girl? You haven't heard what I've been saying to you?"

"Certainly I have!"

"Any damn fool could take one look at you and he'd *know* you were a mighty sick little gal. Your head is healing good but it sure God looks recent like. And the fever's melted all the meat off your bones and you're weak as a kitten. Why, if I took you in there the shape you're in, they'd all *know* I kept you here and doctored you myself and it would be pretty near as bad as taking you in dead."

She stared at him in dismay. He had that careful and earnest logic of the deranged. He had the raw sinewy look of enormous strength. His homemade haircut was grotesque. His eyes, of the palest gray she had ever seen, had an eerie luminosity about them, as though lighted from behind. She had seen animal eyes like that.

With a catch in her voice she asked hopelessly, "When *can* I leave? Please."

"When it's *time!* When nobody could ever know you'd ever had a sick day in your life, Miss Leila. Why, you're going to get so you're fat and sassy and laughing the whole day long. Your hair will all be grown back to cover that scar. You'll be healthy like never before. Don't you fret about things to do around here. There's a thousand things, Missy. I can show you the kinds of wild orchids and air plants, and how the fiddler crabs make signals to each other, and

how comical them baby pelicans are. Misty mornings, early, I can
take you out on the flats, and sometimes I can have you scrunch
down in the skiff and we can go to some beaches I go to where real
good stuff washes up and there's nobody there at all. We'll have us a
fine time, and you've got Sergeant Corpo's word on that. Then, say
along toward fall, you can just say goodby and set off in that fine
boat. If you don't know how to run it, I can teach you easy. And you
can bet that boy Jonathan and your brother Sam will be glad to see
you looking so fine and happy. They see you now, it could scare
them some."

"How do you know about them!"

"I swear, you asked me that three times now and ever' time I tell
you it was from listening to you talking to that whole mess of people when you were sickest."

"But they'll be so *worried* about me, Sergeant!"

He shook his head sadly. "You know if you fret about it, you're
not going to have you a good time on my island at all. You'll spoil it
for sure for the both of us. Now don't you worry about the lady-
stuff you'll need. A gal has her needs and she has to have pretties and
all, and when I get set to go on into town, you can give me a list of
anything you can think of."

He got up quickly and went over to his great jumble of boxes and
containers and came back with a green metal box and put it on the
floor beside her feet. "This here is an ammunition box and they're
good things because the damp can't get into what you put in them."
He opened it and looked expectantly up at her and she saw that it
was full almost to the top with money.

"Where did you get all that!"

"I cash the army check and I don't never need that much for what
I have to buy, so I just bring the rest of it on back and put it in this
box. Been doing it for years and years. I got a box that filled up a
long time back and I had to start a new one. It's over there some-

place. I surely would like to know how much there is all told. Maybe you could he'p me count it out. I used to try but it took so long I'd get all mixed up somewhere in what number thousand it was I got to. So I gave up on it."

He closed the box and put it back with his other boxes. He sat down again and said in a tone of wonder, "I know I got to keep you here like I said, Missy, but I never thought in my whole life I'd be glad to have anybody close by again. Folks make me edgy. But you, somehow, it doesn't bother me one little bit. I swear, when I didn't know if you was living or dying, you were still the prettiest little thing I ever saw anyplace, and I can see now that all you're going to do as you get better is get prettier. It'll be a nice thing, having you here with me for a long long time, Missy."

He seemed to be implying something, and it gave her a little crawling feeling of growing apprehension. She looked wide-eyed at him and moistened her lips and said, "I—I don't want to be—your *girl*, Sergeant!"

He was motionless and then he jumped up so wildly he knocked his chair over. He glared at her and said, "Who said any such thing as that? You think I'm some kind of animal? You think I ought to be locked up? That it? Why I wouldn't lay a hand on you . . . ." He gave a grunt of astonishment and stared down at his right hand as if he had never seen it before. He turned it this way and that.

"Never happen again anyways," he said in a strange voice. "Happen again and I cut you off, finger by finger."

"What happened?"

"When I first toted you up here. I had to look close at you to see every hurt place. This fool hand—it reached itself out and felt your little bare titty." He looked at her in shame and distress. "It was only that one time, I swear, and nothing can't ever happen again like that, Miss Leila, on my word of honor— All I want— All I want . . ."

He stopped and his eyes changed, looking through her rather

than at her. He turned slowly and in a wooden manner quite unlike his normal movement walked to a place to one side of the door where he grasped two uprights fashioned of peeled poles. She could guess from the tension of his body how strongly he held them. They were a few feet apart, and the areas where he held them were darkened with the past times of standing there. He leaned forward, put his head against a heavy cross beam. He rolled his head slowly from side to side and made an almost inaudible moan. He leaned his head back and then thudded it so heavily against the beam she felt her stomach turn over.

"Sergeant!" she cried. "No!"

When he did it again, she made her way to him, clung to one arm, tried to pull his grip loose and turn him. His arm was like marble.

He turned slowly at last and looked at her. He said empty syllables that fitted his mouth loosely and did not combine into words. He wiped his mouth on the back of his hand. She got him over to the bed and he sat down. He frowned up at her. "Get a little bit mixed up now and again."

She felt no fear of him and knew there would never be any fear. The luminous look of those strange eyes was the limpid clarity of a kind of innocence. A child looked out at her. The rigid ethic of boyhood controlled the big tough body. It was as though he had built a tree house, a place to play pretend, and had filled it with toys, and she was another toy, the newest of all.

There would be chances to get away from him just as soon as she was strong enough.

"It'll be just like you say, Sergeant. We'll have a fine time. We'll have fun."

The slow smile lasted a long time. "Surely will," said the Sergeant.

Sixteen

RAOUL KELLY KNEW he was on some special lists. He had caused too much trouble for too many people to expect to go unnoticed. There had been one very clumsy attempt and one very skilled attempt which went wrong only because by some freak of luck the set-gun so mounted in his bureau drawer as to fire into the chest of anyone opening the drawer had misfired. After the second attempt he was able to get a pistol permit without too much difficulty.

He was licensed to carry it for self-protection. It was a Colt Cobra, a 38 Special with a one-inch barrel, and it fitted lightly and without bulge into the side pocket of his trousers. But usually it was locked up in the glove compartment. Guns made him feel foolish and theatrical, as if he were called upon to imitate a quite different sort of man. All through weapons training before the Bay of Pigs he had the idiot impulse to pull the trigger and yell BANG, YOU'RE DEAD. And after the fiasco as he was being led away, he thought it would be far more logical if all those very still, manlike lumps would get up, shrug, grin, wash off the fake blood and go buy each other beers.

He knew that it was with the very best of intentions a small group of compatriots had demanded he acquire the pistol permit from the Dade County authorities. At the same time they arranged an informal roster, and kept a watchful eye on his car and his rented room. After much thought, Raoul had taken his own quiet steps to insure his safety. He had typed out thirty pages of those guesses, hunches and gossip which were very probably quite true, but were so unprovable he could not risk publication. He left out two names. They were both, he was quite sure, clever and highly trained revolutionaries masquerading as anti-Castroites. He showed his notes to both those men and said that should anything happen to him, three close friends had copies and all guaranteed they would get the material published. And he had added that from time to time, as he discovered more probabilities of the same order, he would supplement the notes. There was, he thought, one very comforting thing about the Enemy. They were unfailingly practical. Given a choice of two evils, no emotions entered into their decision to pick the lesser one.

When, leaving the Harkinson place, with 'Cisca beside him, turning from the narrow road onto the highway he had seen the new-looking gray Plymouth sedan still parked in the same spot, he remembered the weapon in his glove compartment. He had not thought of it for weeks.

From time to time during that Monday evening, as he pleaded vainly with the stubborn and unyielding Francisca, he kept remembering the gray car. And at last it provided inspiration.

"Now then, Señorita," he said, her dark eyes looking at him over the rim of the cup as she sipped her coffee, "I must outline the situation."

"Oh, of course. Completely. And then perhaps it will be possible, Señor, to talk of other things?"

"Perhaps. You will not quit your job."

"The job will end itself when she can no longer pay me. Until then it is easy work. She does not interfere in my life. I am content."

"You refuse to marry me."

"Or anyone."

"Or come with me to California on any basis."

"To go so far! No."

"Then, truly, I must not go, because I cannot leave you."

"You will find friends there. I will find them here. I am not so important to anyone, Raoul."

"To me you are."

"But I do not *wish* it to be that way."

"It *is* that way, regardless of what you wish, *querida*."

"Perhaps it should be ended then."

"I would stay near you in any case, 'Cisca. And one day, perhaps this year, perhaps next, they will manage to kill me."

Watching her closely he saw the vapid look which signaled her change from shop-girl Spanish to crude and clumsy English. "Sotch a crazy theeng! Oh boy."

"They've tried twice."

"Ho! To rob sotch a reech man, you bet."

He reached across the booth table, captured both slender wrists in his workman's hands. She tugged, looking angry, but he held her firmly.

"The same people who killed your brother, *querida*."

"Let me go!"

"The people's republic in the land of peace and brotherhood, baby. Because I'm still fighting. Because I sting them with the words I write."

"Please. Let go!"

"You won't read what I write. You want to make believe nothing ever happened. You can't remember Havana, eh? You were never there. There isn't any war. You never scrubbed the soldiers' barracks on your hands and knees out at Rancho Luna. That was some other girl. And when they kill me, you'll forget that too, like everything else."

She made such a sudden violent effort she nearly wrested her hands free, but he did not let her go. She lowered her head, chin on her chest, so that all he could see of her was the lustrous darkness of her hair. A waitress moved near, curious and concerned. He gave her a nod and a smile to reassure her. She moved away, but glanced back, her expression showing a certain dubiousness.

Her arms were completely limp. He released his hold slowly. She remained there unmoving, and he could see the slow lift and fall of her breath under the pale green blouse.

Oh, you are a clever one, Kelly, he thought. Without any trouble at all you push her back into her empty and silent cave. The operation was brilliant, but the patient died on the table.

Slowly she raised her head and looked at him. Tears were streaming down her face. But her eyes had a look of awareness of him and of herself he had not seen before. They were the eyes of Señorita Francisca Torcedo y Sarmantar, only daughter of Don Esteban, only sister of Enrique.

To his vast astonishment she spoke in English, husky, halting, thickened by grief. "Doan be deads. Then nobody. Nobody left. Nothings. Not loving me, please. Sotch a rotten girl! Not to marry, please. But you for safe, I go with. Any places. All my life, I go with. Care for you, anytimes you say. Jesus help me. I swear for it."

She lowered her head again, sighed very deeply. His own eyes were wet as he realized how desperately he had needed this affirmation of her love, kept so carefully hidden. It had been more than his pride which had been affronted by her apparent happy willingness to think of their relationship as a casual affair, something suitable for a housemaid who would be expected to have a boyfran who would take her to movies, to the beach, and to bed. And he suddenly understood why, once she had been forced into revelation, it had to come out in English. There were too many blocks for it to be said in Spanish. She had used it like a code, a way to say things she could not say, like the secret languages children invent.

When he took her out to the car she moved like one recovering from illness. She was remote, emotionally exhausted, shy.

He decided that if English was the way to reach her, he would stay with English. The "rotten girl" part puzzled him. It indicated that there was guilt involved in her long withdrawal, as well as shock and grief and sickness. But what could cause her to feel so unworthy? He suspected that it would be very unwise to try to find out. Maybe some day. Certainly she would not feel guilt at having tried to kill one of those "liberators" who had so clumsily shot the adored papa, or guilt at having been made pregnant under circumstances she had no way of controlling.

As he drove down the dark highway with the girl sitting passively beside him, he suddenly thought of one possible situation which could make her feel that she was rotten. She had spent months as a prisoner. What if one of them, one of the village boys, had taken pity on the little upperclass *pollita*? Some young and gentle lad, who had treated her with a natural kindness, smuggled better food to her, saved her from the more brutalizing kinds of labor. He knew the capacity for warmth and gentleness the young village men of his country often had. A young boy, perhaps as young as she. In her anguish and despair, she might well have responded to him, willingly. But she could not realize that both she and the young militiaman were both victims of the merciless random patterns of history. She would know only that she had given herself to the Enemy, that out of a weakness and helplessness she would misinterpret as callousness and lust, she had lain with the murderer of father and brother. Then, after her rescue, having not the ability to physically kill herself, perhaps because of the mandate of the church, she had killed the guilty Francisca and had become someone else.

At first he thought the diagnosis fanciful, but there was too much weight of detail to support it, and indeed he could not think of any other factor which could have so distorted a person of her strength, spirit and intelligence. A lesser woman could have devised useful rationalizations for indulging herself with the Enemy. To the daughter of Don Esteban, the sister of Enrique, it would be a matter of personal honor, and an insupportable memory. Such a woman could live only with the memory of never having been taken except by force.

He sensed the ultimate irony, that what she thought of as rottenness was in truth a measure of her great worth.

"You'll give Mrs. Harkinson notice?"

"Tomorrow I say it. I work what she say. One week. Two."

"You don't owe her anything."

"I do what is right."

"I will send a letter to California tonight to tell them I accept. When you tell me when you can leave, I will tell the paper. If you can leave soon, we will drive."

"If you say it." Her voice was listless.

He parked outside the gate, walked her to her stairs. She turned, leaned against him, sighed heavily and touched her soft mouth to the side of his chin. "We are in love," he whispered.

"If you say it."

As he turned around and drove out he thought of the pale car. It was still there. He had seen it for an instant when he had turned off the highway. His lights had touched it as he turned. It was fifty yards south of the road to the Harkinson place, on the same side, and backed into the semi-concealment of a small grove of trees. There had been no need to mention it to Francisca. It would only worry her. He had not needed to prove to her that he was possibly in danger. He was no longer as proud of his device of the posthumous publication. If they had learned of this attachment, and had identified her, they would need only to pick her up and take her into the city and hide her, and Raoul Kelly would do anything they asked of him.

He turned south rather than north and as soon as he was around a long curve and out of light and sound, he found a place to pull off the highway. He took the revolver from the glove compartment, left the dark and silent car and crossed the highway and soon came upon a fence. He waited as they had taught him until his eyes adjusted to the night. The loaded weapon in the side pocket of his unbuttoned jacket nudged him from time to time as he walked north, paralleling the highway. Something went scuttling away from under his feet, thrashing off into the grass, giving him a horrid start.

Warrior type, he thought. Cover and concealment. Deadly weapon. A man should have the looks to go with the game. John Wayne would move like a tiger. He'd never turn his ankle and walk into a tree trunk. I am marked by the long-ago movies, Abbot and Costello. I am Lou Costello, whose every venture ends in a prat-fall.

He reached the grove and he could see the pallor of the car. He moved closer and saw the gleam of the rear-view mirror on the driver's side. He saw a dark bulk of someone slumped behind the wheel. Just as he was close enough to the rear of the car to touch it, the door opened and a man stepped out. Raoul's palm was sweaty on the serrated wood of the grip. When he got over the fright of thinking the man was coming after him, he was pleased to see that the stranger was not as huge as imagination had created him. The man stretched, grunted audibly, lifted his knees high in a slow, in-place march.

BANG, YOU'RE DEAD! Raoul thought. He took two steps forward and said, "Don't turn around. I've got a gun. Take it slow and easy."

After a silence of at least five seconds, the man said, "What do you want?" The accent was not strong, but it was of some other region. It reminded Raoul of one of the CIA people at the training area, a young man from Oklahoma.

"Why have you been parked here all this time?"

"What's that to you?"

Impasse. Raoul had a picture of himself taking another step, hammering the gun down smartly against the back of the neat sandy skull, revealed by the courtesy light which had turned on when the car door had been opened. Then you squat by the victim, get his wallet, look at his papers . . . But he could imagine too vividly the sound of steel against meat and bone.

"Are you an officer of the law?" the fellow asked.

"I'll ask the questions around here, buddy." And what do I ask next?

With no warning the car door slammed, and for an instant Raoul stood in total darkness, his night vision stolen by the courtesy light. Then something hammered a monstrous blow into the pit of his stomach. He was turned and his hand was rapped against the side of the car. The gun fell from his numbed hand. He was hit in the throat, and on the cheek and on the chin. The last blow felt very soft, as though it had come through a pillow. He faded, light as a balloon, onto his knees. Hands fumbled at him. He crawled slowly away, stopped and threw up.

In a little while he edged sideways, got hold of the slender trunk of a tree, climbed it hand over hand until he was up on his feet. He turned and leaned his back against the tree. A flashlight shone in his face. He put his arm up to shield his eyes. When the brightness went away he could see the man sitting sideways on the front seat of the car, feet on the ground, revolver resting between his thighs in the glow of the courtesy light. He was pushing the cards back into the pocket of Raoul's wallet.

"How do you feel, Mr. Kelly?"

"I've had better evenings."

"Come on over here and set for a spell."

Raoul got in on the passenger side. His wallet was handed to him. He leaned forward and worked it back into his hip pocket. He said, "Where's the other one?"

"What other one?"

"There's just you?"

"Just me."

"Then I better be glad there aren't two of you."

"It's the adrenalin. A man with a gun on him better move fast or not at all. Here you go. It's empty now. Put it in that side pocket. Put these shells in the pocket on the other side. Newspaperman. Last thing I expected. But I guess it's reasonable to expect that a reporter, if he's bright enough, if he did some digging, would take an interest in Crissy Harkinson these days."

"Who are you?"

"I'll return the favor," the man said. He took out a billfold, unsnapped a card case, handed it over. Raoul looked at the cards. His mind seemed to move slowly and reluctantly. His face hurt. A lawyer from Texas. Samuel Boylston. It made no sense. Boylston. Something about the name. Then he remembered it was the name of the boat guest. A Miss Boylston.

"The girl on the Muñeca was related to you?"

Boylston was looking at him with what seemed to be a new interest. He answered in rapid, fluent border Mexican. "She was my sister. It gives me a very special interest in the entire affair. You might be of some help to me."

The verb forms were simplified, and he used the familiar form of address, as though talking to a servant. It irritated Raoul, the accuracy of the guess as well as the manner.

"Mr. Boylston, I suspect that my Cuban Spanish might create problems for you. And my English is a little better than your

Mexican Spanish. I do not believe I can be of any help to you. A young lady from Cuba works for Mrs. Harkinson. I visit her often. That's all."

"I see. Did you drive in with her not long ago in a green Ford and then come out and turn south?"

"Yes."

"Then it seems a little strange that you should come sneaking up on me with that gun, just because I happened to be parked here."

"Strange? All Cuban exiles are conspiratorial and paranoid, Mr. Boylston. Haven't you heard?"

"Have you met Crissy Harkinson?"

"No. I've seen her, but not near by."

"How long has your girl worked for her?"

"Not long. She'll be quitting soon."

"Why?"

"Mr. Boylston, you ask a lot of questions. She's going to California with me. I have a new job out there."

"Who is the kid in the rusty blue car?"

"Perhaps a friend of Mrs. Harkinson. Or maybe he's doing some work for her. I wouldn't know. I don't talk about Mrs. Harkinson with my friend. She wouldn't know much anyway. She hasn't got very much English."

"Does Mrs. Harkinson go out much in the evening?"

"Very rarely. Can I leave now?"

"You claim to be a newspaperman?"

"It isn't a claim. It's what I am."

"You don't do well in poker games, Kelly."

"That's a flat statement, eh? A judgment from on high. All right. I lose. And I am not so great with a gun, either. What's your point, Boylston?"

"A reporter would try to pump me, my friend. What in the world is this man doing watching the Harkinson place? What's that got to do with his sister being lost at sea? Not you. All you want to do is get away from me. You didn't ask the right questions. So I have to assume you didn't ask them because you know the answers. And if you do, you are part of the whole stinking game too. So you are coming along with me and we're going to have a long talk."

"Coming where?"

"Just lean forward and keep both hands braced against the dashboard, Mr. Kelly. No. Higher, so I can see them out of the corner of my eye. Fine."

Boylston was staying in a poolside cabana at a second-class mainland motel. There were only a few cars at the motel proper. Boylston turned the lights on, pulled the double thicknesses of draperies across the window wall facing the pool. He pulled a straight chair closer to where Raoul sat, sat astride it, his folded arms resting on top of the back, chin on his forearm. There was a taut agility about the way he moved, a look of power under careful control, which made Raoul uneasy. And the man's eyes were as cold as a cat's.

"We have to find out if you are an animal, Kelly." His tone was uncommonly gentle. "Even if we have to hurt you to find out."

Raoul shrugged. "Bad poker player, yes. Bad with a gun, yes. Does pain bother me? Yes. Will it break me? No. I have had some. I have endured some things. Bay of Pigs. Isle of Pines. Maybe a man should have some of those things, to find out about himself. But maybe there is no point in telling you that. Harlingen it said on the card. Border Texas, I believe. So to start with, in your eyes, I am— what are people of Latin American blood called there? Spic? So you can start with an assumption I am less as a human being than you are. It could be wrong."

Boylston looked thoughtful. "Correction. I've never faulted you people on guts. In other ways? Yes. But—recently I've been reconsidering a lot of old attitudes. It's possible I've been wrong about a lot of things. But that's neither here nor there."

"We're lazy people, Lawyer. We drowse in the sun. We strum guitars and sing about broken hearts. We get very passionate and stick knives in each other. We lie a lot. Okay?"

"Don't push your luck."

"I think you were being honest. It was very refreshing. Perhaps I don't think very quickly after being hit in the face. Perhaps I don't react the way you think I should. But I am not mixed up in anything. You'll have to take my word for that."

"When a man acts in an implausible manner regarding something of importance to me, I have to know why. We have to find out some way of trusting each other, maybe."

"A lot would depend on what you are trying to do, what you're after."

"I want to be absolutely certain of something. Not legal proof. I don't think I'm going to get legal proof. Just proof enough to satisfy me. And then I am going to arrange to have Staniker and whoever was in it with him taken quietly to some out of the way place. And the last thing I am going to do with them is toast their rotten hearts over a slow fire on a sharp stick."

It was said with a deadly and absolute conviction which took all melodrama out of it. Raoul had heard the expression about something making the blood run cold. He had never experienced it before. The eyes and the quiet voice filled the room, and he managed, with great effort, to stop looking at Boylston. He felt that humming sensation which precedes a dead faint. He wiped his mouth on the back of his hand, swallowed, and said, "You convince me, Señor."

"Are you glad you're not one of them?"

"I will be very glad if I can convince you I'm not. If you had talked about legal proof, about police, then I would not tell you a certain story about a young woman of aristocratic birth. But now perhaps it is very necessary to tell you. First, does the word *pundonor* mean anything to you?"

"Point of honor? Of course. That's another thing I respect about the latinos."

"Enough to observe the custom?"

"Enough to be honored to be asked to observe it."

"Then, Mr. Boylston, I will tell you everything I know or suspect. And you, in turn, will promise not to go near Francisca, or take any action which will cause others to go to her and question her." As Boylston started to speak, Raoul stopped him and said. "And whatever you do, or however you do it, you will do it in such a way she will not be involved in it, in publicity, in questions, anything."

"I swear I will do my best—but if I find out you have held anything back or changed the facts in any way, the bets are off."

"*Pundonor* works both ways, Lawyer."

Sam Boylston let Raoul go through it, beginning to end. There was such a marked immobility about Boylston, such an absence of random movement, change of position, physical mannerism, Raoul had the feeling no one had ever listened to him as intently, no attention had ever been as consistent and unflawed.

When he was done, Boylston went out to the ice machine and filled the plastic pitcher, came back and mixed two drinks of bourbon and water in the glistening tumblers stripped clean of their crackly packaging of waxed paper. Sam stretched out on one of the Bahama beds, head propped up, ankles crossed. He had expected to have to come back with those questions which would cut through the familiar fuzziness of both thought and expression. He had accumulated a few questions in the beginning, but Kelly had eventually answered them. Sam found himself respecting the quality of this stocky, swarthy, broad-faced man's mind. Unlike most laymen, Kelly had made a clear distinction between fact and assumption, and between first-hand, second-hand and third-hand information.

"Raoul? I've got the name right?"

"You have."

"I need help. I was going to line up somebody I can trust. Import them from Texas. I think you're a better one to help me unravel this. I think we're in business together. I think you better call me Sam."

"I just told you why I don't want any part of it, Sam."

"Not exactly. You told me some very good reasons why you don't want your 'Cisca involved in any way. And the best way you can bring that about is to keep me from making some stupid blunder that will bring the police and the press into the act. Miami is your back yard, Raoul. If that girl is as shaky as you seem to think she is, and if she is in danger from Staniker and company, as you think she might be, then the best thing you can do for her is ride with me."

"My God, you know where the leverage is, don't you? But why do you want Fearless Kelly on your team?"

"Because you're so good with a gun. Because you're so stupid and agile and savage. One little thing, Raoul—didn't it itch like a place you couldn't scratch to know about Kayd seeing the woman in March, and Staniker carrying on with the woman ever since the boat was sold, and keeping it to yourself?"

"By then, by that time, whether it was planned or not, it was done. It was over for that family. Where would my motive be? A big scoop? A terrible concern to see justice done? Okay, it was stuck in my mind where I couldn't get at it, like a berry seed in the teeth. Because, I guess, I have the inquiring mind. The mind that wants to know what actually happened. Like when you get a call and have to leave in the middle of a movie. But we're in a bloody world, Sam. And it grows ever more bloody. People die badly for very small reasons. It was my concern only in the way it could affect Francisca."

Sam sat up and finished his drink. "I am an officer of the court. To that extent, a law man. Given the same kind of situation, I'd probably keep my mouth shut too. That's our disease, isn't it? Don't get involved. But this thing is too close. It was my blood, and the last, aside from my son, still living in the world. And I set her up for it. Not knowing, of course. You can go crazy trying to trace all the way back, playing that game of 'if'. If I hadn't done this, or had done that, if the timing had been different, if I had listened, if I had understood."

"Better to play that game than the other one."

"The other one?"

"The game of righteousness. The one that says I weighed every move, every tangible and intangible, and I made my decision in cold blood, so I am not to blame if something went wrong."

Sam stared over at Raoul Kelly, feeling strangely agitated. "Why should that be worse? What's wrong with logic?"

"For playing games, it's a fine thing. Chess, bridge, solving puzzles. Maybe it's handy for practicing law or making money. But people don't stand around on game boards, waiting to be moved or captured. There isn't any rule book. Freud isn't Hoyle. You can put in fifty cold facts and leave out one hot little emotion, and you come out dead wrong. Kelly's equation. Want to hear it? When it comes to emotions, everybody is usually wrong. So the only chance you've got is to try not to be wrong so often. And give other people permission to be wrong too. What's the matter? I'm upsetting you?"

"I don't know. Maybe. Last year I would have said that was weak, stupid nonsense. I would have been surprised a man could sound so bright one minute and so soft the next minute. I would have felt superior. Now I feel—I might be able to understand Kelly's Equation if I work on it long enough."

"Don't expect too much. That's part of it."

Sam built two more drinks, handed one to Raoul. "Anyway, aboard the boat that rescued Staniker, one of the women heard him, out of his head, trying to explain or apologize to somebody named Christy or Crissy. I got in from Nassau yesterday. Early this morning

I researched what the papers had written about Staniker. I went to that Parker's Marina and talked to the guys that hang around there. It came into focus. He did as little work as he could get away with. A cottage goes with the job. There's a new couple in it now. Staniker's wife was a cowed little woman. A sufferer. She did all her work and a good deal of what he was supposed to do. He took off when he felt like it. His car is parked out there too. An old yellow Olds. Staniker had been cozy with a Harkinson woman. Ran her boat until she sold it. One old boy kept nudging me and winking and saying that the Harkinson woman had belonged to one of the ex-governors of the state. I got on the phone and called a lawyer I know in Tampa. He knows the political scene. He said, as you confirmed a while ago, it had been an old man named Fontaine paying her bills. He'd been a State Senator once upon a time and hung onto the title. Made a pot of money in land speculation. Died last year. Rumor had it the old boy didn't leave Crissy Harkinson too well fixed. I remembered that Bix Kayd had been into a few Florida deals, but my friend didn't know the name. I phoned Brownsville, Texas, and woke up an old boy who would know, and he said Kayd and Fontaine had teamed up a time or two, but not recently."

"What are you leaving out?"

"Very good! I'll get to it in a minute. First I was going to just walk in on Mrs. Harkinson, when I located the house. Then I gave it some second thoughts. I visited Staniker in the hospital. He's as rough as he'd have to be. But his record is clean. A man with larceny in his heart doesn't get to be as old as Staniker with a clean record. Somebody had to push him into it. He won't crack. Maybe he would have, if somebody got to him soon enough, but he's had time to adjust to it. The Harkinson woman could be the planning department. If so, she could be too shrewd to accept any cover story from me. So I thought I'd better wait for her to come out and follow her and try to get enough of a look at her to see what type she might be. If she could send a man like Staniker after the jackpot."

"Which was?"

"The only thing you can pass under the table. Money. With no memory, no record, no conscience. Cash. Eight hundred thousand."

Raoul was holding his glass in both hands. His eyebrows went up and stayed up. "My, my, my!" he said softly, and drank like a child holding a mug. He scowled. "Maybe he didn't get it after all. Maybe he didn't have the nerve to do what the woman wanted him to do. He was burned. He was marooned. I remember something that happened in Havana years ago that took the police a long time to figure out. A store blew up in the middle of the night. The explosion killed two men. They were identified as professional thieves. It seemed they had the extraordinary bad luck to be in the place when one of the partners had set a time bomb to go off, as revenge for being cheated by the other partner."

"Now you get a chance to listen to something." Raoul watched Sam Boylston get out a small battery-operated tape recorder. As he selected the right reel and threaded it he said, "Staniker was interrogated several times. I got it all on tape. I don't have the skill to do a lot of splicing. So I used two recorders and hooked them together, and took off just what I wanted onto new tape. I don't practice criminal law. But you can't get through law school without being exposed to some of the things to watch for. Just listen. Then tell me what you think."

The machine started. For long seconds there was a hissing sound. Then a man's slow, heavy and slightly thickened voice:

"On the Muñeca you've got—you had every control duplicated up on the flying bridge." Pause. "On the Muñeca you've got . . . you had every control duplicated up on the flying bridge" Pause. "On the Muñeca you've got—you had every control duplicated up on the flying bridge." Pause. "On the Muñeca you've got—you had every control duplicated up on the flying bridge."

There was a longer pause and then: "He had a loud laugh . . . He had a loud laugh . . . He had a loud laugh . . . He had a loud laugh . . . ."

Raoul could tell they were not precise duplications of the same part of a master tape. They were said with slightly changed intonations, slight changes in rhythm. There were a few other phrases said over and over: "She wasn't a good swimmer on account of her leg." And, "That means doll in Spanish." "We got into nice dolphin a few miles out. Spent a lot of time."

Sam turned the machine off. Raoul said, "I see the point, of course. He starts to speak of the boat in the present tense and changes it to the past tense. But he does it every time. After the first time or maybe two, he would have learned to adjust to the past tense and he wouldn't make that mistake."

"So it was memorized, of course. For significant details of any story, people will have a tendency to use the same expressions over and over. So repetition means nothing. But what you watch for are the asides. People telling about something which happened do not bring in the same random thoughts in the same exact words every time. When they do it means they have been coached on those things, and they are trying to give the entire story a flavor of plausibility."

"So what was the real story, then?"

"I know one way I would do it. I would kill them. I would lash them to solid parts of the cruiser. I would put the money in the smaller boat. It was fast and seaworthy. I'd open the seacocks on the big one and let it go down in a mile of water. I'd make a fast run, without lights, down to the northern tip of Andros and maybe somewhere near Morgan's Bluff I'd hide that money where it would keep a long time. I'd run north again, and maybe I'd have loaded rocks into the smaller boat to overcome the flotation. I'd sink her closer to the Joulter Cays. But still in plenty of water. I'd wear a life belt and I'd swim to South Joulter Cay and bury the belt in the sand. I'd have a little can of gasoline with me and some matches in a waterproof case, and I would give myself some convincing burns and then wait to be rescued, rehearsing my story while I waited. It's easy to give yourself more of a burn than you intend. And if he'd been picked up in a day or two or three, which was a reasonable expectation, he would have been in much better shape. Next I would come back here and I'd meet with the woman, and we would decide how long it would be best to wait before going after the money, and what would be the best cover story for going after it, the best way to pick it up and run."

"When does he get back here?"

"Wednesday or Thursday or Friday, this week. I'll know in advance. A nurse will phone me. The woman doesn't know me by sight. The man doesn't know you by sight. That's the way we divide it up. I don't think he'll head for her house. That would be stupid. He'll hole up. She'll go to him."

"You seem very sure."

"Even the way she's acted through the whole thing, the moods your girl told you about—it all fits."

"So let the police have it, Sam Boylston."

"Isn't that just what you don't want?"

"Let me start west with 'Cisca. Then blow the whistle. They'll have to prove the same things some other way. About Kayd seeing her. About her relationship with Staniker."

"With what I've got, I don't think you could get a Grand Jury to indict. There's no way in the world I can prove that money was aboard. Who has the jurisdiction? If he was cleared at Nassau, are we into a double jeopardy problem? Could she ever be nailed as an accomplice? Not if she keeps her head, no matter *what* he says. No provable motive. No witnesses. If they could be indicted, and if it came to trial, any clown in town could get them off, and then no matter what came up later, they'd be in the clear forever."

"Then let go of it, Sam. Go home."

"Let go!"

"People like that find better ways of destroying themselves than you could ever dream up. Everybody dies, Sam. It all ends for everybody. So you are a clever man. And you are a hater. So suppose you get away with it. Will your sister know? Would you want to tell your wife or your boy?"

"*I* would know!"

"And you might have twenty years in Raiford Prison to think about how dead they would be. How come you appoint yourself the avenging angel? Maybe this is your chance to grow up, and all you have to do is recognize it."

"I grew up early, Kelly. Very early."

"Maybe that's why you stopped a little short."

"You don't seem to realize they *killed* my *sister!*"

Raoul sat there, looking like a bland Buddha. "Keel my seestair. Sure nuff. We're having some bad years for sisters and brothers, mothers and fathers and friends. The living are worth every final bit of love and energy you can toss into the kitty. The dead are worth tears. Trying to do more for the dead is self-love. It's pride gone bad. It's romantic nonsense." He yawned. "I can see from your expression you don't believe a word of it. Now you have to drive me all the way back down there to my car so I can go home and get, if I'm lucky, three hours sleep."

"How does your face feel now?"

"Lumpy."

"That's the way it looks."

"I'll tell people I kept running into a door. It kept jumping in front of me." He stood up. "I'll follow the Captain. I'm no good with guns. But I follow people pretty good."

Seventeen

EARLY ON TUESDAY AFTERNOON, Leila Boylston asked Sergeant Corpo to help her climb the crude ladder once again, up to the platform he had built high in a huge old water oak. She told him to stay close behind her in case she got dizzy, but she made it without trouble.

She sat crosslegged on the platform, catching her breath. He smiled at her, only his head visible over the edge of the platform.

"Did purely fine, Missy. You sing out when you want to come on down."

"Okay, Sarg."

After he had started down she leaned over the edge and looked down at him. "You'll be going over to the mainland tomorrow? It's the first of the month."

He stopped and craned his neck to look up at her. "Don't you get too close to the edge there now. I might go in tomorrow. I might go in the next day or the day after. Depends."

She pouted. "But you *promised* me things."

"And I guess you'd want to write down what you need."

"I told you three times I've got my list all ready!"

"Guess you did. No need to get cross about it, Missy."

"But I *need* things. You want me to be happy here. You keep saying it, anyway. How can I be happy when I *need* things?"

"I might go in tomorrow. Depends," he said, and went on down the ladder he had fashioned of boughs and wire.

She settled herself and, through the openings between the branches, looked wistfully out across the wide bay. She could see the bright tract houses rimming the nearest part of the mainland shore, not much over a mile and a half away, she estimated. The shoal water near the island kept the larger boats well clear of it. She could see an occasional glint of traffic moving along a road beyond the houses, and by straining her eyes she thought she could see the bright patterns of lawn sprinklers, and the racing dots of children at play.

Looking south she could see an industrial mistiness, a jumble of city buildings much more distant than the residential shore. To the north were some smaller mangrove islands, and to the west the markers of the Intercoastal Waterway and a navigable outlet to the deeper blue of the Atlantic, water breaking white against the protection of a long rock groin.

She tried to quell her terrible impatience. If he did not go tomorrow, he would at least be going in his skiff to Broward Beach very soon. And when he was out of sight, she would put on Stel's swim suit and take one of the floating seat cushions from the Muñequita, and paddle down his channel and across the flats and over across the bay toward those little houses. If she could not hail a boat, she felt she could make it without too much trouble. She did not panic in the water. She could rest, supported by the cushion. She thought with a certain grimness she might well startle one of the housewives over there out of her wits. Skin and bones, and with a back that looked as if she'd been recently flayed, hair like a bird's nest and eyes like an overworked haunt, one with too many castles to spook up.

She could feel the texture of a telephone, see her finger dipping into the O for operator, twirling the dial all the way around. Brrrrt brrrrt. "Operator?"

"I want to place a long distance collect call to Mr. Sam Boylston in Harlingen, Texas, please."

Oh, Sam, gather up Jonathan and come on the run. Come quickly. Please. I don't know what happened.

She stiffened as again some small and vivid pattern moved across the back of her mind and flickered out. She'd had but one small glimpse of it. A huge head, a man's head, sunbrown and bald, resting face down in a plate of food, but nodding back and forth as if he were saying no to something, rolling his face in the food, saying no because he did not want to be there. And she seemed to be looking down at him through some kind of a window from a dark outside place, and he was in the light.

Mister Bix! But why him? The brown head of a large middle-aged man. Drunk, probably. Mister Bix did not get drunk. Perhaps it was from a movie, a color movie, a clever camera angle.

When she felt sleepy enough to take a nap she did not call the Sergeant, but went down all by herself very carefully. He had been banging away at something, beating on metal with a small sledge. He seemed to have a small-boy intensity about building things. He did not do things very well, but he seemed happy with the results. He was sweaty with the effort. He was indignant about her coming down the ladder without help.

"You could have fell! Fool thing to do."

As she fell asleep, she could hear him working away.

That evening he opened the last two cans of beef stew, served it on mounds of rice. She knew she could not finish so much, and then to her surprise she reached the end of it. The breeze had stopped. The mosquitoes and gnats were bad. The sun was beginning to set. Her belly felt so full it made her think of the Thanksgiving dinners way back when they had been a family of four. Corpo had acted strangely shy and evasive during the evening meal. She insisted on helping him wash up.

At last, in too loud a voice, he made an announcement. "There's something I got to mess with you ain't going to care for one bit, Missy."

"Like what?"

"There are times folks don't know the best thing is being done. You're unsettled, and you want real bad to see your folks, but it isn't time yet. You don't understand now, but you will later on. It's something I swear I don't want to do, but it's one of those things I got to do."

"What are you talking about, anyway?"

He went out and came back very soon, carrying curious hardware, and slapping at the mosquitoes on his throat and arms.

"What have you got there?"

"Now just hold your arms out of the way, and I'll see how it works out." He put the band of metal around her waist. He had wrapped it in cloth to pad it. At the back he had made several slots, large enough to accept the U bolt he had fastened to the other end. With the U bolt through the proper slot, he put the open link of a length of heavy chain through the U bolt, and with a grunt of effort, closed the link with a pair of heavy pliers. He ran the other end of the chain down through a hole in the flooring, went out and under the shack and made that end fast. He came back looking shamefaced.

"Like an animal, Sergeant!"

"It hurt you any? Too tight or anything?"

"It hurts like hell!"

"You shouldn't cuss like that, Missy. Where does it hurt you?"

"It hurts my feelings, dammit!"

"Missy, it's the only way I'd feel right going to town and leaving you here. I have feelings about people, about the things they don't say. You could promise me word of honor you'd rest quiet and wait for me to come back. But you'd be thinking it was fit to lie because you'd be doing the best thing for me and for you and your people. Later on you'll know my way is best and when you decide that, I'll know about it and I won't have to fool with fastening you up while I'm gone. The state you're in now, you might do any fool thing, like setting fire to the place so somebody'd come to see what's going on, or trying to wade the flats and signal somebody in a boat, or even try to float yourself on something and get over to the mainland shore. Miss Leila, I had to find out if this would work good first before I could say for sure I'd go over to the city tomorrow. It looks about right. You got ten feet of slack in that old anchor chain, and I'll leave you in reach of everything you need, but nothing you could use to work yourself loose. And I'll be back just as soon as I can and turn you loose. Sorry that chain is so heavy, but it's the only thing I could figure out except tying you hand and foot."

"Get this thing off me! I feel like some kind of a dancing bear."

As he opened the link and released her, he said, "It won't be so bad, and it won't last too long, and I swear it's for your good just as much as mine. I had a replacement one time, a city boy they sent up to Able Company and put in my platoon, felt he knowed everything there was to know, fixing to get himself killed and maybe some of my other people at the same time. Soon as things quieted down I made that boy dig himself a fox hole six feet deep. Gave him a little aspirin box to bury in the bottom of it and fill it up again. Let him rest and then made him dig up that box. Guardhouse lawyer type boy, talking about cruel and unusual punishment and Inspector General and all that. Had him open the box and read the note I put in it. All it said was: Bury this here box again, Soldier. My, how that boy carried on. He like to kill me if I give him half a chance. But from then on he jumped when I said jump, ran when I yelled run, dug when I said dig. Found out finally it was keeping him alive. And he stopped minding everybody calling him Aspirin. Got proud of the name. Missy, I swear those little arms don't look as much like match sticks as they did. You ate real good this evening."

"Mother hen," Leila said hopelessly. "You darn old mother hen."

Crissy Harkinson, basted in fragrant oils, lay sprawled and drugged by the sun heat, plastic cups like a pair of glasses protecting her eyes from the midday glare, wearing only the red and white polka-dot bikini bottoms, tucked and rolled to the narrowness of a G string. A wind screen, backed with reflecting foil, shielded her from any boat traffic up or down the private channel near the shoreline.

When she heard the rapid slap-flop of Francisca's sandals approach across the patio stone, she reached with slow hand, pawed and found the towel, pulled it across her breasts.

"Iss ice tea, Mees Harkysohn, lady."

"On the little table, dear."

She heard the tick of the glass against the glass top of the table, and a twinkling of ice. She expected to hear the sandals patter off, but they didn't.

"Mees Harkysohn?"

"What now, girl?"

"I queet. Eh? No working here, eh?"

Crissy slowly took the cups from her eyes, worked herself over onto her stomach on the sun chaise. The towel slipped away. Propped on her elbows she frowned and said, "Get over here where I can see you, Francisca. That's better. Sit on that stool."

Francisca sat, facing her. She wore her broad smile of stupid delight. "Queeting, eh? Okay?"

"Not for the day, you mean. For good?"

"Oh yes!"

"Now God damn it, stop grinning at me. What's the matter? We're used to each other, girl. And I don't exactly work you to death. You've got a nice place to live. Television. You're paid right up to date. And paid well. Now what's this all about?"

"I go to California now."

"You go to California now. Isn't that just nifty! Where did you get a stupid idea like that? From a boyfriend. Right?"

She shrugged. "He goes too. Yes."

"Which one? Your little fry cook? What's his problem, baby? A wife and kids he wants to run out on?"

"He has no married, no!"

"But you think it's okay to run out on me, huh? Just up and leave? I've been real good to you, Francisca. Are you being fair?"

The girl scowled. She spread her arms wide. "I have no word. To stay one week, two week, what you like."

"Notice. You're giving me notice."

"Ah, yes!"

"Well, doesn't it depend on how long it takes me to find somebody else?"

"Oh, I find!"

"Don't go away," Crissy said, resting her forehead on her fists, trying to urge her sun-dazed brain into motion. Despite the extraordinary delicacy and sensitivity of her face, the poor girl was quite obviously a merry cretin. Garry Staniker had pointed out the ways she might cause them trouble. Crissy had explained that it was a problem they would have to take in order, consider later, if all the rest of it worked out. Now, of course, Francisca had to be on stage for the rest of it. She was a necessary part of the last act, and as the timing was not yet solidly established, it would be foolish to tell her exactly when she could leave.

Crissy raised her head again. "Let's do it this way, Francisca. Suppose you try to find me another nice Cuban girl. Bring me a little letter from her and a picture. If I like the sound of her and the way she looks, then I'll ask you to have her come here to talk to me. If I hire her, then you can leave after you show her around. All right?"

"Oh yes!" She stood up and cocked her head. "Here come sailboat boy. Sotch a big noise car!"

"Have him wait for me in the living room, please. Then you can take the rest of the day off, dear."

The maid trotted away. Crissy stood up, hung the big towel around her shoulders and quickly finished the glass of tea. Holding the towel around her, she went to her bedroom by way of the terrace doors. She spent a long time in her hot, sudsy shower, knowing that the longer he waited and wondered, the easier this next step would be. At last she went to him in the living room. She wore little makeup. She wore a simple, navy blue cotton dress, and she did not smile at him. He came quickly to his feet and started toward her. She held her hand up and said, "No! Sit down over there, Oliver. Please. This won't take long."

"What do you mean? What are you talking about?"

"It was a pretty good game of pretend. While it lasted. Don't look so baffled, Oliver. I know you remember very well that night I tried to send you away for good. I should have. It's more difficult now. But now it has to be done. Garry Staniker is coming back. You knew he'd come back. You knew that would be the end of it. And we've come to the end of it. What do I say? It's been nice? It's been a ball? There aren't any words. You know that. So just go, dear. Very quickly and quietly. We indulged ourselves. We took all there was to take and gave all there was to give. We pretended it was forever.

But it had a price tag. You *know* that. You'll get over me. It won't take as long as you think. I'll never never get over you, but that's beside the point."

"Crissy. God, Crissy, it can't . . ."

"Stay over there, Oliver. Sit down. Don't come near me. It will just make it harder. And we have to do it. Now."

He settled back onto the edge of the chair. Sand-colored slacks. Dark blue knit sports shirt. That good slope and weight and power of shoulder, a symmetry of chest, the sun-whitened curl of hair on muscular forearms, narrow taper of the waist, round strong column of the young throat. A beautiful animal, she thought, almost perfectly conditioned to me now, trained to respond to every subtle signal, disciplined to fulfill my urgencies with whatever haste or patience I require. But the face is so tiresome, with that goofy yearning look—eyes set too close, upper lip lugubriously long, underprivileged chin.

"I can't," he said. "I can't leave you."

"Don't be dull. There's no choice. We have no choice."

"We could go away, Crissy. Right now. Today."

"I expected you to say that. Deliciously romantic, isn't it? You can get a thrilling job. Bag boy in a supermarket. I could be a clerk in a store. And the miracle of our love would light up the cruddy furnished room and make me forget how my feet hurt. How long, Oliver, before you'd start hating me for spoiling your life, before you'd look at me and see a tired, dreary, middle-aged woman? I *had* my dingy years, boy. Up to here. I'm spoiled. I like the way I live. I keep my looks by living just this way. Disappointed in me? Sorry about that. What we've had has been too perfect and too beautiful to do that to it. It's meant too much to me, to have it turn into— resentment and squalor. If we ran, and I tried to sell the house, it would give Staniker a chance to track me down. No, Oliver. We finish it while it's—beautiful."

"But it can't end. Please, Crissy. Let me stay here with you—and keep him away from you."

She stared at him. "You keep Garry Staniker away from me? Excuse me if I hurt your feelings. You are a strong young man, and you are a brave young man. If you tried to send him away from me, do you know what would happen? First, he would laugh. He'd laugh very hard. And then he would hurt you, terribly. Because he would know you had been—with me. He's an alley fighter. And he's not quite sane. It's possible he might make very certain you—would never be able to have a woman again. And when he was through punishing you, it would be my turn, wouldn't it? Can't you understand that I'm an obsession with him? In his mind I belong to him, like his shoes or his toothbrush, and he can do as he pleases with me. I've learned not to displease him in any way. When he comes swaggering in, Oliver, I had better be here and you had better be gone forever. We've known that since the day I knew he was alive."

"There *has* to be something."

She coarsened her tone. "Like in the movies, kid? Sure. The clean-cut hero whips the bad guy. This is life, baby. Cash in your chips and go find another game. You had your jollies with another man's woman. Go brag around the docks. Consider it a part of your education, Junior."

In a choking voice he said, "Don't talk rough like that. Please. I can't stand it. I—*love* you!"

"And I loved you, and now I have to stop loving you or go out of my mind."

"I don't even care what happens to me any more. I just can't let him—come back and do things to you. I don't care. I'll kill him. I swear I'll kill him!"

"How? With the funny little gun your daddy bought you to plink tin cans with? And wouldn't that be a dandy solution? They'd find out the motive soon enough, and maybe for kicks they'd send me up for twenty years at the same time they electrocute you. I told you I'm selfish, boy. If it was a choice between servicing dear Captain Staniker, or working in the prison laundry daytimes and belonging to some dirty old bull dyke the rest of the time, what would my choice be?"

"My God, this is killing me, Crissy! Please!"

"So let's stop talking about it and end it right now before it kills us both. You've got toilet articles here, and that gun and the ammunition, and a jacket and a tie and swim trunks and your sailboat, so let's make a clean sweep and get it all over with now."

She headed swiftly down the hallway to her bedroom, aware of him close behind her. He stopped in the bedroom, looking sick and dazed and miserable. She went into the dressing room and got the 22 rifle and brought it out, started to hand it to him, then walked with it to her desk, took some tissue from a box and wiped the end of the barrel near the muzzle carefully.

"Excuse me for messing up your little rifle somewhat," she said.

He stared at the pink stains on the tissue with puzzlement and then growing comprehension. "Crissy! Were you going to . . ."

She made a wry face. "Stop the world and get off? I thought so. It was a real comedy scene. The dumb broad sitting at her dressing table looking at the three reflections of herself in the mirror, tears running down her face, sucking on the barrel of the gun. I could just reach the trigger with the tip of my middle finger, light as a butterfly's kiss. Very corny and dramatic. Couldn't do it. So I keep on living, kid. Staniker's bitch. Very well trained. I'll collect the rest of your stuff."

She turned away and heard the gun thud to the floor, heard his great breathy bellow of anguish, and then his big arms went around her and turned her and pulled her snug and close. "Oh darling," he said, weeping. "Oh, Crissy. Oh God, darling."

She stood without response for what she considered a long

enough time, then softened and returned the embrace, and reached back through memory to find something which would convincingly flood her dry eyes. She used the mutation mink wrap again. Savannah. She'd had it on layaway for seven months before she took the final fifty dollars to the store, had them wrap her cloth coat, and wore the wrap back to the apartment. Ten days later that crazy little Polack had gotten into the apartment somehow, when Crissy was out. That nutty Polish whore who had the idea Crissy was after her man. So she'd gotten in, bringing a pair of Sears Roebuck clippers for homemade haircuts, and had chopped all that beautiful silver-blue fur off, right down to the stubble, with the ugly hide showing through. She remembered how she felt when she walked in and saw that lovely soft fur all over her bed and the floor, and the tears came convincingly.

"Darling, darling, darling," she said in a tearful voice. "I was trying to be so strong. But we do have to say goodby. Once more, then, my dear. The last time for us. This is our goodby."

Later, in the drowse and lethargy of passion freshly spent, she lay sweetly sprawled upon him, her head on the firm tanned chest, her ear centered over his heart. With slow fingertips she traced the contours of his lips, and she listened to the deep slow sound of his healthy young heart.

"How can I let you go?" she whispered.

"There has to be . . ."

"Hush, my dear. Could we be—very cruel and very sly? Is it worth taking an awful risk, and doing a terrible thing—to stay together?"

She felt his heart accelerate, striking more solidly against the wall of his chest. "What kind of a risk?"

"I would have to see him. Maybe let him come here, or go to him. I would have to—pretend to be glad he came back. I might even have to—let him have me. Could you endure that? Could you still love me after that?"

"You know I could."

"I think it would make me ill, after you. Physically, desperately ill. Darling, I'd try not to let it happen."

"What are you thinking we could do?"

"I know that it must bother him to have lost that boat and those people and his wife. Oh, not the way it would bother most people. He'll just be worrying about how it might keep him from getting a good job again. He wouldn't feel any guilt, not really. He'd pretend to, but he wouldn't."

"What do you mean?"

"Don't you see, dear? It would look kind of—logical if he killed himself." Suddenly his heart was much faster.

"If—it looked as if he killed himself."

"Yes. Are we—strong enough?"

"He doesn't deserve to be alive."

She hitched upward, held him, put her face in the side of his throat, let out a long shivering breath. "We might be able to—find the right chance real soon. Or we might have to wait, Olly. We'll have to plan the best way to do it. The safest way, and be very clever and not leave any clues, and not let anyone see us at all. I'm scared, darling, thinking about it."

He hugged her close. "We'd be crazy not to be scared."

"It's the only way I'll be free. It's the only way I can be yours."

"I know."

"We'll have to—do it together. Help each other do it. Then we'll really belong to each other forever and ever. It's something we have to share. Do you understand?"

"I—yes. Yes."

"If it goes wrong—they might take us away and kill us, Oliver."

"I'd rather be dead than lose you."

"You really mean that, don't you, darling?"

He rolled to his side, so that he could hold her there against him. "Don't cry, Crissy. Don't cry. We'll do it. Nobody will ever know. You'll see. It's all we *can* do. It's the only chance we've got."

"I have to say the word, dear. It's—murder. You know that, don't you? Murder."

"Don't be scared. Please don't be scared."

"Not when I'm with you. I love you, Olly. So much. So much."

In a little while, in the strong circle of his brown arms she moved slightly, changed her position, sighed, slowly lifted her right leg and hooked it around him, her thigh heavy on his waist.

"I'm terrible," she whispered. "So soon, dear. So soon. Thinking of what—we're going to do to him seems to get me excited. That's terrible, isn't it?"

"No," he said in a hoarse whisper.

"Too soon for you?" she whispered, as she reached for him. She touched the hollow of his throat with her tongue tip. "You too," she breathed. "You too, lovely lovely boy. No, dear. Just lie still. Lie very still. Leave it all this time to your Crissy, to your woman. She'll make it so delicious for you."

As she began, she wished she could get that damned mink wrap out of her mind. It was so silly to get mad about it again after all these years. That screwball Polski. The boss girl had warned the Polski about other things she pulled. And that time the Polski disappeared. Crissy had heard, over a year later, that the boss girl had turned the Polski over to the Snowman for one of his lessons in manners and she had then been sent west for the export trade. But it sure God didn't grow any fur back on those mink skins.

Eighteen

ON FRIDAY AFTERNOON, Staniker walked slowly down the steps from the Bahama Airways plane to the cement apron, holding onto the railing. His weakness made him feel slightly chilled in the sun heat of the Miami Airport, and made him aware of the small frictions of the clothing against his body. He felt the pull of the tender, healing skin on his right knee as he took each step, but there was little pain. McGregory had been pleased with how quickly he had healed.

The insurance company had advanced the money for the inexpensive clothing and toilet articles Nurse Chappie had purchased for him. He carried a small flight bag, blue and white. He had cleared U.S. Customs at Windsor Field on departure.

As he walked with the tourist passengers into the terminal he watched for reporters and photographers, but there were none. It was understandable. He had made it clear even before leaving the hospital that he had signed up with Banner Enterprises. And the

story was old now. The Muñeca had been on the bottom in the endless silence and blackness for twenty-one days. And though he knew
it was the last place she would be, he looked for Crissy.

"Captain? Captain Staniker?" A little man trotted up, beaming.
He held his hand out. "Wezler. Hal Wezler. Banner Enterprises. All
ready to go to work, Captain?" He had swift dark eyes, a ferret face,
black hair, tie, suit and shoes, snow white shirt, gold accessories, a
smile that came and went as swiftly as a facial tic. "Let's find a saloon
and get acquainted and I'll tell you how we're going to work it."

They sat at a small table in a cocktail lounge. Wezler turned over
the pale blue check for twelve hundred and fifty dollars. He talked
so rapidly Staniker had trouble following him. Apparently time was
very important. Wezler had taken a small suite. They would hole up
there. Wezler used a tape recorder. He said he wanted a million
words on tape. He'd fly back out to the coast and turn all that tape
into a book. Everybody was very turned on about it, he said. Marty,
whoever that was, was setting up the tie-ins. They were shooting
for hard cover, magazine serialization, soft cover, book club and a
movie deal. It was going to make everybody very rich. Marty was
even thinking of setting up some kind of serial television project.
But they had to get winging right now. These things cool off. So
how about heading for the hotel right now? Great broads around
the pool. Take a break once in a while. Ease off, have some laughs,
then back to the old Ampex.

"Not right away," Staniker said.

"What do you mean?"

"I have personal things to do, Wezler. And I need rest. I have to
get my strength back."

"Marty isn't going to like this a bit, Staniker."

"Too bad."

"If it turns him off he might cut the whole deal down to practically nothing. You're signed on percentage. You'd lose a pot."

"So I'd lose a pot."

Wezler studied him. "So I'll see if I can con him a little on the phone. Only you got to tell me when, so I have something solid to go on."

"A week."

"Come *on*, baby!"

"A week."

"The man says a week. Where'll I find you, Captain?"

"I'll phone your hotel."

Wezler wrote the name of the hotel on the back of a business card and handed it over. "Where are you headed now? You want a lift? I got a rental out there someplace."

Staniker accepted the ride to Parker's Marina. Before Wezler drove off he pumped Staniker's hand and said, "If you can make it five days, four days, you got a new friend, believe me."

"I'll do what I can," Staniker said.

Parker wasn't around. The new couple who worked there were curious about him, but when he sidestepped their questions they turned sullen and indifferent. They gave him the packet of mail which had been saved for him, and the man unlocked the storage shed so Staniker could sort through the things which had been moved out of the cottage. The heat was thick in the shed. Sweat stung his eyes as he sorted some personal clothing and belongings into two suitcases. He carried them outside, refastened the padlock, and went to where the woman was dipping up live shrimp from the bait tank for two leathery old senior citizens. He told her to tell Parker he'd get the rest of the stuff later. When she gave no sign she heard he repeated it. She turned and said, "You think I'm deaf or something?"

He carried the suitcases around to the back of the main building. His old yellow Olds sat in the sunshine. One tire looked soft. The spare key was in a little magnetic box on top of a frame member under the left rear corner of the car. It had rusted shut. He banged it against the bumper and forced it open. He unlocked the car, stuck the suitcases in, left all four doors open for a few minutes to air out the bake-oven heat. He rolled all the windows down. Never have to own another one without air conditioning, he thought.

He got in, pulled the doors shut, put the key in the ignition. Before he started it, he reached under the seat and slid his fingers along until he felt the thin packet of bills, folded once, he had scotch-taped to the underside of the seat. He pulled it loose, put it into his pants pocket along with the Banner check, Wezler's card, and the money left from the insurance advance.

The car did not start. The battery began to fade. And he felt a sudden and quite unexpected wave of terror. If the car wouldn't start, everything would go wrong. He made himself relax. That was ridiculous. If the car didn't start, you walked over to the gas station over there and told Charlie your troubles.

When he tried again it caught. He revved the motor for a while before putting it in gear. He drove out and down the street and across into the Shell station. A boy was working on a car on the lift. Charlie came out of the station, a broad, bald man in gray coveralls, steel glasses, a smear of grease on his forehead.

"Figured you'd be back soon," Charlie said, shaking hands.

"I got the card okay in the hospital. Thanks."

"Hell of a time finding one that wasn't some kind of funny joke. Nothing funny about six people getting blowed up. That tire's way down, Garry."

"Noticed it. Battery is low too."

"I'll check things out. You don't look so great. Whyn't you go in and set."

Staniker went inside the station and sat in a plastic and aluminum chair. A fan turned back and forth, pushing stale air that smelled of gasoline and the perfumed deodorizing block in the nearby men's room. In a little while Charlie came in and handed him an opened icy bottle of Coke. "Cells are okay. Battery level was down and I filled her up. Checked the tires all around. Your gas was full up. Oil is down maybe a half a quart."

"Thanks, Charlie."

Charlie leaned on the desk. "I was thinking, if you'd been below too when she went, they never would have found out what happened. Mystery of the sea like they say."

"Or if nobody had come along for another couple of days, it would have been the same deal."

Charlie sighed. "You just never know. That Mary Jane was a real working woman. None of those people knew what hit 'em, I guess."

"They never had a chance."

"Those new folks Parky hired ain't no improvement around here. They're so sour I don't go over for a beer even. I'd rather drive down to Smitty's."

"Well, I better be getting along. Thanks for everything, Charlie."

"Where you going to go? Maybe move in with that stuff you got lined up down the bay shore? That one you used to work for?"

"You mean Mrs. Harkinson? I tell you, Charlie, I wish I could. But we broke up just a little bit before this last captain job came along. Broke it up big. No chance of mending that one. She was getting on my nerves anyway. I didn't know you knew anything about her, Charlie."

"Maybe I talked out of turn. The one told me was Fran, down at the sundries. A long time ago. Back in February maybe it was. Fran and Mary Jane, those two would tell each other their troubles I guess. Fran's got her share for sure. As I remember Fran was bad-mouthing you for carrying on with that woman. I nodded, solemn as a preacher. Fran should know the fits I give my old lady back when I still had my hair."

"Next time you see Fran you tell her I haven't got a chance of moving in on that blonde. I guess she'll say it serves me right. You know, Charlie, I wish now I'd—given Mary Jane a few more breaks than I did. I'm going to miss her. I miss her already."

Charlie looked at him. "No trouble for you to find a woman. No trouble at all. But it won't be easy to find a worker like her."

As he drove away, Staniker thought that a lot of Crissy's precautions didn't make sense. But because everything else seemed to have worked out, perhaps it was best to go along with the whole thing. Nobody was going to check on anything at this late date. It was over and done, and the only thing left was a good way to go pick up the money. A good, safe, quick, quiet way.

And now he had to play more tricks. She wouldn't tell him who had told her about this one. She had practiced it with him, in rush-hour traffic until they were both good at it. Any limited access highway with exit ramps and three lanes in each direction would do. Even when he knew how she was going to work it and she knew how he was going to work it, they had no trouble losing each other.

You hung in the fast lane, furthest from the exit ramps, and you found a hole in the traffic, and you adjusted your speed in relation to the hole so that when you were coming up on an exit ramp, you could speed up at just the right time, angle across the other two lanes and duck down the ramp. You then took the cloverleaf and got back onto the pike but heading the opposite way, and did it again. That put you back in your original direction, and anybody who had tried to trail you would be swept helplessly past the exit, locked in the river of fast traffic. He killed time, driving north. On Interstate 95 north of the airport, traffic thickened and he obediently played the game. "You see," she had said, "we won't *know* we're really in the clear. They *might* be playing cat and mouse. And what does it cost to play it safe? Nothing. So *do* it? Don't give me arguments. Do it!"

He drove west on the bypass, and after he had turned south again toward Coral Gables, just for luck, he played the game again, the second time cutting it almost too fine, making horns blare in anger and brakes shriek as he angled across.

The row of a dozen identical cottages was in a defeated area near Coral Gables. Heavy, unkempt tropical growth hemmed the cottages in, cutting off any chance of breeze. The pink paint on the hard pine siding was faded and flaking away, exposing gray wood. The woman lived in a larger cottage on the corner, on a bigger lot. She was four and a half feet tall. Her back was badly humped. Her voice had a metallic resonance, like announcements over a bad loudspeaker. Her face was stone gray, her hair the impossible yellow of industrial sulfur. She wore a green smock, blue canvas shoes, and she smelled like a boarding kennel.

She peered up at Staniker. She tapped a front tooth with a fingernail. "You was here before."

"Couple of months ago."

"Just one night like before?"

"Two weeks this time."

"By God, you're the first repeat business in I can't remember. I don't need to show you one. They're all alike. Let's see. Two and a half a day, fourteen a week. Two weeks I'll make it twenty-five in advance, okay? And ten deposit on the utilities. You get that back when you give me the key back. The tax is just on the twenty-five. Seventy-five cents. Come in and sign the book, mister."

He went onto her screened porch with her, signed the ruled notebook with her ball point pen that wrote in red. Gerald Stanley. General Delivery. Tampa. She turned the notebook around, made change, pawed through the keys in the shallow desk drawer.

"I got ten empties," she said, "but there's three of them need plumbing work I can't afford, at least till by some kind of miracle I get nine full up. Mister Stanley, I better give you number ten, on account it's the one furthest down from that one machine shop across the way there that went on night shift last week. It's just up to midnight, but it does screech some. Mr. Mooney, my dear departed, said once we got zoned industrial it would be no trouble selling off the whole thing for nice money. It's maybe a blessing he died before they zoned so damn much industrial there's no market at all for it. Got to hang on by my social security until it gets better, if it ever does. Thank you kindly. You see anything that needs doing, come tell me. If it'll cost money to get it done, we'll move you to another empty."

She gave him the key. "Like I must have told you last time because I tell everybody, the only three rules I got is don't smash the place up, don't steal the furnishing, don't set fire to it."

He drove down the row to number ten. There were no garages, but each had a narrow driveway. The untrimmed shrubbery brushed the sides of the car at the driveway mouth. He turned hard right and parked in front of the bungalow steps. The car was out of sight of the road. The front door stuck. He had to kick it to get it open. The layout was exactly the same as the one he'd taken overnight the second week in April after Crissy had told him to find a place where he could hide, a place where they could safely meet after he came back alone from the Bahamas. He remembered how out-of-place she had looked when she had joined him there after dark.

Living room, bedroom, hallway, kitchen, bath. Old porch furniture, torn grass rugs, crusted stove, plastic ashtrays, swaybacked double bed, water stains on the ceiling, gloom, dust and the smell of dampness, and cockroaches scuttling swift and clever in kitchen and bath. Rust stains in the toilet and the sinks. Patched windowshades, gray curtains, jelly glasses, corroded tableware, a refrigerator that made a chattering, whining vibration when he plugged it in.

He brought his suitcases in. He stood in the silence of the cottage and heard, outside, the early evening songs of the mockingbirds, hiss of truck brakes and grunt of diesel horn, a continuing sound of some heavy piece of automatic shop equipment, a slow, brutal whickity-bump, whickity-bump, mingled with the less regular sound of metal being cut at high speed, a prolonged screeching.

He left and drove to a little Handy-Andy food store a few blocks away. As arranged he called Crissy's number from an outdoor pay booth. It was 532–1732. It was six thirty.

After the third ring Crissy said, "Hello?"

"Charlie there?"

"What number were you calling?"

He told her 532–1710. The last two digits were the number of the bungalow he was in at the Mooney Cottage Court. She said he had the wrong number. He said he was sorry and hung up.

He bought twenty-five dollars' worth of groceries, beer and magazines and went back to number ten. He parked closer to the steps to make room for her small white car beside his. He felt hungry. He ate half a thick sandwich of cold cuts and cheese, but the next big bite turned into a gluey ball in his mouth. He went in and spat it into the toilet, gagging as he did so. He stripped down to his shorts, put a fan on a chair beside the bed to blow the air across his body. Under the weak bedlamp he sipped cold beer and tried to read one of the magazines. He had to keep going back and reading the same part over. Finally he threw it aside. The beer tasted watery. Night was coming. Crissy would come with the night.

He felt as if it had all been one long linked series of events. Everything had happened in the order it was supposed to happen. It was like looking out a train window and seeing the familiar stations one after the other. It had all been designed right from the day they headed out toward the Stream with the Muñequita in tow, to bring him full circle right back to this place. It was as if the train had stopped. It was on a siding somewhere. They had unhooked the engine and taken it away.

. . .

Night was coming, and the Sergeant went over to the table and pumped the pressure up in the gasoline lantern. He cracked the valve and lighted the mantle. It made a hissing sound and filled the shack with its hard white light.

Leila Boylston sat crosslegged on a cushion on a wooden crate. She wore one of the new pair of slacks, the blue ones, and a blue and white checked blouse. She looked down at the dusty sole of her bare foot. Another sob came. A wrenching thing—half snort, half hiccup. So maybe that one was the last. Funny how you could be cried out and have so many dry sobs remaining. Her face felt bloated.

Before he sat down the Sergeant reached and gave her shoulder a little pat. "Now there," he said. The shyness and gentleness of it made her give him a small quick smile.

"I guess my mind was trying to remember all along," she said. "I'd get little flashes, like pictures, that didn't make any sense. Terrible little parts of it. But when I saw you kneeling down there and cleaning that fish." She shuddered again.

"You said part of it, Missy, when you were out of your head. Those were the bad times for you, yelling and sweating and churning around. I thought it was bad dreams."

"She was the last. Maybe she was dying anyway. I don't know. She was running out of the lounge toward the stern when the bullet hit her. Stel. Stel there on the teak cockpit deck in the light that shone out from the lounge, and the boat dead in the water, rocking so far over and back loose things were all thumping and jingling and banging. I was on the roof of the lounge part, holding onto the ladderway that went up to the fly bridge. She was crumpled against the big fish box. Making that terrible sound. With every breath. Like a cawing. And he was below me. Right below me. He kept working the bolt on that rifle and firing at her. But it was just a click every time. It was empty but he kept firing at her. Firing and yelling at her to shut up. He dropped the rifle. It was always up on the flybridge, in clamps. Sometimes Mister Bix fired at beer cans back in the wake with it. Or sharks."

"Now Missy."

"He went running back to where Stel was. He tried to kind of saw at her neck with that fish knife. But her head and neck were—loose. Too wobbly to cut. She kept cawing . . ."

"Missy!"

"He pulled her away from the fish box and straddled her on his knees. She was on her face. He dug his fingers into her hair and pulled her head up and back. And with the knife he . . ."

She stopped. His hands were hurting her shoulders. She seemed to hear the echoes of her own voice in the shack, too shrill, too loud. The Sergeant was shaking her.

"I'm all right. I'm all right now. Let me finish," she said in her normal tone. "I remember the end now."

"It's a bad thing to talk about."

"He let go. He dropped her. Into all the wetness spreading on the teak. I was *glad* the noise stopped, the noise she was making. That's terrible, I guess. To be glad. He stood up slowly and he saw me. It gave him a terrible start. I guess he had lost track or something. I guess he thought she was the end of it. He came slowly toward the ladderway, never taking his eyes off me. He didn't have the knife. He'd left it in that—puddle. I couldn't make a sound. I couldn't move. I couldn't make my hands let go of that ladder, not even when he was out of sight and then he appeared again, and stopped, his head a little ways above the level of the roof of the lounge part where I was standing. He held onto the railings and swung out to one side to look up at me. His eyes were so big and round. And the whole bottom part of his face was . . . soft and loose. And he had a funny little smile. People drop things by accident and they break and they know they're valuable and that's the smile they wear."

She stopped and held her fists against her eyes for a few moments. She frowned at the Sergeant. "His voice was *little*. He was trying to explain something to me. 'It was supposed to be the way I practiced,' he said. 'I didn't mean for it to go wrong like this. Miss Leila, believe me, Crissy kept telling me over and over the time to do it was when you were all together. Bunched. All eating. But when I started there were only four of them. You should have been there. Both of you. Then you wouldn't have to be scared.' I told him to please leave me alone. He said in a very reasonable voice that he couldn't. I should be able to understand why he couldn't. He said it never would have had to happen if it hadn't been for the money. I didn't know what he was talking about. He said it was so much money Crissy was able to make him do it. He told me not to be scared any more, not to look at him like that. He said he'd make certain there wouldn't be any pain, the way it was with Stella. He was mad at Stella for running."

"Missy?"

"I'm—okay, Sarg. I've got it all now, every bit of it. Suddenly he reached very quickly and grabbed my ankle. It got me out of my trance. I tried to run and fell and yanked myself loose, and as I jumped up he came bounding up like—an animal. I knew my only chance was to dive into the water. I knew he couldn't catch me in the water in the dark. I had on a pretty shift. Stel and I each bought one in the Nassau Shop. Mine was orange and hers was pink. He grabbed at me and caught the back of the neck of the shift. They were very loose fitting. A light material but a close weave. I felt it rip all the way down. I spun out of it and nearly fell again. I wasn't wearing a thing under it. I whirled and dived from up there toward the sea, but

then I saw the boat, too late. I was going to dive right into it. I don't
remember hitting my head at all. It was just like diving into—a huge
deep snowbank. And then I was here."

"And what day was that?"

"It was—the thirteenth. It was Friday the thirteenth. I wouldn't
remember what day it was, except Mister Bix was making jokes
about it being a lucky day. That's a spooky thing to remember."

Sergeant Corpo counted it out on his fingers. "Miss Leila, you
were eight days drifting in that boat, coming this way on that east
wind! Busted head. Fevers eating the meat off you. Sun cooking the
hide off you. Missy, you must be hardy as a she-gator. The life must
run strong in you. Rains must have come down on you just in time
to keep you going. Missy, there in't one man in fifty'd make it
through that. And you're getting more bright and sassy every single
day."

She looked pleadingly at him. "Try to understand that this makes
a big difference in—our plans, Sarg. I *have* to get away from here.
They'll think I was killed too. I bet Staniker thought that dive killed
me. I guess it should have. He was insane, Sarg. His face just—it just
wasn't a human face any more. What if he isn't locked up? He could
be doing terrible things to other innocent people. And then it would
be your fault, wouldn't it?"

"That's one way to think about it."

"My brother will think I'm dead. So will Jonathan."

"That much gladder to see you when you come running."

"Please, Sarg! Please! Oh God, please!"

"Now there. Now you know nobody is going to go off into the
dark night. There's time to think on it."

"The longer you keep me the more trouble you're going to
be in."

He looked puzzled. "Looks to me like it's just the other way around." He stood up. "Time people should be in their beds. Anyways, you haven't even opened up half the stuff I brang you back from town. Pretties keep a gal's mind off her problems."

It was night. Gordon Dale was using both halves of his mind to full capacity. He sat at his digestive ease in his leather chair, following the plot of an hour-long western on the television set, while the other half of his mind walked around and around and around the special problems in the brief he was preparing in a civil action for one of his more important clients—like a puppy circling a hedgehog looking for any reasonable place to sink his teeth.

Miriam was on the couch writing to their married daughter in Atlanta, and she said, "If he has family, I don't see why it has to be up to you anyway."

It was statement, but also a question. He did not want to wonder what she meant. It was one of Miriam's small and special talents to come out with a statement so oblique, so unrelated to anything anyone had said recently, you could not ignore it. It would paste itself to some outer layer of husbandly attention and then begin to bore a hole.

"Um?" he said at last.

"Well even if they didn't have any *legal* responsibility, I would think they'd want to take care of their own."

He sighed. He put the brief back on a shelf somewhere in the back of his head. And when the ranch hands tracked the stolen horse herd out the far end of the canyon, the wind had blown the sand and covered all the tracks. So they milled around, arguing with one another.

"Whose family, dear?" he asked. "What are you talking about?"

"Oh, come *on*, Lieutenant!" she said.

Then Gordon Dale knew, with a certain resignation, they were

to have another little chat about Corpo. He had made captain before
VE day. And upon discharge he had been given a termination pro-
motion to major. He had no patience with courtesy titles anyway,
any more than he had with those uncurably boyish men who kept
green the memories of college fraternity or football triumphs or
Let-me-tell-you-how-it-was-at-Omaha-Beach.

"Corpo hasn't any family."

"Apparently that's what *he* told you."

"No, honey. Really. When I found out he was still alive after
thinking he was dead all those years, the doctors said he wasn't a
danger to anybody, but he couldn't cope without some help on the
outside. They'd tried to turn up somebody, anybody, up in Georgia
who'd take over. I looked in the book and found a fellow I knew
from law school practicing in the area, and I had him check it out.
No family."

"Well, it certainly is *strange*, then."

"Exactly what is strange, dear?" he asked patiently.

She put the unfinished letter aside. "Well, I was at the hairdresser
this afternoon, and Jeanie did me. She's the young one I told you
about. Very pretty, and she's real good too. Anyway, her best girlfriend works in that expensive dress shop out on Sea Crescent Circle. The Doll House. They have darling sports clothes. Jeanie's
girlfriend's name is Andra something, and they call her Andy. Anyway, the day before yesterday, Wednesday, your precious Sergeant
had the entire place in a turmoil."

"Now Miriam, if Corpo gets into any kind of trouble anywhere
in the Broward Beach area, the police would call me."

"Did I say he got into trouble? Did I?"

"You said turmoil."

"In the store. Yes. You can imagine how really weird it would be
to have him walk into a place like that. At least he didn't have that
fantastic beard. But that raggedy haircut and that ghastly dent in his

forehead and those stary eyes were enough to make those girls out there pretty jumpy, Jeanie said. When they asked him what he wanted, he had some little lists and he went through them and picked out one that said clothing and handed it to the clerk. When the clerk saw how many things were on it, she took it to Mrs. Wooster, the owner, so Mrs. Wooster came out of the back and told the Sergeant it would come to quite a lot of money. So he took a really fantastic roll of bills out of his pocket and said it should be enough. He had a taxi waiting outside. He said that it was going to be his little sister's birthday up in Georgia and he wanted to send her a lot of nice things. Andra told Jeanie the list was in a girl's hand-writing, and from the sizes she was a little thing, a size eight or ten. It was quite a list. Underwear, blouses, shorts, slacks, sandals, skirts, a sweater, everything. Mrs. Wooster picked everything out, and Jeanie said Andy said she could have made it come out to twice as much money as she did, but even so it *is* an expensive place and it came to almost three hundred dollars. It didn't faze him a bit. He had a drugstore list and a grocery list too. Andy told Jeanie it looked as if there was hundreds of dollars left in what Mrs. Wooster gave back to him, and after he was gone Mrs. Wooster explained about him to the girls, and how you are sort of his guardian or something, and that was why Jeanie told me about it. She started off thinking I probably knew about it. That was why I said that his family should be looking out for him."

"The way he lives, Mim, he isn't exactly a heavy responsibility."

"I suppose he picked up his check at your office Wednesday."

"He was there waiting when I got there. I noticed the beard was gone, and I was going to ask him about it, but he seemed to be in a big hurry. The check he gets and cashes every time is always the check from the month before. Sometimes he loses track and comes in too early, so I worked it out that way to save him extra trips. I don't think it's good for him to come to town too often. It gets him too confused and agitated."

"Should he be walking around with all that money?"

"Honey, I gave up trying to get him to put it in the bank long ago. He certainly gets more than he needs, a lot more, on a total disability pension. He must have a pretty good bundle by now, and I'd guess he's got it buried in fruit jars all over that damn island. Maybe he shouldn't be walking around with hundreds of dollars in cash, but I can't think of any good way to stop him. And I can't think of any less rewarding outdoor sport than trying to take it away from him."

"Well, if he hasn't got any family, I guess some girl is taking it away from him, one way or another."

"Which I am going to check out right now."

As he walked to the bedroom phone he knew it was a good chance that one or the other of the men he wanted to talk to would be on duty at headquarters. He asked the duty desk for either Detective Sergeant Lamarr, or Detective Sergeant Dickerson.

Dickerson was there, but in interrogation, and would call back. The call came back in fifteen minutes.

"Dave? This is Gordon Dale. I'm a little worried about our Robinson Crusoe."

"If there was any kind of a complaint at all, Mr. Dale, I'd have heard about it for sure. Nothing at all in a long time."

"When he was in town Wednesday, apparently he spent almost three hundred dollars on clothes for a girl. He bought the stuff out at The Doll House. She wasn't with him. He had a list. It sounds to me as if he ran into a smart operator at that waterfront place."

"Shanigan's?"

"She'd be a small woman, size eight or ten."

"Mmm. Funny. I wouldn't think Harry would be stupid enough

to let any of them get cute with Corpo. I made it clear a long time ago. Harry remembers good. I told him that if his bartenders ever tried to put the clip on that poor guy, or if those semi-pros he runs down there ever tried any kind of con on the Sergeant, the Department of Regulatory Services was going to find a lot of expensive things wrong down there, like maybe having to move the whole building back a foot and a half because there isn't any exception to the set-back regulations on file."

"Could he be going somewhere else?"

"Mr. Dale, he's a little too buggy-looking to get service in a good place, and all the other places know the standing order not to serve him. And they know him by sight. I'll check it out. But if I wanted to make a guess, I'd say some little hustler is working him without Harry knowing about it. Maybe somebody new in town. The next step would be money for the operation on her poor old bedridden mom."

"Dave, I appreciate your helping me keep old Corpo out of as much trouble as we can."

"It was a long war, and a lot of people got shot in the head, and I had as good a chance as anybody. We're having a busy Friday night here, Mr. Dale. Okay if I report back to you in the morning?"

"I'll be at the office from eight thirty until a little after eleven. And thanks."

It was night, and Jonathan Dye awakened with a start when a waterbird flew over the anchored catamaran, a night bird making eerie hollow cries of agony. He settled back, rolled and looked up at the incalculable stars. They were anchored in the open flats over sand bottom. There was enough breeze to slap little waves against the hulls. There was an almost imperceptible bump, and then another, and he realized that with the tide ebbing they were beginning to touch the sand bottom as Stanley Moree had said they would. In the morning they would still be hard aground and Stanley would stay with the cat while Jonathan walked over to search the four tiny islands and sand spits they had approached in the dusk.

He stretched and felt the pull of his thigh muscles. Never had he reached such a peak of physical condition before. He could not guess at how many miles he had walked through shallow water, swum through deeper water. He had never thought that his tough sallow skin would take a tan. But it seemed to darken more each day. He knew he had lost weight, but he could not guess at how much.

He looked over at the stillness of Stanley Moree, asleep a few feet away on the bow deck, and felt gratitude and affection. Jonathan had known Sam Boylston had been humoring what he considered wishful fantasy when he financed the search. Sam had not concealed it well. Never had Stanley given him the slightest indication he did not believe in this search. Stanley did not say cheering words, make heartening predictions. Those would have rung false. He did his job. He made valid suggestions. He worked as hard at it as Jonathan. Something of value had drifted off, and they would find it. Jonathan wondered if it was the very essence of gentle Bahamian courtesy, or if Stanley did indeed share his belief. He had not dared question him about it, afraid to learn that Stanley might be humoring him as one would any mad person.

Yet Stanley had found that tank key the day before yesterday. He had seen the small object at a fantastic distance through the midmorning glare, on the slope of sand on an island big enough to have given root to a single bush no larger than a basketball. It was a cylindrical white styrofoam float, half the size of a beer can. A short small brass chain was threaded through it, held in place by a brass disc atop the float. At the bottom end of the chain was fastened a bronze tank key, a device with two spindles spaced to fit into the recesses of the countersunk screw top of marine fuel tanks.

Stanley had examined it with great care. He had rubbed at the green frosting of tiny bits of marine growth it had begun to acquire. He had looked carefully at the amount of corrosion on the metal parts. And he had said that it had been in the water less than a month, that the pattern of wind and tides across the Bank would have brought it from the east, that it appeared to come from a good, big boat. One could not say it had come from the Muñeca. But one could be almost certain.

Jonathan remembered a grassy knoll in Texas, a cool night when the stars were brilliant, Leila beside him, stretched out on her back, her hand in his. A parsec is a light year. A light year is nearly six trillion miles. The faint glow of light from the nearest galaxy has been en route a hundred and thirty-seven thousand years, traveling six trillion miles a year toward us.

"The light that's starting from there now," she'd said. "Who will see it? Or what will see it? Or will it shine on a big cinder?"

"We won't know or care."

"So the time to care is now, huh? And wonder. Jonathan, the light from it shines into my eyes and I'm sending it right on back. It doesn't matter it's too little to measure, or there's nothing there to measure it or care. It's on its way back up there. Have a nice trip. Don't get lonely."

"You're a nut."

"I better be kissed, or I'll get the uglies."

He turned onto his side on the catamaran deck, thinking, I'll find you tomorrow. If you were dead the night breeze wouldn't be as soft or the stars as bright. If you were dead I couldn't smile at the way your mind takes those wild dips and unexpected turns. All the stars would wink out and the wind would rise and blow a gale that would never end.

• • •

It was nearly midnight. Raoul Kelly on his way from the bathroom back to his room heard his phone ringing and quickened his pace.

"Raoul?" Sam Boylston's voice said. "That thing Staniker pulled, it wasn't a mistake." He sounded disgusted and irritable.

"She did the same thing?"

"Exact damn same thing you described, and even though I knew it could happen, I couldn't do anything about it. She left at about eleven. I hung pretty well back. She didn't have as much traffic to work with as Staniker had. But she found a little pack, passed on the left, gunned it, swung back and ducked off the pike and I got swept right on by. I tried to backtrack, but it's hopeless. I'm calling from a booth at a gas station. I think I'll go on back and see what time she comes home."

"So Staniker didn't suddenly realize he was about to go past his exit."

"It's clever. And it's also stupid."

"Very stupid. Sure. We lost them both."

"No, I'm thinking of how clever people end up sweating blood when you put them on the stand. There are little tricks here and there, and they can give a perfectly reasonable explanation for each one. But after a while they begin to add up. The jury begins to wonder why so *much* strange behavior. Then you come on with the so-it-just-happened technique."

"What?"

"Well now, Mr. Defendant, so you just *happened* to decide not to bowl that Wednesday night after not missing a league game all season, and you just *happened* to decide to go back to the office that night to finish a report, and you just *happened* to drive twelve miles out of your way to stop and have a beer on the way home, and you just *happened* to have that bag packed in case you had to take a business trip all of a sudden, and you just . . ."

"I get it. But you say you can't make a case anyway."

"What's the story on your girl?"

"I've got a line on a replacement that woman can't have any reason to turn down, Sam. References up to here. She owes a friend of mine a big favor. I can trust her. What she'll do is make an offer to work for about half what she's getting, with the idea it will pry 'Cisca loose, and after we're on our way, she can quit the job."

"And if the Harkinson woman says no?"

"Then I *know* I have to get her away from there fast."

Nineteen

THE THUMPING awoke Staniker. He had the feeling it had been
going on for some time. It took him a few moments to realize where
he was. He looked at his watch, his only personal possession which
had survived castastrophe. Waterproof, self-winding, shock resis-
tant. It was just past midnight, and in the little window in the dial
above the six the date was changing, from 3 to 4.

He went down the corridor and through the dark living room
and glanced out before he went to the door. Her white car was out
there beside his. He unlocked the door and pulled it open.

"My *God!*" she said as she came in, her voice hushed but angry.
"Did you have to keep me standing out there half the damn—"

"Sorry. I dozed off."

"You dozed way off. It's hot as a pocket in here." He smelled the
fresh tang of her perfume. Her face and hair were paleness in the
dark room.

"There's a fan going in the bedroom."

She followed him. "All according to plan, Garry? Just the way we worked it out?"

"No."

Her voice became louder and it was pitched higher as they walked into the bedroom. "But you *got* it, didn't you? You got it? It's *safe*, isn't it?"

"It's in a good place."

"How much?"

"I didn't count it. It's a lot. Maybe more than you said. I don't know. Enough to make you dizzy just looking at it. I thought you knew how much."

"So maybe he lied? Or maybe he used some up. You waited long enough. You nearly drove me out of my mind, waiting and wondering. I thought you couldn't do it."

He sat on the bed, still dulled by the heaviness of his sleep. He swung his legs up and lay back. "I did it."

She roamed restlessly. She wore a simple cotton dress in an aqua shade that emphasized the golden look of her tan. "These places are gummier than I remembered." She sat at the foot of the bed, facing him, crossing her legs, smooth round brown knees exposed. "You don't look so great, Captain. You look soft."

"Hospital does that."

She made a mouth of distaste. "What's the goop on your leg?"

"Kind of a salve to keep the new skin flexible."

"Will the hair grow back in those places, and on your arm?"

"The doctor didn't think so."

"So you've lost your breath-taking loveliness, my friend. But you got rich. Fair trade?"

"Crissy, it—it wasn't like I thought it was going to be. It was different. It was real different. I can't remember all the parts of it."

"You waited long enough."

"It had to happen in the right place. It went wrong."

She stared intently at him. "They're dead, aren't they? All of them?"

"Oh, they're dead."

"And the money is safe. Where is it? Where you said?"

"No."

"What's the matter with you, Garry? Why not?"

He frowned at the wall behind her. "I think it started to go bad with Mary Jane. They were all below, eating. I put it on pilot and went forward and down through the bow hatch. She was in the galley. I beckoned to her. She came into the crew quarters forward and asked me what I wanted. I put my hands on her throat. I didn't look at her. I didn't want to watch it. When it had been—a long time, I pushed her. She fell back on the bunk. Her hair got caught and wound up in the fan. The fan stopped. It buzzed and stank. But when I climbed back up through the hatch, somehow I couldn't figure out how much time it had taken. I didn't know how long I'd been down there."

"You can spare me the details."

"I was afraid it had been so long we might be too close to the coral. I ran along the side deck. I could see them down there in the lounge, eating. I ran up to the fly bridge. The finder still didn't show any bottom. I had the rifle. I started to slow it and then I thought what the hell, they're all down there, and nothing they can do about it, so I cut off the running lights and killed both engines and got down there fast and went in. They always sat the same way when they ate. It was like a booth. Carolyn and Mr. Bix on one side, facing aft. Carolyn on the inside. Roger across from Carolyn, Leila Boylston across from Bix, Stella in a chair facing the booth, at the open end. We still were moving so it was steady enough. I took Bix first, somewhere in the face. He bowed his head down into his plate. Roger turned and half stood up to stare back at me, and the slug hit the heavy bone above the bridge of his nose and knocked his head

back and broke his neck. By then I was thinking the two girls weren't
there. I hadn't had a chance to look in first. Carolyn was screaming
and trying to crawl over Bix's back and shoulders to get out. I don't
even remember shooting, but the scream stopped and she sort of slid
down him, head first, down the side of him toward the open end of
the booth, and slid right down head first between the bench and the
table top until her hips wedged there and stopped her. Her legs were
leaning against Bix and one leg kept kicking."

"Where were the girls?"

"The only thing I can think of, they had to go to the head, and
Stel went to the one next to the master stateroom, and Leila went on
along to the one forward of that. By then the boat was starting to
rock in the trough, and Carolyn's body shook loose and fell down
half under the booth. Stel came running in and stopped and stared
at them and at me and she started to make a circle around me to go
outside. Just as I took aim, she made a run for it and I took a snap
shot and hit her and it knocked her all the way back to the transom
fish box, but . . . it didn't kill her. She kept making a noise. I thought
I was shooting her, but then I couldn't hear shots. There were six
shells in the clip, I thought. I was sure of it. But I could only be sure
of firing four. Maybe I fired five times at the three of them in the
booth without knowing it. I had to stop that noise. I couldn't stand
it and I couldn't take the time to get more shells. I . . . cut her
throat."

"My God, Garry!"

"I didn't know I was doing it until—I'd done it."

"Where was the Boylston girl?"

"The way I figure out what must have happened, she heard the
shots and she was smarter. She went forward and up through the
hatch. She had to see Mary Jane there. And she wasn't—real good to
look at. Then, from up on top of the lounge deck she saw me finish
off Stel. I went after her, almost caught her, and then I got hold of

her dress and that ripped off, and she dived before I could stop her. She dived right into the runabout, head first. It had eased up on us after we lay dead in the water. She didn't see it before she dived. She hit the edge of one of the engines hatches head first. It killed her. It smashed her head or broke her neck or both. I decided I could take care of her later. It would save time. I remembered the little spare anchor aboard the Muñequita. Big enough to take her on down, and easier than lifting her back aboard. I went and got the money. It was in an aluminum suitcase. I knew that I could get back on the track and finish it like we planned. I didn't know how close we'd gotten. I went up and turned on the depth finder and I nearly jumped out of my skin. It showed eighty feet. The wind had drifted the boat in too close, and any minute a wave could lift it and drop it on a coral head. You have to understand why I did what I did."

"What do you mean? What did you do?"

"It racked me up. They were all making—a silence. I kicked the engines on and made a slow hundred and eighty, but tight, and then got out of there, back out until the bottom had been gone for maybe two miles. I killed everything again, and I went down and dragged Stella below decks, and I lashed them all to solid things. I worked fast because I'd gone down into the bilge first and opened her up. I could feel her moving heavier in the swell. Then I put the bottle of gasoline, a half pint whisky bottle, in the pocket of my pants and went out onto the deck carrying the suitcase. Just as I left the lights flickered and went out below as the water got up to the battery cables. I went back and looked and the Muñequita was gone. I got the end of the tow line where I'd fastened it to a center cleat. I saw how it was frayed, and I realized I hadn't even thought about cutting the tow line with the wheels when I turned around. I couldn't see it anywhere. It was probably way back where I'd made my turn."

"You damn fool! You stupid damned fool!"

"I got my knife off the deck, thinking maybe I could cut the

dinghy loose. It was lashed forward. But she was riding low and
heavy and she began to kind of tremble and hesitate and I knew she
was going. I could get pulled down, I thought. So I went over the
rail and swam. That suitcase, thank God, was watertight. It didn't
have enough buoyancy to hold me, but it would float by itself. I
pushed it in front of me. I swam until I was winded and I turned
around and looked and the boat was gone. Absolutely nothing there.
I hadn't heard a thing. Then there was a big belch and whiteness
when a bubble of air came up. I paddled around. There were some
cushions floating. I collected two of them, and then I saw something
lighter colored and it was that styrofoam board of Stella's. It held me
fine. I figured out from the wind and the stars which way I had to
paddle. When dawn came I found I was a little too far north. I made
my way to South Joulter, let the board float off and waded ashore
with the money. The thing I was scared of was boats being around
the corner in the anchorage or further down toward the flats. I ran
and shoved the suitcase into the brush and piled sand on it. Then I
walked around the shoreline. Nothing. I climbed to the highest
point and I couldn't see a boat anywhere. That meant I had a chance
to find a good place for the money."

"My God, Garry, if anybody had the slightest suspicion, they'd
take that island apart and . . ."

"Why should they have? It's a good place. There's some rocky
ridges. Way above high tide. There's a hell of a big old rusty boiler
up there. It must have been part of a wreck long ago, a pretty good-
sized vessel. Take a hurricane to throw it way up into the rocks. It
maybe weighs a couple of tons. One end is rusted away. That end is
half buried in drifted sand, and half full of drifted sand. I'd shoved
the knife into my belt. I used it to dig up a bush that blocked the
open end. Then I dug down into the soft dry sand inside the boiler
and worked the suitcase down into it and smoothed it over. I planted
the bush back in the hole where it had been, and I brushed away my

footprints when I backed away from there. It's safe. It will be safe as long as we want to leave it there."

"But what happened to the boat the Boylston girl was in?"

"I don't know. I don't understand why the air search didn't find it. I thought I'd have to explain about it when I was taken back to Nassau. But while I was on the island I worked it out."

"Oh sure, you worked it out."

"I knew she was dead. So it would have to be one of those freak things. As if she'd come out onto the cockpit deck just before the Muñeca blew. I hadn't seen her. It had blown her into the air and blown her clothes off and dropped her into the boat we were towing. I worried about there being no burns on her. Then when I realized she hadn't been found that first week, they weren't going to be able to tell much about burns when they did find her."

"But why didn't they? What could have happened?"

"It would drift pretty fast. Too much flotation for it to go down. It might get awash. One thing could have happened. She was pretty and she was new. And she was better than ten thousand worth. There are some rough people in those islands. Weight the body and drop it over the side. Run the boat up one of those creeks on Andros, cover it with brush and wait for the fuss to die down."

She shook her head slowly. "Luck, Captain. You were shot with luck. And you apparently almost died of burns and exposure. Oh, that makes it look real good, but if you had, maybe that money would have stayed right there forever. You cut it close."

"The way I did it, I found an old piece of cloth in the sand on the beach and I tied it around the end of a stick and soaked it with the gasoline. The matches stayed dry enough. I held it in my left hand and ran the flame up and down my right side. You could hardly see the flame in the sunlight. I could smell the stink of my hair scorching. It didn't seem to last long enough and it didn't seem to hurt enough, so I used some more gas and did it again. I buried the bottle and the matches and the rag in the sand. It began to hurt worse. The next morning it was a lot worse. It looked so bad it scared me."

She laughed aloud.

"What's so funny?"

"Just thinking about the money. It makes me feel good. It makes me feel like laughing and dancing. It's sitting there, man, and it's waiting for us. You act so sour. Doesn't it make you feel good?"

"Just wonderful. Sure."

"What's wrong?"

"Six people. That's a lot of people. I keep thinking Mary Jane is wondering where the hell I am. Like I should phone. And then I remember. Crissy, you don't know how many people it takes to add up to six. More than you think."

She squeezed his left ankle. "You did fine. What are you so gloomy about? Oh! Did you expect a better show of gratitude? So okay! Only can you wipe that goop off first with a towel. It smells funny." She stood up and reached both arms back to undo the top hook and get the dress zipper started. "No, I didn't mean anything like that," he said sharply. She stared at him, then walked to the head of the bed and leaned over him and put her mouth down upon his. In a little while she straightened up. "When the man says no dice he means no dice."

"Sorry."

"Why be sorry? It's way too hot in here anyway. I was going to make a gesture. Like gratitude. It'll keep." She smoothed the seat of the dress with the backs of her hands and sat back where she had been before.

"What comes next?"

"Don't you remember? It's like we said. You stay holed up here. We can't be seen together by anybody ever."

"It's over. What difference does it make?"

"Don't be so dull! *Somebody* was in that deal with Bix. People like

Bix, like the Senator, like those other buddies of his, they don't trust anybody or anything. They'll think it was some kind of cute way to get the money. And when they can't find you, they'll back track you to me. I can lie *much* better than you can, and I can size up the situation. Did anybody follow you, or try to follow you?"

"I don't know."

"You didn't forget to do like we practiced, did you?"

"No. I did it. I felt like a damn fool, but I did it."

"I'm not sure anyone was following me. But there could have been. I thought I kept seeing the same car. We are *not* going to take any chances. This is the time to be most careful, Garry. Believe me. Somebody may be adding up two and two and trying very hard to get seven. Believe me and trust me." She patted his ankle. "You've done so beautifully so far. Remember, it could be my neck too. Be a good boy. I know this is very very depressing, but I'll sneak down here and keep you cheered up. Think of how we're going to get the money."

He got up slowly and went to the bureau and took the Banner check out of the drawer and handed it to her.

She stared at it and then up at him, her eyes narrow. "Just exactly what the *hell* is this!"

"For my personal exclusive eye witness story of the ill-fated cruise of the Muñeca."

"Are you out of your *mind!*"

"What are you so hot about? Look, it kept the rest of the people out of my hair. Once I was sewed up they knew there was no point in asking questions."

"But you don't plan to *do* it!"

"Why not?"

"You idiot, we want the whole thing to be forgotten just as soon as possible. And what makes you think you need the money?"

"I thought it would be—kind of a natural thing for me to do."

They argued for a few minutes. He told her about his promise to Hal Wezler, and where he was staying. She was silent and thoughtful for a few minutes and then she said, "You can't do it, Garry, because I've decided we don't really have to wait so long to go after that money. It's too much risk to leave it on that same island where they found you. You were supposed to take it to a better place. When we made our plans, we thought it was going to be in a better place."

"How soon then?"

"Maybe—next weekend?"

She watched his face. He sat on the side of the bed. Finally he said, "We didn't do much talking about after. Except we'd split."

"Because we could no longer afford each other, honey."

"I better know how you figure on handling it, Criss. From then on."

"Is it any of your business?"

"If somebody gets interested in how you got rich all of a sudden, it could turn out to be my business."

"They won't. I sold the last decent piece of jewelry. A damned fine emerald. So I've got a stake. I'm going to put the house on the market, and set the price low enough so it will move. I've got the bill of sale on the emerald to show how I happen to have cash. And I am going to turn the house money into cash. And then, dear boy, I am going to go from bank to bank, and I am going to turn that emerald money and house money into certified checks, just as many times as I have to to unload my share of the loot. Cashier's checks. I learned that little trick from Fer. I'm going to sew them into the lining of something and fly to Italy and rent something rather nice on the Italian Riviera. As soon as I'm settled, I'm going to drive up to Zurich and open a lovely account with those checks and have those shrewd little men invest in very safe income things for me and deposit the income in another account I can draw on as I need it. I am going to swing just as long and hard as I want to, and I am going to grow old very very gracefully, and I am not going to have to beg any son of a bitch in creation for anything ever. I should be worrying about you, instead of you worrying about me. You're more likely to fumble it, Captain."

"I've been thinking."

"That in itself is . . ."

"Shut up, Crissy," he said in a tired voice. "While that Hal Wezler was giving me a ride out to Parker's he kept looking at me whenever we had to stop for a light. Finally he said he was going to take a chance on something. He said he was going to stick his neck way out and recommend they make a lot more use of me than they'd figured on. He said that while he was doing the book from the tapes, I should go out to the Coast and he'd get me lined up with some people who'd—teach me how to handle myself in—public exposure situations. Create a celebrity image, he said. Then if I've got what he thinks I've got, it would be a bigger thing than just plugging the book and getting me on things like the *Today* show, things like that. He said I had a good chance of coming up with such a bankable image, it might even help swing a movie deal on the book, with me playing myself. He said I—project something that if it comes through on the screen, it could be big. He said the housewives were hungry for a more mature type guy and . . ."

"Are you serious? For the love of God, are you trying to have me on, Staniker?"

"I figured it out this way. That money. I could rent a deposit box under another name and pay three years ahead. I could just let it sit there. Then suppose it's like Hal said, and I happen to hit? Why should he kid me anyway? They've signed me up for what they want. So I could make good money at it. I could buy the kind of motor sailer I was telling you about. Then pick up my share and I'm off around the world in it, enough to keep going on as long as I live.

If I don't hit, the money is still there, and I think of some other way."

"Oh boy," she said. "You are really it! You didn't want money after all. You wanted to be a celebrity. You were getting too beat to line up the really first class tail the way you used to, but this way you can start getting it again, as much as you need whenever you need it."

"When we split," he said sullenly, "what we do is our own business."

"They get you into a corset and cap your teeth, you'll look just darling."

"Get off my back, Crissy!"

She slid close to him. "Let's not pout. People with that lovely raw wad of money don't have to pout. We have to be a ways and means committee. Can you still borrow that fast boat from your old buddy?"

"The Bertram? Sure."

"And it will get all the way over there and back?"

"Almost. Oversize tanks. Lay an extra thirty gallons aboard in five gallon cans and it's no sweat."

"Garry, how fast could you make the round trip in the dark?"

"There's a weather factor. Give me a fairly flat sea, and allow time to go ashore and get the suitcase, add a reasonable safety factor—ten hours, eleven say. Leave at seven and be back by six in the morning. But when we were planning it, you kept talking about the risk of coming back here and finding a reception committee."

"That's why I've been taking sailing lessons."

"You what?"

"You can run more southerly on the way back and come to Biscayne Bay below Cape Florida, Captain, and when you pass a blonde in a yellow bikini sailing her Flying Dutchman, you drop the pretty suitcase off. Maybe with a float tied to it just in case. She picks it up and sails home and puts the cash in her wall safe, and that night, after you've returned the boat and driven back to this charming hideaway, the blonde brings you your share of the bread. A sailboat has such an innocent look, don't you think? I hired a boy to teach me. The poor dear has the most terrible crush on me."

"It could be a pretty good way," he said at last. "You sure work things out, don't you?"

"There's a lot at stake. Isn't it worth a lot of time and thought and work? What would it come to per hour?"

"I can make a call about the Bertram."

"Not yet. Not until I tell you. You know, this hasn't been much of a celebration, has it? Why do we have to be so tense and gloomy? We're out of the bind, Garry. We broke loose. The hardest part is all over. Tell you what. I'll come by here Sunday night. I'll bring goodies. We'll have our little celebration. It's a funny thing, Garry. Now that I know that this is the only place we'll ever be together again, I really think I'm going to miss you. Isn't that weird?"

He looked at her and looked away. "Ever since the Senator died, things have been weird. I don't know. I get the feeling this isn't me. I get the feeling none of it happened. I don't think I've known for one minute how you ever felt about anything."

"Why should you want to know?"

"I guess it doesn't make any difference. Not any more."

She drove the little white car home in a roundabout way through empty streets, through a coolness of recent rain, the wet streets reflecting the caligraphies of all-night neon. For half the journey she thought of Staniker. There had been just enough toughness, just enough greed, just enough brutality for him to manage it. But now his eyes were wrong and his mouth was changed. He had expended something he'd never regain. It was, she thought, like what happened to a man who experienced a truly professional, cold, savage beating. It left him with all those little apologetic mannerisms, bob of head, ingratiating smile, a wariness very like shyness.

And then she planned herself for the boy. A horn blast behind her startled her and she realized she had slowed to almost twenty miles an hour and the rain had begun again, and she was trying to see through the blurred windshield without thought of turning the wipers on. The car roared irritably by her. She turned the wipers on. She tried to be amused at her absentmindedness, but it left a chilly little hollow of apprehension just under her heart.

The boy was waiting under the roofed part of the stone terrace, outside the locked doors of her bedroom. She turned on a single low light and unlocked the doors.

He held her close, wrapped in his strong young arms. She made herself tremble.

"You were gone so long!" he said. "It was driving me nuts. Why were you there so long, darling?"

"The r-rain is blowing in, d-dear. Please."

He released her and closed the sliding door. She sat in the straight chair by her desk, knees together, fists in her lap, head lowered. He dropped to one knee by the chair, put his fingers under her chin and lifted her head. She saw agony in his face. "Did he—did you have to . . ."

She shook her head in violent negation and shuddered. "He tried to. I—made excuses. He—hurt me. He hit me in the stomach. It made me sick. Oh. Olly darling, he's worse than before. He's—very strange. He wanted to keep me there. I had to promise to go back there Sunday night. If I don't he'll come after me."

"So that's when we do it," he said harshly.

"But can we? Can we really?"

"What's it like where he is?"

"It's—very good for what we were talking about. It's a horrid little bungalow court near Coral Gables. It's the sort of place you would go if you wanted to hide. I don't think there's anyone in the bungalows near him, and it's all so jungly and overgrown you can't see them from each other or from the road in front. It really seems like—well, like the kind of depressing place where—that kind of thing could happen." She frowned. "He *killed* those people, Oliver."

"He *what!*"

"It wasn't any accident. Oh, he didn't admit it. He's much too clever for that. Nobody will ever be able to prove a thing. But that place he's in, he rented it under another name. He said it was to keep reporters from bothering him. I think it's so he can really go into hiding if somebody gets suspicious about what really happened on the Muñeca."

"What makes you think he killed them all?"

"I know him, Oliver. God, how I know him! He said little things that fit together. He said he wouldn't have to worry about money for a while. And he gave me a slimy wink and said the cruise ended before he'd had time to decide which one was better stuff, the little lame girl or her step-mother. I suppose he got careless and Mr. Kayd or the brother caught him with one of them. If he hit one and killed him, he'd kill everybody. That's how he is."

"It isn't wrong to kill a man like that," said Oliver.

He moved closer to her, on both knees. She pulled his head into her lap. She slowly stroked his crisp hair. "He's a monster," she whispered. "We have to be so careful. It's going to be like a nightmare for us, but when it's over—we can go away together for a little while, to some marvelous place."

There was no sound in the room except the breath of the air conditioning, and a faint whisper of the rain outside.

"Get up now, dear," she said. "I want to make a drawing of the floor plan of that cottage while it's fresh in my mind. We've got a lot of work to do. A lot of planning."

She turned her chair to the desk, turned on the desk light, opened the drawer and got paper and pencil.

Twenty

LEILA DID NOT KNOW what had set the Sergeant off just when they were getting the noon meal on Saturday. It could have been the scene she had made the night before, crying and raving and cursing and carrying on until she had exhausted herself.

But he had not seemed angry about what she had done, or about the scene. He had seemed just—saddened, and disappointed in her. After she was certain he was asleep on Friday night, she had rubbed herself liberally with repellent, and had sneaked off the boat without a sound and up the stairs and into the shack and taken the big flashlight which had been aboard the Muñequita. Then, driven nearly out of her mind by those bugs which didn't mind the repellent, in the windless night she had climbed the ladder to the platform high in the water oak, and had aimed the beam through an opening in the branches toward the houses on the mainland shore. It wasn't too late. Many of them had lights on. She worked the switch until her thumb felt sprained. Dash dash dash dot dot dot dash dash

dash dot dot dot. She had to stop to whack the insects on her face and arms and ankles.

"What are you trying to do?" the Sergeant had roared, so close at hand she had nearly leaped off the platform.

She had fought him on the way down and they had both nearly fallen. But she did not start the really large scene until he had strapped her into that impossible belt again and forced the link shut and said, sadly, "If 'n you can't be trusted at all, Missy, then I just have to do this ever' time I have to leave you alone, and ever' time I have to get some sleep. Don't like it any better than you do. But you won't pay attention to good sense!"

"Good sense!" she had yelled. "Good *sense!* You're a *crazy!* Don't you even know it? You got that great big dent in your head where they took your brains out. You're *kidnapping* me! You know what they'll do to you? They'll take you away and they'll lock you up forever in a big room full of other crazies!"

But he had just kept looking mournfully at her, shaking his head, and finally he had gone down and brought her bedding up and taken his own down and gone to sleep on the boat.

This morning he had seemed the same as usual. Perhaps a little quieter. He'd been opening a can of franks and beans when suddenly the can and the can opener fell from his hands. He stood there swaying from side to side in a strange way, and then she remembered what it reminded her of, a long time ago, stopping at that roadside place when she was little, and there was an elephant there chained in the sun, swaying just like that.

She watched him. She moistened her lips. She glanced at the belt and chain over by the post. The shorts and halter top she wore were good enough for swimming. Run and grab a cushion off the Muñe-quita. Jump in and swim his little channel through the mangroves and out into the open bay. A hundred yards of channel. Lots of boats on a Saturday.

He wasn't looking at her, or at anything. Then she saw the water running out of his eyes. She had to tug and pull at him to get him turned around and, in his sticklike walk, over to his thinking place. She put his big hands on the greasy places on the peeled uprights. He moaned and gripped with such a terrible strength she heard little gratings and poppings of muscle and bone and gristle. He thunked his head against the beam so violently, she screamed and ran and got the thin faded cushion from the old wicker chair and folded it once and held it against the beam. He butted his head against it.

"You're not crazy, Sarg," she kept telling him in a pleading tone. "You're not. I'm sorry."

His hands fell to his sides. He looked at her, half frowning, and he walked over and sat on the bed, face in his hands.

"Missy?" he said at last.

"I'm right here, Sarg."

"Things spin around and around and get sucked down, like they went down a drain."

He shook himself like a big, tired hound and stood up. "Takes it out of me," he said.

"That lump on your head is getting huge."

He felt of it with cautious fingertips. "Whomped me a good one that time."

He started toward the kerosene stove then stopped and looked at her. "I wouldn't have knowed you'd left, Miss Leila. Why didn't you?"

"It never entered my mind."

He picked up the can and the opener. "Lost my hunger, but you could eat some I expect. If you'd eat real good—and sleep as much as you can . . ."

"Yes?"

"And if you could run that nice boat down to the city all by yourself and promise word of honor you wouldn't remember a thing about where you were or who doctored you . . ."

"I promise, Sarg. Honest. Cross my heart."

"Three or four days more, I could let you go."

"Do you mean it?"

"It's a promise for sure. Can you wait just that little bitty time more, Missy?"

"Oh, yes!"

"Then I don't have to put that danged chain on you. I sure to God hate to see you fastened up that way. In the night I decided I just couldn't do it one more time, no matter what."

Gordon Dale liked to work in the silence and emptiness of the law offices on Saturday morning. He solved the problems of the brief, and when he was ready to leave he remembered he hadn't heard from Detective Sergeant Dickerson. He was told that Dickerson should just about be arriving at his home. He phoned the home number. Dickerson had just walked in. His voice was weary.

"Who? Oh, Mr. Dale. To tell you the truth, I forgot all about it. Just when I was ready to go off at midnight, we had a real dandy. I wish to God they'd been one motel further away. That would have taken it over the city line. Fellow on vacation got slopped and beat his little kid to death. His wife put the body in the car and tried to be an ambulance, and took out two palm trees and a light post. So I worked on through. The post showed the kid had a lot of old breaks, green stick fractures that had healed without attention. A lousy night, Mr. Dale. I'm sorry I didn't get around to . . ."

"That's all right. No rush. Get some sleep, Dave."

"Soon as I can get anything, I'll get back to you, Mr. Dale."

• • •

Sam Boylston lay propped up on two pillows on one of the Bahama beds in the motel cabana. He wore blue swim trunks he had purchased at a dime store in the shopping center a block away. He talked on the phone to Corpus Christi. He was listening for the third time to the kid's excited tale of danger and injury. He made the right sounds in the right places. He could look out through the window wall and see the three girls horsing around, taking turns off the low board—the fat girl with the red sunburn, the skinny dark one with a loud laugh, and the little chunky one with the deep tan and the straight hair bleached egg white.

"Well," he said, "you sure had yourself a time, Boy-Sam. Want to put your mom back on?"

Lydia Jean came back on the line. "*That* was a long talk," she said. "Oh, just a minute." In the background he heard her shouting something to Boy-Sam. "Sorry. He was going to go running out without his sweater. There's an edge in the wind for this time of year. Out of the north."

"Was it a bad break?"

"A very clean simple fracture, and he really didn't cry very much. He turned white as ghosts. You were very very patient with him, dear. He's being a terrible bore about it. He can make a description of falling out of a tree last practically forever. He had to be so sure you found out he didn't cry very much. Sam, all the time he was talking to you, I kept thinking of what you told me about Jonathan. How long is he going to—keep doing that, keep looking for her?"

"Until he accepts the fact she's dead."

"With Leila, that isn't easy. She was so much more alive than— most of the rest of us."

"I know."

"Are you going back to Harlingen now?"

"Pretty soon, I guess. Why don't you go down and open the house and wait for me there?"

"I thought of it."

"So why don't you?"

"Sam, dear, my heart bleeds for you in this whole thing. I know how you felt about your sister. I loved her too. You know that. And I should be with you. Time of need and all that. I don't want to be cold and hard, but it would be coming back for the wrong reason. I've invested—too much heartache in this to come back for anything but the right reason. You'll have to understand why I had to leave. And when you *do* understand, I can come back to you."

"Same old paradox. Try this for a partial answer. Remember Rosalie's brother?"

"Of course."

"I was wrong."

"I beg your pardon?"

"I said I was wrong. Dead wrong. Does that mean anything?"

After a long pause she said, "It's interesting. I think I would like to know why you think you were wrong, Sam."

"I know now that I let Rosalie down and I let you down."

"Indeed! I see. You did not live up to what we expected of you."

"What's the matter with you?"

"But you were perfectly content with yourself, of course. You *knew* it would be stupid and out of character for Sam Boylston to go down there and defend that fellow. But because I wanted it, you should have gritted your teeth and—humored me."

"What the hell do you want of me!"

Her voice sounded far away. "A little more than that, I'm afraid. A little more than that. Take care of yourself, Sam."

She was gone. He rolled onto his shoulder and slammed the phone back onto the cradle. The chunky young girl appeared just outside his window wall, shading her eyes, peering in at him. She grinned, made a beckoning gesture, pointed toward the pool and made swimming motions. He shook his head no, and she made a pouting face and shrugged and went away.

He could not stop asking himself what Lyd wanted of him. Talking with Theyma Chappie in her little apartment, when, to his confusion and dismay the tears had begun without warning, he had felt close to an understanding, as though suddenly it would be revealed to him, the way a light bulb appears over the head of the comic strip character, and he could say: Of course! *Now* I know.

But if he could never understand, and could not alter some inner perfectionistic coolness, some chronic insistence upon a world of reasonable cause and effect, why could she not accept the flaw for the sake of the rest of it? A presentable man, of scrupulous marital fidelity, fair in his dealings, achieving through all the long shrewd hours of work a position of status, social and professional, and the income to give her a life without want or drudgery. Father of her healthy son. Would she prefer a sickly romanticism, a variant of a Jonathan, baying his lover way across the Grand Bahama Bank? She could not seem to understand that it was a world wherein, if you faltered, They ripped you down quite casually and went on Their way.

Yet Lydia Jean was not a dreamer. She had that practical streak, that capacity for acceptance of the things she could not change. If he was forever incapable of change, she would not be so merciless. It meant she believed in something within him which he could not identify. And it meant that she believed that if he could grasp it, use it, the benefit would be as much his as hers.

It was paradox, and as so many times before during the months of their separation, it seemed to spin faster and faster in his mind until a kind of centrifugal force flung it out and away.

He looked out at the pool. The other two had left. The brown chunk solemnly practiced dives from the low board. He had bought the trunks and gone swimming because his body had begun to feel stale. He was accustomed to exercise. The chunk had challenged him to a race. He had heard her friends call her Toby. The races had given him the excuse to extend himself, the challenge to stretch the long muscles, empty the bottoms of the lungs. When it was just two lengths, she could beat him in free style, most of her advantage coming from the quick racing turn she knew. Three lengths was the best for them, a tossup. When they had tried four lengths, he had won as decisively as she won in the two-length competition.

Then he had gone in and phoned Lyd. Optimism born of exertion. But it hadn't worked out.

He watched the Toby girl. She was trying swans, and getting good elevation off the low board. She would eel out of the pool, climb up onto the board, stand at a measured distance from the end, use both thumbs to hook her pale wet hair away from her eyes, stand very still, then take her steps, land at the very end, and take a maximum spring from the fiberglass board. In the sealed room with the air conditioning humming, it was a silent performance out there.

Her suit was black and white, formed of two panels, front and back, with red lacing up the sides across the two inch gap between the panels, brown healthy young flesh bulging in diamond patterns against the tension of the lacing. Her thighs were too heavy. Her hips and breasts were hearty, shoulders broad, waist narrow and limber. The muscles of her back, contours softened by the little layer of woman-fat under the wet brown hide, moved smoothly and with precision.

Drowsy from exertion, depressed by Lydia Jean's response, he drifted into erotic fantasy. He brought the brown girl into the room, drew the transparent blue draperies across the window wall, pressed the night-lock button on the door. He would take her gently out of the suit. Her body would be wet, scented with soap, chlorine, and the healthiness of flesh. Tremblingly apprehensive, goose-pimpled, pleading softly while he pressed her gently down and . . .

Outside, as if on cue, the Toby girl went halfway out the board, turned around, sat and stretched out, face turned toward the sun. A great grinding spasm of lust catapulted him up out of drowsiness, a wanting that was as vivid as great pain, obliterating everything but itself, as pain does. In the constraint of the built-in support of the cheap swim trunks, he bulged hard as marble. Shocked by the intensity, he sat up and caught his breath and took a derisive look at the lonely man far from home. The chunk could not be more than sixteen years old. Under the ragged edge of the bangs which half concealed her eyebrows was the round uncommitted face of childhood. A real conquest, fella. They'd come after you with a net.

But as the hotness of immediate and overwhelming need faded he was uncomfortably aware of the residue it left in the back of his mind, an urge to pull down all the walls, tumble them in upon himself, go plunging out into the streets and commit acts of such vileness and terror and pointlessness that when at last they brought him down, all his chances would be gone forever, all careful things undone, all accomplishment forgotten. And then, because it would be past rebuilding, no one would ever expect him to even try. And he would be free. There were other ways to be free. To disappear so cleverly he could never be found. Or to find that hiding place, where they had hid from you long ago, and looked as if they were inwardly smiling at how easy it had been. They were like tinted wax. Scent of a thousand blossoms. Dark wood and silver handles, organ playing as the people came in, making little rustling and creaking sounds as they sat down. They coughed. And then the man came out from the side with the book, and put it down, opened it, looked out at all of them and cleared his throat . . .

"You could on sudden impulse harm yourself," Theyma Chappie said, as clearly as if she sat there beside him.

Again, on cue, he saw one of the motel maids, in white uniform, a Negro, walk across his line of vision on the far side of the pool, passing in front of the cabana directly across from him. She was much darker than Theyma, but he saw, perhaps made more evident to him by the uniform, the same slenderness, the same high-hipped, gliding walk, saucy bulge of rump.

He reached for the nearest reality and had the operator make the call person-to-person to Mr. Taylor Worth, Boylston and Worth, Harlingen.

"Things are beginning to pile up, Sam," said Worth. "I got a postponement on the Gianetti thing, but hizzoner was a little puckered. How long do I have to stall?"

"I don't know. Not much longer, maybe. I can't say for sure. I appreciate your holding the fort by yourself."

"People are wondering about some kind of ceremony for Leila. You know how many friends she had. Sorry to bring it up, but there's a big memorial service for the Kayds tomorrow. People keep phoning up. Anything you want me to tell them?"

"Just that it will have to wait until Jonathan and I get back, and that's indefinite at the moment. Tay, have you heard any locker-room gossip about Bix?"

"Well, there was a hell of a lot in the beginning. You know how it would be. A pretty shifty type. Then when they finally got the whole story and that captain was cleared, it all died down. Now it's beginning to pick up again."

"Why?"

"You should be able to figure that out, Sam. Because you're still hanging around that area. Why? As a special personal favor tell me why."

Sam Boylston reached quickly and found a plausible answer before the silence lasted too long. "I was checking around when I first got to Nassau, before we found out what happened. I came across the bits and pieces of a deal Bix was putting together. Of course the structure fell apart, but the pieces are still lying around."

Taylor Worth chuckled. "And that offends the Boylston sense of order?"

"And greed."

"The ultimate motivation."

"Keep it quiet. Later if I can find a way to put the pieces together, we can pick up some blocks of that Sunshine thing of his, then let the news leak out a little."

"You awe me, Samuel. Keep me posted. I'll keep stalling. Right now I've got to run."

As he was taking his shower, Sam found himself thinking that it could be done without any deal. Just quietly pick up Sunshine Management at depressed prices over-the-counter, then leak word that Sam Boylston was getting into the act. The golden touch should be good enough to average out maybe three points if the holdings were unloaded again carefully enough. It would make the shareholders feel right at home, he thought. The same kind of a deal Bix would have rigged—and Sam couldn't stomach.

Oliver Akard was in the empty house of his parents in the empty afternoon. Dust motes winked in the shafts of sunshine. His father was working overtime at the shop. His mother was at a Saturday afternoon benefit bridge.

He had slept so late she was gone by the time he got up. It had been a relief not to have to face that martyred, wounded look, the audible signs of affliction. It had been almost dawn when he had come home, and on an impulse to challenge them, instead of turning off the engine and coasting into the driveway, he had driven in, parked in his usual place beyond the carport, revved the engine three times, the holes rusted through the muffler adding a snare-drum resonance to the insult to the neighborhood peace.

An hour after his late breakfast he was hungry again, made two thick sandwiches of peanut butter and drank most of a quart of milk, drinking it from the cardboard package as he watched television baseball. The game seemed meaningless, and he could find nothing on the other channels to hold his interest. He left it turned on, and soon the sour soundtrack and dramatic voices of an old movie eased the silence of the house.

He had packed a dufflebag with most of what he would need, and put it in the back of his closet behind his winter coat. He could put the toilet articles in at the last moment. He had composed the note he would leave and had hidden it in his desk. Crissy had helped him with it:

> *I have to go away alone for a couple of weeks to think things out. Nothing has been going right any more. I'm sorry for all the worry I've given you lately. I have some money. I have to get things straightened out in my head before I do something real crazy.*
>
>   *Your Son, Oliver*

Crissy was certainly fussy about having things exactly right. She thought one word ought to be changed and she wouldn't let him cross it out. He had to write the whole thing out again.

He felt irritated with her, the way she had acted as if he wouldn't be able to remember things from one minute to the next. She had made him draw the floor plan from memory, even to putting in the street and the little box to indicate where he would park, and a dotted line to the bungalow door. Number 10. Mooney Bungalow Courts. And he had to write out that little list of what to bring with him.

When he had tried to protest, she had leaned her face into his, her eyes startlingly round and bright. Her voice had been very slow and distinct, her mouth shaping each word as though for a deaf person, and she had put in some words which had shocked him. He had not known she could come on so heavy.

She had told him not to come by until dusk. He planned to leave the house well before that, so he would be gone before either of them came home. The hands of the house clocks moved with a terrible slowness. Yet when he would realize that another hour had gone by, and he was an hour closer to what they were going to do, the bottom seemed to fall out of his stomach. It was better to think beyond that part of it, and think about going away with her. Perhaps in a week, she said. That's why the note said he was going alone. So they wouldn't come after him to get him away from this terrible, terrible woman.

Going away with her would be the reward for doing what he had to do tomorrow night. She wouldn't tell him where. She said it had to be a surprise. He would adore it. A lovely, lovely place. Long, lazy days and nights of love.

He went back to the kitchen and opened the refrigerator, and as he reached to get the milk carton and finish it, he caught a faint scent of fresh limes, and it made his heart stand still. The shampoo she used had that lime scent, familiar now from all the times of breathing her in, face in that softness and crispness of her hair. There was one perfume she wore only for bed, a strange heavy bitter-sweet muskiness that seemed to put a sharper and more desperate edge on his need. And there was often the faint odor of rum and oranges in the hot gasping moisture of her breath against his face, and under these mingled smells, another one, the elusive, distinctive scent of herself, of her flesh and of the using of the flesh. Sometimes when it had just ended and she rested in his arms, these richnesses seemed almost unpleasant, and would remind him of the times when he was tiring and she was still demanding, how fleshy and vast she would seem to become in the bed's darknesses, something so remorseless and devouring it would seem to him, in that half delirium of fading response, that some animal thing was after him, grasping, straining, grunting, churning at his helplessness.

He could look at her later at a distance, dressed, so slender and tidy and graceful, and marvel that the night-thing could be so completely hidden away, all the soft machinery dismantled and dispersed.

He walked through the house, touching things. This table. This hassock. These white bricks in the fireplace wall.

Raoul had taken Francisca to the beach Saturday afternoon, all the way up to North Miami Beach. Commitment had created small tensions between them. They talked too rapidly and gayly about nothing, and lapsed often into silences which were not comfortable. He had the curious sensation that he was taking pictures of her, a mechanism in the back of his mind clicking, filing a color print away. When she swam alone and then came smiling up the little slope of beach toward him, yanking the swim cap off, shaking out her dark hair, pelvis tilting in her slightly self-conscious stride in her brief, one-piece, candy-striped suit, scissoring thighs in the flawless even dusky gold of ancient ivory, the camera clicked again and again.

When she lowered herself to the big beach towel beside him, the camera in his mind backed away from the two of them and took the incongruity of that lithe elegance in the gross company of such a squat broad hairy fellow with a pocked peasant face, hair thinning. Then the camera took closeups of her beside him, droplets of sea water on her bare shoulder, and an oblique glance of her dark eyes before she looked toward the sea, her profile perfect as new coins against the beach glare, against the background of all the beach people stretching into the distance along the broad band of whiteness bordering the cobalt blue water with its dancing mirror glints.

It disturbed him to have the camera-feeling, as if he were storing up the memories of her for the empty years ahead. He and Sam

Boylston had debated how much danger she might be in. It had to be weighed against the danger of destroying the adjustment she had achieved. It was her hiding place, and were it destroyed, she might seek that other hiding place again, the withdrawal, the meek, passive, unresponsive silence he had seen when he had visited her with her brother.

With time and love and understanding, he felt there was a good chance of slowly merging the 'Cisca of now with the Francisca who once had been. And then, little by little, the housemaid would disappear, along with the shop-girl mannerisms, the saucy walk, the shallow pleasures.

But will she then settle for a Raoul Kelly, he thought. It would be a bitter irony to discover that her acceptance of him as a "boy-fran" would be outgrown, along with her delight in soap opera, her collection of movie magazines, her taste for bright, tight clothing and semi-theatrical makeup.

As the afternoon did not seem to be going well, he decided to take the risk he had weighed and wondered about. He went up to the big parking lot and came back with the folder from his files. It contained a selection of the articles he had done in Spanish-language newspapers, cut to size and Xeroxed on the newspaper machine on 8½-inch by 14-inch sheets, and fastened into a clasp binder. He had made the selection with great care, leaving out those things which might trigger too many memories for her.

"'Cisca, I want to show you why I am unpopular with certain people."

She opened the folder, read a few lines and closed it. "You said you are. That is enough for me."

"There is something else."

"Indeed?"

"Boys climb to the very tops of the tallest trees. They do very dangerous things upon their bicycles. If the girl is watching. This is my work. It is what I do. I would wish you to admire how I balance in my tree tops."

She shrugged almost imperceptibly and opened the folder again. After a few moments she said, "But I do not have the political mind, Raoul."

"For much of that it is not necessary."

"But such difficult writing, and on the beach?"

"I am without mercy. Read, woman!"

She made a face at him and sighed and continued reading. He watched her, and he saw her change. By leaning a little bit he saw which one she was reading. It was the appraisal of the policies of the Twelve Families of the Republic of Panama, and some intimate biographies of those individuals most active in blocking the reforms of the judicial system. She was frowning as she read, her lips compressed. It surprised him that her submerged intelligence should have been awakened by that article. It was one of the more complex ones, and it led with a documented care to the thesis he reiterated in article after article: In countries where men of good will work to achieve honesty and equality under the law, education, literacy, good health standards, the opportunity to lead a better life than one's forefathers, Communist subversion becomes futile.

"Shall we swim now?" he asked.

"Not now. You go if you wish," she said absently.

He swam. When he came back, she had rolled onto her stomach and was propped up on her elbows, reading the pages in the shade of her body. He toweled himself, popped open a fresh can of beer from the cooler.

Finally she was done. She closed the folder and put it aside. She was lost in thought for a long time.

"How do you learn these things?" she asked abruptly.

"Research, study, interviews. There is always a pattern, always a slow movement in one direction or another."

"This is a very very important thing you do, Señor."

"One would like to believe so."

"Does anyone listen?"

"Fewer than one would hope."

It was the steady, thoughtful look of Francisca Torcedo y Sarmantar which met his gaze. "One cannot doubt that they would relish silencing such a man. One man who so carefully stabs at the tenderest parts. I could not know, Raoul. I think it is very possible that you are a great man."

"Perhaps you have been too long in the hot sun, *querida*."

"Greatness is to use the quality of the mind to change these slow directions of history, no?"

"But I am merely . . ."

She rapped the cover of the folder with her knuckles. "Tell me. This work in California, will it give you a way to make more men listen?"

"Yes."

"Then you should permit nothing to interfere. Nothing!"

"I have accepted. You will come with me."

And he saw the little signs of change again, as she edged back into the role more comfortable for her. Small changes in posture, in expression. She laughed, brash and merry, signaling the English that put his teeth on edge. "Crazy sumbitch, you! Eh? Get turned on by sotch a estupid little broad. Looking at your head, I think. So I go with. Okay. Because you crazy as hell, man! Swimming now? Can't catch." She hopped up and ran fleetingly toward the gentle surf line.

He left her at the Harkinson house at quarter to five. He had an article to finish and turn in, and he said he thought he could be back by eight. She had told him that Crissy Harkinson had said she wouldn't need her that evening.

Raoul did not return until eight thirty. He went up the stairs carrying the two warm cartons of Chinese food he had promised to bring. The plan was to heat it up on her little stove and eat there and make the ten o'clock feature three miles away wherein James Bond would cavort his way through windrows of women to be beaten sodden by the minions of some chap of incredible rascality before, at last, outwitting him, slaying him in horrible detail in wide-screen color, with gadgetry devised by M.I.T. dropouts, and then at the fade-out, taking his bemused ease betwixt perfumed breasts of such astonishing pneumatic dimension he would have a slightly exasperated and apologetic look, like that of a man trying to take his bass drum into a phone booth.

The servant quarters were dark and silent. He had noticed that Crissy Harkinson's little white convertible was gone. The Akard boy's car was in the parking area, a clumsy, underprivileged shadow.

He opened the screen door and went inside. " 'Cisca?" he called. " 'Cisca?"

Fright and apprehension seemed to bulge his heart. He put the food aside hastily and began putting lights on, expecting that it would be one of those plausible domestic accidents. But the small rooms were empty. The candy-striped suit hung from the shower rail.

She came pattering up the outside stairs, calling, "Raoul? Raoul?" His heart lurched and his knees turned watery, and he knew that he could take no chance with her, not from now on, not ever.

She had on sleek white slacks and a fussy little red blouse and far too much lipstick. She gave him a quick little hug and kiss, and then laughed at him and said she had given him a clown face. She hurried and got a kleenex and dabbed the red from his mouth. As she busied herself with reheating the food and laying out the dishes and silverware, he said, "The boy is at the house waiting for her?"

"Oh no. She is there too. Why would you— Of course, her little car is gone. She took it in this morning to be fixed. But by noon it was not done, and they stop work at noon. They will finish it on Monday. A garage man drove her back here. They will deliver the car on Monday. She was very angry. She called me over to speak with her. We talked for a long time. I have good news."

"What?"

"When we are eating. Then I will tell you."

They sat down at the small table she had set by the window, and she got up almost immediately and dug into the pocket of her slacks and took out folded bills and sat down again.

She held the money up and said, "This is until the end of this month of June. She talked to the one you found, that Amparo, on the telephone. Amparo will come here on Wednesday and after I show her where everything is kept and explain how things must be done, then I may go. And she will give me a letter. I think I can find work in California. Maybe I will work for an important actress. Mmmmm. This is very good food, Mister Kellee!"

"What else did she talk about?"

"Oh, one minute. Something else to show." She hurried into her bedroom and returned with a savings account book, handed it to him gravely. "Inspect it, please."

The total, deposited in small amounts over two years was just over eleven hundred dollars.

"Obviously you could have no idea you were associating with such a rich girl," she said loftily. "I shall pay my share of the expenses of the trip. I would like to know what it is they do to these very small shrimp."

"I am honored to have the attentions of such a rich lady. What else did Missy Crissy have on her buzzard's mind?"

"She is not so bad as all that! She asked that I do a special favor for her tomorrow night. She is upset. She confided in me. She had tears in her eyes. Sometimes it is possible to feel sorry for her."

"What about?"

"She and the Captain Staniker had a great quarrel before he went
away to the Bahamas. That is something I did not know. She told
him she never wanted to see him again. She said she was tired of his
coming over and complaining about all his troubles, and drinking
her whisky and getting ugly and mean. She ended the affair. Now
the Captain has returned. He had telephoned her. He insists on seeing her. She begged him not to come here. When he telephoned the
second time last evening, the boy was with her. She said the boy
became very agitated. She says the boy has an infatuation for her.
She admits there was an affair with the Captain, but she looked into
my eyes and said there had been no relationship with the boy. That
is the kind of lie one cannot expect a housemaid to believe. But I
suppose it is a matter of her pride. Even though she knows I know,
she cannot say it. It would make her appear foolish, this seduction of
a silly boy who could be her son. She said the boy is acting strange
and violent, and thinks to protect her from the evil Captain. She
cannot make the boy understand that she can protect herself without help."

"Where was the boy while all this was going on?"

"We spoke in the kitchen, sitting with cups of coffee, like old
friends. Perhaps in a way we are. She said that all of this has exhausted her. Perhaps the boy was asleep in her bed while we spoke.
I could not say. She said that tonight she is going to be very firm
with the boy and send him away forever. Doubtless he will make a
great scene. She says she cannot endure such nonsense any longer.
She says the Captain is a bore and the boy is a fool. She does not
want any ugliness here which will bring the police. Tonight she will
finish it with the boy and that will be the end of it. And so tomorrow she asks that I remain here all day and all evening. We shall close
the big gates. Lock them with the chain and the padlock as when no
one is here. She will turn the switch which silences the phone.

Should either one arrive, the Captain or the boy, I can go onto my porch and shout to them that she has gone away, and they can see from the gate her car is gone, an accident of some convenience. She explained she wishes to have a very quiet day alone. I shall fix lunch for her, fix an early dinner, and she will take sleeping pills and go to bed early and see if she can sleep the clock around, or longer, to restore herself. She says she will lock the doors to her bedroom to avoid any chance of the boy bothering her when he comes to remove his sailboat. She said he has promised to come by, in the boat of a friend, at dusk tomorrow and take it away from here. She suggests that I might go around to the bay side of the house at nine o'clock to look and see if the boat is gone, and look in at her to see that she is not being bothered by the boy. She has engaged herself in crude behavior I think, and now wishes to escape, and rest, and perhaps find someone more agreeable." She gave him a wicked wink. "It is possible of course that she is no longer young enough to accommodate such a hearty young man without finally becoming exhausted, even such a type as she is."

"So we do not go back to the beach tomorrow?"

"It is a pity. When you leave me tonight, you can help me close the gates. They are heavy." She looked at the clock. "Look! The time! Oh, we will miss the beginning! Hurry!"

As she sat beside him in the new hard-top movie house at the shopping plaza, gasping and squirming at the magic excitements of Bond, digging her nails into his hand and wrist at the moments of deadliest danger, he followed the plot with a portion of his attention, and at last devised a plausible way to handle the situation.

The boy's car was gone when they returned. When they were in the little apartment she chattered about the movie until he said, "Lovely lady, I, Señor Jaime Bond, must ask your assistance in helping me elude the deadly agents of Schmaltz."

"Ah!" she said, eyes sparkling. "I am service you, hah?"

"I think your native tongue might be more accurate, Señorita, even though the English version has a certain unique charm."

"So. How may I be of service?"

"I shall leave now, but I shall only *appear* to leave. In truth I shall drive away, conceal my car in a small wooded place not far from the entrance to the road which leads here. We shall have left the gate ajar. I will steal back on foot, slip inside, close it the rest of the way and fasten the padlock. I will then creep quietly up to these quarters which by then will be dark, and here I shall hide all night, all day tomorrow, and all of tomorrow night until the deadly agents start seeking me elsewhere."

The sparkle of fun faded to dubiousness. "You are serious?"

"Of course. I shall take great care not to risk showing myself to your employer, Señorita. She too is an agent of Schmaltz. A very clever one. And I shall have much needed rest and recuperation. We shall be very sly. We shall speak in whispers. And you shall take comfort in knowing you have served The Cause."

"She would be very angry if . . ." She paused and shrugged. "But she never comes up here. Anyway, the job is nearly at an end." Her frown disappeared, and her eyes shone with mischief again. "You ask a great sacrifice of me, Señor. I shall force myself to endure it and help you outwit the forces of evil." She moved closer. "I shall even share my toothbrush!"

"No one could ask more."

As he went quietly up her outside stairway after hiding the car, walking back and chaining and locking the gates, he felt the small weight of the revolver against the side of his right thigh as he climbed each step. He opened the screen door and locked it behind him with hook and eye. When she did not answer his whisper, he knew she was in the bedroom. He wedged the revolver down, out of sight, between the cushions of the couch.

As he entered the dark bedroom she said, softly, "Could you be Señor Jaime, sir, who outwits everyone?"

"You have made a correct identification."

She giggled. He undressed in darkness. He slid into her bed, took her into his arms, feeling the vital warmth of her under the sheerness of fabric. He was prepared for all her cheery, greedy acceptances, her happy little love games and chortlings. But she was strangely rigid in his arms, fists against his chest. Her body was trembling and he heard a little catch of her breath in her throat.

"What is wrong, *querida?*"

"I—I don't know. I feel very shy. Very strange. Why should I be frightened of you?"

"Just rest in my arms. Let me hold you."

He held her quietly until her body relaxed. But then, at his slightest caress, she would give a little start, a little gasp. Tenderly, gently, carefully he brought her along until all at once she wrapped her slender arms around him with a desperate strength and with her breath fast and hot against his throat, she said, in a voice an octave lower than he had ever heard her speak, and in that special accent of the best blood of the tropic city of his birth, "You are my life. You are my heart. You are my love. You are my soul."

With stinging eyes he knew that he, Raoul Kelly, had at last wooed and won the lovely daughter of Don Estebán, to have, to hold, to cherish for as long as he might live.

Twenty-one

IT WAS ALMOST nine o'clock when Crissy looked again at her watch. She was standing at the bureau in Staniker's ten-by-twelve bedroom. A mirror was fastened to the wall above the bureau. Enough of the silvering was gone from the back of it to make a fragmented image of the room behind her as she fixed more drinks. She moved slightly so she could see Staniker's face. The buff-colored windowshade was pulled down to the sill. Though the window was wide behind it, there was no air to move the shade. The rusty electric fan, for all its whining and whirring, did not seem to stir the air.

Staniker lay on the double bed, in pale blue boxer shorts, his mass and weight deepening the hollow in it. He was propped on two pillows. There was an oily gleam of sweat on his face and body. His big face was slack, his speech slow and thick.

She poured him another bloody mary from the big, widemouth Thermos, holding the ice back with the fingers of her free hand after two cubes had clumped into the glass. She took it to him, feeling between the cool glass and her fingertips the crackly crust of color-less nail polish she had applied to the pads of fingers and thumbs. He took the glass from her, and in lifting it to his lips, spilled some on his broad chest, wiped at it with his other hand.

She went back to the bureau and fixed herself a weak bourbon and soda. She wore navy blue slacks. She had rolled them up to just below her knees. The dark kerchief was in the pocket of the slacks. The waistband of the slacks was damp with sweat. She had taken off the forest green silk shirt with long sleeves and tossed it onto a chair. The roots of her hair were damp. A drop of sweat ran down be-tween her breasts to soak into the brassiere band under her breasts, and another trickled from her armpit down to the side of the slacks. She wondered how long he was going to hold out.

"Absolooly dead," he said in a tone of heavy complaint. "Grayse broad'na worl' could walk ina here bare ass, n'I couldn do a thing forrer, blieve me. Worryn bout it alla time, baby. Alla time."

She came with her drink to sit on the side of the bed. "Crissy'll fix, honey. You drink up and get just a little more stoned and Crissy'll take care."

"Sure, sure, sure. Suppose to make it worse."

"Drinking? It works both ways, friend. It'll stop a motor that's running and start up one that's dead."

"Whadaya know about it anyway?"

She looked mildly at him. "All there is to know. Drink up, buddy boy. When I met the Senator I was a first class hooker. That's *how* I met him. I got talent you need. Drink up."

When he lowered the glass there was an inch left in it. He stared owlishly at her. "Figures. B'God, it figures."

"Did I make the marys too spicy, Captain?"

"Just right, baby. Got a real stick in 'em. Hittin me pree good."

Damn well told there's a stick in them, lover, she thought. Four of the big bombs, the blue and yellow ones. Fer brought them when

I was having trouble sleeping. Never take more than one, he said. After the first one, I wasn't likely to. It scared me. It reached up and yanked me under, like a barracuda hitting a floating gull. That left two, and I flushed them down, just in case.

"Gedda work, kid," he mumbled. "Get busy."

She lifted the glass out of his slack hand and went back to the bureau. She had made a small sample first, taken a cautious sip. If there was a taste to the drug, the tomato juice, salt, pepper, lime juice, tabasco, worcestershire and vodka overwhelmed it.

"Better have a fresh one handy," she said. "This is a celebration, Garry. Right?"

"Funny about at guy knowing about the money . . ." His voice trailed off. She ran back to the bed. His eyes were closed. She shook him.

"Hey! Garry. What guy?"

"Uh. Brother." His eyes wavered, trying to focus.

"What brother, dammit?"

"Boy—Boys—Boylston. Nice fella." His eyes closed and his jaw sagged. She shook him. She plucked a fold of belly flesh and twisted it. She thumbed his eyelid back. She straightened and took a long breath and let it out.

She took both glasses into the bathroom and rinsed them out. She took them back to the bedroom and packed the glasses, Thermos, the bottle of soda and bottle of bourbon back into the dark overnight bag she had brought. She took it into the dark living room and put it down by the front door. She remembered how she had worried about him not seeing her car out there. But when he had asked about it, and she had said with a practiced casualness, "I can't get the damned thing into reverse gear, so I had to leave it down the street," he had accepted it without question.

She found the living room light switch beside the door, clicked the lights on and off once, quickly. She looked out the window and saw Olly emerge from the shrubbery and come quickly to the front door. It stuck. She yanked it open and he brushed past her.

"Is he . . ."

"Out cold. Yes. You don't have to whisper, honey."

"What took so long?"

"He's a big man. He kept hanging on and hanging on. Come on."

Following her down the short hallway he whispered, "Why have you got your shirt off?"

"Because it's hot as the hinges of hell, friend."

Oliver came to an abrupt stop just inside the bedroom doorway and stared at the big man asleep on the bed. He licked his lips. His adam's apple slid up and down his throat as he swallowed.

She went to the bed and undid the snaps at the waist band of the underwear shorts.

"Why are you doing that?"

"Will you *stop* whispering? Please! I'm doing it because it would look damned funny if I didn't. Will you *please* help me instead of standing there like a statue!"

He helped her work the shorts off the sleeping man and pull them down and off his limp feet.

"Take the head," she said. "Come on. We've got to get him over to the edge of the bed first. Once more. Fine. No, you idiot! Not by the wrists. We don't want to drag him. Sit him up and get your arms under his arms and lace your fingers across his chest. There!"

She turned around and backed and lifted his legs and locked a big ankle into each of her armpits, and held tightly to her left wrist with her right hand. "Now!" she said. She heard the boy's gasp of effort as the big body came free of the bed and hung between them in the air. The weight of him pulled her back a half step and as she bent forward to compensate for the stress, she felt the sweat bursting and trickling all over her face and body. "Come on," she said in a voice grating with effort, and walked under the burden, taking small steps. The bathroom was directly across the short hallway from the bedroom, and the tub was opposite the door, against the wall, under a window.

It was narrow and deep, standing on claw feet clutching white balls. The porcelain was chipped down to the metal at many places along the curve of the rim. Rust lines ran from the two faucets down to the drain. The faucets were on the ends of pieces of galvanized pipe which came up through the floor boards and through the yellow and white linoleum, high enough for the elongated nozzles, which retained a few flakes of the original chrome, to extend over the rim of the tub. A white rubber stopper was tied by a piece of string to the cold water pipe. She had left the light on, and the buff shade pulled down. She walked to the faucet end, turning slowly, bent under the weight, as he walked his end of the sleeper to the sloped end of the tub.

He pulled her backward and she said through clenched teeth, "What are you *doing?*"

"Got to get—around the end—of the tub."

There was a great tug as he let go, as he let Staniker slide down the slope of the head end of the tub. It yanked her back and the backs of her thighs hit the rim and as she released his feet, she toppled backward, twisted, braced herself by getting her right hand against the opposite rim. She was poised there, unable to push herself back to her feet. Oliver stepped quickly around, caught her left wrist, pulled her back to her feet, saying, "I should have said I was letting go . . . ."

"Stop *flapping!* Let's get it *done!*"

He lay in the tub, canted toward his left, head leaning against the far rim. His right leg was hooked over the outside rim. She took hold of the heel and lifted it and dropped it in. It thudded, bonging the tub metal. He slid down a few more inches, feet resting against the faucet end, knees bent and spread, big brown hands laying slack against the contrasting whiteness of his inner thighs.

They were both breathing noisily from the exertion. She wiped her forehead with her forearm. Looking down at Staniker she said, "Now it's up to you, Olly. Take over, dear." There was no answer. She turned her head sharply. Oliver was standing looking fixedly at Staniker. He was breathing through his mouth, and his under lip sagged away from his teeth.

"Oliver!"

He started, looked at her with a puzzled expression. "He looks so—so—"

"Harmless? Dumb? Helpless? Take my word. He isn't. Go ahead. Get started. Put the stopper in. Turn the water on."

Moving slowly and clumsily, he did as she told him. The faucets coughed rusty water, then cleared into two solid streams drumming against the metal tub.

She touched the boy's arm. "I'll wait in the living room. As soon as there's enough water, turn it off and do it and we can go."

She went in and sat on the couch in the dark room. She had hoped to be able to send the boy to do it. But he had begun to come apart. When he came out, she would go in and make certain he had done it completely. But it had to be the boy, because if something went wrong, it would have to be her word against the boy's. Nobody would be able to prove she'd even been there. And if he killed, it would give him a guilt that would break him completely if they were picked up. She sat wishing the boy had had just a little more iron, so she could have sent him, so she didn't have to wait around, holding his hand. Besides, he'd sworn to do it. Fair is fair. She heard the faint thunder stop as he turned the water off. Time passed. He did not come out.

She stood up and walked swiftly to the bathroom. He was sitting on the toilet lid, his face in his hands. On the floor she saw the new single edge Gem blade and the waxy paper in which it had been wrapped, and the cardboard strip which had protected the sharp edge. She looked at Staniker. His chest rose and fell. The water was tinged slightly with rust, and that was all.

She knocked the boy's hands away from his face, stooped and looked into his face. "You promised!" she said in a harsh whisper.

He looked at her—a big child on the verge of tears. "I tried. I tried and tried. I—I just can't. Oh God, Crissy, I can't."

She bent and picked the blade up, picked up the wrappings and, as he stood up, she put the wrappings into his trouser pocket.

The boy said, "What are you . . ."

"Shut up. Just stay out of my way, you damn baby."

She bent over the tub and picked his right hand up and, holding the blade by the reinforced edge, pressed his thumb against the oily side of the blade, and then pressed his fingertips against the reverse side, the tips of the index and middle fingers. Then she grasped his thick palm in her left hand and held his hand under the water, the underside of the wrist downward. Holding it, she reached under it with her right hand, put the blade edge against the underside of the wrist, and then, pushing down with her left hand, pulling upward with her right, she pulled the blade deeply through, through the resistances of flesh, gristle, tendon. Darkness pumped into the water, threading, lightening to pink at its furthest curling. Quickly, grunting with the effort, she cut through the other wrist as deeply and finally, dropped the blade between his thighs. It ticked audibly as it touched the bottom of the tub.

She spun away from the tub, unsteady, her ears humming, feeling chilled by the pre-fainting feeling blood gave her. Oliver stood there, gray and gagging. She ran at him, shoving at him with her wet hands to get him into the hall, to get him moving, cursing him in all the obscene words she knew. When she slapped him, he came out of it, and went off to get the car.

In the bedroom, with a despairing haste, she put the silk shirt on over her wet body, tied her hair into the kerchief, snatched up the small suitcase she had brought. She heard herself making a small whining sound with each breath. She made herself stop. She paused for a moment in the bathroom doorway, held her breath and heard Staniker's deep, slow breathing.

She went through the dark living room and opened the front door. As she did so she heard Oliver's car stop on the other side of the brush just short of the mouth of the driveway. The idling engine ran raggedly. She took a deep breath and made herself think of how she had arrived and how she was leaving, to be certain she had left nothing behind. Nothing, not even a fingerprint. With the coated fingertips she pulled the door shut and tried it. It was unlocked. She had not released the catch on the bolt inside, and it seemed pointless now to make it appear that the cottage had been locked. They would have enough to think about, the people who investigated it, and this would be just another significant clumsiness.

She hurried out, peered up and down the empty street, and scuttled into the dark car. He stalled it, and the starter motor ground for endless seconds before it caught again. After they had reached a street where there was more traffic, she saw one of the oncoming cars blinking its headlights off and on.

"Lights! Lights! God damn it, wake up!" she said.

He turned his headlights on. A few minutes later he missed a turn, and when he went around a block to get back on their route, he went through a stop sign. She made him pull over and get out and go around the car as she slid behind the wheel.

The night was misty. She drove within the speed limits, obeying all traffic signals.

"It isn't like I thought," Oliver said in a husky voice.

"What did you expect? Jokes? Violins? We agreed we had to do it. You said you'd do anything for me."

"I'm sorry. I couldn't. I just couldn't. Crissy—it was wrong."

"So preach me a sermon."

"If—we made a phone call, maybe they could get there in time."

"In time for what? He's *gone*, baby. Long gone. I saw a girl once with a hemorrhage they couldn't stop. One of those big rosy Irish types. She got knocked up and a girlfriend tried to do the job with a piece of tubing and a piece of wire. She dwindled way down, all gray and shrunk up, and she looked fifty years old when she died."

"You're different," Oliver said wonderingly. "You're not the same at all."

She looked ahead through the mist, slowing for the last turn. "I'm Crissy," she said. "Your dear Crissy. Look what your dear Crissy did, all for the sake of love. I'm the same. The world is the same world. You make it or you don't make it, honey. Nobody picks you up and brushes you off and gives you another run at it. You do what you have to do before somebody does it to *you*."

"But it wasn't like I thought," he said.

"When it's for real, it never is, Olly."

She saw the obscure shell road and made her turn. It was a mile and a half south of the turnoff to her house. She drove slowly until the headlights shone on the palm bole she'd had Oliver place across the road when they had driven out, hoping it would discourage any lovers or fishermen who sometimes used this road to drive down to the shoreline.

He got out and lifted the end of the log and walked it out of the way and got back into the car.

"Remember what comes next?" she asked.

"I sail you back and leave you off at your place and bring the boat back here and drive home. Tomorrow I hitch a ride over and walk in and sail the boat up to Dinner Key."

She put the car in gear and drove ahead slowly. "And if they question you, you don't know anything about anything."

"Oh God, Crissy! I—I can't even stop thinking of how—heavy he was . . . ."

"You'll be fine," she said. "Believe me, darling, you won't worry about it at all. Everything will come up roses."

As she neared the end of the road she looked to see if the headlights picked up any gleam of metal from parked cars, but the area was empty. They had found the place while sailing. She slowed and parked near the foundations where an old frame house had burned down years ago. She parked on a slight down slope. Headlights shone on his sailboat tied to the small remaining section of an old rotten dock. She turned the lights off and got out. The wind from the west was still blowing gently, moving the mist that was coming off the water.

They went down to the sailboat. She said. "Oh, here's the car keys. Wouldn't that be great, to go off with them."

He put them in his pocket. He leaned and put the case aboard. He said, "I—I'm sorry I couldn't do . . ."

"It's over, dear. It's done. That's all that matters. Darling, before we run the sail up, would you look at the main sheet there near the transom on the port. There seems to be a turn of the jib sheet around it and it could get jammed in that roller thing. The flashlight is in that little . . ."

"I know." He stepped aboard. She followed him. He got the flashlight and knelt, peering at the lines.

"It looks all right to——"

At that instant she stabbed the muzzle of the single-shot 22 rifle into the socket of his right ear, pulling the trigger as she did so. It made a quick, hard snapping sound. He dropped and the light went out and he began a savage thrashing down there in the bottom of the boat. She backed quickly and sat on the dock planks and pulled her feet out of the way. Elbows and knees and heavy bones thudded against the bottom of the sailboat. He made the effortful grunts of combat. The boat rocked, swaying the tall naked mast back and forth. There was a quivering drumming sound of unseen arm or leg against some solid part of the boat, a muscular tremor faster than she would have believed possible. Then there was silence. The small rocking stopped, the mast motionless. The breeze from the west held the hull a few inches away from the dock, affixed by bow and stern lines. She slid aboard cautiously. He was face down, head toward the stern. She wrapped his right hand around the action of the rifle, pressing the fingers against the metal. She wrapped his left hand around the middle of the barrel, thumb toward the butt. Then she placed the weapon down, butt toward the stern, close beside him, pushed his thumb through the trigger guard, pressed it against the trigger.

She took the little packet of scratch paper out of the hip pocket of her slacks. It was slightly damp. The last draft of the note. Floor plan of number ten. She worked his wallet out of his hip pocket, put the packet in with the few dollar bills he had, and replaced the wallet. She became aware of acrid odors of urine and excrement. She freed the bow line first, as Oliver had taught her to do under such circumstances of wind and mooring. As the bow swung slowly out, she ran the mainsail up and belayed the halyard around the cleat in the way Oliver had taught her. She freed the stern line. The boom swung to starboard, and she let off on the main sheet, and, other hand on the tiller, her feet braced near his back, she sat and sailed northward up the shoreline, staying well enough out for the mist to hide her from anyone on the shore, yet not so far out she would fail to see the corona of the outside floods she had left on against the

THE LAST ONE LEFT

mist. She came upon that haloed light sooner than she had expected. The only sound was a gurgle of water around the transom and rudder, a faint rattle of halyards against the stick.

She went by the lights and, staying well out, brought it around, close hauling it, pointing it close to the wind, peering into the mist, rehearsing the things which had to be done quickly. When the dock appeared she found she was too far out. When she turned toward it, she turned right into the eye of the breeze. The sail flapped. She thought, with a touch of panic, she would not have the momentum to reach it. She scrabbled, caught the boat hook, leaned and caught the edge of a dock piling. As she pulled the stern in, the breeze caught the close-hauled mainsail, heeling the boat and almost breaking her hold. But then she was able to grasp a dock line in her right hand. She put the case up on the dock. She found the loop and slipped it over the tiller. She let out on the main sheet until the boom was angled far enough out to port. She wedged the sheet into the safety cleat, stood quickly and scrambled onto the dock, banging her knee painfully against the edge of it. She rolled and looked out and saw the Skatter moving out into the mist. The rattle and gurgle died. The mainsail was a tall blur and then it was gone. It would go aground, she was certain, on the western shoreline of Eliott Key.

She snatched the case up and moved swiftly, limping slightly, into the shadows of the shrubbery near the foot of the stone stairway. She waited and listened and watched, and then moved quickly from deep shadow to deep shadow, moving behind the flood lighting. Dressed in the dark clothes, she walked quickly along the terrace to the sliding doors to her bedroom. She had left the draperies a foot apart. She looked into her bedroom. It gave her a strange feeling to see, in the glow of the night light, the woman shape under the light blanket, blonde hair snuggled into the whiteness of the pillow. She put the case down, lifted the corner of the mat outside her door, took the thin spatula, slid it through the crack and lifted the catch free. She put the kitchen implement in the waistband of her slacks, rolled the door open, picked up the case and edged through, into the bedroom coolness, into the place of all her scents and lotions and fabrics. She yanked the draperies shut, reached through and locked the sliding doors again. Took three slow steps and fell to her knees, and then rolled slowly onto her side. She pulled her knees high, tucked her head down, held her clenched fists between her breasts. After each long slow exhalation she felt a clenching and tremoring of her belly muscles, somewhat like the residual quiverings after orgasm. She felt the texture of the rug against her cheek and temple. She smelled her own sourness, a sharp pungency of nervous sweat.

At last she got up very slowly. It took a great effort. She took care of the case first, rinsing the glasses again, drying them on one of her soft towels before putting them back into the rack on the bar. She rinsed the Thermos. One sliver of ice was left. She reached in through the wide mouth and dried the inside carefully and put it back in the compartment under the bar. She replaced the bourbon bottle and soda bottle and bottle opener in their customary places. She put the overnight case in the luggage locker in her dressing room.

After her long, hot shower, and after she had toweled her hair to dryness, used her array of sprays, astringents, lotions which were so ordinary and comforting a part of her bedtime routine, she put on a short nightgown and turned her bed down. She took the pillow she had used for the torso, the rolled bath towels she had used for the legs, the wig and wad of toweling she had used for the head, and put everything away carefully. She had had to go out onto the terrace a half dozen times and come back in and pat and plump and adjust until the shapes of round hip, dip of waist, shoulder, sprawl of legs had looked real to her. She rolled up the damp soiled clothing she had worn. She spread the slacks on the floor, put the shirt, bra, pants, socks and boat shoes on them, and rolled it all into a tight, stubby cylinder and tied it with twine, then remembered the kerchief and got it and stuffed it into one end of the cylinder. They were all old, all ready for discard. She put the bundle in the back of her closet and washed her hands.

She unlocked the inner door, drifted silently through the dark house and put the spatula back into the kitchen drawer and went back to her bedroom, leaving the inner door unlocked. The inter-com master was fastened to the wall just inside the door to the dress-ing room. She depressed the button under the designation Apt, pressed the speak bar and said in a drowsy voice, "Francisca? Fran-cisca?"

She released the bar and waited, and just as she was about to try again, the girl said, "Yes? Yes? Yes?"

Crissy frowned. There was no teaching her not to put her mouth so close to it and speak so loudly.

"Sorry to wake you up, dear. What time is it, anyway?"

"From—uh twelve in the night is maybe ten minutes later."

"Is that all? I had to get up and then I couldn't go back to sleep. I took a hot shower and that didn't help a bit. If I take another one of those pills, I'll feel terrible tomorrow. Would it be too much trouble to bring me some hot cocoa, and maybe some crackers?"

"Oh, no! No troubling!"

"Just put a robe on, dear."

"Soon, soon," the girl said in her high, happy voice.

Crissy opened the draperies to the same gap as before, opened the inner door a few inches, turned off all but the night light and the bedside lamp, then rolled and turned and tossed until the bed lost its too-fresh look.

Francisca knocked and came in with the cocoa and crackers on a small lacquered tray. She wore a quilted robe in a lurid shade of bright lime yellow. Crissy hitched herself up, put another pillow behind her back and reached for the tray.

"Thank you, dear. This is pretty silly."

"No is," Francisca said firmly.

"Did he come by and collect his sailboat? I tried to see but it's too misty to see the boat basin."

"Is gone."

"Did he give you any trouble?"

"Oh, no! Never see him."

"You don't have to wait for the tray, dear. Go on back to bed. I think this will do the trick." She put her fist in front of a wide yawn. The girl said goodnight and went out and closed the door quietly.

Just as she was lifting the cup to take the last few sips, Crissy began a violent and uncontrollable trembling. Cocoa spilled on the front of her nightgown and on the top sheet. She put the tray aside quickly, and when it kept on and on, she went across to the bar and poured a half tumbler of dark rum. She had to hold it in both hands. Her teeth chattered against the thick rim. Once it was down she was almost certain she would lose it. But then her stomach accepted it. She turned off the light and curled up in her bed in the same position as when she had lain on the floor.

The trembling stopped like something slowly running down. While she was thinking about getting up and taking a pill, she fell off the edge into sleep.

Twenty-two

AS DUSK BECAME NIGHT, Mrs. Mooney had begun to fight a familiar battle with her conscience and with her desire.

After she had fed the three old dogs, she turned the lights out in the house. She plodded from room to room, muttering to herself. From time to time she would climb the stairs and go into her bedroom and stand at the window overlooking the row of rental cottages and see through the leaves those fragments of yellowish glow from a light in Number 10, a light in that Mr. Stanley's bedroom shining through the pale worn shade.

The logic of it was beyond question. With such dense shrubbery, the cottages had a lot of privacy. And on a night so hot, there could be but one reason for pulling the shades down.

She had fought it and won the other night. But tonight it was stronger. Like a terrible gnawing. It was so unfair that it should keep going on and on into these years when she thought it would be over, when she would have rest and peace.

She roamed the dark house, muttering her complaints, and explaining how terrible a thing it was, telling it all to Mr. Mooney, years in his grave now, reminding him that it had begun way back even when he was still alive, and how he had caught her at it once and given her the beating she deserved, told her they could send her off to jail, told her she was an evil woman, and even after she had promised she would never do it again, he had been nasty-polite to her for weeks.

She turned the television set on and sat to watch it, then found herself roaming back and forth across the living room in the pallid flickering light of the horses running, the men shooting and shouting.

The next time she went upstairs she avoided looking out the window and instead went to her big desk in the corner and turned on the desk light and opened the big scrapbook atop the litter of old invoices and receipts.

The three old dogs had already gotten into her bed for the night, and they lifted their heads to look at her, their eyes glowing in the reflected lamp light. She turned the pages, and looked for a long time at the clippings about her marriage to Michael Mooney on the Fourth of July in the center ring of the Coldwell Brothers Circus in Topeka, Kansas. Mr. Mooney had one of the best small-circus dog acts in the business, and she had worked the act with him, had done clown on the side, and had sewed a thousand costumes for the dogs during all the circus years.

All gone now but the three old dogs, all of them single-trick puppies, all eagerness, in the last months before it all came to an end. All gone but Jiggs and Tarzan and Maggie, fat and going blind.

Maybe, she thought, Mr. Stanley had been taken sick and it would be an act of Christian charity to go check on him . . . .

And remembered that she had told herself exactly that same thing back in April when that same Mr. Stanley had taken a cottage for just one night. When their car had local plates and they checked in alone, for an overnight, you knew what the rascals had on their minds.

If I hadn't slipped that last time, she thought, it wouldn't be gnawing so terrible now. Maybe it wouldn't count as a separate sin, but as a part of the sin of the last time.

She closed the scrapbook, reached and turned the desk light off, hit the closed book with her fist. The mind kept making up the shiny, easy excuses to make everything seem all right, and afterward you knew the reasons were dirty, but by then it was done and you were eased and you could say never, never, never again; you could say it was over forever.

She wondered if that Mr. Stanley had noticed how it had unsettled her to have him show up again. Usually you never saw them again. Her heart had bumped and her hands had been shaky. He was one of the ones who had to share the blame of it, leaving the lights on for it instead of liking darkness for it like decent folk.

As she went slowly down the stairs, sliding her hand on the bannister railing, she wondered if it would be the same one, the tall blonde woman with the beautiful slender tan body, but a very strong woman for all the slenderness, a match and more for the hammering brutishness of him.

Held out this long, you have, she thought. So heat yourself up a mug of warm milk and drink it down and go to your bed like a decent-minded widowed dwarf lady, with three old dogs depending on her. It's late, Little Maureen. Somewhere around ten or later even. Drink the milk and kneel by the bed and pray to God to take away the gnawing and burning because you are too old now for evil.

"Never again!" she said aloud. She bit the inside of her mouth, tasted blood, groaned, trotted into the dark kitchen and folded the little aluminum stepladder she used to reach the dish cupboards. In her cotton housecoat, carrying the ladder, she slipped out into the dark, hot night and threaded her way in her hump-backed stealthy crouch along familiar paths that led behind the cottages. Moving swiftly and breathing shallowly, she set her ladder up under the lighted window and climbed it and stood upon the top of it, hands against the siding for support. She put her eye to the narrow opening between the shade and the framing of the window screen and looked into the room and into the tumbled emptiness of the sagging bed. Disappointment was as sharp as toothache. She saw a pattern of light on the floor which indicated the bathroom light was on across the hallway.

With an anxious agility she climbed down, folded the ladder, and trotted around the rear of the cottage and, as she set it up under the lighted bathroom window, she had a vivid, sweet, dizzying memory of that pair two years ago and more, ah, how they'd sloshed and strained in the suds, and all the while the girl, plump as a little dumpling, squealing and giggling, had teased the poor rascal shamelessly, giving him such little samples he was near out of his mind with the need of it, a torture Mr. Mooney would not have permitted for an instant.

She climbed up the ladder and put her eye to the opening and stood tiptoe tall so as to look down into the tub. She stopped breathing for two long seconds, then turned and stepped off the top of the little ladder into space. The tilt triggered the old reflexes and skills of the clown years, and she jacked her knees up, tucked her head down, rolled her right shoulder under, and relaxed her body completely at the instant before impact. She rolled over and back up onto her feet, gave a little hop to regain balance, and then leaned against the side of the cottage for a moment, feeling dizzy. Poor old Little Maureen, she thought. One little rollover makes her all shaky inside.

She folded the ladder and raced back to her house along the overgrown paths, the leaves brushing at her. The number to call was in the front of the phone book. "Miz Mooney talking," she said in a voice like a contralto kazoo. "I got one needs help bad and needs it quick, in my number ten cottage. Maybe he's breathing, maybe not, anyway in a tub so blood dark I can't see if it was wrists he cut. What? Sonny boy, there's no way in hell you can find it unless you stop talking and let me tell you where my place is. So kindly fermay the boosh and get your pencil out . . . ."

At eight o'clock the following morning a brisk young man named Lobwohl sat at a steel and linoleum desk with his back to a big tinted window. He was reading the preliminary reports on the Mooney Cottages business and making notes on a yellow legal pad, and pausing from time to time to sip coffee from a large, waxed cardboard cup.

Two men, heavier and older than Lobwohl, came sauntering in. As one of them sat down, Lobwohl said, "It starts like one of those weeks. Did you get hold of Harv?"

"He should be started on it by now. I told him what you wanted. A complete job on the second time around, right? Every latent, every grain of dust, every thread, every hair. He said to tell you there's one thing that makes it easier than usual."

"Nothing ever makes anything any easier."

"It was empty for two months before that midget rented it to him, and sitting empty and hot as a bakery, so Harv says the oils in all the old prints are dried out, and the way they take the powder, he can tell old from new right off. Anyway, his team should be working there now. He requisitioned one of the big lab trucks with everything on it."

Lobwohl, nodding approval, continued his note taking. The other man, standing at the window, said, "I'm telling you. That damn Shaeffer. One forty-seven season average, and last night he rolls a six hundred series. Two twenty-eight the last game!"

"Shaeffer in Safe and Loft?" Lobwohl asked as he made a note.

"So they edge us out by five pins," the man said with disgust.

"Okay, Bert, Barney, let's get to it," Lobwohl said. The man turned from the window and sat beside his partner, facing Lobwohl. "We have the make on him as Staniker. So his name was on the check in the bureau drawer and on his discharge from the hospital in Nassau. And the prints match, and he looks like Staniker's daddy. So we are very clever people. But he is G. Stanley from Tampa as long as we can keep the lid on it."

"Why should we?" Barney asked.

Bert said, "He likes the bright light they shine on you. He makes those faces. Any minute, CBS signs him."

"We'll move faster and better if it's just another four lines on page forty, at least for now. I checked upstairs. If we start making the big effort, somebody wonders why. So it's just us. Here's what we've got from medical. Ten o'clock last night, plus or minus an hour. Pretty good load of barbiturates, but hard to tell how much exactly with all the blood gone out of it. But here is the clincher. No false tries on the wrists. One cut each, and as deep as you'll ever see. The point is this. The cuts went so deep they destroyed the motor ability of the fingers. So he could cut one that way, but not both, unless he held the blade in his teeth, and that's not very damn possible. Here's what I go for. Somebody half cute. Wanted him dead. Didn't figure the wrist business. Forgot to fix the catch so the door would lock itself. Let's hope he was so sure it would go over he didn't worry about prints. It's about time we were due for one where prints would do us some good. How long has it been now?"

"Three years anyway," Barney said.

"A hundred and fifty dollars in the same bureau drawer. We've got two directions to go for motive."

"What's with the G. Stanley bit?" Bert asked.

"That leads into one of the motives. The dwarf-lady said he was a one-night customer back in April. At that time he and his wife were living at that marina. The word is that he was stud. This time he signed for two weeks. The layout is fine for a sneak job, if you don't mind a little squalor. The husband could have showed up instead of the lady and figured it that it would seem reasonable Staniker would be depressed by losing that yacht and those people and his wife and being the only one to get out of it alive."

"And," said Bert, "if you go the other way, it's somebody doing it *because* he lost the boat."

"You're a better cop than a bowler," Lobwohl said. "I remember a sob story about a girl on that boat. Her boyfriend and her brother came flying over from Texas to be in Nassau while the search was still going on. See if you can get me that clip without anybody smelling anything. Then we see if either or both are in the area, or maybe left the area this morning. I can have that checked out other ways once you get me that article. Meanwhile, you two dig into Staniker's love life. He got to town Friday. He took that place Friday. I want to know exactly who he was banging before he went cruising. Move fast on it. And quietly." He tapped one of his phones with his pencil. "And come back to me on this outside line, not through the radio net. Start at that marina and work out from there. Neighborhood. Bars. I don't have to tell you your business."

"We'll call in just before noon anyway to see if Harv has anything juicy."

Bert Kindler and Barney Scheff arrived at the Harkinson place a few minutes past eleven on Monday morning, drove through the open gate and got out of the department sedan slowly.

A maid in a blue and white uniform, and a man in dark pants and a blue shirt, suit coat over his arm, were coming down the open staircase from an apartment over the garages. Both were apparently Cuban. The maid hurried toward them with smiling greeting.

"No, not Mrs. Harkinson," Scheff said after they had identified themselves. "We want to ask you some questions, honey. What's your name?"

"Why question? Why?" the girl demanded.

"Your name," Kindler said.

The girl looked very frightened. She backed away slowly. "Why?" she asked again.

"Honey," Scheff said, "maybe you haven't got papers, huh? Maybe we just put you in the car and take you down and . . ."

"No!" she said. "No! Oh please!"

"'Cisca!" the man said sharply in Spanish. "Go back up to the apartment and wait. They will not take you anywhere!"

As she went running up the stairs they stared blandly and curiously at the man. "*Comprendemos un poquito, hombre*," Kindler said.

"My English is adequate. Her name is Miss Francisca Torcedo. What do you wish to know?"

"What's your name?"

"Raoul Kelly."

"You work for the Harkinson woman too?"

"No."

"Kelly, what makes you think you can stop us from taking that little broad in for questioning if we want to? Man, I get a reaction like that from anybody, my ears grow points," Scheff said.

"I think I can stop you if you will listen to why it would be a bad idea. If you won't listen, I can't. You look as if you've both been in your line of work long enough to want to listen."

"Talk a little," said Kindler.

"First, her papers, and mine, are in perfect order. She does not have much English. She is of a family which was very wealthy and important in Havana. When the Castro militia came into the city, her father was shot and killed in the confusion. She went into the street and wounded a militiaman. They took her to a military compound and kept her there. She was mistreated. There was serious emotional damage. Her brother and I were in the Bay of Pigs invasion. He was killed. I was captured and exchanged later. He told me to look after her. I am going to marry her. She is getting better, little by little, day by day. Taking her in for questioning might push her way, way back, out of anybody's reach, and she might not come out of it. I am close enough to her to be able to answer any question you might want to ask her. If you try to bother her, I will try to stop you, believe me."

Both officers looked sleepy. "Kelly means it," Scheff said.

"What we could do," Kindler said, "we could stand in the shade." They walked to the nearby shade. Kindler said, "If you are like we call unresponsive, then we take her in where we got somebody can speaka the spic."

"And you take me too, I suppose. Horizontal, if I make a fuss. Cubans are tricky. You got to watch them."

"He's real sensitive, Bert," Scheff said.

"You know what I think about Cubans?" Kindler said. "I wish there wasn't any other kind of civilian in Dade County *except* Cubans. You know what that would do statistically, man? It would cut crime almost in half. I could spend more time with the wife and kids. So unpucker yourself, bud."

Raoul grinned ruefully. "So all right. My mistake. What do you want to know?"

Scheff gestured toward the main house. "Word has it here and there the boss lady is prime gash, and it was old Fer Fontaine set her up here before he died. Bert and me have a thing about bothering anybody who has real good friends in politics. Anybody we might know subbing for the Senator?"

"No."

"So then if we happen to be trying to locate somebody by the name of Staniker, and if we leaned on her some, like saying we know Staniker kept on using her as a shack job after she sold the boat he operated for her, she wouldn't phone anybody in the court house or in Tallahassee."

"It's not very likely."

"Would she say it wasn't like that with Staniker?" Kindler asked.

"I don't know. She might deny it. She might admit it."

"Then Staniker wasn't just making a brag to his marina pals?" Scheff asked.

"No. But whether she admits it or denies it, I imagine she'd tell you the same thing she told Francisca, that she and Staniker had a quarrel before he took the job aboard the Muñeca, and she told him to stay away from her. And she'd tell you that since Staniker came back from the Bahamas last Friday he's been bothering her by calling her up and asking to see her."

"So," Scheff said idly, "last night she went to see him to tell him to stop bugging her?"

Raoul explained that Crissy Harkinson hadn't been off her property since Saturday afternoon, and explained about the car and the locked gate.

"But she didn't know you were right here all the time with your girl, Kelly?"

"No. I've never stayed here before. But it seemed like a good idea to talk Francisca into it. That locked gate wouldn't keep out anybody who wanted to get in. Staniker used to thump Crissy Harkinson around sometimes. I thought he might get loaded and come around and Francisca might try to keep him from bothering Mrs. Harkinson. And there was another unknown factor too, a kid Mrs. Harkinson just broke up with because he was acting strange. The locked gate was to keep both of them out."

Scheff and Kindler both began to speak at once, then Scheff let Kindler take it. He said, "Was the kid getting any?"

"I *know* she would deny that. But he was. She hired him to teach her how to sail, and it went on from there."

"Name?"

"Oliver something. Nineteen, twenty. A big, husky kid. Kept his sailboat in her boat basin. Flying Dutchman. I looked it over once when Mrs. Harkinson was out. You could probably trace him through the name of his boat. The Skatter, with a k."

Raoul saw the two men glance at each other with identical expressions of bland satisfaction. "And," said Scheff, "I guess the reason the kid began acting weird and getting on her nerves was because he knew she used to be Staniker's piece, and he knew Staniker was back and he knew Staniker was bothering her."

"She told Francisca the kid knew Staniker was bothering her."

"So she gave Oliver the old heave? Like take your sailboat and go, Sonny."

"He came and got the boat in the early evening last night. She'd taken a pill and gone to bed early. She asked Francisca to take a look later on and be sure the boat was gone and the kid wasn't hanging around the area or bothering Mrs. Harkinson. I went with Francisca when she took a look."

"What time was that?"

"A little after nine last night. Then Francisca went and looked into the bedroom and Mrs. Harkinson was there asleep."

"Good-looking woman?" Kindler asked.

"I've seen her at a distance. Well built. I would guess about thirty, but Francisca is certain she is close to forty."

"And fooling around with young kids," Scheff said. "I got a boy nineteen. My old lady is thirty-eight. Look, why is your girl working for a bum like the Harkinson woman?"

"Until day after tomorrow."

"How long has she been working for her?"

"A year. A little more than a year."

"What's the Harkinson woman's background?"

"I wouldn't know. Francisca wouldn't know either."

"Where's she from?"

"She said something to Francisca once about living in Atlanta."

"She's in the house now?" Kindler asked. Raoul nodded.

"Look her over?" Scheff asked Kindler.

"She'll keep, Barney. The kid might not."

"Can I ask a question?" Raoul said.

"Sure, Kelly."

"Why are you looking for Staniker?"

"Routine. Just routine," Kindler said.

As they walked toward the car, Francisca came timidly out to the railing of the shallow porch and looked down. They all looked up at her. Her eyes were huge and her mouth was sucked into a small bloodless button.

Kindler called up, in wretched but understandable Spanish, "Señorita, you are a very beautiful lady. We do not take you away. This man of yours is a good man."

She looked startled and then beamed down upon them happily. "Kaylee is beauty-ful fella!" she cried.

Raoul felt heat in his cheeks. Both officers laughed and 'Cisca waved busily to them as they drove off. "Sotch nice!" she said to Kelly.

Ten minutes north of the Harkinson turnoff, Scheff and Kindler stopped at a shopping center and phoned Lobwohl's outside-line number.

"This is Bert," Kindler said. "Did Harv get . . ."

"Better come on in," Lobwohl said. "A flippy kid did it and then shot himself. Had a note on him saying he was afraid he was going to do some crazy thing. Had a map and a floor plan of number ten. Even had the wrappings off the blade in his pocket. Coast Guard spotted him dead in a sailboat grounded off Eliott Key."

"Named Oliver maybe?" Kindler said.

After a long silence Lobwohl said wearily, "All right. All right. Come on in and show off, you smart-ass."

"Is it all going to break now? The ID on Staniker?"

"Yes. Why?"

"When it breaks wide open and the news people get a look at the motive, we're going to get swarmed worse than anything since the Mossler thing. Look, the broad that Staniker and the kid got to is a Mrs. Cristen Harkinson, late thirties, blonde, a swinger. The late Senator Ferris Fontaine had her stashed in a very lush bay house down here a little southeast of Goulds, all very private. He probably built it for her and deeded it to her. And she had a cruiser . . ."

"And up to the time she sold it, Staniker worked for her, running the boat. I've been reading the clippings, Bert."

"She broke off with Staniker. He gets the job running the Kayd boat. She lines up the kid to give her sailing lessons. So she takes one kind of lessons and gives another kind. Staniker comes back from the islands. He wants to start making it again with Harkinson. This bugs the kid. He gets so hairy about it she tosses him out too. What I'd guess, the kid thinks he gets cut loose because she's going to pick up with Staniker again. A green kid would be way out of his league with a live one like that. So how did the kid know where Staniker was? You see what kind of can of worms that opens up?"

"They'd both become nuisances. She could aim one at the other and either way it came out, Bert, she'd be rid of both of them. Two rejected suitors taking it out on each other. But she would have to be pretty cold to set them up like that, wouldn't she?"

"She was home in bed, and I think that will check out. And I think that even if she conned the kid into killing Staniker, she'll deny it up down and sideways, and nothing we can do. I am just saying that the hints in the papers are going to stop just short of actionable, and it is going to be dirty laundry week, and a mob scene at her house, guys in trees with telephoto lenses, the whole treatment."

"So?"

"Protective custody? She'll have to make a statement anyway. She's the link between Staniker and the kid. We've got to go through the routine of the murder one indictment anyway and . . ."

"I try to keep from telling you your end of the business, Bert."

"Sorry about that."

"So you want to bring her in. And you happily married and all that. Or maybe you collect autographs."

"Well, I like to see Barney have a little fun on the job too, but I was thinking that if we have her before she knows who did what to who, and make it a long slow ride, and fake her out a little, there might be something we could make stick later on, because there will be all kinds of pressure we should do something about her. The exposure is going to heat up every weird and rapo in the files, and with a full moon coming up, the cronkies are going to line up three deep, breathing through their mouths anyplace they think she might show."

After a silence, Lobwohl said, "All right, but we don't know how much clout she might have, so go very, very easy."

"We have this little roll of red carpet we carry, and . . ."

"Somehow, Kindler, when you make those little funnies I keep thinking of all the kicks Mercer and Tuck are having bringing the Akards in to make a positive on the only son they're ever going to have. The kid was born and raised here and there is no j.d. record on him at all, so the mother is going to keep telling Mercer and Tuck that he was always a good boy."

"I'm sorry, sir."

"No apology necessary. I shouldn't chew you. And by now I've been around long enough so I should stop bleeding."

"When you do, it's time to get into another line of work."

"Before you unroll your little red carpet, the lady will be apprised of her right to have an attorney present while her statement is being taken, and she will be permitted to phone and arrange to have said attorney either meet her here or meet her at her house and drive in with her while you follow along."

"So what do I tell her about why we're bringing her in?"

"Hey! There's no next of kin on Staniker. Central records hasn't sent back a match on the prints yet."

"Oh I like that! Duty of a citizen. Ex-employer, et cetera. Voluntary all the way. And a good jolt for her that ought to knock loose something useful—if there is anything. Meanwhile, maybe somebody could start backtracking her, develop a line to somebody who knew Fontaine well enough. And there's a chance she lived in Atlanta. While we're in the place I can let light-fingered Scheff see if he can pick up anything with a chance of enough prints on it to get a principal registration."

"Pretty remote."

"Let me get Harv to tell you how it worked a couple times where we knew a single print registration wouldn't do us any good at all."

Halfway along the shell road to the Harkinson place they met Raoul Kelly trudging toward the highway.

When they stopped, Raoul came over to the car, wearing a troubled frown.

"Kelly," Barney Scheff said, "we're taking the Harkinson woman in. With any luck we'll keep her around awhile. And you maybe better clear your little gal out of there today instead of waiting until Wednesday. You got a car?"

"I left it parked down the highway, in a grove."

"If nobody clouted the wheels and the engine, after we leave she should lock the place up and pack and leave with you, because if we scared her that bad, she's going to get a lot worse time from the spooks who'll come swarming around the place."

"What's the matter? What are you talking about?"

"When we were here before, we knew somebody faked Staniker for a suicide. Stuck him in a bath tub and cut his wrists. From what we got from you, it looked like Oliver might fit, and they found him floating around in his sailboat. After he fixed Staniker, he killed himself. The woman is the motive. You have no idea how miserable the newspaper guys and the rest of them can get when they get a sniff of a story like this. Those bastards will really shake up that Francisca. What you do, Kelly, you stash her someplace where they can't get at her. Then if we have to get a statement or anything, we'll keep it as quiet as we can. What we'll do, we'll get in touch with you if we need her. Where do you work?"

"On the *Record*."

Bert Kindler said, "I hope to God you work around the presses or peddle ads."

"Reporter. But I do features. Latin American politics. Foreign affairs. Stop looking at me like that. Look, you did me two favors. Both large. So I am going to run to a phone and get the city desk and yell they should stop the presses. Scoop. Gimme rewrite. Here's my card. Home address."

"And," said Scheff, "when they start beating the bushes looking for Francisca Whosis, everybody knows she's Kelly's girl. So you can make a very fine deal for an exclusive maybe?"

"I won't have any idea where she is."

After a long thoughtful stare, Scheff said, "Let's buy it, Bert. But if he leaves us with any egg on the face, all we have to do is tell his boss what kind of a piece of news his boy sat on. Let's go get Crissy-wissy and take her bye-bye."

Twenty-three

BARNEY SCHEFF HAD SPENT four years of his professional life on the Miami Beach force. He had worked the big hotels along Collins, called in by the house detectives and protection agencies to work upon every form of bunco the guile of man and woman has been able to invent.

When Mrs. Harkinson met them at the door and let them in, he knew at once that he was in the presence of class merchandise. He had seen hundreds of them. The ones this good were usually celebrity imports, lined up for a full season by somebody with the scratch to pay the exclusive freight. Ten, twelve years ago that was the way she would be making it. Mink to the floor, glittering at ears, throat and wrist and fingers, swaying on the tall heels with the hair piled high, moving in the clubs and the show bars at the side of some little fat guy with his head tanned dark brown all over from playing pool-side gin for high stakes. The small men wore the big young blondes with the same pebble-eyed indifference with which an iron curtain diplomat might treat the aides who follow a pace behind him.

Such women were one of the necessary outward manifestations of that special kind of coarse and curious money which accumulates in the lock boxes of casino owners, union officials, dealers in casino properties, in the raw products of addiction, in oil tankers, night clubs, prize fighters, television properties—in all the more or less legal services and products which, if a man were greedy enough and ruthless enough, could provide a way of channeling off cash without leaving any trace in the official books and records.

So they kept the tall blonde for that season or that place in tow, at the Beach, or Vegas, or Palm Springs, or London, or Acapulco, or Puerto Rico. She sat in the box at the track, a stick of tickets in her fist, squealing the smart money horse home. She leaned forward at ringside, face avid, cawing for blood. And in the night in the hundred and fifty a day suite, under lights turned low, while the cigar end smouldered and stank in the bedstand ashtray, she earned her keep in effortful requested ways. She would not get too drunk, or get quarrelsome, or make demands, or steal through the darkness to thin the pad of bills in the platinum clip, or give any wolf anything but immediate frost, not the smart ones. She would be a fun kid, because it was a smallish world and everybody knew everybody sooner or later. If you got labeled trouble, if you got too cute, the easiest fate would be no phone call from the next friend of a friend, no more first-class jets, no more silk sheets, no more thirty-dollar Chateaubriand for two. Or it could be a cancellation with a little more to remember if the friend of a friend was in one of the tough trades. Barney Scheff remembered taking one in who'd had her teeth uncapped with a pair of pliers. Between faints she was hysterical, yet not crazy enough to tell who'd done it.

Yes, this Harkinson was one of the great broads, years past the peak of it, but hanging in there so well, you had to marvel at what it had to be costing her in time and effort to keep the illusion of youth. Not only the masks and packs, and the oils and skin foods and lotions and the careful measuring of sun to keep that flawless brown gold of the expensive tennis-club tan, but on top of that, the daily measurements of every dimension to the quarter part of an inch, followed by exercises that would exhaust a stevedore. Then, once you had the pretty machine all assembled, you had to imitate the unconscious tricks of youth, no matter how tired the flesh. You had to walk pert, more trimly and quickly, smile saucy, exaggerate all expressions and all gestures, move the head quickly, and run the voice up and down as many notes of the scale as you could handle.

But, baby, the years are written on the backs of your hands, in bulged veins and thickened knucklebones, and written in the horizontal lines across your throat and in the little striated patterns on the slightly puffed flesh under the eyes.

She'd use every possible way to keep the machine going, from pep pills to those long, hearty romps in the sack at regular intervals to keep the girl-making glands humming.

She was obviously ready to go out. She wore a little beige dress in a linen weave, very unadorned, very simple, yet fitted so artfully and elegantly to that brick-house build the price tag almost showed. And elegance in the careful-casual tossle of the sun-streaked hair, sheen of nylons on the very special legs, a couple of expensive ounces of high-heeled sandals, white purse by the door with white gloves on it, and on the table beside the purse, one of those bright little hats they pull on to keep their hair from snapping around when they drive their convertibles.

There was a business with the eyes she did very well indeed, swinging the glance away slowly and then popping it back onto you, like being snapped with a little whip. Broad across the brows, heavy and prominent bones in the cheeks. Nose a little small, upsnubbed over a short upper lip. Lips of equal unusual heaviness in a considerable amount of mouth.

So there she was, one long arm away, all fresh and fragrant and resilient, unable to make any motion without effective and graceful display of a promise of goodies for me and thee, eyes making her cool speculations the way the man-smart ones can't help doing, while the mouth made the words of another kind of conversation.

If something like this, Barney thought, really vectored in on that sailboat kid, it would be like going after a goldfish by sticking a twelve-gauge into the fish bowl and pulling both triggers.

"Well—if it is something *really* important," she said. "I'm waiting for them to bring my car around. It's been in the garage since Saturday morning. I have an appointment with the hairdresser, and then I was going to go . . ."

"We're asking you to do a favor, or maybe more like a citizen's duty," Kindler said. "What we've got to get is a positive identification on a body."

She put her fingertips to her throat and made her eyes round and sat on the broad arm of a low chair. It pulled the hem of the short little dress about four inches above her knees.

"My God, who *is* it?"

"We're pretty sure he's a fellow worked for you, Mrs. Harkinson. Staniker. Captain Garry Staniker. We can't locate any next of kin."

"Automobile accident?"

"No. What he did, he killed himself. He was holed up in a fleabag over near Coral Gables and he got loaded and sat in the bathtub and cut his wrists. What it looks like, he got depressed over the bad luck on that cruise, and getting burned and being the only one got out of it."

She swallowed with an apparent effort and said, "I'm not going to be a hypocrite and tell you this is any horrid shock, men. Garry wasn't one of my favorite people." She shook her head and gave them a wry, disarming grin. "While he was still running my boat, he seemed like a nice guy. And really attractive in a kind of outdoorsy way. When—a very dear and close friend of mine passed away, I was very alone. And Garry was very sweet and understanding." She stood up with a lithe quickness, made a little shrug, and a mouth of distaste. "But he tried to keep hanging on. Male pride, I suppose. Some men won't admit it when something is over. He got to be a damned tiresome bore. He couldn't get a good job. He'd come by and drink and tell me his problems and get mean drunk. It was a relief when he finally got a decent boat to run and took off."

As she turned away, Barney Scheff read Bert Kindler's quick glance. They had been teamed for five years. All the people they worked on fell into some familiar category. Approach had to be adjusted to the individuals. Staying in any pattern was a sure way to come up empty oftener than you should. You developed a feeling, like an extra sense of smell. Like with that Raoul Kelly, they shared the decision to play it his way, but had one of them been dubious, they would not have gone along. The weirds were easy to smell out, as easy as the chronic losers. Amateurs could be suckered by traps so old you had to brush off the cobwebs before you used them. But the cute ones took you onto uneasy ground, especially when they were intelligent and confident. A clumsy truth and a plausible lie could sound almost alike. The frankness of her implication of an intimacy between her and Staniker could be either because the news he was dead had shaken her up, or because she was one of those women who got a little bit of jolly out of letting practically anybody know that if the stars were right it was possible to get a hack at all that merchandise, or because she sensed there was a chance it would be checked out later, and if they came up with a relationship she had not implied in any way, they would wonder why she hadn't.

Kindler's glance said, "My turn" and Scheff's slight shrug said, "Have fun."

"I guess losing that boat and those people would give him some new problems to tell you, Mrs. Harkinson."

She spun toward him, head a-tilt, and said, "Do you ever get a funny kind of superstition about people? I mean somebody is all right, and then they sort of turn into a loser, and everything starts to go wrong for them. You get the sort of spooky feeling you don't want them anywhere near you. As if it could rub off and they could turn you into a loser too."

"I know what you mean," Kindler said.

"He wanted to tell me his problems all right," she said grimly. "He phoned me as soon as he rented that place last Friday. He was going to come right out. I told him I'd made it very damned clear back in April we were all through. He said he was going to come and see me anyway and if I tried to keep him from coming here, he'd— give me a thumping I'd remember a long time. Garry was a brutal man, Sergeant. And I couldn't afford to let him know I was scared of him. But I was. I've been terrified he'd force his way in here. So—I can't be sorry he's dead. But—there's something funny about it."

"Like what?"

"I wouldn't say he was the kind of human being who'd brood about losing that boat and those people. He'd worry about not being able to find a job. But on the phone he didn't seem depressed at all. Just kind of arrogant. He told me he had a big check in advance for an exclusive story on the whole thing. I don't know how to say this—just that if he had money in his pocket, he felt good. And he just wasn't sensitive—the way I guess people are who commit suicide."

"Well," said Kindler, "to get back to the point here, we'd like for you to come on in and take a look, just for the record. A formality."

She stood hip-shot, elbow resting in her palm, chin against her thumb, looking broodingly at the floor. "I want to do the right thing. And you have been nice about this, both of you. Please understand. I know it's only a formality, really, but it wouldn't be just a formality to me. It would be a very personal thing. And it would be like—confirming that something still exists that died a long time ago."

Kindler said, "Look, we're asking you as an ex-employer. That's all."

"Then if that's the relationship, I think you'd better get maybe the man he worked for at that little marina. I just don't care to be—identified with the whole thing. I'm really sorry."

"We can't force you," Kindler said. "Can I use the phone and find out what they want us to do?"

"Of course."

Scheff had an idea he knew was at least as good and possibly better than Kindler's. It could even be the same idea. So he said, "I'll check in, Bert."

He dialed Lobwohl's outside line. After the first four seconds Lobwohl caught on that Scheff was talking for the benefit of someone who could hear his end of the conversation. Scheff reported the Harkinson woman's refusal and started to ask for instructions and then said, "What? No kidding! You know, that's a funny thing because that's just what this Mrs. Harkinson was saying. She said he wasn't the type. Yeah. Sure. Well, nobody touched his money there and it wasn't hard to find, so you can forget that angle. She might have some ideas. What? Well, it's on account of she knew him real well, right up to a little while before he went to the Bahamas. Yes, that's what I mean. Yes, that's what I'd say it was. We can ask her, but if she didn't want to do the other, why should she do this? I see. Sure. Well, put it this way, she's a smart lady and I don't think we'd have to do it that way."

He hung up and stood up and said, "Somebody tried to make it look like suicide. But the lab boys say he was killed. You were right, Mrs. Harkinson."

"It's—easy to understand. But it's still dreadful."

"I'm sorry to have to do this to you, Mrs. Harkinson, because I guess if you hadn't been a little shook you wouldn't have let us know Staniker and you had a relationship. But we do know it, and we can't just forget you said it, and I was duty bound to report that."

"I wish you hadn't."

"They say you should come in and they'll take a statement."

"But *why?*"

"When somebody is murdered and it isn't robbery, then what we have to do is find out who would want to kill him and why, and the quickest way to get a line on that is to interrogate somebody who knew him real well, would know what his habits were and so on. What I should explain, it's a little different than the identification thing. You can come along voluntarily, but if you say you won't, then because you might have some information bearing on a known murder, we'd have to set it up to take you in anyway. You could refuse to answer questions once you're there, but that would be up to you. What you can do if you want, you can phone your lawyer to meet you there, or go in with you."

"Are you charging me with anything?"

"No m'am. Not if you come in voluntarily."

She spread her arms wide, and with rueful grin said, "Why don't I learn to keep my mouth shut? So you've convinced me. Voluntary cooperation. There isn't a thing I can help you with as far as I know, but I'll go in. And I certainly don't need a lawyer. But there's one errand I'd like to do on the way in. Some material I have to leave off with my dressmaker. Can we do that?"

"Sure can," said Kindler.

"Excuse me a few minutes while I get it ready. Then we can go."

When she closed her bedroom door behind her, she hurried to

the closet in her dressing room, and pulled out the twine-wrapped package of the clothing she had worn. One of her suits had been returned in a white cleaner bag. She wrapped the bundle neatly, tied it with twine, snipped the twine with her nail scissors.

She stood quietly and made herself review every possible thing which might turn up in a painstaking search of the house. After putting the single shell in Olly's little rifle, and hiding the rifle under the edge of decking where she could grasp it quickly enough, she had dropped the extra shells into the bay as she had sailed the Skatter down to the place where Olly was waiting for her in the dark in his car. The notes and plans had been burned in an ashtray and the ashes flushed down the toilet. He'd taken his other belongings home.

It was strange, she thought. You brace yourself for the police. You wait. You expect them to be narrow deadly people, and poisonously clever. But when they arrive, earlier than you had expected, it is just two placid dumpy apologetic men with mild heavy faces and an air of clumsy courtesy.

The car was delivered as they walked out. She had the man put it in the carport under the servant quarters. He brought her the key and the copy of the service charge. She put them in her purse and as he was unhooking his scooter from the rear bumper, she called to Francisca and told her she would be back in a couple of hours.

Kindler sat in the cage, and she sat up in front beside Scheff. Scheff drove very sedately. She directed him to a large shopping plaza. "It will just be a minute," she said. "She works daytimes and sews at night. Don't go away." She left her white purse on the car seat. She went toward the shops and turned into a long arcade. When she was out of sight she quickened her pace. She went through the arcade and came out behind the buildings. Trucks were parked back there. Garbage cans were lined up behind a supermarket. She looked around. A man rolling a loaded dolly out of a big truck seemed oblivious of her. She plucked the top from a garbage can, dropped the package onto a viscid mass of brown lettuce and rotten fruit, picked up a stick from a shattered crate and pushed the bundle into the garbage and replaced the lid. Flies swarmed like small chars in an updraft, a blue-bellied buzzing audible in the sunlight. She re-entered the arcade.

When they were back on the highway, Scheff said, "That maid of yours a Cuban? Pretty little thing."

"Francisca is very good natured. But she's no mental giant. She tries to do what she's told, but sometimes she doesn't understand and other times she forgets. I'm losing her, darn it. You get them to where you can trust them to do things the way you want them done, and they take off. There ought to be a way to make them sign up for three years, like the army."

At two o'clock on Monday afternoon, Sam Boylston sat in his pool-side cabana with Raoul Kelly and Francisca. Her manner was constrained, puzzled, apprehensive.

"Promising for Wednesday," she said. "I keep telling."

"Miss Torcedo," Sam said softly.

"Si?"

"Raoul and I must talk. If all your belongings are out there in his car, maybe you have a swim suit. It's a very nice pool. I think a swim would be relaxing."

She looked questioningly at Raoul. "Why don't you, *chica?*" he said.

Raoul went out with her to unlock the car. They came back and she changed in Sam's bathroom. She seemed happier. After she had gone out, with swim cap and towel, Sam said, "She's a lovely one, friend. Congratulations."

"You know, you're very good with her, Sam. She has a good reaction to you. With a stranger she usually goes into her shell. On the way here I told her we can trust you. What was it when we came in? You were okay and then strange for a minute."

Sam said, "Something that will keep happening to me, I guess. I don't know how long. When she walked over and sat down—Leila had that same slimness, and she moved the way your girl does, handled her body the same way. And I knew I'd never see Leila again, see her cross a room like that." He pinched the bridge of his nose, cursed softly. He leaned back. "Take it from the top. God *damn* it! That sappy kid kills Staniker, then himself. They take her in. What are they trying to get her for? A morals charge?"

Raoul Kelly went through it all, pausing only to organize the material into as orderly a presentation as possible. And again he was aware of how totally and intently Sam Boylston could listen.

"So now I need advice, Lawyer," Raoul said.

"From a lawyer who's been up all night two nights in a row waiting for the little white car that wasn't even there? I wondered about your car there, parked and locked, and I figured you'd tucked it out of sight and moved in with the girl. What's the problem? I'll try to think."

"I want to get Francisca out of range of this whole mess. I was going to leave Thursday the ninth. Only a very few people know about me and Francisca. But that's a few too many. I have to know how much trouble I can get into if I leave in the morning. The stuff in my room I was going to take to the paper, I can mail in. I could leave her here and go close out the bank account, pack what I need, get a friend to crate up the rest of my stuff, the files and research and so on and hold it all until I send a shipping address. I have to report out there on the nineteenth. A Monday. Those two cops were good guys. When they find out I'm gone, they're going to be very, very unhappy. What can they do to me, to us? I don't want to mess up the new job. I don't want her extradited and brought back here by some damned matron. But I can't let her get caught up in the kind of fantastic publicity mess there's going to be. How should I handle it?"

Sam Boylston stood up and roamed the room, stopping to look at Francisca swimming quite prettily and gracefully. He turned and clapped his hands once. "Here it is, client. You are going to go pick up your money and your gear, mail your stuff, with a note of explanation that you are leaving a few days earlier than planned. Come back here and sign a statement that I am representing you and the girl. Then we'll use my tape recorder and you can question her in Spanish. I'll put the necessary identifications at the beginning. Take her through everything she knows they might use against the Harkinson woman. Set the background first. How long she worked for her and so on. We want to establish the relationship with Staniker, and the relationship with the boy. How late the boy was at the house, how often, the times she'd hear him drive out. And get in everything she remembers about that last day of March when Kayd visited Crissy Harkinson. Finally, go over the weekend, the locked gates, going to see if the boat was there, looking in at her, bringing her the cocoa."

"How can you represent us if you aren't . . ."

"You are going to leave when we have a good tape, Kelly. And you are going to drive right on through to Texas, and down to Harlingen. I'm going to give you the address of my house there, and by the time you get there, my wife will be expecting you and she'll know what to do. I advise marriage as soon as my partner can get the usual restrictions bypassed. And if anybody gets ugly, I'll see that there is a doctor and a judge who see eye to eye on the inadvisability of her being returned here. You sit tight. I can represent you. You'll be in the state where I'm licensed. I can get a local man to work with me here if it comes to that. If it hasn't blown over by the eighteenth, you leave your wife with my wife and fly out to California and report in, and we'll get her out there to you as soon as it makes sense to do so."

Raoul Kelly stared at him in a long silence and shook his head and said in Cuban Spanish, "You are a one! Truly."

"El fantástico, seguro, hombre."

"I should make big protests, Sam. Can't impose. All that. But for her sake, if it would help her in any way, I'd go beg bread in the streets."

Raoul went out to the pool and spoke with Francisca and then hurried away.

Sam phoned Lydia Jean at her mother's home in Corpus.

"Sam? Where are you? Why are you still over there?"

"It's a long story, honey. But right now I want you to do me a favor."

"Such as?"

"Two friends of mine are leaving here this evening and driving right on through. What I want you to do, honey, is go back home and open the house up and . . ."

"Now just a *minute!*"

"It isn't a trick. You're the only one I'd trust to handle the situation. The girl is an emotional disaster area. She and her guy are in a strange kind of a jam. He can explain it to you better than I can. And it is important to get them married as fast as we can arrange it, as *you* can arrange it. I think you can put more leverage on my partner than I can in a situation like this."

"Married?"

"If it could be done with a few trimmings, I think it would help. And at the house. I know this is a hell of a thing to ask . . ."

"Who *are* these people?"

"His name is Raoul Kelly and he looks like somebody's gardener, but don't be deceived. Francisca Torceda is her name, very beautiful, and racked up so bad maybe she makes it, maybe she doesn't. You could have a lot to do about that, and it could be worth it."

"These are important people, Sam? Is that why you want me to . . ."

"They are *very* important people. I am going to have my neck way out for them here, and somebody might chop it pretty good."

"Very important. Yes, dear. I understand you perfectly."

"She's a housemaid and he's a newspaper reporter, and they'll have every personal thing they own in that car with them, and if I can get them out of this jam, my fee is going to be five dollars, and I probably won't see either of them again ever. But they are very important."

"Is that the truth?"

"I swear it."

"I wasn't going to do it."

"I know. Why should you? Sam Boylston always looks out for Sam Boylston, and uses you or anybody else."

"Or," she said slowly, "Sam Boylston makes a big, fat gesture. He imitates an honest to God human being for a little while, and I might fall for it. Oh, Sam! What are you trying to do to me?"

"Set you up, kid. I hired this couple from an acting studio. See if you can trip them up, then you can hate me forever."

"I've never hated you!"

"Resent me forever, then. Do I keep my word?"

"So scrupulously it's almost irritating."

"Word of honor, then. I won't come near the house until they're gone and you've had a chance to go back to Corpus. I happen to need some help from somebody—with more than their share of sympathy and understanding, at least toward everybody but me."

"Now why do you have to . . ."

"Will you do it? Please, Lyd . . . Lyd?"

"Oh, I'm still here. I'll drive down early tomorrow."

"Thanks, dear."

"Are you going to get into some kind of trouble there?"

"I don't know. And I can't seem to give too much of a damn. Maybe—maybe no matter how careful you are, no matter how well you play the percentages, They bitch you anyway, one way or another. They get at you through the side door. The rain comes down, baby, and we've all got sixteen buckets and seventeen holes in the roof."

"Have you had some drinks?"

"Not yet today, but it's a creative suggestion."

"You sound so strange. When will those people get to Harlingen?"

"I'd guess it's around seventeen hundred miles. I'm going to tell him to take a break midway. Make it late Wednesday."

"Will he be able to tell me why you're acting so strange, Sam?"

"I don't know."

Kelly's girl swam for a long time. She was showering when Kelly returned.

Lobwohl swiveled his chair and put his heels on the corner of his desk, ankles crossed. "Let's let her stew another ten or fifteen minutes before we give her another session. Agree?"

Scheff nodded. He reached and picked up the ID sheet which had been transmitted over the wire from Atlanta and looked at it again. Cristen Harkinson, ten years younger. Smudged pictures, indistinct in outline, flawed by wire-relay technique. But in both the full face and profile the look of surly defiance was quite obvious. Also known as Crissy Harker, Chris Harkins, Christy Harvey. Five arrests. Soliciting, public prostitution, conspiracy to defraud. Two convictions, with each time, a hundred dollar fine and a suspended sentence.

"Between the lines," Kindler said, "you read pretty good protection. Not a free-lance situation. What it was, there's always pressure on the operation. League of decency, PTA and so forth. So they run like a roster on the hookers, an arrest once in a while. It takes the civilian pressure off the department, and it's a good way to keep the broads in line. A high-price call circuit, they get uppity, and give each of them a record of convictions, it locks them into the circuit and keeps them from getting ideas, or leaving the business."

"But she left," Lobwohl said. "From the only rumor I could pick up, she was one of a pack they brought down to stock a party at Key West around eight years ago, and that's where she met Fontaine and he took her over."

"So what was she then?" Kindler said. "Twenty-seven maybe? Twenty-eight. You could guess special enough to be a good earner, but easier to pry her loose than if she was twenty. I'd say what Fontaine did was maybe ask a favor of a friend in a political way in Georgia, and maybe he had to sweeten it with cash to make them let go, and maybe he didn't. Anyway, as the name was the same here as there, we didn't have to work through a print classification for the ID on her."

Lobwohl, frowning, tugging at his nose, said, "All these nice prints on record, and Harv can't pick up a partial down there of any one of them, but we have that palm print on the rim of the tub, nice and fresh and clear, and Harv says the size could indicate a woman, but you know and I know what will happen if Lab asks her to please press her little patties against the Stockis block and then against the pretty white paper. She has to be tough and smart. The longer we can keep this absolutely voluntary, the better chance we have of catching her in contradiction. I'd sure God like to prove she was there, egging the kid on."

"How about this?" Scheff said. "Let me be dumb guy. It won't be too hard to act like she gives me some ideas. I let on you've got a good reason to believe she was at number ten, and you're going to try to trick her, and maybe she should yell for a lawyer. Then we see how she jumps. If she yells for the lawyer, we could take a chance on booking her and taking the palm print for Harv."

"Give it a try," Lobwohl said.

When Scheff sent the matron out to wait in the hall, Crissy Harkinson jumped up and threw her cigarette on the floor, stepped on it and said, "I am getting damned sick of being stuck here all day long, Sergeant."

"Scheff. Barney Scheff. Just be a little patient, Mrs. Harkinson."

"Patient!"

He winked at her, held his fingers to his lips, then pointed at the ventilation grill. All the interrogation rooms were wired, and he guessed she would realize that also. But she looked astonished and indignant. He went up to her and put his mouth close to her ear and in an almost soundless whisper said, "I want to do you a little favor, Crissy. Maybe sometime I can drop around your place and explain why I'm doing it. Okay?"

She gave an abrupt little nod.

"What I think you better do, you better shut your mouth until you get a lawyer in here."

"Why?" she whispered.

"I don't know what they got, but they got something that makes them think you could have been in that number ten cottage. It makes the whole thing look different, and Lobwohl is tricky. He could fake you out and maybe put you in real trouble."

He turned away from her and said loudly, "These things take a little time. We appreciate your cooperation, Mrs. Harkinson."

"I just want to get it over and get out of here, Barney. I wish they were all as nice as you."

"I say live and let live," Scheff said, and winked at her again. She was staring at him and though she was smiling he was aware of cold speculation, of that kind of suspicion which will never accept a cop at face value. "I'll go see if I can hurry it up some."

A few minutes later they came back in, Lobwohl, Scheff, Kindler, the clerk with the tape recorder, and the clerk with the stenotype. They seated themselves around the oblong table as before, and Lobwohl smiled disarmingly at her, and read the identifications and date and time into the record before saying, "Once again, Mrs. Harkinson, I wish to establish for the record that you are here voluntarily, that there are no charges against you, that you are here out of a willingness to help us in our investigation of the death of Garry Staniker. You have been apprised of your right to have your attorney present if you so choose. Am I correct in saying that this is your understanding?"

"Yes sir."

"And do you wish to have an attorney present at this time?"

"No sir."

"Then I would like to get back to your recollection of what Staniker told you over the phone."

"Some of it was over the phone, and some of it was in person."

"I don't quite understand."

"When a person does a dumb stupid thing, you kind of hate to admit it to anybody, right? I told you I was frightened of Garry and what he might do. But I decided I could maybe—run a bluff. I guess that when you don't tell the police the whole story, it just gets you in trouble. So I guess I better tell you now to clear the air. Friday night I went to that grubby cottage. I had a horrible time even finding it. I thought that the more I refused to see him, the more he'd keep bothering me. I didn't want him coming to my home, so I thought that if I went to him and told him right out that I didn't ever want to see him again, it might put an end to it. I guess I was thinking that he was like a mean dog. If you don't look or act scared, they'll leave you alone—you hope."

"Did it work?"

"God, no! It was a vile experience. It was suffocatingly hot in that crummy little cottage. He was half tight. If his burns hadn't still been hurting him, I know I wouldn't have been able to fight him off. He said ugly things to me. He showed me a check he had gotten from Banner something or other, to tell his story of the accident in the Bahamas. He told me how important he was going to be. He said they were going to make a movie and he was going to play the lead. I begged him to stop bothering me. He said he'd think about it. He said no woman had ever walked out on him and no woman ever would. He said he always did the walking out. On the way home I decided I'd better go away for a while, just pack a bag and get in my car and go. I thought I'd go Saturday afternoon, but I had to get the car fixed and it wasn't done in time, so I had my maid lock the gates and I told her that if he came around, she should tell him I'd gone away. As a matter of fact, when you two men came to talk to me, I had no idea Garry was dead, and I was going out to do some errands, and then I was going to leave today in the late afternoon, or at least by tomorrow morning."

"Were you at that cottage long?"

"I got there at midnight. I think I was home by three in the morning. It was sort of spur of the moment. I've had better ideas, believe me. But I really think going away for a while would have solved the problem. He would have had to get busy on that contract he signed."

"Did he give you any idea why he registered under a false name?"

"I think he was worried about somebody close to the Kayds or the Boylston girl thinking he had lost the yacht because of carelessness or incompetence, and coming after him to beat him up."

"And that was the only time you were ever in that cottage?"

"Being there once wouldn't give you any reasons to want to go back."

"What rooms were you in?"

"The bedroom and the bathroom. Oh, and I sat in the living room a while. Why are you asking me that? Oh, I see! Wow, even though it so happens I can prove I never left the house Sunday night, it would look pretty strange if you found evidence I was in the cottage. I guess I had a good motive, too. But I couldn't do anything like that. I really couldn't. Blood. I'm the kind who can prick a finger with a needle and faint dead away."

"A lab unit has collected every scrap of possible evidence from that cottage, Mrs. Harkinson. There is a fresh palm print which was dusted and photographed. From the size and characteristics, it seems to be a female hand. It was on the rim of the tub. How could your palm print, if it is yours, have gotten there?"

She looked puzzled. "On the bathtub? I don't see how that could be mine. Oh! Just a minute. On the far side of the tub, next to the wall? If that's where it is, I know how it happened. He made me cry. I went into the bathroom to repair the damage. I was standing at the sink. He came to the doorway and gave me one hell of a shove." She stood up and backed away from the table and showed them a bruise on the outside of her right knee. "I went staggering back and hit my leg against the tub and I would have tumbled right in if I hadn't sort of turned in time and stuck my hand back and caught that far edge." She sat down again. "Is that where the print was?"

"Would you voluntarily let us take a palm print, Mrs. Harkinson."

"I don't think so."

"We wouldn't require fingerprints also."

"I think that if the police are asking you to give them prints and all, then there ought to be charges or something, and I ought to have a lawyer. I mean you seem to be asking a hell of a lot, and I'm getting sick of this place."

"I believe we're through now."

"And I can go?"

"Any minute, just as soon as we bring in the statement from the first series of questions for you to read over and sign. They might be ready now, in fact. Why don't you all wait here and I'll go check on it right now."

"I'll go see," Scheff said and hurried out. He found Tuck working at a desk in the bull pen. Tuck, a slight, sallow man with heavy bags under his eyes, was pecking out a report.

"We're about to hit her with phase three," Scheff said.

"How are you making it?"

"Like nowhere. By now she is probably the only person in Dade County who doesn't know about the dead kid. What did you get?"

"We didn't get a thing until we split the Akards up. Then after a lot of hemming and hawing, she told me that she hadn't dared tell the kid's old man, but a week or so ago when she had fought with the kid about his attitude, he admitted he was getting it from an older woman. He said she was twenty-eight. He wouldn't tell his old lady who it was. Some girl saw the Akard kid in his sailboat with the Harkinson woman, evidently, and told the girlfriend the kid had dropped when he got tangled up with Harkinson, and the girlfriend told his old lady. It gave her enough to pry it out of him, but she didn't dare tell his old man." He shook his head. "It's days like this, Barney baby. Those are good people. Their life from today on is lousy. There better be a special corner of hell reserved for kids who kill themselves, and for the Crissy Harkinsons. Is she getting edgy at all?"

"If she is, she could have been a great actress, Tommy."

"Remember Ackles, retired two three years back? He used to say the top-dollar whores are the best actresses around. Whatever act the mark wants, shy, scared, bold, college girl, spooky, cold, take charge, exotic, comedian, athlete—whatever he seems to want, that's what he gets, because that's where the bonuses and the repeats are."

Scheff went back to the interrogation room and, as planned ahead, gave the Harkinson woman a bleak look, and took Lobwohl over to a far corner and whispered to him. All he had to tell him was what Tuck had turned up, but they kept it going longer to match the amount of information he was supposed to be imparting.

Lobwohl went back to his chair. He regarded her for a few very long moments. "A boy died today, Mrs. Harkinson. He was a suicide. He had a serious head wound. They couldn't save him. There were a few moments of semi-consciousness toward the end. He said he did it for you. He said he had to protect you from Staniker. We have all the proof we need that he did it. It was curious you did not mention your visit to Staniker on Friday night until a little while ago. It is more curious that you have not mentioned the boy. It makes me wonder just how much—suggestion was involved, Mrs. Harkinson."

Scheff, watching her closely, saw an expression of wild astonishment. She put her fingers to her throat. In a hoarse whisper she said, "Olly? Olly Akard? Dead? Oh God, oh dear God!" She lowered her head, hands hiding her face. "But it was just *talk!* Just brave kid-talk! That's all."

"But he had to get Staniker's address from you."

She looked up sharply. Her tears were flowing. "No! I swear he didn't. I don't know how he could have found that place . . ." she frowned. "Unless—unless he followed me. When I got back, he was waiting at my place for me."

"What was your relationship with the boy?"

"He—He was a very wonderful boy. I was really fond of him. I wanted to learn to sail. At Dinner Key they said he taught people.

And while he was teaching me, he—got a sort of a crush on me. I guess it was sort of flattering for a while. But then I realized it wasn't a good thing for him, to feel like that about a woman practically old enough to be his mother. I made a very bad mistake. I told him about the relationship I had with Garry. And one of the times Garry phoned last Friday, Oliver was there. He made such a scene I told him if he kept it up, I wouldn't let him see me any more. He kept it up. Saturday I told him to go away and stay away. You can ask my maid, Francisca. She knows the locked gate was to keep him away too. He came early Sunday evening and got his boat and took it away. He had somebody bring him by boat, I guess. I didn't see him. I went to bed very early. I was exhausted, emotionally. I told him that his ideas about me were childish and foolish and absolutely impossible. I told him to go back to his nice little girl. Betty I think her name is. You must believe me! I had no *idea* Olly would do such a crazy thing. Even if he thought of something silly, like beating Garry up, how could he find him? No, this is a terrible terrible thing."

"You imply that the relationship was innocent?"

"If you mean did I have intercourse with that nineteen-year-old boy, I certainly did not!"

"But that boy was apparently willing to stage a clumsy murder for your sake and then sacrifice himself, Mrs. Harkinson."

"Oliver was—a very romantic and idealistic boy. I guess that when I saw how he was beginning to feel toward me I should have laughed at him and called him a silly kid. Okay, I let him kiss me. I let him dream a little. I let him talk about life, the way kids do. It's like—being young again. He made crazy plans about us. Impossible, of course. Maybe I was being as silly as he was. The difference was he could believe it and I knew it was nonsense. I'm a woman alone. If I'd ever told that poor kid the kind of life I've really had, it could have driven him out of his mind I guess. It was just—sweet. A game.

I stopped playing that game when he got so worked up about Garry being back and phoning me and demanding to see me. Saturday I told him to stay away from me. I told him—in a pretty ugly way, I guess. I felt responsible for letting him get such nutty ideas and not stopping him sooner. I tried to jolt him, shake him up."

Lobwohl said, "As this crush, as you call it, developed, Mrs. Harkinson, the boy became sullen and difficult and withdrawn. It worried his parents. The girl he used to go with told his mother about someone seeing an older woman in the sailboat with Oliver, a blonde woman in a bikini. She could not make Oliver tell her who the woman was, but he admitted he was physically intimate with the woman."

Her eyes went wide, and her voice was thin as she said, "Told his mother *that?* But it wasn't *so!* Why would he want to hurt her like that? It doesn't make any sense at all. I guess he was trying to—break loose."

"In what sense?"

"His mother wanted him to become a minister. His girl, Betty something, was going to become a nurse. Then they were going to be missionaries. It was all planned, and he said that he hadn't been able to tell them that he was losing his faith. Maybe he thought that if he told her—that lie, she would stop trying to push him into the ministry." She shrugged, sighed, wiped her eyes with a tissue. "It's the only thing I can think of. Can I go now? Can I please go? He was such a fine boy. And I'm to blame. It makes me feel sick."

Lobwohl opened the folder in front of him and took out the wire copy of the Atlanta ID card and with a long reach, he put it in front of her. "We're all deeply touched by your sensitivity, Crissy."

She looked at the card without expression. She looked at Kindler, Scheff and Lobwohl in turn, a measured three seconds for each one. "Very cute," she said. "Real fancy nifty cute, you sick-minded bastards. Real careful timing. Let me ask *you* something. Do you think for one minute that if this is *all* I am, or all I *could* be, a man like Ferris Fontaine could have endured me for the last seven years of his life? I never conned him. He knew the score about me. You know what a hustler learns first of all? Don't trust anybody. And I learned to trust that wonderful old man. You know what he gave me back? Some dignity. Some self respect." She rapped the wire copy with her knuckles. "I remember this kid pretty well. She had a lot of hate in her. She kidded herself. She drifted into the trade telling herself it was just for a while. She thought she was better than the others she worked with, in New York and Savannah and Atlanta. Then she found out she was just another hooker. Then Fer came along, and after a long time she got her pride back. Every cell in your body is supposed to change every seven years, right? So don't get me mixed up with some rental playmate in Atlanta a long, long time ago."

"I will remind you again that we can suspend this until you are represented by counsel, Mrs. Harkinson."

"Where can you go from here? You don't need any more from me!"

"Your attorney will advise you that you are providing essential evidence regarding motive in a homicide investigation. He will tell you that even though we have sufficient proof as to who committed the crime, and even though that person is now deceased, Florida law requires that evidence be presented to the Grand Jury for preparing an indictment, and that the subsequent suicide must be handled as a separate matter. He will inform you that we can hold you in interrogation for twenty-four hours, or until early afternoon tomorrow, and at that time we can bring charges against you, if we find sufficient basis therefore, or, if we feel it is in the best interests of the proper investigation of the case, we can ask for a court order which will empower us to hold you in protective custody until such time as the Grand Jury decides whether or not you should be asked to give direct testimony during their deliberations."

"Hold me for the best interests of what, damn you?"

"You are news, Mrs. Harkinson. Big, gaudy, melodramatic news. You are bright enough to figure it out. What's their approach? Infatuated youth slays only survivor of the Muñeca disaster to protect blonde mystery woman from unwanted attentions. Future minister a suicide after slaying rival for favors of ex-mistress of deceased State Senator. Heartbroken mother says Akard boy was a model boy until blonde twice his age started taking sailing lessons."

"Do you characters peddle that crap to the reporters?"

"Mrs. Harkinson, when we identified Staniker, it took these two men an hour and a half to follow the trail right to you. There are perhaps a hundred people from the papers, television, radio and the wires services jamming up the place downstairs, dreaming up cute tricks to be the first ones to get to you. It's even too late now to have someone drive you back to your house to pick up what you'd need in the way of clothes and toilet articles. You can make a list and explain to a matron where she can find things, and we'll send her to your place to pick them up."

"My maid knows where my things . . ."

"She has been advised to leave the premises after locking the place up. We have men posted there now to keep people from breaking in."

"What are you trying to *do* to me?"

"Protect your constitutional rights, Mrs. Harkinson, and protect your person not only from the news media but also from what is usually referred to as an aroused populace."

She pressed her fists against her eyes, shuddered and said, "I think I'll take that free phone call, mister."

Just as Lobwohl got up and turned on the lights in his office, Tuck came to the doorway and said, "They got the kid's car finally. Coast

Guard chopper spotted it. Deserted spot on the bay shore maybe two miles below the Harkinson place."

"News out yet?"

"No, sir."

"I want the top lab team on it. Harv and his people, and I want them to comb the area. Keep it sealed until they've got daylight, and then they can impound the car when they're done."

"They're still on the Harkinson place."

"Move them off it. They can go back to it. And where the hell is that maid?"

"Bert and Barney are on it. They'll find her and bring her in."

"I know, but when?"

"Who did Lady Harkinson get hold of?"

"Palmer Haas."

Tuck whistled. "She went to the right place. Feisty little bastard. Miserable as he is, you got to give him credit."

"He's making all the motions, but he knows damn well the worst thing we could do for her right now is release her."

Tuck grinned. "He listening to what we got?"

"Avidly."

"Funny, isn't it. A very cagey broad like that being half smart. She should have screamed for Palmy before she was brought in."

"It's the big myth. Innocent people don't need counsel, they think. Asking for one makes a bad impression, they think."

"But we still came up empty. Remember that."

Twenty-four

RAOUL KELLY'S CAR was parked beside Sam Boylston's rental car at the motel. Sam walked the couple through the soft night to the car. Raoul unlocked it and held the door for 'Cisca. The trunk was full, the back seat stacked with luggage.

Raoul came around the car and opened the door on the driver's side. "Around Biloxi or a little ways this side of it we'll hole up," Raoul said. He moved away from the car, drawing Sam with him. "How are you going to handle it?"

"I'll wait and see if they unravel it without help. When I lost her Friday night, it's obvious she was going to meet Staniker. He told her where the money is. Once she knew that, she could sick the kid on him. That poor damned kid. If he hadn't been rocked so bad he killed himself afterwards, and if he'd been charged with murder, I think he was too infatuated to tell them it was in any way her idea. And even if he did break, I don't believe she would have left him with any kind of direct specific quote he could remember. It's obvious she expected it to happen Sunday night. That's why she wanted verification she was home."

"But if it looks as if she's going to be cleared, Sam?"

They could see the lighted pool beyond a corner of the building. Sam watched The Chunk race off the high board, kicking and yelping on the way down, a rangy boy in close pursuit.

"I'm not as civilized an animal as I thought I was," Sam said. "The instinct is to find a way to move in on her and let her think she's conning me. Simple Sam Boylston. Crissy baby, this has been a wretched experience for both of us. I'd like to lease a boat and go back over there and take a look at the area where it actually happened. Keep me company, Crissy baby. Just the two of us. Raoul, that water is so fantastically clear. I can't reach Staniker. He left the party. She's the last one left now. That water is too beautiful to drown in. But Leila is down there somewhere. I dreamed about the Muñeca last night, or rather this morning after I got back here. I was in a little boat in the sunshine. I had one of those glass bottom buckets they use. I was looking straight down. It was all lighted up. I saw every one of them down there. They walked around in that slow funny way of people underwater. Carolyn's hair and Leila's hair floated. I could see their mouths move but I couldn't hear what they were saying. I knew my boat was drifting away from the spot, and looking down at them was like saying goodby because I knew somehow I could never find that exact same spot again, or tell anyone how to find it. I made some kind of noise that woke me up. I was sweaty."

"My friend. My good friend . . ."

"Very, very nice, I think, to let her get her hands on the money. She should have that thrill. Then do you know the best way to do it? What you do is hit her right on the button. Nice short little right hand punch, just slightly overhand. Then you wire her ankles together. You find about ten feet of water. When she wakes up, you talk about the nice money and you talk about how smart she is, and then you roll her off the boat into the pretty water. She'd last a long time I think. If it was going to be over too soon, you could give a little assist with a boat hook. You could watch it all."

"Could you?"

"I don't know. That's the part I don't know. I talked about the money to Staniker in the hospital. He'd tell her I visited him. What I'll do is give you enough running room, then I'll go in and do some dickering. Accept the Francisca tapes as is, boys, and I'll play you some other tapes."

"Information you withheld?"

"Because, boys, there wasn't enough motive to make sense. Does a man who wants to shed his wife take five other people along?"

"More than that, on airplanes."

"But the bomb is remote. It's almost abstract. The nut doesn't know the names, see the faces, let the eyes see him. The nut is in a bed someplace with his heart pumping and the radio on. Boys, it was just today I heard there was a fat basket of cash on that boat, so I came running. And damned if I know what's on the Francisca tape because my Spanish isn't that good."

"Kayd is on there. So why didn't I come running?"

"That's one you won't have to answer. But you and I know the answer. Better roll it, Raoul Kelly."

Before Kelly got in, Sam bent and looked across at the girl beyond the steering wheel. "*Bien viaje. Buena suerte*," he said.

"*Mil gracias*," she answered, smiling. "*Adios, Señor*."

He turned to shake hands with Raoul, but received instead the gruffly sentimental *abrazo* of the semi-Americanized latino.

"I will tell Mrs. Boylston you are a remarkable man."

They backed out. The girl waved. The car waited at the mouth of the drive until a traffic gap large enough to accommodate it came along. Moments later they were lost in the anonymous patterns of all the east-bound flow of red tail lights.

He stood in the night shadows watching the traffic. He had an awareness of all the weight of the night city around him, of all the animal tensions of this single moment in time in this place, a shrewd and tawdry city, shining like toyland between the swamps and the sea. The night was weighted with derelicts and dancers, terminal breathing in wards, clenched fists of women as they pushed each time the pains came, chips in perfect alignment on green felt as men thumbed up the corners of the hole cars just enough to read the news, giggling young men in a chickenwire apartment painting the body of one of their chums a lovely gold, ambulances and tow trucks moving away in separate directions with a load of torn flesh or a load of ripped metal, thousands and thousands of picture tubes all telling the same jokes at the same instant to a hundred thousand living rooms, frantic rumps ram-packing the beach sand under the spread toweling, the simultaneous squirts of red tomato and yellow mustard in a hundred different places to disguise the flannelly taste of fried meat, a thousand simultaneous sobbings, thrashings, swallowings, vomitings, ejaculations, coughings, scratchings, cursings, shy touchings, whisperings, kickings . . . .

He had never considered himself particularly imaginative. Never before had he felt this way about a city, and he knew that it could only be possible in a strange city, and at a time when grief and uncertainty and introspection had sharpened and heightened awareness.

This great Gold Coast became a gigantic cruise ship moving through time rather than space, constantly assimilating the foods, the newborn, the gadgetry, spewing aft the unending tonnage of garbage and waste and dead bodies and broken toys, rolling imperceptibly in the slow tides of history, the passengers unaware that no city is forever, that it will end one day and the eternality of time will cover it in a silence of dust, sand and vines. Each passenger, whether first class or steerage, was compelled to accept the constants of pain and time, greed and need, joy and love, fear and lust, and the iron paradox of self-awareness.

Each passenger knew beyond doubt that he was the only one aboard who could truly experience the ultimates of love and loss, that he was the only one with a secret destiny which would be made manifest to him some day, and that on that day everyone would come to understand what should have been evident to them all along.

So I am an impertinence, he thought. The weight of the night city is the weight of indifference, because they are busy with their own changings of bandages, their own cautious reachings to find out if, after all, there is anyone near enough to touch.

And using my life to buy better accommodations aboard ship is only another way to keep from thinking too often how short the journey is for each passenger. Bix Kayd and Carolyn, Roger and Stella, Staniker and his wife, Leila and Oliver Akard, they are back there in the darkness left forever at that exact moment when they left the big cruise, and we go wallowing along toward one as yet unmarked minute in time, one for me, one for Lyd, one for Boy-Sam, one for Cristen Harkinson, one for Nurse Theyma Chappie, one for The Chunk.

There was a concept, a justification, almost within reach. It was like awakening in the night from a dream, knowing you have The Answer to Everything.

Like the old joke, he thought. Okay, so life *isn't* a grain of rice. Get a box, lawyer. Go yell the word from a park somewhere. Become one of those incredible people who have one simplified credo and try to make it fit every wrong in the world. Organic food.

Communist conspiracy. Early rising. Do unto others. THINK. Balanced diet. Zen tennis. Auto-hypnosis. Rosicrucianism. Fasting.

Step right up to the cave of mysteries and yell your solution at the audio-lock. Somebody is going to yell the right word some day, and when the door swings open and suddenly we all know the answer to that primary question—Why?—we may find it unendurable to live with that answer.

On Tuesday afternoon at four o'clock, June seventh, Sam Boylston sat across the steel desk from John Lobwohl. Kindler was over at the right, straight chair tilted back against the wall. The Staniker tape ended. Sam pushed rewind, and the little machine began to whirr the tape back onto the reel.

Lobwohl yawned. "You're all we needed, Mr. Boylston. A Texas lawyer messing up the scene, making like spy movies. Okay, it was your sister who died with the Kayd family. But what's the point in you trying to cover for Kelly and that maid?"

"I explained that. And Kelly explained it to Kindler and Scheff. I'm trying to make a point here. We'll never get to it unless you let me go through it in my own way, and ask the questions later."

"You're in a pretty poor position to try to make any points, Boylston. But go ahead."

"Would you say that those tapes give a fair basis for suspecting that accident was fishy, Captain?"

"How did you get those tapes anyway?"

"They can't be used as evidence of anything, so that's beside the point, isn't it? I want to know how you'd interpret them."

Kindler asked permission to speak. Lobwohl nodded. Kindler said, "It's a set piece all right. Memorized. But what I wonder is this. Staniker had a week alone on that island over there. He lost a good

boat and a lot of people. He was a hired captain. It was his liveli-
hood. So I think all that week, he'd be going over and over it, how
to say it, because he'd know there'd be a lot of questions if and when
he was rescued. So it would sound like that, like it had been memorized. And we can't exactly bring Staniker in and sweat it out of
him, Mr. Boylston."

"What can you nail Mrs. Harkinson with, Captain?"

"As far as I can see, absolutely nothing."

"But you'd like to find something you could make stick?"

"So bad everybody around here can taste it," Kindler said.

Lobwohl said, "We've got her stashed. Apartment hotel. Kind of
a compromise deal with her lawyer, Palmer Haas. Sneaked her out
at noon today. Two men outside her door at all times. Damn it, we
have some blanks to fill in. We've got to have that maid of hers."

"Let me ask a hypothetical question. Just imagine I happened to
have a tape of the maid's story, very detailed, covering everything of
interest to you. In Spanish, because she has little English. I listened
to the whole thing. I have enough Spanish to follow it. And suppose
I made proper identifications as the tape starts."

"As a lawyer, certainly you know that tape is not . . ."

"Captain, I'm not talking about admissibility. I'm talking about
leads and angles for investigation. And suppose I could give you a
very pertinent and substantial piece of information, one that might
change your thinking on the whole matter. Would you then, if you
think the information valuable enough, slack off on trying to bring
Francisca back here?"

Lobwohl pondered the question, sighed and said, "You told me
you do not handle criminal cases. Do you know anything about po-
roscopy?"

"Only that it takes a good man to get it across to a jury without
confusing them."

"Right. The sweat pores on the ridges of prints have as distinctive and unique a pattern as the prints themselves, and we use it when we have fragmentary prints." He opened a large folder on his desk and said, "Come around here, Boylston. This is the palm print we found on the rim of the tub in that number ten cottage. Here is the palm print Mrs. Harkinson let the Lab take for comparison purposes. We have twelve characteristic points of similarity, making it a positive match. She explains plausibly how she happened to leave the print on the tub on Friday night when she went to see Staniker. Now look at this area here." He pointed to the pad at the base of the thumb. "This next glossy is a blowup of that portion of the hand, using a waxy material to bring up the pore structure. Ink hides it. Here is an impression of that same area. It came off the barrel of the 22 rifle. Here is another taken from the aluminum tiller bar of the sailboat. All we can really nail down is four points of similarity on the gunbarrel impression, and five points on the tiller impression. No absolute value as evidence."

"What does she say?"

"What she says now is filtered through Palmer Haas. She says that as she was taking sailing lessons, it would not be surprising to have some sort of print on the tiller bar. She says also that Oliver brought the gun over because of the palm-tree rats. He shot five of them and buried them next to the roots of some kind of plant out there."

"Scheff found them," Kindler said.

"She says that she remembered the gun and before she took her sleeping pill, she took it down and put it in the boat so he wouldn't have the excuse of coming back for it. Right now we are trying to locate any friend of the Akard boy who could have brought him around to get the sailboat out of her little boat basin Sunday evening."

Lobwohl, yawning again, got up and went over to the chalk

board on his office wall. Swiftly he drew a shoreline, a crude outline of the Harkinson house, a symbol for the sailboat, a box to show where the boy's car was parked.

"Here is what we have to wonder about, Boylston. Was the palm print made Friday night or Sunday night. Lab found two blonde hairs in the cottage, and microscopic comparison of root structure and cross sections show they came from her head. Were they left there Friday or Sunday night? What would the scheduling be if they were left there Sunday night. The boy comes and gets the boat, because apparently she was still there when it was gone. He picks her up, sails down to where he left the car. They go see Staniker and kill him. Drive back in his car. The boy sails her back to her place and leaves her off. Then he can't stand the thought of losing her forever and the idea of having helped kill somebody, so he knocks himself off. You see the hole in all that, of course."

"Motive," Sam Boylston said. "She would have a lot easier ways of shedding a boyfriend. What if I could give you all the motive you'd need?"

Lobwohl, teetering from heel to toe, regarded him somberly. "You wouldn't get on my nerves so bad, Boylston. That's all I can give you."

Sam Boylston hesitated and then took the two tapes in their metal boxes out of his jacket pocket. "These are the Francisca Torcedo tapes. In Spanish, so you'll need a transcript in English."

Lobwohl held them out to Kindler. "Put Lopez on it."

"Don't say anything fascinating until I'm through in the kitchen," Kindler said as he left.

"They goofed," Lobwohl said. "Scheff and Kindler. When they couldn't come up with the maid, they had to tell me how it happened. Telling it practically made their teeth ache. They're the best I've got in homicide. Want to know a funny thing? If they hadn't goofed, I wouldn't still have the case. There are some people upstairs who like to reach down and take over the jazzy cases, if everything is going smooth. It is a celebrity angle. But if things are going a little sour, they'd rather have it stay down here where the pros are. No glory in having to make explanations."

When Kindler came back he had Barney Scheff with him. Scheff was introduced. He did not seem entirely pleased to know Sam Boylston. They sat down.

When Lobwohl nodded at Sam, he said, "If you check it out you will find that Bixby Kayd and Ferris Fontaine were associated in some business ventures. You will find that the members of the inner circle sometimes held their conferences aboard the boat Fontaine gave his mistress. I can guess that Kayd was aboard that cruiser for one or more of those meetings. When you get the transcript of the Francisca tapes, you will find out that Bix Kayd visited Cristen Harkinson at her home on the last day of March, a little over two weeks before he arrived back in Miami and hired Staniker. He had a rental limousine and driver. You should be able to trace that. Questions?"

Lobwohl no longer looked tired enough to yawn. "Is this the implication? Kayd was trying to locate Staniker through Crissy Harkinson?"

"Because he could have heard and remembered that Staniker knew the Islands well. And because he would know Fontaine wouldn't have used a hired captain who couldn't keep his mouth shut about private affairs and business deals. This is speculation, of course."

"And so?" the Captain asked.

"And so there happened to be eight hundred thousand dollars in cash aboard the Muñeca when that accident happened."

The three police faces had the same listening look as, in the silence, they reshuffled the facts.

"Son of a bitch," murmured Barney Scheff. "Why cash?"

"To swing a land deal, buy some votes on a Board."

"Will we be able to prove that money was aboard?" Lobwohl asked.

"Not a chance. The people who can verify it would lie like hell to save their skins from the tax man."

"Have you ever heard of withholding evidence?" Lobwohl asked with dangerous courtesy.

Sam Boylston looked hurt and astonished. "Without information about the money, I didn't have a thing worth telling, Captain. I got a lead on the money this morning, from a friend of a friend, and here I am."

"This gets out," Scheff said, "and the news guys are going to fall on the floor and foam at the mouth and giggle themselves to death."

Lobwohl hit his own forehead lightly with the heel of his right hand. "Friday she goes to see Staniker. He tells her where he cached the money. If she was sure he wasn't lying, and the money was reasonably safe, the best thing for her would be Staniker dead."

"And," said Kindler with a certain note of awe, "he was the deadest looking dead I ever did see. He was a husk, like something shed him and crawled off."

"Captain," Sam said, "what is the time of death on Staniker?"

"Ten o'clock, plus or minus an hour."

"When you get the transcript of the Francisca tape, you'll see that it takes Mrs. Harkinson out of the picture. I could understand enough of it to realize Raoul Kelly was being very thorough about nailing down the exact times. Francisca looked in and saw Mrs. Harkinson asleep in her bed at quarter after nine. There was a night light on. Later, at quarter to midnight, Francisca and Kelly heard the pump running and knew Mrs. Harkinson was using water in the main house. At ten past midnight Mrs. Harkinson called Francisca on the intercom and asked for some cocoa and crackers. She said she had awakened and taken a shower to see if it would relax her enough to go back to sleep, but it hadn't. With the gates locked and with no car available to her, I guess it would check out that she just wouldn't have had time to sail two miles, drive with the boy to Coral Gables, drive back, sail back to her place. It could be done, I suppose, if Staniker was all ready to hop into the tub and hold his wrists out. But you say he took on a pretty fair load of alcohol and barbiturates. It would take time for that to work."

"Assuming," said Lobwohl, "that the maid wasn't given a little present of money to establish those times, Mr. Boylston."

"No. Not that one. Or Kelly."

"So you're a great judge of character, eh?" Scheff asked Sam.

"Knock it off," Lobwohl ordered. "Let's see where we are. You represent Kelly and the maid, Boylston. We've got tangible evidence that the Akard kid killed Staniker. If he'd cut one wrist and fixed the door so it would lock when he left, we might have bought it as suicide, at least until we got a look at what was in the kid's wallet. Harv says with the kid it was definitely suicide. The arm was long enough and the barrel short enough, and the muzzle was right in his ear when he thumbed the trigger. And I don't see how we've got a chance in the world of proving the Harkinson woman pressured the kid into killing Staniker. We keep the Harkinson woman on ice until the Grand Jury indicts Akard on a murder first charge, then takes up Akard as a new matter and accepts our file and calls it suicide. Now let me make a little prediction. The Harkinson woman will disappear. She'll sell that house. And some day she'll go pick up all that money. So I wonder a little about you, Boylston. You're convinced she was the moving force behind Staniker's killing the people, taking the money, and convincing a lot of people it was an accident. We have you and we have your sister's boyfriend, that Jonathan Dye, to wonder about. You just don't look like somebody who's going to say it's too bad, she got away with it, let's go home and forget it. There's something about you Texans. Maybe it's a vigilante attitude. A sense of family. Blood for blood. You're a lawyer. You should know better. But I wonder if you do."

Sam heard his own accent thicken as he said mildly, "And I wonder if it's any of your business to wonder, Cap'n."

"Where is the Dye boy?"

"Looking for Leila. Searching the Great Bahama Bank. Leased a catamaran and hired the fellow who owns it. He's sure she got out of it somehow."

"He must be out of his damn mind!" Scheff said.

Sam sighed audibly. "Before all this happened, I would have appointed myself to bring him to his senses. Sure. I would have told Kelly it was foolish to take Francisca out of the state. What the hell good is logical behavior? It's a cold satisfaction, gentlemen. I can verify that. I have always been a very logical type. You have to let people be as irrational as they want to be, and maybe there are better reasons than you know. Maybe what Jonathan is doing isn't a crazy one-man search party and nothing but that. Maybe out there on those flats he's putting up a bridge, a way to cross from a life with Leila in it to a life without her. He knows she wouldn't have even been aboard that boat if I hadn't sent her off with the Kayds to try to bust up the romance. I wanted to bust it up so she'd marry into the kind of status I thought was important, so I wouldn't have to explain to people that my sister was off do-gooding in the jungle someplace for a very small dollar. Jonathan offended me because he doesn't give a damn about the things I thought were important. I was awake at dawn this morning. I was making up a conversation, explaining to Jonathan what I was going to do. I could develop certain contacts, and I could afford to pay the fee to have some specialists pick up the Harkinson woman very quietly and take her to the right place and turn her over to me. But Jonathan kept asking me why. I told him because I expect it of myself. Then he asked me if I expected it of myself, or expected it of the man I have been imitating all my life. Good question. He wanted to know if I thought Leila would approve. Another good question. But I can't just let go of it! Not all the way!"

He noticed that they were looking at him with strange expressions. He realized why, and shook his head and laughed at them. "The lawyer has flipped, huh? Ever notice how uneasy people get if you try to say some of the weird things that happen inside your head? I used to hold everything back. That's part of the incantation, because if you let go, They come after you. I'm going to try to tell people what I think. It's going to raise hell with my law practice. But it's the only way I can think of to stop being completely alone in the world."

"You've been under a lot of strain," Lobwohl said.

"Starting before any of this started. Anxiety building up for years. The pursuit of perfection. But I imagine I'll take one small hack at playing God. Some photographer is going to get a good shot of Crissy Harkinson. I'll arrange to get some prints. I'll turn them over to somebody who went into the deal with Bix Kayd and took a whipping. I'll just tell them there's a good chance she knows exactly where the money is. There'll be no place in the world she can hide."

Twenty-five

ALL DAY WEDNESDAY Corpo kept thinking of chores he had been meaning to do.

An hour before sunset Leila Boylston marched up to him where he was nailing a crude brace to the side of the stairway.

"This is about enough!" she said.

He turned and smiled at her. "Getting hongry, Missy?"

"Now don't you start that. Sarg, you made a sacred promise on your word of honor. I'm all ready to go. I've *been* all ready since morning. And you've been dragging your feet all day. I'm really getting *very* angry with you."

"I've been thinking on it, Miss Leila. Make more sense to get a nice start in the morning, don't you think?"

She stamped her foot and began to cry. Ten minutes later she was still snuffling as the Sergeant slowly threaded his narrow channel at the wheel of the Muñequita, towing his skiff on a short line astern.

"Kindly please stop them crying noises," the Sergeant said. "I'm doing like you want, okay?"

"I c-can't help it, I'm so huh-happy."

"Happy to get shut of the ol' Sergeant. Sure."

"I'll come back to see you. I promised. I'll bring Jonathan and Sam. They'll want to thank you for everything."

"Hardly likely," he grumbled. "Never will see you again, Missy. Never figured on liking anybody around. You did get me real edged up a lot of times, but mostly there was more good to it than bad."

"Thank you."

"No cause for thanks. You wrote down the count on that money?"

"Right on your calendar. You shouldn't keep all that cash around, really. And I'm going to pay back what you spent on me."

"It was a present. I keep telling you. I never held with trousers on girls, but you look right good in that there pair."

When he came to the mouth of his channel he slowed, then edged out very cautiously. A tug was taking a big dredge north along the Waterway. About a mile to the north-west, a red runabout was towing three water skiers.

"Clear enough, I guess," he said and moved out, following the natural channel across the flats, and then, as he reached deeper water, he turned south and looked back to see how the skiff rode as he increased speed.

"What we'll do," he called over the louder noise of the two engines. "I'll take you down close enough so you can see a place where you should tie up. You go in slow with it. Nothing fancy. You understand how?"

"I steer toward the side of the dock and I pull these two things back to half way and kind of coast, and before I bump I pull them back all the way to reverse, and then push them to half way and turn off the keys."

"I'll stay in the skiff close by and when I see you've made it, I'll go on back home."

"And I won't remember a thing about who took care of me, Sarg."

About a mile and a half south of his island, Corpo saw a fast launch coming from the direction of town. He eased well off to starboard so they would pass at a good distance. After he was by he looked back and saw the launch make a big fast white-water turn and start coming up very fast behind him.

Corpo stood with his hands locked on the wheel. He heard the pursuing boat slap through his wake. It came up beside him, twenty feet away on the port side, siren growling as it slowed to his speed. He did not look over at them.

"Sergeant!" the familiar voice shouted. "Sergeant Corpo! Kill those engines! Now!"

He pulled the throttles back. The bow lifted and then settled. He put both drives in neutral, turned both keys. He moved back from the wheel and still not looking toward the Lieutenant, he sagged down into a sitting position on the deck. He closed his eyes and rocked slowly back and forth. When your eyes were closed, voices sounded funny. Like the people were talking into empty barrels.

With vivid flashing eyes, body rigid with anger and indignation, Miss Boylston looked directly at Dave Dickerson, then at Gordon Dale, then at Chief Cooley. "I am *not* going to be given a sedative, gentlemen! I am *not* going to be knocked out. And the business of Sergeant Corpo is *not* going to be set aside so you can take care of it later."

"All I said was . . ."

"I heard what you said, Mr. Dale. Should I call you Lieutenant the way Sarg does? You and I happen to be the only people in the world he gives one damn about, and I am not going to talk about anything to anybody until I have some kind of guarantee you'll leave him alone."

"I don't rightly see how we can do that," said Chief Cooley.

"Lock him up, eh? The wonderful answer to everything. I would like to speak to Mr. Dale in private."

Cooley sighed, nodded at Detective Sergeant Dickerson and they left the hospital room. "Mr. Dale, are you getting tired of being responsible for Sergeant Corpo? Is this just a wonderful opportunity to stick him back into a veterans hospital for the rest of his life?"

"You're very young, Miss Boylston. He held you there on that island over two weeks. He didn't seek medical attention for you. He did not report finding the boat and finding you. He told me that in front of Chief Cooley. It's out of my hands."

"If you want it out of your hands. That's my point. When he found me he thought I was dying. I guess I should have been. I think if he tried to bring me in when he found me, I could have died on the way. He is simple, and he is confused, but he certainly is smart enough to know what would happen to him if he brought a girl's body to the city dock. He is confused about what happened. When I regained consciousness he was going to bring me in. But I begged him not to. I pleaded with him."

"Why?"

"I couldn't remember what happened. I knew somebody wanted to kill me. I didn't want them to find me. I wanted to stay right there on his island where I felt safe. He was very sweet and very gentle, and he did not do anything out of line at all. Why do you people want to punish him for doing what I asked him to do? How was he to know?"

"Then your memory came back."

"Don't look at me in that skeptical way. I remembered, and I asked him to bring me here to town. That's what he was doing when you and that cop started showing off, blowing sirens and waving a gun."

"Dickerson picked up the name on the transom with the glasses. The Muñequita. What was any cop supposed to do?"

"That's beside the point. He's no danger to himself or anyone else. He's a gentle person. He was released in your custody. He admires you. What's the matter with you? Does it spoil your image to have to look out for a disabled man who saved your life?"

"Now just a minute!"

"Don't get stuffy with me. You remind me of my brother. He's a lawyer too. You're all defensive because you haven't been doing your job, Mr. Dale."

"I've done everything possible to . . ."

"To let him go his own way. So you've let him accumulate over twenty-three thousand dollars in cash in two ammunition boxes in that crazy shack of his."

"That *much!*"

"If you cared, you'd know how much. We have something in common. He saved my life too. Why don't you buy the island from the state? Would it cost more than he's got?"

"I don't know. Probably not."

"If he can't own property, if he's legally incompetent, borrow the money from him and buy it and lease it to him for the rest of his life for a dollar. When he dies, dedicate it as a bird sanctuary or some damned thing. But right now, please, get those fools to let him out of the cage they've put him in and let him go back to his island. This is a lousy time for you to give up on him."

He looked at her. "The minute I heard about his shopping spree I should have gone out there. But I didn't. Too busy. Too indifferent. Too much trouble. So I'm annoyed at myself, and I feel guilty, so the Sergeant is a handy target. Okay, girl. I'll fight them off and pry him loose one more time."

"As many more times as you have to."

"But humor me a little. Let me keep telling myself it's the last time."

The nurse gave Sam Boylston a shy and luminous smile and ducked out of the room, closing the door gently. He approached the bed, shocked at her emaciated look, yet with a great joy that it was indeed Leila. On the way up, traveling at high speed in the official sedan, he had convinced himself that it was a case of some stupid girl hunting for publicity. With her eyes closed Leila looked emptied of all her familiar vitality.

As he neared the bed she opened her eyes and looked quite vaguely at him, then gave a yelp of joy, grinned widely, stretched her arms out to him and began to cry. He bent awkwardly over the bed to hold her in a close embrace.

"Hey," she said. "Hey, Sam. You're not supposed to cry too. You play things cool."

"Very cool. Very remote. Sure, honey. I've taken up crying lately. I might have to use it on a jury sometime."

He pulled a chair close to her bed. She blew her nose. "You know something, Sambo? I've never been really sure you love me. I guess you do. I guess you sent me on that crummy cruise because you love me. Where's Jonathan?"

"Hunting for you. In a homemade boat out there on the Bank. Maybe they've made radio contact by now. He—He knew you weren't dead. Everybody knew you were. Everybody but him. Fool performance. He wanted to do it. I gave him some money."

"You? Financing foolishness?"

"I wanted somebody believing in it, even if I knew it wasn't true."

"If I'd died, he'd have felt that I wasn't in the world any more.

He'd have felt the emptiness. I would if he died. You go into one room, and you can tell if the whole house is empty. You can always tell. Damn it, they made me take a sedative. They keep prodding at me and saying Hmmm and Hmph. It scalds them they can't find something wrong, really wrong."

"Leila, have they told you how they want to handle this?"

"Yes. Complete loss of memory. But—I do remember. God, I remember! Have they found that crazy man?"

"Take it easy, Leila. A man named Lobwohl wants to talk to you. Friend of mine. I'll call Lyd while he's talking to you. Is there anything I can get you?"

"Jonathan, and quickly please."

At nine o'clock on Thursday morning, the red and white float plane came snoring and chattering down to circle the catamaran. Jonathan realized how silent his world had been. Sounds of the sea birds, slap of waves, creak of mast, the long exhalations of the wind. He thought the plane might be in trouble. It straightened out and ran downwind, then turned and landed, heading directly for them. Stanley turned the cat directly into the eye of the gentle breeze. The sail flapped. The plane stopped a hundred feet away, and then with short, sharp bursts it came toward them. Two dozen feet away the engine coughed and died. A man in weather-bleached khakis climbed out and stood on the float.

"Jonathan Dye?" the man called.

"That's right, who are you?"

"Can you heave a line over?"

Stanley caught some wind and moved closer. He threw the line, and the pilot caught it deftly, made it fast to a brace. Stanley dropped the sail and pulled the catamaran and float plane together.

"What do you want?" Jonathan asked.

"Want to give you a plane ride, boy."

"No thanks."

"Had a time finding you the way the glare comes off these flats. I would say that from here it is just under a hundred miles a few points off due west, there's a little Boylston girl wondering what's taking me so long."

Jonathan stared at the pilot. He was a crickety old man, charred by the sun, brows and hair bleached white, tiny bright blue eyes, teeth like spoiled corn.

"Flew wet goods out of these islands, you know, until that goddam FDR blew the business all to hell. The little bit you can tote in one of those old buckets, all struts and fabric and spit, it had to be prime goods to pay off. Ask anybody. They'll tell you Jake Lord has flew everything that can get off the runway. Get your gear together now, boy."

"She's alive?" Jonathan asked. "Leila?"

He saw the mouth moving, knew the man was making words, but he could no longer hear them. He felt as if each of these long and silent days had been pulling some part of him to an unbearable thinness and length and tension, like a silvery ribbon reaching from him to the most distant pieces of rock and scrub they had searched.

"She's dead!" he bayed, as the strand broke. Then Stanley Moree was close to him, grin big, eyes wet, chopping his fist into Jonathan's upper arm, telling him he was one crazy mon, and he would bring his woman back one day, and they would sail and sing and laugh.

When the float plane turned back into the wind and lifted, Jonathan looked down and saw Stanley waving from the deck of the cat.

On Friday, in the early afternoon of the tenth day of June, John Lobwohl had lunch with Palmer Haas in a booth in one of the back alcoves of Fritzhoff's.

Haas, a small man in his middle thirties, had the aggressive tough-nut face of a workmanlike welterweight, one of the spoilers managers avoid when they are bringing a promising boy up through the ratings.

"Now what the hell, Johnny! What the hell!" Palmer Haas said in his abrupt rasping voice.

"Now don't plant your feet. Okay? I know and you know that you're not going to enter into any conspiracy against your client."

"You've got a better name?"

"Let's call it a search for truth."

"Real idealism, Captain. Makes my eyes sting a little."

"Any client deserves the best you've got. This one, this Cristen Harkinson is as poisonous as they come."

"Johnny, would you say to a doctor don't treat that fellow, he beats up on his wife and kids?"

"All right. You have a professional obligation. Everybody is entitled to every protection under the law. And we're both stuck with the antagonist theory. I am a cop. My job is to accumulate a solid file, one with a reasonable chance of conviction, and present it to the States Attorney. Then you and him fight. Except for my people testifying for the prosecution, I'm out of the picture from that point on."

"Except you throw them too many files with big holes in the middle, you get shifted into some other line of cop work, Johnny."

The waiter brought the two steinkrugs of dark draft beer. Lobwohl took several deep swallows and set the stein down. "That confrontation rocked her, Palmy. You saw that. The last thing she ever expected was somebody to show up off that Muñeca. The Boylston girl tired fast, but she gave us a picture of how Staniker acted and what he said, and how he sawed the Kayd girl's throat open that was as convincing as anything either of us are ever going to hear."

"But it was essentially bush, my friend. And having that Sam

Boylston, the brother, right there was bush too. He never took his eyes off my client. You want to see what murder looks like before it happens, it was right there in his eyes. But it was a damn fool tick. You know better."

"It shook her. But you put on your big act about trickery and so on and it gave her time to steady down."

"I get paid to put on my acts."

"Let me ask you this. In complete confidence. An opinion between friends. What if the Boylston girl had been found in time for us to grab Staniker alive? Now forget all this crap about jurisdiction. Pretend it happened in my back yard. I've put my cards face up for you. Kayd visited Crissy Harkinson. Staniker gets the captain job. The Boylston girl's story verifies what her lawyer brother dug up about the money. Don't you think, based on what we both know and can guess about Staniker, that he would sing it all loud and clear, and implicate Harkinson?"

"Why should I make guesses about something that didn't happen?"

"Because if the timing was different, we could have nailed her to the wall."

"If your aunt had balls she'd be your uncle, Johnny."

"She is very good, this Crissy. And she's running in enough luck to make it work out for her. Once the Muñeca took off, she recruited a patsy for what she had in mind. Not some smart-ass kid, but exactly the kind of dumb idealistic kid she could con into taking care of a little problem called Staniker. The size of the stink has startled her a little. She didn't guess how much there'd be. All she has to do is ride the wave, keep her head down, and eventually she's home free."

"Which means, Johnny, you can't build a solid file."

"That's my problem."

"And that confrontation, that little masterpiece of Perry Mason drama, was bush-league desperation. You sweetened me into a little friendly cooperation, and then you pull that on my client."

"The file isn't solid. But there are some funny bits in it that don't match up."

"I bleed for you, Captain. You conned her into a hell of a lot of so-called voluntary interrogation before she had the representation she should have had from the start. That was your big chance, and I think she was a little too cute for you. You blew it."

"Let me tell you something, Palmer Haas. Or ask you something. This file we've got. If she was pure dog, a dismal ugly woman, and if almost anybody in this area was representing her beside you, I think I'd take a chance and try to go with what we've got. But she's got too much presence and looks and quickness of mind, and you'd use your challenges to set up a jury that would give her the most brownie points based on those assets."

"And charge her with what, man?"

"Accessory. Murder one."

"Come *on!* What do you take me for?"

"Palmy, do you remember how we got to know each other? Six years back, wasn't it? That Todd couple. There were two places in the cross examination where you could have objected and didn't. Why?"

"Simple ignorance, Captain."

"I contend that you knew they were guilty as hell and I contend you knew that was the only place where it could be opened up, and I contend that pair of butcher abortionists sickened you, just as that retired Atlanta whore sickens me. I further contend that in these past six years you've lowered your sights, Counsellor. You're hooked on your batting average, and the better the average, the bigger the fees and the more of a celebrity you become."

"Thanks for the lunch. I don't have to take this crap from anybody. See you around."

John Lobwohl found himself quite suddenly alone in the booth. You have to try. That's the only constant. But, he thought, maybe the flaw is in trying harder when you can feel no pity, trying a little harder to nail the cold, clever, amoral ones, perhaps out of some pitiful compulsion to try to improve the world. The world penned up the sheep with the tigers, and nothing you could do until you could prove that was real lambs wool between the great white fangs.

Palmer Haas slid suddenly into the booth. "Six guys at the bar gave me the jolly greeting when I was on my way out, Johnny. It gave me that good old warm glow. I'm a real celebrity. What's really on your mind?"

"I'm going to give you all the funny pieces out of the file. If it ever comes to trial, you might dig up most of them beforehand, but not all. After you get these pieces, then I ask a favor. When you say no, you've gotten all our ammunition free."

"Interesting risk."

"First item: She said she'd never been to those Mooney cottages before. She said she had a hard time finding them, a week ago tonight. We took some sneak shots of Harkinson. I assembled a set of ten similar photos, ten women, blonde, about the same age bracket. Staniker had been there one night back in April, as G. Stanley from Tampa. I sent Mercer and Tuck to see that little hump-back lady that operates the place, on the very slim chance maybe Crissy had been with him and the dwarf lady had a glimpse of her. She said she couldn't remember any woman, and then when she went through the pictures she got a reaction to the Harkinson woman. She got flustered. She went into some kind of a wild story about remembering an outside screen wasn't hooked on the cottage they were in, and going to fix it so the wind wouldn't blow it off, and seeing the two of them in there. It turns out she's a peeper, and goes scooting around in the night with her little aluminum kitchen ladder. She nailed the ID a little more solid by describing the car the blonde arrived in, a little white foreign convertible, parked beside Staniker's Olds in front of the place. She watched some pretty strenuous fun and games, apparently. That was at about the same time, according to Crissy, she was breaking up forever with Staniker. And it means she lied about never having been there before. Conclusion: They were setting up a hideout for Staniker after he got back from the Islands.

"Second item: She claims she did not tell the Akard boy where Staniker was. She guesses he probably followed her. Yet on that same Friday night Sam Boylston tried to follow her, and she pulled a very smart trick, exactly the same trick Staniker pulled on Raoul Kelly when he tried to tail Staniker that same day."

Palmer Haas asked what ruse was used, and Lobwohl described it. "Nothing much yet," Haas said. "Keep going."

John Lobwohl recounted the deft way Crissy had tricked Kindler and Scheff into letting her dispose of a bundle of something or other when they drove her in. "We phoned Kelly in Texas," Lobwohl said, "and he questioned his girl. As far as the maid knows, Crissy never bought yard goods, never used a dressmaker. We combed that shopping center and came up empty. Conclusion: She wanted to get rid of something, and improvised a good story and dropped the bundle in a trash can, and it is long gone."

"What would have been in it?"

"Something worth getting rid of with as much cold nerve as a burglar." With his hands he showed the dimensions of the bundle as Kindler and Scheff had described it.

"Anything else?"

"Yes. And it doesn't make any sense either. Mercer and Tuck searched the Akard boy's room. There was a dufflebag in the back of his closet, packed for a trip. They found a duplicate of the note found in his pocket. It was under the blotter on his desk in his bedroom. It was almost identical to the note on the body. There was one change. The note on the body said at the end, 'I have to get everything straightened out in my head before I do something real crazy.' The one in the room said 'things' instead of 'everything'."

"As if one was a first draft?"

"Which one?"

Haas drained the stein and set it down. "The trouble with this, beginning to end, the ones you want to ask questions, they just aren't around any more. Questions from your point of view, of course. My job is to defend my client to the best of my ability."

"You know what's holding her together, don't you?"

"How do you mean, Johnny?"

"All that pie in the sky. She hangs on through this and she'll never have any pain again. As Boylston said this morning, now that we know Staniker didn't have the use of the Muñequita, the places where he could have hidden the money narrows down."

"What direction are you going?"

"There's an interrogation room over at Female Detention. You said this morning, Palmy, that we by God better have charges to file or we better leave your client alone. You said you were all through advising her to cooperate in any way. You said you wouldn't let your client be used for fishing expeditions."

"And I said it loud."

"I would like to have you bring her in again, smuggle her in through the back way and up to Room C, third floor, east wing. Very routine stuff. All very polite. You and me, two of my people, recording clerks, and Sam Boylston if you agree."

"I haven't agreed to any part of it."

"I ask permission to have her taken down to the little ID section downstairs for a photograph. Nothing to be construed as being in any way a charge against her. I explain that we are being swamped by crazies who claim to have seen her in a hundred different places, and this will just help weed out the ones who are sick-minded."

"And I just sit there and say, go ahead, Johnny, old buddy."

"It just happens that the matron who'll take her down there belongs to the same church as the Akards. She's called Little Annie. She's been teamed with another matron named Norstund for a couple of years. There will be a little misunderstanding."

"Now come *on*, Captain!"

"I swear to you on my word of honor that there will be no brutality. Those two are competent people. They will pay absolutely no attention to anything she says. They'll probably be talking to each other about their favorite soap opera. If Harkinson puts up a fight, they'll subdue her without hurting her or marking her. They'll merely put her through the complete physical search routine, from hair roots to rubber gloves, that they give suspected female pushers. They'll scrub her down in a disinfectant shower, put her in gray twill and paper slippers and bring her back up to Room C."

"Have you lost your mind, Lobwohl?"

"This isn't social register goods, Palmy. This isn't a first horrid contact with ugly reality. But it's been a long time for her. A long, lush time. Maybe she's forgotten what that special kind of indignity feels like."

"How can I justify letting a client in for . . ."

"Why do you have to? You don't even know there's going to be a little misunderstanding. The basic request is reasonable."

"Just a lousy moralistic Christer cop after all."

"But here is what I lay on the line. So you can get your kicks, Counsellor. If Lady Harkinson rides with it, you can cover yourself by making an official complaint. Then, you see, I can't stay out of it and let the two matrons take the grief. I stand up at the hearing and say they did it on my orders."

"Do you know what that might mean?"

"I do indeed."

"Johnny, you want this one real bad, I guess."

"This bad. If I can't nail this one, I think I will stop giving much of a damn about any of them from now on."

"She's tough. She's hard as stones, Captain Johnny. I tell you what. I'll bring her in. I'll have her there at four. A picture? I can advise her to cooperate. But forget all this other stuff. Okay?"

Lobwohl said slowly, "You couldn't bring her in if you thought I was fool enough to try anything as stupid as that. You wouldn't be living up to your obligations to your client. Okay. We'll have a final chat with her, take a picture, apologize and let it go at that."

"Takes about fifteen minutes to get a good picture?"

"Twenty, sometimes. You know how it is."

"I'll just have to be patient. Thanks again for lunch. Your kids want my autograph?"

"Next year, maybe, Palmy. They're still hooked on the Green Bay Packers. Retarded, I guess."

Twenty-six

SAM BOYLSTON WATCHED the door swing shut as Crissy Harkinson left with the matron. The name for it was presence, he thought. Control so perfect there was mockery behind it. Today a little green dress with white trim. White gloves, shoes, purse, and jaunty little white hat on the sunstreaked casual hair. Wraparound glasses, very dark. Sensuous flavor of perfume still hanging in the air after the sway of the round hips under cool green fabric had disappeared into the corridor.

Scheff sighed and lifted a laundry case onto the table top and took out the bricks of white paper wrapped in manila bands.

"More funny tricks, Captain?" Palmer Haas asked.

"What this is," Scheff said, "it's from that time we had to fix up a dummy ransom, the guy was already dead before the FBI got into the act even."

"Mr. Haas," Lobwohl said, "I am not going to make any statement or ask any question about what might appear to be on the table when she comes back into this room. She knows nothing about any money according to her testimony thus far."

Sam Boylston reached into his inner jacket pocket and took out the thick envelope and slid it down the table to Scheff. Scheff opened it and began to doctor each brick of paper by sliding a bill under the brown band on both sides of it.

Haas said, "I wish to make an official objection to Mr. Boylston being here."

"You objected last time too," Lobwohl said.

"Why should he be permitted to help you with your shabby little tricks, Captain?"

"If I requisitioned this much cash, how long do you think it would take me to get it?"

"Maybe two weeks," Kindler said, "and with a guy assigned to it who wouldn't let it out of his sight."

"The way you're handling this, Lobwohl, is offensive to me," Haas said. "I'm letting you get away with . . ."

"With murder?" John Lobwohl asked.

Scheff finished doctoring the packages. He stacked them in an orderly and impressive heap on the table top.

Haas looked at his watch. "Isn't this taking too long, just for a photograph?"

"Maybe," Lobwohl said lazily, "I've got people down there beating her with rubber hoses."

"I'm beginning to wonder. I think this case is too big for you, Captain. The publicity makes you dizzy. You keep getting these delusions. I don't like this money nonsense. The minute my client comes back through that door I'm going to tell her to keep her mouth shut."

"You do your job and I do mine," Lobwohl said.

"You shouldn't use your office to try to punish immorality, my friend. You are an officer of the law, not an avenging angel. I demand that I be taken to my client right now."

Lobwohl asked Kindler to go see what the delay was. Kindler went out. As the door started to swing shut he pushed it open and said, "She's being brought back right now, sir."

Kindler had a tone of awe in his voice. He moved back into the interrogation room, holding the door wide. Little Annie, five ten, wide as two women, face of pale granite, nocolor eyes, gray hair pulled into a tight bun, marched in a swift choppy stride. Behind her came Crissy Harkinson, in a clumsy jolting trot, hair stringy damp, head humbly bowed, clad in a gray twill prison dress three sizes too large for her. Sam saw that Little Annie was using a come-along, a small loop of chain that went over the prisoner's thumb and was tightened by turning a short metal bar the guard held in the palm of the hand. It would cause pain only when the prisoner tried to hold back.

Little Annie took her past the table and over to the blank wall. She slipped the chain off the thumb. Head still bowed, Crissy Harkinson backed against the wall. She was breathing hard. She knuckled a strand of the damp hair away from her eye. There was a vivid odor of lysol in the room.

Sam had the feeling that the shocking transformation had made everyone forget their lines and their plans.

"I must ask you to let me answer any questions asked," said Palmer Haas in what struck Sam as a strangely mild tone.

She lifted her gaze a little further and saw the money. She held her breath and then began panting as before. She seemed to be chewing an imaginary wad of gum. She knuckled her hair back. She made a whinnying giggle. "She thought it was *laughs* one left. Not last. Laughs. Grabbed that silly nigger bitch and ran her into the crapper after lights out, beat on her for laughing. Oh Jesus, what a great place he picked, huh? Big old rusty boiler, he said. Half full of sand. Nobody'll look there. Shit! That's the ball game. Poor little Olly didn't have the balls to cut his wrists even. Had to do it for him. Should have known you bastards would win. Botched the boat thing, let the little bitch float off. Ran over his own tow line for chrissake."

The silence in the room was intense, awed, as deadly as fatal disease. She made a chewing sound. "Knew when it was sour. Stuck his little toy gun in his ear. Had it right up against the gunnel where I could pick it up in the dark. Sweet dumb jackassy kid thumping and banging around in the bottom of that boat. Nothing at all left in his head but getting laid. Nothing. Hit my knee getting off onto my dock. Aimed him off, southeast, loop on the tiller bar. Know what?"

"That's enough!" Palmer Haas shouted at her, getting to his feet.

"I thought it was all roses," she said. "Then I looked in at my bed and it was like something suddenly sliding sideways in my head. That thing I fixed in my bed was *me!* And the thing outside looking in, it was made of a wig and a pillow and towels."

Haas moved toward her saying, "Stop talking, Cristen!"

She straightened herself from her hunched over position, her face showing strain. "I don't know. I keep getting these cramps all the time, like I should woops my cookies, but I can't make it." She shook her head. "Funny. Like when I was thirteen, waiting down in that storage place off the furnace room, in the dark, wondering about rats, waiting for Mister Liborio to come and do it. I made him get me a whole five pound sack of that candy, then I didn't have to give a shit whether old Satchel-Ass laid a demerit on me or not, but you know, it spoiled the game, jumping the squares to see who'd win, because what's the point in winning when you got enough hid to make you sick of candy?"

Haas, standing near her, reached to take her arm, apparently to try to get her attention, to make her stop. When he reached, she dodged violently, arm coming up to guard her head from a blow. Still holding her arm up, she stood in a crouch, and looked up at Haas, wary eyes looked out from under the crooked elbow, mouth making the childish chewing motions.

"I'm your lawyer," Palmer Haas said gently. "I'm not going to hurt you."

She lowered her arm and straightened up. "Oh hell, I know that. Let me tell you. I can make out. All you smart bastards don't change that. I bet it all, baby, and I lost it all. So I take the lumps. Don't worry about me. Write up something I can sign, and then get off my back. I'm not going anywhere I haven't been before."

"Mrs. Harkinson, I am your attorney and . . ."

She moved around him, closer to Little Annie. "Now I'm tired," she said. "I feel awful tired. I think I want to go lie down somewhere." She smiled at Little Annie in a humble, shy, placating way, and in a gesture that Sam knew would haunt him as long as he lived, Cristen Harkinson held out her thumb for the come-along chain.

Little Annie looked at Lobwohl. Lobwohl nodded. Little Annie took Cristen by the upper arm and walked her out. Kindler held the door. Little Annie went at the same swift muscular stride, and Cristen jounced along beside her in the obedient half trot, bowed head bobbing, paper slippers making a scuff-pat sound on the institutional flooring.

The door closed. Sam had the feeling they were all exhaling at once, tensions fading. Scheff sat with his eyes closed.

"You realize, of course," Haas said angrily, "that no part of that is in any sense admissible."

Lobwohl stared at him. "You are going to go through all your motions, Palmer, and we are going to go through all ours, and if there is any sense and justice in the world we are all going to find some nice quick legal way of avoiding courtroom circuses, and we are going to put that sick dirty animal away with a load of consecutive sentences that will still have a long time to run when they box her and take her out the back gate. And we all live with it in our own way."

Haas slowly wiped his face from forehead to chin with his open hand. He gave John Lobwohl a weak smile. "Right now I think that my colleague here from Texas and I are going to go quietly off someplace and get plastered. Maybe Boylston and I are the only ones who really know the names and numbers of all the players."

After five rings Lydia Jean said, "Hello? Who is it?" She sounded blurred by sleep, slightly querulous.

"This is a drunken husband," he said carefully. "Sodden, disreputable."

"Sam! Are you really drunk?"

"I have discussed it carefully with a dear friend. After conducting certain tests, we have adjudged each other drunk. Yes."

"You certainly are very stately about it."

"It is a solemn occasion, dear wife. There is the matter of a certain paradox which needs exploring. I tried to explain it to my good friend, Mr. Palmer Christopher Haas, member of the Florida bar, and he suggested I should explore it with you."

"Explore, sir."

"I telephoned you when I learned that it was really Leila, not some girl they thought was Leila. I was sober. I cannot remember what I said. I am drunk at the moment, but I feel I will be able to recall this conversation perfectly. All I remember of the other one is a desire to tell you good news, and to tell you I love you. Did I relay that message adequately?"

"Yes, indeed."

"I wish to say it again while drunk."

"Please do."

"I love you, Lydia Jean."

"That was very nice dear. Thank you. I love you too."

"I have been learning mysterious things about mysterious people. A certain dusky nurse named Theyma Chappie had messages for me. A certain Raoul Kelly pointed out a vague trail through the underbrush. My drinking companion, Mr. Haas, who is now asleep within range of my vision, has decoded some invisible writing."

"About what?"

"It is supposed to be about me. And thus, indirectly, about you. But it disappears, like—like a dab of cotton candy on the tongue of a summertime child."

"That's a very lovely turn of phrase, Sam dear."

"They seem to come imbedded in the liquor somehow. At any rate, what I am is me. I want to be looser."

"You sound looser."

"What I promised, you take care of things for Raoul and 'Cisca and you would have fair warning to zip back to Corpus. But I am going to be me, and you are going to be you, Am I right?"

"I—suppose."

"The only change, if there is any change at all, dear wife, is that now I know it is not so great to be stuck in the world as a Sam Boylston. It is not so easy for either of us to live with it."

"The wedding is Monday, dear. High noon. She is a darling. And he is a very wise good dear dumpy little man, and we are frantically laundering her English."

"You aren't answering my question, Miss Lydia Jean."

"Jonathan is flying back tomorrow with Leila. They phoned me just at dinnertime. I asked if you were coming along. They said they didn't have any idea."

"Let's get back to the promise I made you about . . ."

"You could, of course, stay solemnly drunk over there amid those flesh pots, Sammy, or you could get on the dime and come home with the kids and lend a hand around here, like being a best man and mixing punch."

"But I want to know what you are going to . . ."

"How can you know if I don't know?"

"Excuse me. T'was brillig and those slithey toves were all over the dang place."

"I beg your pardon?"

"The gospel according to Palmer Christopher Haas. He says logic is man's most destructive illusion. All thinking is done with the glands, and the logic part gets stuck on afterward to neaten things up. So—when I couldn't follow what you were saying, any answer is okay."

"Darling?"

"Yep."

"Catch that plane. Get some sleep now, and catch that plane."

On Sunday the twelfth day of June, Howard Prowt, humming happily to himself, read the water over the Bimini bar with the skill acquired in these weeks of cruising the islands, and when the hue of the morning water deepened to a dark rich shade, he put the HoJun on automatic pilot on the course which, allowing for wind, the flow of the Gulf Stream and compass deviation, should bring them in sight of the sea buoy off Fort Lauderdale in four plus hours.

He clambered spryly down to the cockpit deck. The girls, June and Selma, were cooking bacon in the galley below, and chattering back and forth. Howard peered over the transom to check on his water circulation through the engines. Kip came back from the bow along the side deck, carrying the made-up bow lines. As he stowed the lines he said, "All clear forward, Skipper."

"Good deal. Hatch too?"

"Dogged down tight."

"We'll take some water forward when we get into the Stream."

Kip lit a cigarette and said, "Damn, I hate to have this thing ending. I was saying to Selma in the night, we've never had a better time."

"Glad you people could make it."

"Howard, I swear to God you've taken off two inches around the middle, and you've got a tan there, man, that won't quit."

"The thing about cruising, the boat is moving all the time and you're balancing yourself against it and so all day long you're getting exercise without hardly knowing it."

June called them to breakfast. Howard perched where he could watch the open sea ahead. Getting to be so many pleasure boats with automatic pilot there was no guarantee anybody would get out of your way. Kip got the eight o'clock news on the transistor, a Miami station.

They had all been following the Staniker case, theorizing about it. The announcer said that an informed source had said that it now appeared, based on new evidence, that the Harkinson woman was going to be indicted for the murders of Staniker and the Akard boy.

"Well, I'll be a son of a gun!" Kip said. "That old gal must be a real pistol."

"A face that sunk one ship anyway," Selma said tartly.

"Some part of her at least," Kip said.

"Here we go again, kids," June said.

"Honestly though," Selma said, "it was really like a miracle the Boylston girl lived through such a terrible ordeal."

As he put his plate aside and picked up his coffee cup, Howard saw his wife look obliquely at him and look away. And he knew only he was sick of that particular expression.

He cleared his throat and said, "Are we all friends?"

"What have I done now?" Selma said.

Without looking toward June, Howard said, "I should have told you kids this sooner, I guess. Confession is good for the soul or something. When June and I brought this bucket across the Gulf Stream alone, I wasn't scared. I was plain terrified. I didn't know there *was* so much water. I was green, and I didn't know what the boat could take and I didn't know how to handle it in seas like that."

"Howard!" June said.

"Anyway, we saw that Muñequita, bobbing and drifting along, sliding up and down those big damn swells. June thought she saw something for a moment, like a child's hand. I tried to come about and see if I could take that boat in tow, but I couldn't make myself do it. That's how I tore the radio cable loose and busted the television. It was such a sad chicken performance that when we got into Bimini, I didn't open my mouth."

June said quickly, "Howard, really! It probably wasn't that same boat at all. And what I saw was a rag flapping or something. Honestly, if you can find *anything* to blame yourself for, you'll do it. It's like a compulsion with you." She looked at the others. "I begged him not to try to get near that boat. But you know my Howard. He has to try. You know, if it *was* that same boat, and if she was aboard it, can you imagine the mess if we came too close and sort of hit it and tipped it and rolled her out of it. It was just some old hulk that floated away from someplace, dear."

Kip said solemnly, "I want to do all my cruising with somebody with the good sense to get scared at least once a day."

"Howard dear," Selma said, "you make this boat feel safe as a church, you really do."

June came to take Howard's cup to refill it with hot coffee. She let her fingertips rest on his hand for a moment as she took the cup. She looked into his eyes. It was not the same look as that other look. He could not read this one either, but he knew it was better. He knew a lot of things were better.

"What's he saying about visibility?" Kip asked.

They listened, and the announcer said that with the change of wind during the night to a mild two to three knots out of the southwest, the whole southeast coast of Florida was becoming blanketed with smog from the fires burning in large areas of the Everglades.

Howard Prowt went out on deck and climbed to the flying bridge. Already the horizon was blurred ahead, and the sun, rising behind them, was haloed.

By eleven it had become so murky Howard Prowt halved his speed and recomputed the effect of the Gulf Stream and reset the automatic pilot on the new course. There was a small stench of burning in the heavy air, and the sun above the smog made an eerie light on the cruiser and the nearby sea, a light tinged with saffron. They all made jokes and laughed too quickly at them. "If you look up, kids, and see a man standing up there about forty feet in the air, he's on the bow of a freighter."

A small tired bird fluttered aboard, some kind of a warbler, and flew below and sat on a bunk with his bill agape. The women made tiny voices to him, and cooing sounds, and provided water and crumbs, but he would not touch them.

Ten minutes later a blue heron flapped out of the murk and perched on the big basket-work fish trap Selma had bought in Nassau. It was of Haitian design, and she planned to make some kind of decorative hanging thing out of it beside her pool. Howard had lashed it fast in the port transom corner, and the heron landed on the upper bulge of it which extended above the transom.

The heron had a brooding silence about it, a self-possession which seemed to match the strange overcast. His eyes were a startling savage yellow. The limited visibility made the sounds of the engines louder, as well as the sound of the bow wave. They seemed to be going faster than they were.

"Howard's Ark," Kip said. "We are rescuing the animals, one by one. Welcome aboard, boids."

"A vote of confidence, dear," said June, patting Howard's arm.

"In about twenty minutes now, people, let's hope we edge up to some hunk of mainland we can recognize. Pretty soon now I'll put her on manual and slow her to a crawl."

"Aye aye, sir. Want a lookout forward?"

"I'll tell you when, Kip."

When Selma went below for something she startled the small tired bird and it flew out on deck and landed on the fish trap about six inches from the heron's talons. Howard said it would make quite a picture. The long and the short of it. June scurried and got her Instamatic and edged closer to the birds as Howard watched. Suddenly, with both slyness and a terrible indifference, the heron reached one taloned foot out to the side and clenched it on the small bird. He dropped the body and it fell down through the wide mesh of the fish trap.

"God *damn* it! God *damn* it!" Howard yelled, and without conscious impulse he hurled his half can of beer at the heron. It missed by a yard, spewing beer as it turned through the air. The heron gave a rusty gawking sound and flapped away.

"Look!" Selma called. "Hey, look right straight ahead! Isn't that a building, a tall building?"

Howard hurried to the controls and just as he switched to manual control and dropped his speed, he saw the sea buoy about fifty yards off his port quarter.

June came and stood beside him. "Right on the nose again, honey. Old Captain Hornblower himself."

"Sure, sure, sure," he said, irritably.

She put her fingertips on his wrist. "I know. It made me feel lousy too. It was so cute, having the birds riding with us. But I guess it wasn't like on purpose. You know? It's more like kind of an instinct."

"Maybe, if it occurs to you, you'd get some lines out?"

"Please don't get in one of your moods. It's been a lovely trip. It really has, sweetheart." She patted him and went and got the lines. As she took one line forward he thought of a giant claw reaching down out of the dirty mist overhead and clenching her once and dropping the broken body over the side.

I'd throw beer cans at it, he thought. Do that to my wife, will you, you crummy buzzard.

"What's the matter with the crew?" he roared. "Where's the Captain's drink? Shape up, you people!"

About the Author

JOHN D. MACDONALD was an American novelist and short story writer. His works include the Travis McGee series and the novel *The Executioners,* which was adapted into the film *Cape Fear.* In 1962 MacDonald was named a Grand Master of the Mystery Writers of America; in 1980 he won a National Book Award. In print he delighted in smashing the bad guys, deflating the pompous, and exposing the venal. In life he was a truly empathetic man; his friends, family, and colleagues found him to be loyal, generous, and practical. In business he was fastidiously ethical. About being a writer, he once expressed with gleeful astonishment, "They pay me to do this! They don't realize, I would pay them." He spent the later part of his life in Florida with his wife and son. He died in 1986.